THE
COUNTESS
OF
STONEMASON

THE COUNTESS OF STONEMASON

V. C. LOVE

ISBN: 979-8-89109-649-3 (Paperback)
ISBN: 979-8-89109-648-6 (Ebook)

Synopsis

Long ago, in the 1700s, a peculiar girl with royal blood is born in France. Andrea is rebellious, curious, adventurous, and most of all, stubborn. She grows up to become a very eccentric and important person who enjoys numerous adventures from France, to Spain, and throughout the New Spain. Follow Andrea, the Countess of Stonemason as she amasses great fortune and power, fights against love, and behaves as she pleases. This powerful woman descends into madness and becomes entwined with dark and evil forces, fighting fiercely to be the master of everything and every man she takes an interest in. Despite her astonishing beauty and having everything anyone could ever desire, she is never satisfied. She had everything she wished for…almost everything. In the end, she faces a fate so fearsome, the legend is still talked about to this day.

Do you dare discover the truth of the Countess of Stonemason?

Contents

CHAPTER ONE

A Royal is Rising

France 1700s

It was a warm summer day. The leafy trees were tall and green everywhere around the big, beautiful residence of Madam Cecile and her only daughter Marie. Madam Cecile had happily accepted on having a birthday celebration for her young and handsome neighbor, Pierre, at her house at his insistence. Many nobles and some of the most important people of France attended the reunion accompanied by their respective families. The house was full of joy, laughter, and close friends as it used to be many years ago before Cecile became a widow. Cecile's husband was a rich businessman who was well-liked, respected, and visited by his many friends, the powerful nobles of France. This celebration was like the many they used to have when Cecile's husband was still alive, but this one seemed different.

Pierre wanted to have his twenty-fifth birthday party at Cecile's house due to his father's house not being a feasible option. The count's beautiful mansion was not suitable for his birthday party as it was under major construction and extremely dusty. Pierre got his wish, and his birthday celebration was at Cecile's house.

Everyone outside in the gardens was full of excitement. Many youngsters danced around the colorful flowers. They played hide-and-seek and ran around the great, vast gardens while the bunnies hopped from one rosebush to another. Ladies chatted happily while the men made jokes and laughed with a contagious exuberance.

However, the interior of the house had a different ambience. It seemed as if no one was there. Suddenly, someone abruptly entered the quiet mansion. It was Pierre, the handsome birthday gentleman. He looked around and seemed frustrated at not finding what he was looking for, until he stopped and stared ahead. He was immobilized by her beauty and smiled at her. Marie saw him and immediately hurried down the stairs to greet him. She hugged Pierre and he kissed her cheeks desperately. They kissed passionately and touched each other's faces. Tears rolled down Marie's cheeks as she smiled and caressed his face. He continued kissing her cheeks, her whole face, and her hands desperately. He said, "Oh, ma chérie, what are you doing in here all alone? I have been looking for you everywhere."

Marie answered, "I have missed you so much, Pierre."

"Me too, but we have to be patient."

"I thought we were going to be together forever."

"We will, ma chérie, but not yet," said Pierre.

"I don't think we can wait anymore, and I cannot hide our baby much longer," she said, while uncovering her growing tummy.

Pierre fell on his knees, touched and kissed Marie's abdomen as he said, "My little one, I love you so much already; you will be a great count someday, just like your grandfather." Then, he carefully covered her belly with her blue silk cape. It was as blue as her big, beautiful eyes. Marie wiped her own face with her hands. Pierre finished wiping Marie's tears, held both of her hands in his, and bent to kiss her forehead. A couple of children ran into the house and giggled. "Pierre, your father needs you outside to hear his announcement."

Pierre looked into Marie's eyes and caressed her soft, shiny, black curls. She said, "Go, your father is waiting for you." She let go of his hands.

He took a bouquet of white-and-red rosebuds out of his satchel and placed them in his beloved's soft hands. "I took all the thorns off one by one, so they would not hurt you. You will have their beauty and perfume, but their thorns will not harm you, ma chérie."

Marie smelled the bouquet, and said, "It must have taken you forever to remove every single thorn."

"You deserve everything, ma chérie, all the time, all the patience and all the love in the entire world", said Pierre. He added, "This bouquet of rosebuds is special just like you."

Marie smiled softly, caressed her own face with the soft bouquet, and smelled its beautiful scent. Then, she said, "Go, Pierre, your father is waiting for you."

Pierre walked to the door slowly, still looking at her. Marie watched him while she smelled her special bouquet with soft white-and-red rosebuds. She looked at Pierre with eyes of profound love and adoration. He turned around and looked tenderly back at her. Then, he turned, lowered his face, and hurried out to find his father in the gardens as the children had mentioned.

"Pierre!" Marie yelled anxiously, but he did not hear her. She wanted to say "I love you," unfortunately he had already left. She looked in his direction, but he was already outside. She continued slowly down the stairs, little by little, one small step at a time. She stayed still for a few minutes in the middle of the long, elegant staircase looking at the door to the gardens. She could hear the cheering and clapping outside. The same children who came to let Pierre know his father wanted to see him, came into the house skipping and melodiously screaming while excitedly repeating, "We will have a wedding party, Pierre is getting married!"

Marie held her harmless white-and-red rosebud bouquet with her two hands against her chest. Then, she leaned against the wall and with one hand she held her abdomen under her soft cape. She took her hand out of her cape and held her forehead. She was confused. *Did Pierre arrange the wedding plans for us to get married, but forgot to tell me? Or does he want it to be a pleasant surprise for me during his birthday party today? Or maybe he wanted to tell me the date for our wedding was already arranged. Maybe, I didn't let him say the good news because as soon as I heard his father was looking for him, I asked him to go see him. It does not matter. The reason for doing it in this unexpected way is not important. Finally, we are going to be together forever, and this is the most important thing right now.*

Marie walked outside to find out what was happening in the gardens. *Is my wedding with Pierre already being announced happily by his father?* She smelled the carefully arranged white-and-red rosebud bouquet her love had made for her. Marie enjoyed the enchanting aroma of her roses and imagined her wedding with Pierre. Both of them standing at the entrance of the church. They were dressed in white. There were big, beautiful, perfumed, white-and-red flowers everywhere. They were both looking at each other as Pierre kissed Marie's cheek. Everything was perfect in Marie's mind as she smiled completely enamored and caressed her own face with the soft, perfumed flowers. She smelled her beautifully scented white-and-red rosebuds one more time. For the first time, she was ready to publicly announce their union. She was ready to start a new life with the love of her life.

Marie felt ready to be part of her engagement celebration with Pierre, and an overwhelming feeling of happiness invaded her mind and her whole body. She was feeling comfortably warm inside, and the beautiful shining sun rays felt good on her head, face, arms, and on her entire body. At last, she started to feel the happiness that she had been waiting on for so long. Marie was filled with joy, but she was also extremely nervous at the same time. She was feeling a little doubtful. *What is my mother going to say about this? Is she going to accept me leaving her house to marry and live with Pierre?* Marie took a deep breath and, eagerly, stepped into the gardens with a subtle smile.

She stood still as a statue watching Pierre's father, the count, embracing a beautiful, young, redheaded lady with one arm, and Pierre with the other. "Cheers for the happiness of this young couple who will be husband and wife in a few weeks, and to the union of our families," Pierre's father announced. Marie felt light-headed. She was not sure about what was happening. She wanted to leave, but she could not move. She wanted to look away from Pierre and his newly announced fiancée, but she found herself staring at them instead.

Pierre's mother and grandmother were crying next to Marie. The announcement of Pierre's wedding took them by surprise too. Pierre's mother was saying, "Twenty-five years have passed very fast, a day like today Pierre was born, now he is getting engaged."

Pierre's grandma answered, "He is a man now, Daughter, don't you forget that." She added, "I am crying while realizing that I am getting older every day. Why are you crying, dear?"

Pierre's mother looked at her own mother, and replied, "These are tears of happiness, Mother, weddings make me emotional. And I was not expecting my own son's wedding this soon."

Marie's face was paler than ever. Usually, her cheeks were naturally rosy, but not at this moment. Her face turned paler and paler with each passing moment. She was feeling colder and colder with every second that passed on this warm summer day. Her whole body started to shake with the coldness she was feeling from head to toe. Her hands felt weaker and weaker with each second. Her hands opened slowly, revealing the enchanting white-and-red rosebud bouquet, completely devoid of even a single thorn. The bouquet her love had carefully arranged for her, lifelessly crashed to the floor. Marie felt the strength in her body leaving her. She started to feel dizzy. She leaned on a tree and held it with both hands to avoid falling down. Then, she sat on a bench without taking her eyes off the new couple.

Two beautiful horses with a lovely, decorated carriage came into the garden, one stunning, majestic, black, and shiny, the other beautiful, splendid and white as snow. Pierre's father walked the young couple to the horse-drawn carriage. Pierre looked confused, but he was following along with everything his father was saying. Pierre's fiancée looked proud, tall, happy, and glamorous. His father offered the beautiful girl's hand to Pierre. He took her hand to help her step into the carriage, and he got inside with a big leap still with a serious, worried expression. The gorgeous redhead gave her just-announced fiancé a kiss on the cheek and smiled a big smile at him proudly while holding his hand. Pierre just looked at her nervously and quietly. As Marie watched the young couple, he looked very handsome and charming. Marie stopped shaking. Now she did not feel cold anymore. She could feel and hear her heart pumping blood faster and faster with every passing second. She could feel torrents of blood rushing from her body into her head. Her face was feeling hotter and hotter and it did not look pale anymore, or rosy as most of the time. Now, her face looked bright red. Her eyes were watery and giant teardrops started to fall down her cheeks.

Pierre's mother gave Marie a soft white handkerchief, and said, "Here, dear. I know how you feel." She added, "Weddings make me cry too."

The horses began trotting majestically, carrying the new couple into their new life. Marie's beautiful, scented, harmless, well-arranged white-and-red rosebud bouquet ended up in pieces as the horses trampled it on their way out. The sun was suddenly covered by clouds. The wind began to blow harder and all the soft, scented, scattered white-and-red petals from the bouquet ended up at people's feet. They stepped on the petals without noticing and continued with the celebration.

Marie blew her nose with the handkerchief Pierre's mother gave her.

"Madame Marie, Madame Marie!" The scream interrupted Marie's flashback.

"Your daughter, the Countess of Stonemason wants you at the table, dinner is served." Marie nodded to the child and continued thinking about the past as she walked back toward the house.

Young Pierre was standing at her balcony. He said, "My father never told me his plans of marriage for me." He added, "I am as surprised as you are. This is going to be a good business for him." Pierre got closer to Marie, and said, "Let's leave France, Marie; we could go to Spain and start a new life there, without anyone telling us what to do and how to live our lives."

Marie said, "I cannot leave my mother."

Pierre sighed, looked into her big, blue eyes and gently held her arms. "Ma chérie, we are both twenty-five years old, our parents should know by now that someday we will live our own life, have someone to love and form our own family."

Marie insisted, "It would be devastating for my mother if I leave her like that." She added, "I am the most important thing for her and her only family. She would die out of sadness and loneliness without me."

Pierre, looked at Marie with his big brown eyes, and said, "Your mother is not going to die just because you leave France and marry me, Marie." He added, "We have the right to make our own choices and be happy with the person we love."

"No, Pierre, you don't understand, I cannot leave my mother like this."

Two months later, Marie was screaming desperately during labor. Her house employees assisted her in delivering the baby as her mother was out on church activities with her friends.

When her mother returned home, she was greeted by the cries of her little grandchild. Cecile entered the door, and asked, "Whose baby is crying?" She hit the floor with her cane, and added, "I have told all my employees before to not bring their children to my house during work hours."

The maid looked at the cook in front of her. Then, she looked at Cecile, and said, "My lady, that baby is not an employee's baby."

Cecile looked at her. Then, she looked at the cook, and asked, "What does she mean by that?"

The cook said, "She means that the baby is not the child of one of your employees; it is yours, my lady."

Cecile hit the floor again with her cane, grumped, and asked, "Mine?" Then, she asked, "Do you know my age?" Cecile slowly sat down on an elegant comfortable chair as she fanned herself with a fan. She stopped, opened her eyes wide, and looked upstairs. Then in a loud voice, she said, "Marie!" She desperately asked, "Where is Marie?"

Her two employees looked at each other. The lady said, "She's upstairs."

Cecile walked upstairs slowly. She opened her daughter's room. There she was lying on the bed with a baby in her arms. Marie had prematurely given birth to a beautiful baby girl. She was looking at two of her employees who were near the bed. One of the ladies asked, "What is her name?"

Marie answered, "Andrea."

Cecile saw them and fainted. The three employees who were in her daughter's room tried to help her regain consciousness.

Meanwhile, Pierre was getting married to the lady his father chose for him. The church was full of giant white flowers.

Everybody looked happy, except for Pierre. He had a serious expression with a melancholic look in his eyes. His casual smile looked forced, trying to be polite, but his mind was absent. He was wearing a black suit with a white shirt. His golden hair was well-groomed, but his big brown eyes looked sorrowful. He looked particularly handsome, but his pleasant appearance could not hide his sadness.

Five years later, Andrea was playing with her father as usual. He had the habit of visiting her twice a week and more often when he could, since the day she was born. Pierre asked his daughter, "Who is the most beautiful girl in France?"

"I am, Father," replied little Andrea, so self-assured. Her hair was not as black as her mother's, and it was not as blond as her father's either. Hers was a golden brown like the cinnamon trees, and it matched with her skin color. Her skin was golden brown from all the time spent playing in the sun. Little Andrea's eyes were not blue like the sky or her mother's eyes. They were not amber like honey or her father's eyes. Andrea's eyes were a bright intense green. They were as green as the vegetation all around her where she spent hours and hours playing every day. Andrea was growing up to be eager and more curious each day. She asked her father many questions when she saw him. She loved being with her father. Pierre tried answering her questions accordingly for a child to understand and to the best of his ability. He loved pleasing his daughter. Andrea asked, "Why do you have to leave, Father?"

Pierre answered, "I have to go, but I will be back soon."

"But I want you to stay here with me, Father, or take me with you."

"Your mother would not like it if I take you with me, and I cannot stay here either."

Andrea asked, "Why don't you live with Mother and I, Father? You have to live with us because you love us. Don't you love us, Father?"

Pierre calmly but with sad eyes, said, "Yes, I love you both."

Marie said, "Come here with me, Andrea, and let your father leave."

"No, Marie, let my daughter be here with me." He added, "Let her ask me anything she wants." Pierre looked at his daughter, and asked, "Who is the most beautiful girl in France?"

Andrea looked at her father with a big smile as she replied, "I am, Father." She added, "I am the most beautiful girl in France."

The memories replayed in Marie's mind over and over again. The boy ran back and stood in front of Marie again. He said, "Madam Marie, your daughter the Countess of Stonemason is waiting for you at the table." Marie snapped out of her daydream. She abruptly came back to the present, and gently said, "Yes, Jose, I will be there soon."

Three years had passed and Andrea was now eight years old. Andrea wept while Marie looked at her, and said, "You are not going to go with your friends to that tall tree again." Andrea cried inconsolably. She said, "But I want to go, Father, I want to go."

Pierre looked at Marie, and said, "Let my daughter do what she wants, Marie."

Marie answered, "No, it's too dangerous. She already fell when she was trying to climb a small tree, and she had to stay in bed all morning because her back was hurting really bad." Marie shook her head no, and said, "Now Andrea is feeling better, but you can see that she is still hurting, and she wants to go again and climb up an even bigger tree this time." Marie looked at Pierre, and said, "She could have another fall and hurt herself even worse than before."

Pierre held Andrea's arms, looked her over, and asked, "Did you get hurt, my beautiful one?" He looked at her from head to toe, and added, "Where does it hurt, my little queen?"

Andrea smiled while jumping and holding her father's hands. She said, "It doesn't hurt that much anymore, Father." She added, "I am all right."

Grandma Cecile used to say it often, and again she said, "All children fall down." She added, "I don't see what is so special about this one that she should not fall like all the other children."

Pierre looked at Marie, and said, "Marie, nothing bad is going to happen, I am going to go with my little queen."

Marie, preoccupied, intended to explain her important argument. She said, "But—"

Pierre interrupted her thoughts when he said, "Let my daughter do what she wants, Marie." Pierre and his daughter left to go climb any tree she wanted. Marie stood still, worrying, and quietly watching them walk away from her. Grandma Cecile told Christine, "Go with them, Christine, and help Andrea if she needs it."

"Mother!" said Marie. "Christine's mother passed away recently. She is only three years older than Andrea, and she is filled with sadness. How can she help Andrea?"

"I don't know," Grandma Cecile answered. "That girl is very cautious and well-mannered. Even now after her mother's death, she still knows how to manage herself around others, helping them while still taking care of herself. Maybe Andrea will learn something from Christine." She added, "Come on, Marie, you have to give Christine some credit." Grandma looked through the window, and said, "She has learned so fast with the few lessons she has received from Andrea's tutors when Andrea has refused to take her classes; you know, because your daughter always does as she pleases." Cecile frowned, and said, "You have allowed her father to spoil the little brat way too much."

Many hours had passed until Grandma Cecile spoke again, "I still think that little brat of yours is spoiled rotten by her father, and you never do anything to put an end to it." Andrea was running outside the house. Grandma Cecile said, "Speaking of the devil, there she is." She added, "I am going to take this little brat to church so she can learn the sense of decorum that her parents refuse to teach her." Cecile held her granddaughter's arm, and ordered, "Let's go, Andrea, we are going to church."

Little Andrea looked at her arm. Then, she looked at Cecile, and said, "Grandma, I don't want to go to church. I am going back to play with my friends. I just came here for a drink of water."

Grandma Cecile insisted, holding Andrea's hand. "Your friends can wait. I am going to teach you something important today, and you are going to be a lady of faith so you can follow the right path in life."

Andrea asked, "What path, Grandmother? I know all the paths in the woods, and I just want to go there and play with my friends."

Grandma Cecile gave Andrea an umbrella, and said, "Here, in case it rains on our way back." She added, "Don't worry, child, we will return soon. You are going to meet new friends your same age, with good manners, not like the savages you are always running around with, and you may even like it. Let's go."

Andrea asked, "We are just going to be in church for a little while, Grandma?"

Grandma Cecile replied, "Yes, child, just a little while, and Christine is coming with us too." She added, "We are going to church, Marie." Marie nodded and continued looking at them quietly.

Grandma Cecile and Andrea left holding hands. Cecile held her cane with her left hand while Andrea carried the umbrella in her right hand. Christine walked in silence behind them. On the way to church, they passed some trees and one of the trees caught Andrea's attention. "What is that giant cocoon, Grandma?"

Grandma Cecile answered, "There is no such thing child, keep walking."

Andrea insisted, "It is a giant cocoon, Grandma. What does it have inside?"

Grandma Cecile said, "I told you there are no giant cocoons." They continued walking fast. There were a couple of beautiful ladies walking toward them. One of the ladies was tall, slim, and blue-eyed with dark hair. The other lady was tall, slim, and brown-eyed with blonde hair. They were both exceedingly beautiful, feminine and had their long shiny hair falling freely down their backs. The two ladies wore a lot of gold jewelry on their hands, around their necks and they had long ostentatious gold earrings. Their skirts were wide with big colorful flowers.

Then, both ladies approached Andrea's grandmother. The one with dark hair and blue eyes asked her, "Dear, madam, allow me to see the palm of your hand and tell you what the future holds for you."

Grandma Cecile said, "I do not have any money with me, and I am in a hurry."

The other lady insisted. "She will read your future so you can prepare for a better life. Let her see your hand."

Grandma, bothered by the insistence, madly replied, "I do not want you to read my hand, we are going to church. The Good Book says not to partake in these acts." She added, "Besides, I am not giving you any money."

The blonde-haired brown eyed woman asked, "Since you do not want to spend any money, your earrings will do for now, say yes, eh?"

Grandma Cecile looked at the ladies with a frown, and said, "Do not insist anymore, I said no and it means no. I am not giving you my favorite earrings or anything else for that matter."

The dark-haired blue-eyed woman insisted. "Today is your lucky day, madam. I will tell you your future for free if you accept, just let me see your hand."

Grandma Cecile shook her head and sighed. Andrea looked at them with big eyes, and asked them, "Can you read my future?" Andrea, extended her little hand, then ordered, "Read my hand and tell me the events that await me and my family."

Both ladies looked at each other surprised and amused, and they giggled at the precocious little girl. Grandma Cecile, with a louder and rougher tone of voice, ordered, "Get away from us. I want to teach this girl good things. I do not want her to put her faith in fortune-tellers."

Andrea insisted, "Common ladies, here is my hand. I am allowing you to read it, what are you waiting for?"

Both ladies looked at each other and laughed. The brunette said, "You will have to wait, little girl. I will read your hand when you are older."

The blonde lady added, "We will be waiting for you to grow up. Then we can tell you all about your future."

Christine, as usual, observed everything quietly. Grandma Cecile said, "Unbelievable, one cannot go to church in peace without fighting with the devil on the way there." She held Andrea's hand and walked hurriedly. Christine quickly followed behind them.

At church, people of all ages welcomed Andrea, and she played with the other children. After about an hour Grandma Cecile and Andrea were walking back home. Grandma was holding the big umbrella over herself, her granddaughter, and Christine as it was drizzling a little bit. Andrea asked Grandma Cecile, "Grandma, I did a good job at church, didn't I?"

Grandma Cecile replied, "Yes, child, you did. You are both coming with me to church more often from now on."

Grandma, hopeful, looked at the two girls, especially Andrea. "This is going to be good for you. Church will help you become beautiful and obedient young ladies."

Andrea said, "Let me hold the umbrella, Grandma. The rain has stopped."

"All right, child, since you were such a well behaved girl in church, you can hold the umbrella the rest of the way home. Anyway, it is only misting now."

Andrea said, "All right, Grandma." Andrea ran ahead about six feet away from Cecile and pulled the branches of a tree as she rapidly poked a huge beehive with the umbrella several times.

Grandma Cecile screamed, "No, Andrea, don't do that!" The beehive fell off the tree after several repeated hits with the umbrella. The umbrella fell next to Cecile. The bees came out of their hive and immediately attacked Andrea, Christine, and Grandma Cecile.

Andrea ran and yelled, "Run fast, Grandma, run!"

Christine stood still and covered her face with her hands. Grandma tried to scare away the bees with her cane, but it fell just out of her reach. Then, she tried to run, but she twisted her ankle. She picked up the umbrella, used it as a cane, and walked as fast as she could behind the girls. Grandma Cecile yelled, "Run, girls, run faster!"

Andrea and Christine ran home quickly while Grandma Cecile walked with her umbrella as fast as she could, but not fast enough to leave the bees behind. Marie was by the door looking out the window when she saw the two girls run inside the house and close the door swiftly behind them.

Marie, confused, asked, "What happened?"

Andrea answered, "The bees are after us, Mother, and they got Grandma."

Christine said, "Grandma needs help; a big beehive fell off a tree and she can't run fast."

Marie went out to help her mother. After a few minutes, they both came inside the house. Marie said, "Christine, go get the doctor for Grandma Cecile."

Christine said, "Yes, Mother Marie."

When the doctor came inside the house, Grandma Cecile was in bed moaning. Her whole face was red, swollen, and deformed, as well as her arms and legs. The doctor asked, "What happened to her, Marie?"

Marie answered, "Bees, Doctor, the bees from a beehive stung her." Marie was crying silently.

The doctor said, "Cecile, you might be a little too old to be playing with beehives. How do you feel?"

Cecile, moaned and spoke slowly in a low and shaky voice, "I wasn't playing, this is all the little brat's fault." Cecile could hardly open her swelling lips, but she carefully moved her lips again to communicate with the doctor. She said, "The little brat poked and hit the giant beehive with the umbrella. As you can see these are the consequences of her mischievous actions." Grandma Cecile continued moaning in pain and complaining by gently moving her lips. She whispered, "This little brat is a pain in the neck and everywhere else." The doctor shook his head in disapproval.

Andrea interrupted in surprise. She asked, "How was I supposed to know what a beehive looked like if I had never seen one before?" She added, "It looked like a giant cocoon."

The doctor looked over his glasses to see Andrea. He asked, "How is it that you haven't seen a beehive before when you are always running through the woods with your friends?"

"No, I have never seen one before. At least not that big."

The doctor looked at Andrea with a serious face. He nodded, then said, "I see, but you should not poke and hit something just because you do not know what it is."

Grandma Cecile slowly said, "This is all your fault, Marie. I refuse to continue risking my life for the sake of teaching your naughty daughter good values. I cannot see you, Doctor. I cannot see anything." She shook her hands in front of her eyes. Then asked, "Am I blind?"

The doctor replied, "It is probably only temporary. We will see in a few days once the swelling comes down."

Cecile continued to moan and complain. She said, "I can barely open my mouth to speak and it hurts so much. Why did I have to be punished with a brat for a grandchild?" She was weeping inconsolably. She cried, "Why me?"

Andrea opened her eyes wide and pulled Christine's hand. She whispered, "Let's get out of here, Christine!" They ran outside the house. Andrea said, "Let's go play by the biggest tree."

Christine said, "We should stay home and see how we can help Grandma."

"Mother is there with her, let's go."

"I don't feel like going anywhere until Grandma Cecile is better."

"She will be better tomorrow, let's go play."

Christine said, "Let me ask if we can go play for a little bit."

Andrea said, "I will wait for you by the tallest tree, hurry up."

Seven years had passed and Andrea was now fifteen years old. Andrea was furious and yelling at Marie. "All my friends are going to the beach, except me, because you won't let me!"

Marie calmly replied, "I said, you could go if I accompany you and if you promise not to set foot inside the water, but you refuse to listen to me."

Andrea said, "Why would I go to the beach if I am not allowed to be in the water?" She rolled her eyes. Then added, "I want to swim, Mother."

"Andrea, it is dangerous. Many people have drowned and died in those waters despite being very good swimmers."

"That is not going to happen to me, Mother." She crossed her arms. Then said, "Besides, nobody actually saw those people die. Maybe they just left the country."

Marie was disappointed in her daughter. She answered, "I am sure they are dead, Andrea. Do you think they just decided to leave France by swimming away and abandoning all of their loved ones?"

Andrea said, "I don't care, Mother." She shook her head. Then said, "That is not going to happen to me. I am going to swim and I am going to be fine."

Pierre entered the house. He asked, "What is all this commotion?"

Andrea cried louder while hugging her father. Then said, "Father, I want to go swimming with my friends to the beach and Mother won't let me." She added, "Mother enjoys ruining my life. She wants me to be stuck inside this house forever. Her plan is for me to be bored and miserable all day just like her."

Pierre looked at Marie while caressing his daughter's hair. He gently asked, "What is wrong with going swimming, Marie?"

Marie sighed in frustration. She said, "Pierre, you have already known for many years how many people are swallowed by the ocean while swimming in it."

Pierre laughed out loud. He said, "So this is the problem, huh? People who have died before?" He added, "Marie, people have died there and will continue to die. That is not going to stop my daughter from swimming and having fun in the water."

Andrea said, "Nothing bad is going to happen to me, Father. I know how to take care of myself."

Grandma Cecile said, "Here we go again, the brat always gets her way since her incompetent, dumb, and permissive parents haven't a clue how to raise her."

Marie said harshly, "Mother!"

Pierre ignored Grandma's comment. He said, "Marie, Andrea is intelligent, and she knows how to take care of herself. She is going to be all right while having a splendid time."

Marie said, "But—"

Smiling, Andrea interrupted with a loud voice. She said, "I am intelligent, and I want to go swimming."

Pierre said, "Let my daughter go swimming, Marie. She is young, let her have some fun." Pierre grinned and looked at Andrea. He said, "Let's go, Andrea." Mesmerized, he looked into his daughter's eyes, and asked, "Where is the most beautiful girl in the world going?"

Andrea, with a big smile, replied, "Swimming, Father." With an even bigger smile on her face, she said, "I am going swimming!"

"PIERRE!!!" exclaimed Marie, with a worried voice.

Pierre said, "Come on, Marie, let my daughter do what she wants." He added, "Let her have some fun."

Andrea's grandmother took her cane and walked quickly to the door. She hit the floor with her cane. Then said, "I am going to tell everyone how you continue to spoil this insolent brat." She added, "People should know that you do not discipline her. Then, when she does something horrible, they will not blame her. They will blame you two instead."

Marie said, "What are you talking about, Mother?"

Pierre, still looking at his daughter with a profound fatherly love, said, "Time continues to pass quickly, ma chérie. You, my dear Andrea of Stonemason, continue to grow more beautiful and intelligent every day."

Andrea caressed her own hair. She said, "Yes, I am, Father!"

Andrea was now almost eighteen years old. Her father looked at her mother. He said, "I have been thinking a lot about Andrea's future. I have decided that making a journey to Spain would be in my daughter's best interest. She still has much to learn about how the real world functions." He added, "Maybe in one or two years she will be ready to travel by herself." Before Marie could say anything, Pierre hurriedly asked, "Where is Andrea?" He looked out the window and firmly ordered, "Find my daughter, Marie."

Marie answered, "Andrea has been outside all day. She must be busy and has found something fun to do under the sun. You know she likes to do that."

Pierre said, "I will go find her myself." He mounted his horse and looked around the fields for his daughter. The sun was high in the sky, shining and warming up everything under it. After galloping with his horse for a few minutes, something caught his attention. He guided his horse to slow down. Pierre saw a couple rolling on the warm grass and kissing passionately. When he got closer, he could recognize the adolescent boy. It was Myles. The son of a rich merchant, but he was not of royal birth like Andrea's father's family. Then, he recognized the beautiful and elegant girl who was with him. It was his daughter, Andrea. Pierre, with his eyes wide open, looked at them quietly. He could see them clearly, but he could not hear what they were saying. Andrea and Myles continued kissing passionately.

Myles caressed his girlfriend's curly hair. He said, "I can't wait for us to get married and be together all the time."

Andrea kissed him tenderly. She asked, "Are you sure that is what you want?"

Myles kissed her while he looked into her big, intense green eyes. "More than anything in the world." He added, "Andrea, I love you so much!"

Andrea kissed him again. She said, "I love you too, Myles!"

"I am so happy here with you that it seems unreal, like a sweet dream that is going to end soon."

"It is going to end when we want it to end, and not one moment sooner," she said.

Myles said, "I want to have my father speak to yours about our marriage plans."

"Wait, darling. I will speak with my father first."

Myles asked, "What if your family does not approve of us getting married?"

Andrea said, "That would be their problem, I choose my own life." She added, "I do as I please. I want to be with you, Myles." She hugged him and they both rolled over the warm green grass as they laughed happily.

Pierre shouted in a pleasant but firm voice, "Andrea!"

Still on the grass, she looked up and saw her father. She sat up and fixed her hair with her hands. She stood up, shaking off the leaves and grass from her beautiful dress. Pierre, now looking at them both with narrow eyes, gently said, "Let's go, ma chérie. I need to speak with you."

Andrea finished shaking the grass off her fancy dress. She answered, "Yes, Father." She waved to her boyfriend and smiled. Myles smiled back tenderly and waved good-bye to her. His heart was beating fast. His pupils were dilated while still looking at his beautiful girlfriend. He had a big smile on his blushing face.

Pierre, looked at the young man in love, and said, "Good-bye, Myles."

Myles was still looking at Andrea. Then, he turned his attention to Pierre for some seconds. He said, "Good-bye, sir."

Pierre left with his horse. Myles continued to stare at his sweet love. Andrea got up on her horse and followed her father. Pierre and Andrea rode toward home. They were quiet for half of the ride back. Marie was watching them from a distance. Finally, Andrea's father broke the silence and looked at his daughter. He asked, "What was that?"

Andrea looked at him serenely. Then, she looked at the horizon proudly and sure of herself like she had always been.

Pierre, still looking at his daughter, asked, "You can't possibly think that is love, do you?"

Andrea looked at him quietly as she smiled and remembered her sweet love, Myles. Pierre said, "I remember when I was your age. Believe me, you don't know what love is. You might think you are in love, but you are not." He added, "It is just this age and all the energy that comes with it confusing you."

Andrea looked at her father and her smile slowly disappeared from her beautiful face. Then, with a serious expression, she calmly asked, "How do you know what I feel, Father?" Then, still with no smile on her face, she asked, "How can you be so sure that I am not in love?"

Pierre replied, "I know it is complicated, but you are not even eighteen yet, ma chérie." Disappointed, he shook his head. Then, calmly asked, "Love, love, love, what is it good for eh, my beautiful, wonderful, intelligent and amazing daughter, Andrea?" Still shaking his head, he asked, "Haven't you learned anything about love?"

She stopped her horse and looked at her father. He got near her and held her chin. He said, "Listen carefully, honey. Love is good-for-nothing." He added, "Your mother loves me very much. Is she happy?" He immediately replied, "No, she isn't. I love her very much. Am I happy?" He answered his own question, and said, "No, I am not happy. Love does not let you think straight. It makes you want to behave irrationally. And all for nothing, because no matter how much you think your sweetheart loves you back, your love is going to be unrequited. And when you think your beloved would do anything for you and your love, you will find out he won't." He sighed, got closer to his daughter, and patted her head. "Because as much as he can love you, his love is not going to be as great as yours and you will suffer for this love." He looked into his daughter's eyes. Then said, "Understand it very well, my beautiful child. Love is suffering and you don't want to suffer. Even when you find the greatest form of pure love it still holds you back. Love stops you from having a great life." He added, "You see, I cannot even think of my own great future because I prefer to think about yours. Do you see where I'm going?" His tone of voice intensified when he said, "And let's not talk about marriage because it does not work either. You marry and you become the unhappiest you have ever been. And you want to know about babies?"

Andrea looked at her father with a serious face and interrupted him. She slowly said, "Do not say anything else. I understand perfectly well, Father." This was somehow confusing for Andrea, but she was still sure of herself like most of the time. She looked at her father. Then said, "Do not worry, Father. I will avoid the great suffering you and mother have gone through. I will not suffer for love or for anyone. I will have a great future." Andrea had her mother's shiny curls, her father's persistence, and a profound desire to please her father.

When they arrived at the house, Pierre looked at Marie. He said, "Marie, it is time for Andrea to see the world, to visit new places and meet new people." He added, "I would like her to go to Spain with the new teachers I hired to guide and accompany her."

Marie said, "She has very good teachers already."

"Yes, but her new teachers are even better." He added, "They are knowledgeable on how the whole world works. They will teach her many new things that she still needs to learn. Especially, the way power, politics, and royalty work."

Marie said, "Pierre, you said earlier that this was going to happen in one or two years."

Pierre said, "No, Marie. I realize now my daughter is ready to go. We don't have to wait any longer."

Andrea, with her adventurous young heart became excited and lightly jumped up and down. She screamed, "Spain, I am going to Spain!"

It did not matter anymore, but Marie could not stop thinking about it. Her memories of her past tortured her every day and at all times. Maybe her own and her daughter's life could have been different, she thought. If only she had made better choices for them both. But it was too late for lamentations now and the past could not be changed.

CHAPTER TWO

In Spain

More than three years have passed since Andrea arrived in Spain. Andrea walked with her four new teachers: two of them French, Dianne and Charles, the other two Spanish, Valerie and Salvador. As they were walking and chatting animatedly, Andrea stopped and looked at the handsome, charming young man in front of her. "Myles!" Andrea said, opening her intense green eyes wide when she saw him. He was tall and slim. He had tan skin, big blue eyes, and black wavy hair. His eyes reflected the tender love he felt for her. "What are you doing here in Spain?" she asked.

Myles inclined his head, then looked at her tenderly with his big blue eyes. He asked, "You don't know what I am doing here in Spain?" With his deep, sweet voice, he calmly said, "Come here with me and I will tell you what I am doing here in Spain."

Her teachers talked among themselves. Dianne said, "She has a royal meeting to attend in two hours, and she needs to change her clothes to be presentable."

Andrea looked at them, and said, "This will not take long, but I need to talk to Myles." She added, "I will see you at the palace soon." The four teachers looked at each other, confused.

The handsome Myles offered Andrea his arm and she took it. Myles led her to the cathedral and once inside, they sat on a wooden bench in front of the altar. Myles held Andrea's hands in his and with his big blue eyes he looked into Andrea's big, bright, and intense green eyes, while saying, "I am here in Spain because after more than three years of waiting for you in France it felt more like thirty, and I lost my peace of mind. I could not eat. I could not sleep. I could not do anything without missing you."

Andrea looked at him with narrow eyes. She said, "Myles, it has been more than three years since the last time we have seen each other. How can you still think about me?" Andrea was looking at Myles attentively with her big, bright, intense green eyes. There was no smile on her face. She couldn't understand his reasoning. She stopped looking at him and started looking at the altar.

He looked at her with his big, blue eyes. Then said, "You promised me you would return. That you would not leave me, not for too long, remember?" He held on to her hands and kissed them one by one. Myles said, "My dear love, my sweet Andrea, neither the time nor the distance could have made me forget you. I still think of you from the last day we were together in France, my love. Do you still remember that last wonderful day we spent together in the meadows in France?

Because I cannot get it out of my mind, and it is still as clear as the time it happened. Andrea, the profound love I feel for you made me follow you to Spain. I waited as long as I could, but I cannot do anything without you anymore. I have been waiting for you since the time you left France, and my mind has not been able to dissolve our memories together. The truth is that I would not manage to forget you, ever." He sighed, and said, "The time has felt much longer than it has been. Sadness has followed me everywhere since you have been away. Everything seems different and dreadful when you are not with me. I am deeply in love with you and in this sacred house of the Lord, I want you to know that I want to be with you forever. I want you for the mother of my children. I want to grow old with you by my side." His deep and sweet voice was clear and sincere. As he looked at the love of his life, he could not even blink.

Her eye contact with him was direct but she could not disguise how surprised she was. *How could he still be thinking of the promises he swore to me three years ago? How could he still be swearing the same promises before me after three long years away from each other?* She could not understand it. However, he was talking from the depth of his heart. Andrea laughed out loud. "Us together until we are old? That is a very long time, and having children? Children?" she repeated, still laughing out loud while feeling confused and amused at the same time. "Children?" she said, annoyed. "The little, naughty brats are a pain in the neck." Andrea slowly moved her hands away from Myles and put them on the wooden bench in front of her. She quietly looked at the altar as thoughts ran wild in her mind.

Myles took a beautiful, big red flower from the altar and gave it to Andrea. He said, "You are everything to me, the meaning of my life. My love for you has no end. Andrea, my love for you is greater than anything I have ever felt before for anyone."

Salvador, still looking at the young couple from a distance, looked at Dianne and Valerie, then said, "That flower is as big and lively as his young heart, but he still has a lot to learn." He added, "Oh, how I remember the times I fell in love. I had to learn the hard way that they did not care for me the same way I did." He sighed.

Dianne looked at Salvador. She said, "Aw, you are feeling nostalgic."

Charles interrupted Salvador's memories from his youth and with a smirk on his face, he said, "But it is better to have loved and your love not been reciprocated than to have never loved." Dianne and Valerie giggled.

Myles was still declaring his profound love to Andrea. He looked at her with hope, and asked, "My love, what are you thinking?"

Andrea looked at him a little confused, serious and quiet. Myles, still looking at Andrea with eyes of profound love, insisted, "Say something, my love. Please, tell me how you feel. Tell me anything. My love, I am here to put my heart and my life in your hands. I have tremendously missed looking into your bright beautiful eyes that I adore. These three years I could not stop thinking of this day when I could finally hold your hands in mine again. Even right now, feeling your hands in mine, I still do not know if it is true that I am smelling your hair or if I am just dreaming. I am so happy to have you here with me. You cannot even begin to imagine how deep my feelings for you are. Let's get married, my love. What is your answer, Andrea? How do you feel about us? I cannot live without you; I love you so much!"

Andrea, still looking at him puzzled, answered, "Thank you, but I cannot do this. I have bigger plans for my life."

One of her teachers, Charles, interrupted, "My lady, we have to go. It is late and you have an important event to attend." Her other teachers stood next to Charles waiting for her answer.

She looked at them, and said, "Yes, I am ready to depart with you." Andrea stood up from the bench where she was sitting with her ex-boyfriend. The big, red, lively flower that Myles had given her fell to the floor. Charles stepped on it by accident. Andrea picked up the crushed flower with only a few remaining petals. She looked at Myles indifferently and gave back the flower to him, saying, "Good-bye, Myles." Andrea walked away quickly with her four teachers, and she never looked back.

Myles watched them walk away from him still half expecting her to turn around. He looked at his crushed flower, looked at the floor, and sat back down on the bench. He placed his right hand on his forehead attempting to hold himself together. Meanwhile, he was still looking down at the wilted red rose in his left hand. He closed his fist along with his big, blue eyes. A little blood dripped from his left hand and tears fell from his eyes. He opened his eyes, got up from the bench, and placed the crumpled flower in a vase with white chrysanthemums. He walked slowly in the same direction that his impossible love went. He stopped for a moment, saw Andrea's back while she was walking away from him. Then, he turned around and started walking in the opposite direction. He walked away slowly while looking down.

Meanwhile, at the palace, where many nobles including Andrea and her teachers resided, everything was quiet. Andrea asked, "Why is it so quiet in here?"

Dianne said, "Everyone went to the royal party. We should do the same."

At that moment, a gentleman interrupted them. "Not everyone likes parties, but we could go together if it pleases you, my beautiful lady." He kissed Andrea's hand.

The duke, a redhead of average height with hazel eyes, was pleasantly plump. He was also a flirtatious widower about twice Andrea's age. Her teachers looked at each other puzzled. Andrea answered, "Well, Mister?"

The duke hurriedly replied, "I am the Duke of Roux, darling, just call me Duke."

Andrea smiled, and said, "Very well, Duke. We will see you at the royal party. There are still some things we must take care of, but we will see you shortly."

The duke answered, "As you wish, my lady. I will see you there as you have requested."

He left and Andrea's teachers started to murmur. Dianne asked, "Requested? Requested? You did not request to see him."

Valerie agreed. "He was the one who requested your presence."

Charles said, "Delusional, opportunistic man."

Salvador asked, "Do you like him, sweetheart? He must be your father's age."

Andrea smiled. She calmly said, "Your minds are going a little too fast for me." She added, "Are we going to the royal party?"

Her four teachers replied, "YES."

Dianne said, "This party is very important, and you should be there."

Charles remarked, "This is an opportunity for you to become more well-known amongst the royalty here."

Valerie added, "Some of the most important French and Spanish royals will be there, it is essential that you get to know them."

Salvador chimed in, "And you are going to have so much fun at the party." The five of them laughed in unison.

Andrea said, "I have been very happy with the four of you here in Spain during these last three years. I want you all to know that I enjoy your company and that I appreciate your friendship very much."

Dianne said, "We love you too, dear."

Valerie agreed, "Yes, we do."

Salvador concurred, "Yes, dear, it has been lovely getting to know you and guiding you here in Spain."

Charles joined in, "Yes, I agree with all of you, but this is not the time to get sentimental." He added, "We have an important royal party to attend."

Andrea stated, "Let's go to the party."

Dianne exclaimed, "I have marvelous wigs for all of us!"

Valerie declared, "And I have prepared the finest white powder for our faces."

Charles sighed, "I'm so relieved to have such meticulous, good friends like you ladies. We have everything we need! Let's go get ready."

Andrea interrupted. "What do you mean, get ready? I just changed my dress and fixed my hair, I am ready."

Her teachers laughed together. Dianne said, "You are smart, but too young. You cannot go like this to such an elegant royal party."

Valerie added, "Nobody goes in their natural state ever, that is offensive to the royals and shows no class."

Andrea declared, "I am not going to wear such horrible wigs and disgusting dust."

Surprised, Charles and Salvador exclaimed, "AN-DREA!"

Andrea continued, "My hair and skin are more beautiful than those horrible items, and I refuse to wear them."

Dianne said, "You are still very inexperienced." She added, "You just need to get used to these fancy items. You will see soon enough."

Andrea said firmly, "I said no, and I am not going to wear them. If I were you, I would not wear them either. Royal fashion is extremely ridiculous and inconvenient. I am far too beautiful to wear any of these unsightly and unnecessary items."

Salvador replied, "Well, since none of us can convince you to wear the wig and fine white powder, you may go as you are."

Charles added, "However, I have to warn you that there is a great possibility that you are not going to be permitted to enter the party."

Valerie stated matter-of-factly, "There is a dress code, if one does not respect the etiquette and the other nobles, you are not allowed inside the royal party."

Andrea assured them, "They will let us all in, do not worry your pretty little heads." She added, "Regardless, I refuse to wear that horrendous wig and dust, even if they do not let us in."

They all agreed to attend the royal party together and to allow Andrea to go in her natural state. All of them stepped into a carriage pulled by four horses ready to begin their new adventure.

Meanwhile, Myles was still walking slowly through the streets of Spain with his head down. He felt so alone. He didn't know where to go or what to do. He was still perplexed he did not receive the response he was expecting from the love of his life. He walked past a bush with red roses. Their fragrance made him look up at them. He looked at the flower in front of him, it was big, red, and beautiful. Promptly his big blue eyes were watery and huge drops started rolling down his cheeks. A robust, middle-aged man in a fancy black suit saw him. He asked, "Why are you so glum, my friend?"

Myles wiped his face with his arms and gasped. He replied, "I'm all right."

The man hugged him from the neck with one arm. Then said, "You look like you need the remedy for sadness and worries related to love, come with me." The man let go of Myles and pointed with his hands to a place near them. He added, "I have exactly what you need."

Myles followed him and they entered the tavern the man was referring to. Once inside, the man sat on a stool, looked at the tavern owner, and said, "Serve this young man a drink, the best you have to forget a great love."

The tavern man said, "Yes, sir, coming right up." He served him the drink and Myles drank it in one gulp. Then he frowned, coughed, and held his cup up, waiting for more.

The tavern man gave him a new drink, and Myles tossed it back again. The elegant gentleman who brought Myles into the tavern, said, "I see you understand how this love remedy works. You just continue doing it until you feel better."

Meanwhile, Andrea and her teachers were arriving at the royal party and the duke was already standing outside waiting for her. The duke smiled a big smile when he saw her. He kissed her hand to greet her. Then, he offered his arm to her. Andrea took the duke's arm and together they walked toward the entrance of the royal party. Andrea's teachers walked quietly behind them. At the entrance, the guards looked at each other and whispered to one another. One said, "Look at their appearance!"

The other one answered, "Shhh… they are with the duke!"

Two more guards came to the door. One said, "You may take your break; we will cover you." The four guards talked for a little bit.

Andrea, her teachers, and the duke went inside the ballroom without any issues. They were not even noticed by the newly arrived guards. Dianne exclaimed, "Oh, this lovely music!"

The duke, waving one hand in front of him and placing the other one behind his back, gallantly looked at Andrea. He asked, "May I have this dance, my beautiful lady?"

Andrea smiled and extended her hand to him. The two of them danced gracefully. Many men looked perplexed at the beautiful Andrea. Ladies discreetly looked at her and murmured terrible things about her and her friends. One royal lady said, "She is so full of herself, look at her dancing happily and she is not even well presented for such a high-class party."

Another royal lady answered, "She does not respect the rules of etiquette all of us royals have always respected, so ill-mannered."

Another one added, "How can she show up without a beautiful white wig and no powder on her face? She is shameless. Why did they let her in here like that? She should not be here. They must throw her out immediately."

The duke went to the restroom. Meanwhile, Andrea was dancing with a handsome young gentleman, a marquess, and both were talking animatedly. The duke came back and declared, "Excuse me, but you are dancing with my date."

The marquess said, "I don't think you can call her your date anymore since she is happily dancing with me and does not seem to miss you at all."

Andrea said, "Excuse me, gentlemen, but I am not interested in any of you at the present moment." She continued, "I need a drink, excuse me." She left them arguing while she headed toward her friends. Then suddenly a young, handsome prince asked her to dance with him. She happily agreed. Both men stopped arguing when they noticed her dancing in contentment. A messenger came and told Andrea that the king wanted to see her in private. She went to see the king.

Afterward, she continued dancing glamorously for the rest of the night with the most important royal gentlemen at the party. It was late when Andrea and her friends finally decided to leave the party to go home and rest. The five of them agreed and went home.

Early the next day, Andrea and her teachers were still sleeping when someone was knocking at their door. "Who is it?" asked Charles.

The messenger answered, "A gift and a message for my lady of Stonemason." Dianne opened the door and looked at the basket full of new and expensive gifts. She looked inside her purse, gave the messenger some coins, and said, "Thank you, you may leave now." The young man bowed and left.

Dianne woke Andrea up saying, "Andrea, your royal admirer has sent you beautiful and lavish gifts today."

Andrea, still half asleep, answered, "Who?"

Dianne said, "The duke. Look, these are the finest fabrics, wigs, and jewels imported from France."

Valerie had awakened with the news and was also checking the basket. "And the most expensive white powder for your skin."

Andrea said, "I don't even like those things, but the fabrics and the jewels might be useful. Perhaps we should send them back."

Dianne asked, "Send them back?"

Valerie shrieked, "Are you crazy?"

Charles said, "It would be very discourteous of you to give back such fine gifts."

Salvador affirmed, "Even if you are not interested in the duke, you can still keep the gifts he sent you if you please." He continued, "Nobody asked him to give you anything. It was done at his own risk."

Looking at her teachers, Andrea said, "All right, you can have them all."

Dianne replied, "Thank you, dear."

Months later, the group of friends was together as usual. Charles looked at Andrea. He said, "Several months have passed and the duke continues to shower you with expensive gifts, still with no success in winning your heart. He doesn't seem to make any progress in capturing your attention, dear, or is there something I don't know?"

Andrea asserted, "No, I do not think so!"

They all heard a loud, familiar sound. Valerie, intrigued, looked at her friends, and asked, "Trumpets?" They all went outside to see what was happening. Six young boys were on their knees playing the trumpets. Three on one side, and three more on the other. In the middle was the duke, walking toward Andrea. A boy holding a red cushion with jewels was following the gentleman. The strong duke had a smile on his face. He stretched his arms waiting to have Andrea's hands in his. The boy with the jewels got on his knees. The duke held Andrea's hands, and said, "My dear, Andrea, I give you these jewels with all my love." He placed a bracelet around the wrist of his dream woman. The bracelet was thick, big, and made of gold. It had little intricate figures and was adorned with fine, colorful, shiny gems. The figures were many stars, the moon, and the sun, all made of gold. Then, he closed the clasp and immediately slipped a big gold ring on her finger with colorful shiny gems. Andrea gave a serious look at the jewels on her hand. Then, she caressed her own hair with both hands. The duke said, "My dear, it is time to formalize our commitment and get married soon."

Andrea, looked at him, and asked, "Marriage?" She added, "I do not think so!" She stretched her arm looking down at the jewels on her hand with narrow eyes. Then, showing her hand with the jewels to the duke, she said, "Take your jewels with you, remove them from my hand. I will not marry you, Duke."

The trumpets played triumphantly. The duke's face turned red when he said, "Silence those trumpets!" He looked at Andrea. Gently he said, "Do not answer right now, dear, take your time to think about it, do not rush to answer."

She said, "There is nothing to think about, I will not marry you now or ever."

He knelt in front of her and held her hands in his. He asked, "Why not, dear, we have been getting along so well?"

She said, "Marriage does not work, and I am not interested in walking with you to the altar."

He stood up and bent to kiss her hand. Then said, "I will leave, but if you change your mind, send a messenger and I will return."

Andrea looked down at him with narrow eyes. She replied, "I will do no such thing, good-bye."

The duke declared, "I will see you later, dear." Then he left.

Valerie looked at Andrea. She asked, "Are you sure you don't want to marry the duke, dear?"

Andrea said, "Please, no more talk about marriage."

Charles asked, "Do you like your new jewels, dear?"

Andrea, glanced at her hand, and said, "They are all right." She looked at Dianne. Then asked, "What about the princesses you were going to visit today?"

Dianne replied, "Thank you for the reminder, dear. Would you like to come with me?"

Andrea said, "It is not my desire at this moment to go see those two boring and mindless brats."

Dianne, looked over at Salvador, and asked, "Would you like to come with me and visit the two princesses who got hurt horse riding last week?"

Salvador answered, "I don't like the idea of visiting them, it is such a tedious endeavor. But since you want to go, I will gladly go and keep you company."

Dianne smiled. She said, "That is good enough for me, let's go." They both said good-bye to their friends and left. They were walking together and conversing enthusiastically when Dianne almost tripped over a man sleeping on the street. Luckily, Salvador caught Dianne by her waist. They looked at each other and smiled. The man on the ground immediately grabbed their attention. Dianne said, "I thought it was only a big bump on the street, but it is a person. Look at this disgusting fellow. From the look of his appearance, he has not showered in weeks. His hair is all disheveled, his clothes are as dirty as an old rag, and his shoes are missing."

Salvador added, "And with that smell, I can assure you his main interest has been drinking day and night." Salvador gently moved him, and said, "Come on, careless man, move away from the pathway and let us walk in peace."

The smelly young man started mumbling words and continued sleeping in the same place. Salvador tried to move him again, but he rolled himself back to where he was before. Dianne said, "Forget it, he is too drunk to wake up. Let's not waste our time with him. He cannot even speak clearly; he is just mumbling who knows what."

The dirty, drunk man rolled over and continued mumbling incoherently, "Andrea. Andrea, my love. Where are you, my love? Andrea, let's get married, I know you love me."

Salvador and Dianne looked at each other, both surprised. Dianne asked, "Andrea? Whose Andrea? Our Andrea?"

Salvador replied, "Oh my, look at him. Well, he looks like Myles, Andrea's ex-boyfriend."

Dianne got down on her knees, looked closely at the drunk man, and slapped his face gently with her purple gloves. "Myles, is that really you?"

Myles opened his big blue eyes and looked at Dianne for a few seconds. He said, "Andrea, my love, you came back to me."

Dianne, with a frown turned her head to avoid Myles's breath, and said, "So handsome, but too stinky, talk the other way."

Salvador was on the opposite side and covered his nose as soon as he felt Myles's breath on him, saying, "Andrea, Andrea."

Dianne stood up and exclaimed, "HE IS MYLES!" She added, "Poor fool, how could he end up like this?"

Salvador answered her. "You already said it, because he is a fool, that is why." Salvador held him and moved him carefully to one side of the street. He said, "Now, you are kind of out of the way so nobody will step all over you and hurt you." He added, "How can you look this skinny and be this heavy?"

A gentleman was walking by, and Dianne looked at him. She asked, "Excuse me, sir, do you know this man?"

The gentleman answered, "Not very well, but I will tell you what I know about him." He continued looking at Dianne. Then said, "He has been dedicated to the drink for some weeks. He stumbles drunkenly through the streets, and other times he rests on them with a tired face and his emotions numbed by the alcohol." He added, "He is penniless and drinks out of the pity of the citizens of this city."

Salvador asked, "What good is that kind of pity?"

Dianne replied, "Thank you, sir."

The gentleman answered, "You are welcome, madam."

Later when Dianne and Salvador went back home, they told Andrea the news about Myles. Valerie glanced at Andrea with concern. She whispered, "Poor Myles, he is a disastrous, homeless, drunkard. He has lost his manhood to alcoholism and still he can only think and speak of you."

Andrea, with a confused and indifferent tone, very slowly asked, "Why are you telling me all this, Valerie? Am I to be blamed for all the vagabonds in Spain? Did I ask all of them to do nothing but drink every day, become alcoholics, and waste their lives away?"

Valerie replied, "No, Andrea. It is not your fault, but I still feel a little pity for the dumb young man."

Dianne added, "Foolish man, wanting the love of a woman knowing she does not love him."

Charles said, "A man wasting his life away over a woman who doesn't care about him. There are so many women in the world. Where is the logic in that?"

Salvador mentioned, "I am going to have to go and check on this dreamer every day, just to make sure he is all right."

Dianne looked at Andrea. She said, "Don't worry, dear. Salvador will take care of Myles to make sure nothing bad happens to him."

Andrea looked at Dianne, then her eyes moved to Salvador. She said, "Why should I be worried about him or any other unintelligent man who wants to throw his life away? Do you think others are held responsible for his life just because he chose not to be responsible for his own actions?" Andrea slowly said, "Trust me, I am not worried. I refuse to waste my time on an individual who dedicates his time to drinking, no matter what his excuse is. I do not want to hear anything else about this matter." Andrea's four teachers quietly looked at her.

Early the next morning Salvador went to go look for Myles. Valerie accompanied him and they found him with a guitar in his hands singing.

Myles' Song

"My Love"
I used to be so happy
I used to enjoy my life
I did not care for anything
and everything was just right.
Then, I met my love one day
The greatest love to find
It made me see the world
Like never in my mind.
Everything was wonderful
My dreams were only of love
But then my love has left me
As lonely as ever before.
Oh, my love, where are you?
Why can't you love me back?
Why can't you love me again?
I miss you very much
You can ask me for anything
And all you want I'll give you
If only you would care about me
If only you would like me back
My love, come back to love me.
My love, my dear love, be the
same as in the past

When you used to like me
When you used to love me back
Only you are my happiness
Only you are my life
Can't you feel my heart?
This heart that beats for loving you
Come back, my love, come back.
I will be here waiting for you
Don't take long to be back
I hope you don't wait too long
To miss me and take me back
I met my love one day
The greatest love to find
It made me see the world
Like never in my mind
Oh, my love, where are you?
I love you very much!

Myles was crying again. He wiped his eyes with his dirty sleeves and continued singing and playing an old guitar.

Myles' Second Song

"My Beautiful Love"
I have a love, my beautiful love
with eyes as bright as the stars
with lips as the sweetest fruit
with hair like the gentle pigeon
whose best friend is the wind
with a body as warm as the sun
I want your eyes to see me
I want your lips to smile
I want your hands to touch me
I want your arms to hug me.
My love, my beautiful love

with eyes as bright as the stars
with lips as sweet as the sweetest fruit
with hair as the gentle pigeon in the wind
with a body as warm as the sun
I want your bright eyes to see me
I want your sweet lips to smile
I want your soft hands to touch me
I want your warm arms to hug me.
My love, my beautiful love
The one I love the most.

Salvador watched Myles attentively as he continued singing the same two songs over and over again. Many men surrounded Myles, and some of them clapped their hands. Salvador said, "Look at him, with so much love that he created these songs out of his heart."

Valerie put her hands over her chest, and exclaimed, "He is so romantic!"

One man gave Myles a drink, another one gave him a bottle of wine. Myles started drinking again. He started crying once more, and said, "Andrea, my beautiful Andrea, where are you?"

Some men left, while a few remained and tried to console him with more alcohol, and others asked him to play his guitar. Myles remained on the ground under a tree as he continued to sing, drink, and cry. He bellowed, "Andrea, my sweet Andrea, why don't you love me?"

CHAPTER THREE

The Trip

Pierre strolled through the gardens at Cecile's house on a warm evening, like many others before this one. He was looking for Marie and continued pacing around the garden until he found her. Marie was looking down, watering her pleasantly scented giant pink roses. Pierre looked at her and smiled a sweet loving smile. "Marie, my sweet love," he whispered.

Marie looked up at him, and immediately asked, "Pierre, where is Andrea? I haven't heard anything about her since she left France."

Pierre's sweet smile vanished while he looked attentively at Marie. Then he answered, "She's all right, ma chérie. It is the way it should be. Don't worry about Andrea, she is fine." He held Marie's hand and looked at her tenderly. "Now tell me, how are you doing?"

Marie took her hand away from him. She said, "How can you say Andrea is fine, when you're not there to see her?"

Pierre calmly replied, "Andrea is smart, and she knows how to take care of herself. Don't doubt her, she is perfectly fine and she always knows what she is supposed to do." Smiling playfully, he gestured by placing his fingers on his chest, thumbs in the air, and said, "You know, she learned from the best."

Marie, with a slightly louder voice, asked, "Does she really know what to do? Do you really think she is all right? Or do you just not care what she does, as long as she's with the royals in high society like you have always wanted for her?"

Pierre's face turned serious. "Marie, what is the problem now? You are just making a problem where there isn't one." Calmly, he added, "Marie, you need to find something important to do with your life to help you take your mind away from Andrea." Pierre shook his head. "I am telling you; she is perfectly fine."

In a calmer voice, Marie asked, "How can I take my mind away from my daughter? Andrea is very young, and it doesn't matter how knowledgeable and intelligent you say she is." Marie added, "She is young and she doesn't have enough experience to be living by herself. I just know it. I just know something is not right with her. A long time has passed and she hasn't written any letters to let me know about her life in Spain."

Grandma Cecile was listening from the window. She interrupted the conversation by hitting the floor with her cane. Then said, "Well, Marie, your knowledge about this is no good when you do not do anything about it. Is it?"

Marie changed her tone of voice to a nicer one, and told Cecile, "Please, Mother, this is very important."

Pierre continued looking at Marie. He said, "Marie, I am telling you, stop making problems where there are none. Stop this nonsense. Andrea is perfectly fine, just stop it."

Grandma Cecile rolled her eyes and shook her head. Desperately, Marie said, "I am not going to stop it. Can't you see how worried I am? Don't you understand, Pierre? I am not going to stop thinking about her until I see that she is all right. I want to see her with my own eyes, not hear it from your mouth. She is my daughter. I want my daughter back. I have to make sure she is safe. I should have never let you take her away from me, but you have always been winning her over with gifts and letting her have her way all the time." Marie placed both hands on her head and turned around. She exclaimed, "Andrea never listened to me! I should have never been so soft with her and with you. I should have taken better care of her and guided her with my own intuition instead of letting you buy her with gifts and trips. You have always let our daughter have her way." She looked at the sky. Then said, "I should have stopped you from influencing her into thinking royalty, power, and riches were the greatest achievements in life. My daughter is lost, and I don't know where to find her."

Pierre looked at Marie tenderly, got closer to her, kissed her on the cheek, and calmly assured her, "Andrea is not lost. She's in Spain and perfectly all right, Marie."

Grandma Cecile took a sip of her hot cocoa, looked at them both, and said, "The little brat is still a pain in the neck wherever she is."

Marie pulled herself away from Pierre. She stated firmly, "I am going to Spain."

Pierre retorted, "You are not serious."

"Oh, yes, I am serious, very serious and not you or anyone else is going to stop me from traveling to Spain to see my daughter. This is something I should have done a long time ago."

"Don't interfere, Marie. Let Andrea live a happy and successful life."

Marie shook her head, and said, "No, I have been waiting for my daughter to come back to me for a long time." Marie paced around the room, and said, "Andrea was only supposed to go away for one or two years, but instead of her returning home, she has stopped writing. I don't even know if she is healthy and well. How can you say she is happy, when we have not heard a single word from her for more than a year? I don't believe you anymore, and I don't need your permission, Pierre. I am going and that is final."

Grandma Cecile looked at Marie. She asked, "What about me? You just care about your impertinent daughter. Are you really going to leave me here all by myself? Andrea is young, and I am old. I need you more than her."

Marie looked at her mother. Then announced calmly, "You are welcome to come with me if you want, Mother."

Grandma Cecile hit the floor with her cane, raised her voice, and said, "You know I am too old to travel. You are my only family, and you just don't care about me. You are going to find me dead when you come back, and it will be all your fault."

Marie serenely said, "You are going to be all right, Mother. I said I am going to Spain, and that is what I am going to do. I need to go find Andrea; it is my responsibility."

Grandma Cecile said mockingly, "Responsibility, ha! If you really knew anything about responsibility you would not have had her in the first place."

Pierre touched Marie's shoulders gently and looked at her. He said, "I wish you were this decisive when I asked you to leave France with me and start a new life together, Marie. Our daughter and our own lives would be so different now."

Marie's eyes watered, and she softly whispered, "I have thought about it many times, Pierre. This has been one of the greatest regrets of my life."

Grandma Cecile affirmed, "Of course you have regrets. You have been a very bad daughter. I have suffered so much because of you, Marie, with all your poor decisions. That is why now you are going to pay for what you have done to me with your daughter's and your own bitter tears. You will be looking for one, but you will find two instead. You are going to find her with a newborn or pregnant, one of the two, and that is going to be your fault too."

Marie looked at Cecile. She calmly said, "Andrea having a baby is the least of my worries, Mother."

Angrily, Cecile shouted, "You are a bad daughter! Oh, what am I going to do all alone without a family?"

Pierre looked at Grandma Cecile and spoke in a sweet low voice. "Marie has not done anything wrong. Her biggest mistake in life has been never thinking or caring about herself. She has always been trying to please everyone around her, sacrificing her own happiness for others all the time. Unfortunately, she has not been able to make anyone happy as she might have thought with her unhappy life."

Marie calmly and firmly said, "Pierre, then you understand why I cannot continue to do the same thing all over again. I am not going to hide my feelings or wait for everything to turn out the way I want. This time, I wish to see my daughter and that is exactly what I am going to do. No one is going to stop me, neither you nor my mother."

Grandma Cecile angrily and desperately said, "I am going to tell everybody in France that you want to leave me all by myself. I am old and sick, and you don't care about me. I am going to die because of you and your rebellious ways. If you leave France, when you come back you will find me dead, and it is going to be all your fault. Everyone is going to know because I am going to tell them. You have to take care of me. I am your mother, and your mother must be first. I should always come first. You have to wait for the brat to come back or write you a letter whenever she wants. You two have spoiled that girl all her life. She has always done as she pleases and this time will be no different than before, but don't abandon your mother, you ingrate daughter."

Marie sighed, "I am tired of waiting all the time. I have waited for so many years for one thing or another. I already waited very long to hear news about Andrea, but I am not going to wait any longer. Good-bye, Mother. Good-bye, Pierre."

Marie took out a trunk from a large wooden chest and left.

Cecile shouted, "I will tell everyone about your evil ways, you lousy daughter! Everybody will know you have abandoned me, leaving me to fend for myself! To die all alone and unprotected!"

Marie looked back at her mother, then walked toward her, and said, "I am sorry, Mother." She was having second thoughts about leaving her mother. Marie looked at her mother once more. She said, "You can come with me if you want, let's go."

Cecile said, "You are crazy, and a terrible daughter. I cannot travel at my age."

Pierre said, "I will be around as always, madame. I will make sure you are all right."

Marie looked at Pierre, then back at her mother. She said, "Thank you, Pierre. Take care, Mother."

A few hours later, Marie was on a carriage on her way to Spain. Her trip companions were two ladies and a gentleman, the three of them royals. The two ladies were talking among themselves. The gentleman was listening to them quietly while Marie was lost in thought. Franchesca was saying, "That young woman who mixes with the royals all the time, some are even thinking of giving her a title and nobody really knows how she is going to get that royal title."

Catalina asked, "What are you saying? If you ask me, everybody knows she will buy it with the only valuable things she has which are her youth and her great beauty."

The gentleman interrupted, "I cannot deny how beautiful she is," he said, and sighed. "Oh, she is sooo beautiful, such beauty as I have never seen before in all my life, and I have seen many beautiful women in my lifetime. You can be sure of that, but no one as beautiful as her."

Franchesca said, "I do not think she is that beautiful. I think she has men bewitched."

Catalina agreed. "Bewitched!" she said assuredly, with wide eyes. "You are right, they are bewitched; that's what it is."

Franchesca said, "That is why no man can resist her, because she has magical powers."

The carriage stopped abruptly, and the horseman asked, "Would anyone like to come out and stretch their legs for a little while?"

The gentleman immediately agreed and got out of the carriage, while Franchesca said, "Invitation accepted, just what we need, some space to move and fresh air."

Catalina agreed. "Oh yes, we need to do this more often."

The horseman said, "Yes, we should, but we need to continue on the road to our destination so that we can get there in good time just as all of you want."

Marie was quietly listening to their conversation from a distance because her thoughts had taken her far away, even though she was sitting so near. She was thinking about her whole life, about the little girl she had raised, and wondered how she would find her when she arrived in Spain. *Would Andrea be all right? Would she still be the same impulsive, immature girl, or has she matured and learned during these three years? Would she be healthy and busy with her new life? Is that why she stopped writing letters to us? Or is her health not as good and that is why she stopped writing? Or is it worse? Is she very ill and nobody knew how to reach her mother? Or is it even worse than that and she did not want me to know she was in trouble? Maybe the issues she is having have nothing to do with her health. Am I a grandma?* Marie smiled subtly. *If I am a grandma, this is not as bad as other people might think. I actually think it will be very nice when I can see Andrea as a mother. I want to see my grandchild. I am going to love my grandchildren very much. What if she is in jail? No, news like this would have come already. What if she has been kidnapped? What am I going to do to find her? What am I going to do to bring her back? What am I thinking? She cannot be kidnapped; this is just me exaggerating, or could it be? I do not know what to think. What if she met a nice, handsome boy? She got married and moved far away from Spain? Where will I find her? I mean, it is very good that she is happy with her charming husband, but I need to see her to find peace of mind. What if she does not want to see me because she thinks I am a bad mother? On the other hand, I don't think I have been such a terrible mother, but I have not been a very good one either. I am sure there are many mothers who are a lot better mothers than I have been. Or maybe she is a drunkard now? No, it couldn't be. What if she just moved to a new place where I cannot find her because she does not want to see me ever again? What if I get old looking for her, and I never find her because she is hiding from me? She is hiding because she does not love me. I never let her do anything she wanted to do, but she did it anyway since her father let her do it. I am sure she would not be hiding from her father, but is she hiding from me? Is she alive?*

Marie was plagued by the agonizing and endless possibilities of Andrea's whereabouts. The two royal ladies continued criticizing the beautiful young, soon-to-be royal lady. The horseman said loudly, "Ladies and gentlemen, it is time for us to continue on our journey to Spain, please go back inside the carriage and find a comfortable spot to enjoy your trip."

Marie continued living in her tormenting thoughts while the horseman offered his hand to help her into the carriage. Then, the royal gentleman offered his hand as well to help her step up inside the carriage. Marie was submerged in her thoughts as usual. She did not notice the help offered from the gentlemen, and she got inside the carriage by herself. *What am I thinking? I should not assume the worst, or should I?*

The gentlemen looked at each other and shrugged their shoulders. The royal gentleman said to the horseman, "Some are absent from the present day and others are absent thinking about other people's lives, but most of them are not where they are supposed to be. I do not know what is worse, to talk to a quiet woman who won't listen to you because she is far away from where she seems to be, or to listen to the ill intentions of women who feel threatened by another who is much prettier than they have ever been?"

The horseman replied, "It is hard for me to answer that question, sir. I would just want the company of any woman who gets close to me even if she has any of those defects. I think I would still enjoy her company one way or the other. However, I would hope that she someday changes her ways for me."

The royal gentleman urged the two ladies to join them inside the carriage. "Ladies, forget for a moment how much you hate the beautiful soon-to-be countess and let me help you inside the carriage."

They both frowned at him and exclaimed in unison, "We don't hate her!"

Franchesca whispered, "Just because she does not have good taste and does not know how to powder her face for royal parties like us royals, does not mean I hate her. I just dislike her a little bit or maybe a lot."

Catalina said, "You have to admit she has terrible manners, does not follow the rules of etiquette, and does what she wants all the time with others. Especially with all the men that surround her."

The royal gentleman added, "I do not know about all that, but she looks very pretty without all the royal requirements, the makeup, and the wigs. She is a natural beauty." He offered his hand to help the two ladies, and one by one they accepted his hand and stepped into the carriage. Once they were inside the carriage, the royal gentleman tipped his hat, and said, "Have a nice trip, ladies." Then, he went to sit next to the horseman.

Surprised, the horseman asked him, "Was the carriage not comfortable enough for you, sir?"

The royal gentleman answered, "It is not the place, but the company, and I know already I am really going to enjoy talking to you from here until we get to Spain."

The horseman smiled, and said, "We still have a long way to go, sir."

The royal gentleman said, "I have a feeling it will not feel that long talking to you, horseman."

The horseman replied, "Well, thank you, sir." Both gentlemen smiled at each other.

The royal gentleman said, "People do not change their ways for anyone; you should know what you are getting yourself into and not get false hopes up for any woman just because she is pretty. However, you are free to love a not-so-nice lady if that is what you choose, I just do not want you to have false hopes for her to change."

The horseman said, "At my age and position in life, any woman would meet my present requirements, sir."

The royal gentleman said, "Which are none, I presume." Both men laughed out loud and continued chatting animatedly.

Meanwhile, the two royal ladies inside the carriage were intrigued about their unknown female companion and started asking Marie questions. Franchesca touched Marie's arm, and asked, "Why are you going to Spain?"

Marie looked at her. Franchesca repeated the question while touching Marie's arm. Marie answered, "I wanted to travel to Spain since I was young. I have even dreamed for a long time about living there. However, I have never visited, and I would like to see what I have been missing all this time."

Catalina said, "You will like it for sure. Spain is a great place to live and meet new people. You can come and stay with us for a few days if you want, you look like a nice, classy lady."

Marie replied, "Well, thank you, but I might not be as classy as you two; you two are royals, and I am just a regular French citizen."

Franchesca said, "Yes, you are, but you are much different than most French royal citizens, they are tramps, and you seem very honest and real."

Marie answered, "Thank you for your trust, but it hurts me a little to know that you think the royals from my country are that terrible."

Franchesca said, "They are, most only come to Spain to do very bad things."

Catalina added, "I hope you don't feel bad about it, we are just telling the truth."

Franchesca said, "Of course, you are not to blame for the mistakes of the very disgraceful French royals, but the good thing is you must be one of the good citizens."

Marie said, "I feel good about you two being so kind to me. Thank you for considering me a good person. I hope you continue to feel this way when you get to know me better. Tell me, do you know many French people like me who live in Spain?"

The two ladies answered together, "Not many."

Franchesca said, "Most of the people we know are royals, and most of them are detestable people like we already mentioned."

Catalina said, "We do not know many regular French citizens but seeing you I assume most of them must be kind of good, and not like their royal compatriots."

Marie said, "I am glad you know we are not all the same even when we all come from the same place. I am going to take it as a compliment because that's what it is. Isn't it?" Both royal ladies laughed.

Franchesca said, "Take it as you please, dear."

Catalina said, "I am sure you are a lot better than any of the royals who only go to Spain to lie and steal."

Marie asked them, "Where are you going exactly?"

Franchesca answered, "To the palace, of course. Where Spanish royalty belong, and as I said before you are welcome to stay with us for a few days."

Marie asked, "Are you sure it is going to be all right for me to stay with you both?"

Catalina answered, "Oh, but of course, it is all right; do not worry, dear, you will be welcomed there because you will be with us. You will see."

Franchesca said, "We like French people, we just do not like royals, but we like regular, nice French citizens like you. It is a lot more than just liking them, and to be honest with you, we both have been in love with French men before. Sadly, it did not last."

Catalina said, "Men are men, and they will always be the same no matter where they come from—French or Spanish— they are all the same."

They continued talking to Marie for a very long time until Catalina got quiet and looked at Marie. She said, "We have been talking way too much, but we have not given you the opportunity to say anything. What can you tell us about yourself, dear? Are you married? Where is your husband? Do you have children?"

Marie answered, "No, I am not married, but I do have a daughter."

Franchesca said, "Poor thing, you are a widow; your daughter must be as sweet and gentle as you are, and I would love to meet her in person." She waved her hand in front of Marie showing her one of her big, fine rings. Then said, "This beautiful ring was a gift from my first husband who was a real gentleman, it is so tragic that he died so young."

They all heard gruff voices giving directions to the horses. "Whoa, whoa!" The horses came to a complete halt, and the carriage stopped abruptly. They heard the galloping of horses and many brusque voices outside of the carriage. The different unknown loud male voices continued. A man opened the carriage door and maliciously looked at the three ladies inside the carriage. He stated, "Ladies, we are collecting your jewelry and gold, please put it all in the hat."

Marie took off her rings, bracelets, and simple necklace and put them inside the man's hat. The two royal ladies looked at each other, and one of them asked, "Collecting them for what?"

The man answered, "Hurry, hurry, for the needy people, give them to me now." He pulled their heavy necklaces from their necks and placed them inside his hat. The ladies complained and rubbed their necks in pain.

Franchesca said, "You brute, you hurt my neck."

"Come on, ladies, I have been very gentle and patient with you two, but I do not have all day. Will you give them of your own free will or should we take all of you women with us?"

The royal ladies hurried, they pulled their rings and bracelets and dropped them inside the hat. The man laughed cynically. Then said, "Thank you, ladies, and welcome to Spain."

The thieves left, and the gentleman said, "I apologize, ladies, for the behavior of those ruffians. I wish you had not been put through this difficult ordeal. Most of us Spaniards are good people. You will see for yourselves when we get to our destination."

CHAPTER FOUR

GOING TO THE NEW SPAIN

Andrea and her four teachers were still celebrating her possible new title. Charles, with a drink in hand, looked at her, and exclaimed, "Congratulations, dear, you are soon to be a countess as your father always wanted even before you were born!" The four of them raised their expensive drinks, and shouted, "CHEERS!"

Andrea raised her drink as well and feeling prouder than ever before, celebrated with her mentors. She said, "Thank you to all of you for being such extraordinary teachers and exceptional friends. Everything is exemplary, and I am delighted."

A young man came to them with a message. He said, "The saint bishop is here and asked to see my lady of Stonemason."

Salvador looked at Andrea. He asked, "The bishop, the greatest ecclesiastical authority in the neighboring surroundings, is here to talk to you, dear?"

Charles mused, "I wonder what assignment brought him here?"

Valerie looked at Andrea. She asked, "Do you want a blessing or to talk with him about certain matters now that you will soon become a countess?"

Andrea shook her head.

Dianne looked at Andrea. She said, "Would you ask him to come in, dear?"

Andrea with a smile on her face, looked at the messenger, then asked, "What brings him here?"

The young messenger took a bow. He replied, "I don't know why the saint bishop is here, but his excellency will tell you personally the reason for his visit, if my lady of Stonemason allows him in."

Andrea said, "Oh, but of course, please allow the saint bishop in."

Valerie whispered, "I hope he is here to congratulate you on your prospective new title, and surely he will ask you for a rather large contribution to one of his many causes."

The young messenger opened the door and let the bishop in. The bishop extended his hand which had a big ring with a fine stone centered on it. He said, "Good evening, important men and women of our congregation." Andrea's teachers one by one kissed the bishop's ring. Then, he looked at Andrea and extended his hand. He announced, "Dear, young lady of Stonemason, who may someday become a countess, there is an extremely important matter that I must communicate to you."

Andrea's teachers were leaving to allow Andrea and her important visitor some privacy to talk, when the bishop said, "You may be present to hear what I have to say as it involves all of you as well." All of them signaled Andrea to kiss the bishop's hand. Andrea hesitated and with disgust kissed his ring. They all sat down after the bishop. He said, "My lady of Stonemason, we have decided to help you find a new place where you will be happier in this life and with more opportunities to secure a good place for your soul in the next life. You will be accommodated with many other powerful nobles on a new journey to a new fruitful and wonderful land. It is a warm and sweet paradise full of obedient people to serve you. There you will find a husband, reconciliation with the Lord, possibly happiness, and a new and better way to live. You will find what you deserve, my beautiful young lady of Stonemason, as the granddaughter of a count."

Andrea answered, "What do you mean, Your Excellency? I have not asked for an evaluation of my happiness or anything of the sort."

The head of the church looked at her, and replied, "There was no need for you to request it, everyone in Spain knows about your deplorable ways of living and we have decided to help you, as it is our duty to have special care for the lives and souls of all royals."

Andrea of Stonemason, with her eloquent style of speaking, looked down at the bishop with a serious face. She asserted, "I appreciate your concern about my life, but I do not need you to be distressed about it. I am content just the way I am, and there is no need for anyone to change my life. I can change it myself when I have the desire to do so. I must warn you, that it will not be soon, as I am very comfortable with the life I have been living." Andrea added, "Now, if you will excuse me, I have more pressing matters to attend to, and I am sure you must have other important things to do besides just importuning me." She stood up, looked away from him, and walked to the door to leave.

The saint bishop of the church looked at her and waved his hand at her sternly. He said, "Your sinful ways have come to such a scandalous state that we can no longer hide it from the people. You are a bad example for the royal women, the town women, and all the women in general." The bishop calmed down a little, and said, "However, since you have royal blood coursing through your veins, and we have known your grandfather the Count of Stonemason and your father for so long, we had to do something to help you." The bishop added, "We appreciate your grandfather and your father very much and we could not leave you to your sinful fate. We have decided to allow you to have the freedom and the riches a noble like you deserves to be happy. Unfortunately, you cannot have it here anymore. The highest church tribunal, the saint inquisition, and all the noble counsels of the court have decided to send all of you on a trip to a new, beautiful, far away land. You are traveling to the New Spain to start a new life and to redeem yourself from sin."

The young Andrea of Stonemason paced slowly around the big room. She stopped, stood straight, and looked directly at him, then said, "Let me see if I understand what you are saying, Saint Bishop. Since sinners are not allowed on this land, you are sending me away from this place, along with most of the royal court. Of course, you will not forget to include yourself and some of your colleagues as well." Andrea had a triumphant smirk on her face.

The high priest looked at Andrea, narrowed his eyes, and with a loud shaky voice, he grumbled, "I was warned about your insolence, but it is worse than what I had imagined. Your insolence is one more sin to add to your list of the reasons why you are leaving this land. You will be leaving tomorrow morning with the other nobles who need to find redemption for their sins and a new life. You will have a new beginning." He stood as he continued to scold Andrea. "I will take my leave, as I have many important duties that require my attention. Do not waste this opportunity to become a better person and find salvation for your soul."

Valerie inclined herself to kiss the bishop's hand good-bye. She said, "Your Holiness, have mercy on us."

The bishop looked down at her. He replied, "Begging will not change this decision."

Dianne inclined herself to kiss the bishop's hand. She asked, "What if we promise not to do it again, not that we admit to any wrongdoing, but if we promise not to do what you don't like in front of people and if we do what you want us to do, would you then forgive us?"

The bishop looked down at her. He said, "Please, no false promises."

Charles got near the bishop to say good-bye to him properly by kissing his hand, and said, "We can give you anything you would like for your noble causes."

The bishop held his hand while Charles kissed it, then said, "If you would have shown such a kind heart to cooperate with my noble causes before, I might have considered it, but this sounds like bribery, and the answer is NO."

Salvador kissed the bishop's hand. He asked, "Please, Your Excellency, tell us what we have to do to remain in Spain?"

The bishop looked down at him, raised his eyebrows along with his face, and said, "You have done plenty already. There is absolutely nothing you can do to remain here in Spain." The bishop extended his hand to Andrea for her to kiss it good-bye like her friends did. He said, "Someday you will understand, and you will be grateful for what I have done for you here today."

Andrea's face was furious and with a piercing look toward the bishop, she asked, "Grateful?"

The bishop agreed, "Yes, besides, I will pray for your souls. Especially yours, dear, young and beautiful descendant of royals."

Andrea ignored the hand that he had extended toward her and did not kiss it. She looked briefly down at him as she spoke. "Do not waste your time, nor bother to pray for me. Anyway, I do not think a sinner's prayer will be heard."

The bishop was furious as he cried out loud, "GUARDS!" Two men entered the big room and Andrea's four teachers tried to follow them. The saint bishop left with the guards, and they locked the door behind them leaving Andrea along with her four teachers trapped inside.

Dianne wailed, "Oh, Andrea, we have let all hell loose against us! They have exiled us. Their plan is to send us away with the worst high class criminals to live in a new and distant land."

Charles said, "I have heard of many of the punished nobles being sent there, and they are all horrible people."

Valerie agreed, "I heard about it, too, and I have to agree they are all the worst living creatures I have ever had the misfortune of meeting."

Dianne said, "I knew about this trip too, but it never occurred to me that we were some of the candidates to leave Spain like criminals. This is terrible news." She sighed and sat down, hugging the elegant couch.

Salvador said, "I know I should be worried like all of you, but not all the people going with us are as bad as they say they are. Look at us, for example, we are good people." Everyone looked at him with a serious face. Salvador added, "If us as an example is not enough to convince you that there will be good people on that ship, let me tell you that most of the Jesuits who will accompany us on this trip are very kind people who have dedicated their lives to do good. These kind men have helped everyone around them, especially the forgotten, the poor, and all the people who are suffering. It does not matter who they are or where they come from. They just want to help the needy. Their main focus is helping others without judging them. They are practically saints, real saints, even when they do not proclaim to be. You might not believe it, but you will see for yourselves when you meet them. Holy beings are what they are, and I am telling the truth without exaggerating."

Andrea with a blank stare, stated, "Real saints exist, that is good to know, for a moment I thought they were all like the bishop who everybody has to call a saint when HE is clearly NOT."

Valerie suddenly said, "I am realizing now that not everything about this trip is as bad as we think if the Jesuits are going of their own free will."

Charles added, "Perhaps we are going to be just fine."

Andrea complained, "But I heard that land is new and filled with uncivilized people. I was just beginning to enjoy my time here in this marvelous land, my beautiful Spain. They must have waited a little longer until they formally gave me my royal title." There was a harrowing noise and the four of them looked at each other concerned. It was the sound of many horses galloping together.

Charles said, "The riders of those horses must be Spanish soldiers."

"Where are they going in such a rush?" asked Andrea to her teachers. Neither of them knew the answer and they were curious to discover it. They all rushed outside the door.

The horses stopped right in front of them. There were at least forty riders. The higher ranked soldier who was riding in front of all the others dismounted his horse and walked closer toward them. He said brusquely, "The ship is ready and is only waiting for a few guests, including you five, would you like to come with us, or do we have to drag you there?"

Salvador assured calmly, "No need for violence, Sergeant, we are going to go voluntarily."

The sergeant ordered, "Step into the carriage then, all of you."

Charles replied, "I can see patience is a good quality you do not possess."

Valerie said in desperation, "We must gather our belongings before we depart!"

Dianne agreed, "Yes, Sergeant, we will not take long, you will see."

The sergeant frowned. He sighed, "Very well, ladies, we will escort you to get your belongings, but you will have to hurry up as the orders are to take you immediately to board the ship."

Dianne and Valerie said, "Thank you, Sergeant."

Disappointed, Andrea asked, "Thank you for taking us all against our will to an unknown and dangerous place?" She shook her head in disbelief, and added, "This is outrageous, besides the bishop said the trip would be until tomorrow."

The sergeant said roughly, "I am sorry, madam. Will you get in the carriage, or should I help you into it NOW?"

Andrea boarded the carriage last, after her four teachers. She said, "It is impossible to reason with the riffraff." The sergeant led the horses and guided the carriage as fast as he could toward the palace where the five of them kept their belongings. He stopped the carriage in front of the palace entrance and the rest of the soldiers came to a halt.

Charles and Salvador got out of the carriage and helped the three ladies down. As soon as they stepped into their chambers, the domestic help was ordered to pack all of their belongings inside big chests. They had about twenty wooden chests which were quickly filled with fancy clothes and jewels. The help continued packing their elegant bed sheets and pillows imported from France.

Surprised, the sergeant asked, "Where in the world would all of these fit? Have you seen the space inside of the carriage?"

Andrea blinked her big, intense green eyes indignantly, and calmly replied, "That is not our concern, you are the one in charge of finding where to place our possessions."

The bishop arrived. He said, "Do not bother bringing all of these things with you on the ship, leave them here as a donation for the needy instead."

Valerie said, "The poor would not know what to do with these extremely fine worldly goods, it would be such a waste."

Dianne added, "That would be as good as throwing it all into the sea."

Salvador said, "Dear Monsignor, please let the ladies bring their belongings."

The bishop said, "Does that mean you two gentlemen will not bring anything?"

Charles answered, "We gentlemen have our own basic needs too, Monsignor. We need to be well presented to be able to accompany such fine ladies. I am sure you understand."

Andrea called on the soldiers. She ordered, "All of you, come and grab a chest each. There will be a reward for each of you who can bring these goods unharmed."

The sergeant was going to say something, but before he did, his soldiers hurried inside and grabbed a chest each. About ten soldiers were left without chests. They asked, "What about our reward?"

The sergeant said loudly, "Soldiers, we are leaving now." They all hurried to mount their horses.

The bishop looked at Andrea and her four tutors. He asked, "Would you like my blessing before you go?"

Dianne, Valerie, and Salvador got closer to the bishop. "Yes, please give us your blessing."

Charles got closer to the bishop, raised his shoulders, and looked at Andrea. The bishop asked Andrea, "What about you, child, come closer so you can be blessed too."

Andrea looked the other way. She asked, "Is your blessing going to stop this trip and allow us to stay in Spain?"

The bishop answered, "I am afraid not."

Andrea hurriedly replied, "Then, I do not want it."

He ignored Andrea and blessed her four companions.

One by one they slowly stepped onto the ship. The soldiers placed all the chests on board. The sergeant told Andrea, "Lady of Stonemason, your possessions are all on the ship as you asked. Please now compensate my soldiers."

Andrea replied, "Having the honor of being allowed to touch my expensive belongings should be sufficient compensation, be glad I do not charge you for such an honor; anyway, here you are." She gave him an embroidered sack of coins and the soldiers left swiftly.

The ship sailed into the ocean. The sky was partially obscured by clouds on that cold winter morning. A very tall and strong gentleman sat upon one of the chests. Andrea looked at him with her big, intense green eyes. She ordered, "DO NOT touch my valuable possessions, go find a less expensive place for you to take a seat."

Salvador looked at Andrea and at the unknown gentleman. He interrupted, "These chests are made of very hard wood, you would not be comfortable; I am sure you will find a better and more comfortable place to sit, sir." Then gently, he pulled Andrea's arm, and whispered, "Do you know who that man is?"

She quietly shook her head.

He said, "Of course you do not, or you would not be speaking to him in that tone. He is a very feared murderer and the son of a Spanish royal who has hurt men for less than you can possibly imagine." He continued, "Andrea, dear, I want all of us to get to the New Spain alive; please try to be nicer to all of these people on the ship.

Andrea answered, "Me, the most beautiful and important lady in the world, fearing these low-class individuals?"

Salvador said, "Do not do it for them, do it for me, just do it." He added, "Please, dear, consider my wishes, will you?"

Andrea sighed, and replied, "All right, Salvador, I will do as you say, not because I am afraid of him or the others, but because I want to be considerate of your wishes."

Salvador winked, "That is good enough for me, dear."

The other three teachers looked at him with fear. "What is his name?" asked Andrea.

Dianne answered hurriedly, "That is not important right now."

Charles insisted, "It is good to know the people with whom we are traveling here."

Valerie whispered, "Everybody calls him 'Fast Shadow.'"

"I wonder why?" asked Andrea.

Salvador said, "You do not want to know, dear."

"What about the other man next to him?" asked Andrea.

Charles replied, "That one is his cousin 'Little Shadow,' but you should not be fooled by the 'little' in the name. He is as dangerous as his tall cousin, just stay away from them both."

Andrea looked at them curiously, "That is going to be hard to do as we are stuck here traveling with them on the same ship."

She added, "Look at their big mustaches and long sideburns. The tall one is slim and the short one has a belly. Both are dressed in all black, a sight impossible to forget.

Salvador looked at Andrea, and said, "Do not trust either of them, the shorter one is as dangerous as the tall one, let us just mind our own business and get to this new land in one piece."

Charles said, "Agreed, the three of you understand, right ladies?"

Valerie said, "Yes."

Dianne covered her eyes with both hands. She whispered, "Yes, but this is very horrible."

Andrea said, "I understand."

Darkness was upon them. The sky was filled with bright stars. The waves were swinging the ship from one side to the other, like a mother rocking her baby while she sings a lullaby. The only difference was that no one on this ship could stop the swinging. Dianne and Salvador were complaining. Dianne moaned, "Can anyone stop moving this ship? I feel very sick."

Salvador agreed. "Yes, my darling. I feel the same. This is the worst vertigo I have ever felt."

Charles said, "You need to rest and get used to the movements of the ship."

Andrea and Valerie agreed. Valerie exclaimed, "Yes, stop it, please!"

Andrea sighed, "I wish this ship would stop moving! This is the worst illness I have ever experienced in my entire life."

Valerie said, "This is no illness. Just a little dizziness from the water movement, you will see how we grow accustomed to it in a few days."

Dianne said, "This might be an opportunity for all of us to repent of our sins."

Andrea replied, "What sins?" They all laughed and continued feeling sick.

Salvador was throwing up overboard. Dianne was lying down. Andrea, Valerie, and Charles were holding onto the railing of the ship. The wind ruffled Andrea's hair and dress. Her long eyelashes were bothered by the wind. She covered her closed eyes with her hand. She opened them again. The reflection of the moon shone in her big, bright, intense green eyes every single time she opened them. A loud roll of thunder made her clench her fists on the rail and shut her eyes tightly. The winds started to blow stronger. The waves continued to grow taller and crash louder with each passing moment.

Charles said, "I thought this could not get any worse, but a thunderstorm is fast approaching."

Andrea asked, "How can it possibly get any worse?"

Little Shadow and Fast Shadow were looking at them attentively from the other side of the ship. Little Shadow said, "Look at them whiners, complaining about every little thing."

Fast Shadow said, "We should throw their belongings into the sea before the ship sinks with so much weight."

Little Shadow agreed. "All those heavy chests, let's do it."

A big wave rose higher and higher until it fell with a crash and splashed all of them. Andrea sighed. She could not breathe freely with all the waves coming towards her at once, and the strong winds added to her desperation. The ship's crew were running and screaming, "Everybody, below deck now!" They all scurried inside as fast as they could, but it was not fast enough to avoid the waves from soaking them completely.

Andrea and her four teachers were all wet, dripping with water from head to toe. Andrea started to shake, and said, "I am too young to die here in the middle of the ocean."

Dianne said, "I don't want to die either."

Valerie asked, "Who does?"

Salvador replied, "Nobody is going to die here."

Charles said, "The ship's crew know how to handle these rough storms at sea. We will survive, all of us."

Many sunny days and tumultuous nights passed on the ship. Andrea said, "I have asked the captain when we will arrive at our destination, and he has given me good news. I do not know if I should believe him or if he is simply toying with my feelings."

Charles asked, "What did he say, darling?"

Andrea replied, "He said we will soon arrive at the New Spain!"

Valerie and Dianne both held hands and grinned.

Salvador looked at the horizon, and in a loud voice said, "Look, ladies and gentlemen, land in sight!"

Andrea screamed, "The New Spain!"

The five of them jumped up and down cheerfully as they hugged each other.

When the ship landed on the shore they all felt instant relief wash over them. Andrea said, "We are on land, at last, after so many weeks on the sea." The five of them hugged each other and were happy to be on solid ground. The captain of the ship said, "You all are very lucky that we didn't have any major storms during this trip."

Once on land, the place looked crowded, and they followed a priest holding the statue of a baby Jesus. One priest invited them to join them in their pilgrimage to walk and pray. He said, "Follow the Lord with us."

Valerie said, "We do not have time for this, we are tired and want to sleep."

Another priest got near them and showed them a bowl with money. He said, "Give some money to the child."

Dianne asked, "What child? I did not know statues drink milk or consume food."

A priest answered, "It is not as you think, my lady, it is for the work of the Lord. Would you like to be blessed?"

Valerie said, "We are already greatly blessed, and we are in such a hurry."

Charles looked at his friends. Then whispered, "So many people are following that statue, and giving what little money they have."

Salvador said, "They have something we lack, faith in the one who is so much greater than ourselves."

Valerie looked at Salvador, and said, "Very well, Salvador, as always you are right, now let them have your money and follow them."

Salvador chuckled, "Valerie, dear, I just said we don't do that."

The people continued to sing with candles in their hands, some held flowers, and others whispered their own prayers. Andrea looked at her friends. She scoffed, "This is utterly insane, too many ignorant people gathered here together and wasting my time with their ridiculous beliefs. I cannot stand this any longer." She added, "Let us get out of here, before I lose my mind." She held hands with Charles and Valerie. Then said, "Come, let us make haste. We must walk the other way to waste less time trying to get out of this big crowd."

Andrea almost bumped into an old priest. He saw her desperation and offered her a rosary. "Here, beautiful young lady, pray with us and your mind will find the peace you need." Andrea frowned and did not accept it. The priest gently placed the rosary around Andrea's neck. The priest offered his hand to her, and said, "Join us, my sweet child. Do not be afraid to follow the path of the Lord."

Andrea glanced dismissively at him. She said, "No time for that, Priest, there are more important things we must do." She stormed off in a hurry. Frustrated, Andrea looked at her friends, and asked, "When is all this going to end, or is it possible that this crowd has no end?"

Salvador held her hand. He reassured her, "Patience, dear, everything has an end, even this."

Charles said, "There is only one way to get away from this crowd right now, follow me." Charles led them behind the bushes and through the tall grass. They all followed him away from the crowd.

Andrea took off the white rosary from her neck and threw it as far as she could, it fell on the grass. Andrea laid down on the warm grass and closed her eyes. She felt the rays of the sun penetrate her entire body. It felt like a warm and gentle caress that engulfed her from head to toe. Andrea sighed with content, "We might be able to be happy here in the New World after all. This is not as bad as I thought it would be."

Charles sat down by her side. He agreed, "Yes, dear, we will be fine, you will see."

Valerie, Dianne, and Salvador sat on the grass around Andrea—all of them had triumphant smirks on their faces. Everything was going to be a lot better than what they had originally predicted, or so it seemed.

CHAPTER FIVE

Life in the New Spain

Dianne looked at Andrea and her friends. She exclaimed, "Life has been good to us here in the New Spain!"

Valerie agreed, "Everything has been a lot better than what we had predicted."

Salvador looked at his friends. He said, "Who could have known that the New Spain was going to be the place where we were going to find riches and freedom."

Charles looked at Andrea, then said, "This is the place to be, and who knows, you might even finally get your royal title you have desired for so long, dear." He added, "You are not any regular woman anymore, Andrea of Stonemason; you are soon-to-be royalty, you will soon be the Countess of Stonemason."

Andrea looked at Charles. She stated, "Yes, I am soon to be royalty, but I was never any regular woman to begin with. I am beautiful, I am magnificent, and now I am soon to be a countess as well." Andrea added, "And do not forget rich, I am also very rich. Any day now, I will fulfill my father's wishes of becoming a countess like my grandfather who was a count when he was still alive many years ago."

Charles opened his arms to embrace her. He said, "Congratulations, dear, for all of your achievements, including relocating to live here in the New Spain."

Andrea hugged Charles. She said, "Thank you, Charles. You four have taught me well."

Valerie hugged Andrea, and exclaimed, "You have learned well everything we have taught you, darling."

Andrea smiled, flipped her hair and then replied, "That is true, you are very good tutors, but I am also an excellent student."

Salvador opened his arms wide to embrace Andrea. He said, "Congratulations, dear, I am sure you will soon fulfill your wish to become a countess, and you are also extremely rich."

Dianne mentioned, "Everybody is getting ready to go to the royal party, and we have everything ready for you to be presentable."

Valerie handed Andrea a long, white wig while Salvador gave her the pale white powder makeup and red dust for her lips.

"Hold on!" said Andrea. "We have talked about this before, remember? I am not going to wear that, and I would not wear it either, if I were you."

Dianne said, "What do you mean? These are the most fashionable items only owned by the fanciest and richest royals we know."

Valerie added, "Besides, remember that no person has been allowed to enter the royal parties without these fancy required items."

Andrea replied, "We always find a way to avoid such horrible items. This wig is heavy, warm, and looks old-fashioned, and this makeup is so pale and dry." She put her hand under her chin, and added, "I do not want to look like a ghost; I am the most perfect and beautiful just the way I am." She frowned while moving the wig aside, and said, "I do not need any of these hideous royal items. You have to admit, even being used only by royalty, these things are just terrible looking and very uncomfortable to wear."

Charles agreed, "Andrea is right. We should not wear these intolerable items either. Just admit it, we hate this fashion as much as she does, but we would not admit this to anyone else. Let's just go as Andrea wants, anyway it is not like we have not done it before."

Dianne said, "They will not let us in like this. This is the New Spain, we should be living in better new ways, remember?"

Andrea rolled her eyes, "You sound just like the bishop. Anyway, I am sure they will let us in."

Salvador winked at Andrea, "There is only one way to find out."

Valerie sighed, "Here we go, together to the royal party showing our natural skin and hair like no one else there."

Some playful young children ran barefoot on the street. A boy shouted, "The sheep heads are coming, and they are having a nice party! The sheep heads are coming, and they will dance at their sheep party." The two black-haired boys with dark eyes were running around having fun imitating the aristocrats without even stepping foot inside the royal dance room. A little blonde, blue-eyed barefoot girl took off her common gray rebozo from around her back and placed it on her head. She started to dance while tiptoeing and caressing the rebozo on her head, "I am very beautiful and very rich and you will let me in; I will dance in this party because I have my big white wig."

The carriages were coming and going. Elegant nobles were entering the party. All of them following the official etiquette by wearing the white, wavy wig and the high heels. The ladies had their faces pale white with the powder they wore on their faces, and their lips were all bright red. All of them were wearing the required clothes and items to be able to get inside such a prestigious royal party. All of them except Andrea and her friends. They were all showing their natural hair and skin. No white wig or white powder on their faces. This was quite unusual. The four entrance guards looked at each other and stopped the couple in front of Andrea's group. A gentleman was not wearing the tall red high heels required by all the male royalty. A guard noticed this with only a glance, and said, "Excuse me, sir, but you cannot enter dressed like that."

The distinguished man complained, "My feet hurt and they are swollen. It is upon my doctor's insistence that I do not wear my royal party high heels. They could not fit on my swollen feet even if I tried. That is why I have to wear these simpler shoes."

Another guard shook his head with a serious expression and explained, "We are sorry, but the orders are that no one can enter without all of the royal fashion requirements."

The elegant man frowned and raised his voice a little. He declared, "You have no idea who I am, and you will hear from me if you do not let me in."

The four entrance guards discussed the matter in a very low voice amongst themselves. Then one of them said, "We are sorry, sir, but the rules are for everyone."

Another guard added, "If you return with your royal party shoes, you can come inside, if not, there is nothing we can do to help you."

Another guard added, "As much as we would like to let you in, we cannot do so as we are just following orders from above."

The lady accompanying him held the gentleman's arm, and whispered, "It is time for us to take our leave, dear, let's go home, we don't have to be here." They lowered their heads and left together.

The party was full in no time. The music was loud. There were small groups of ladies sitting down and chatting together. Many men were standing and chatting in big groups. There was a big table full of gentlemen talking animatedly. Many couples were dancing. Most of the guests were already inside the ballroom as they arrived on time. Some of the young children from the working-class families were still playing on the streets. They saw some of the royals wearing their required and pretentious royal items. The little boys continued to yell, "The sheep heads are coming, the sheep heads are coming!" The little blonde girl continued to dance and caress the rebozo on her head pretending it was her big wig. Meanwhile, another little girl with big chocolate brown eyes, brown hair, and soft brown skin was sitting down on a stone quietly watching as the other three children played. The little children saw Andrea's group which made them stop their playing and dancing to look at them attentively instead. They were absolutely stunned. The little blonde girl was mesmerized with Andrea. She said, "You are the most beautiful lady in the whole world, and you don't even have a sheep head." The little girl opened her eyes wider, and added, "I don't need my wig; I don't want to be a sheep head anymore. I want to be just like you!" She immediately took the rebozo off her head and threw it on the ground into a big mud puddle. Then, she fixed her short braids and slicked her blonde hair back with some saliva. The boys picked up the muddy rebozo and placed it next to the feet of the other little girl. She stood up, picked up the muddy rebozo, put it on her head, and started to dance. One boy took off his shirt, put it on his head, and started to dance as well. The other boy saw it and did the same thing. He also took off his shirt and started to dance with it on top of his head. The four children held hands and danced together happily. The boys sang, "We are the sheep heads!"

Andrea glanced at the children and laughed out loud. Then, she looked at her friends and they all laughed in unison as they watched the innocent children play. Andrea, still laughing, asked, "Would you still like to wear the fashionable and very expensive royal wig?"

They shook their heads and laughed.

Andrea's group walked to the door to enter the royal party. The guards first looked at each other, then they looked at the newly arrived guests. One of the guards looked at Andrea in disbelief. He asked, "Why are you dressed like this, madam?

Don't you know the etiquette rules?" The guards all spoke in low hushed voices.

A gentleman approached the guards. He announced, "Let the five of them in, viceroy's orders." The guards let them in. Everybody stared at Andrea and her friends. Women were murmuring horrible things about them. The men were happily desiring her company, and one by one asked Andrea to dance. She danced with many important gentlemen, one after another. The viceroy saw Andrea, and asked his friends, "Do you know that beautiful young lady?" The ladies glanced at the viceroy's wife, but she avoided eye contact and lowered her head. He sent a young priest who was sitting at his table to escort Andrea to his table.

The young religious gentleman asked Andrea, "My lady, I have word from the viceroy to bring you back with me to his table to meet him."

Andrea answered with a flirtatious gleam in her eyes, "We may go to that table as soon as I give you the honor of a dance." She came closer to him and with her big, bright, intense green eyes looked him straight in the eye as she placed his hand directly on her waist while she held his neck tight and close to her.

The priest did not know what to do. He was as red as a tomato. He was sweating and gently attempted to step away from her. Then, he stuttered as he meekly said, "M-m-my lady w-w-we should go back so you can meet the viceroy. He is waiting for you."

The viceroy observed them from afar. The viceroy's wife smiled, and said, "She does not look interested in meeting anyone else from this table. She looks quite happy dancing with that young and handsome priest, might I add."

The viceroy stated, "Young people enjoy dancing and chatting amongst themselves, there is no rush for them to come to this table. I know they will arrive here soon enough."

The viceroy's wife added, "They make a good couple, both young and beautiful. It is such a shame that he is a priest."

Meanwhile, Andrea and the priest continue to dance. Andrea whispered in his ear, "I love your scent, what is your name?"

The young priest answered nervously, "I am Friar Peter, to serve you and the Lord."

Andrea smiled, and playfully said, "Very well, you will serve me one of these days, I will look for you at the chapel where you live."

The young priest insisted, "My lady, please don't let the viceroy wait too long, come with me and meet him as he has requested."

Andrea replied, "He can wait, I am really enjoying your company and I can meet him some other day."

The young priest insisted, "No, my lady, please, I implore you, he is anxiously waiting to meet you. He must have some very important royal matters to discuss with you. And I should not be dancing with you or with anyone."

Andrea laughed. "You are no fun, maybe it is the place we are in. I think we need some privacy to help you relax." She headed over to the viceroy's table as she held and playfully pulled the young priest's hand along with her. The young priest looked nervous, embarrassed, and completely mortified as he tried to gently pry his fingers out of Andrea's hand. Andrea held his hand again, but this time tighter and moved her face closer to his. "Tell me, Peter. What is a real man of the Lord doing in a place like this? Not that I am not enjoying your company, quite the contrary. I am marveled to have found you here!"

The young priest answered while still attempting to separate his body from Andrea. "Please, my lady, the viceroy is awaiting you."

Andrea moved even closer to him this time and whispered breathily in his ear. "Do not be afraid, handsome. Let us go see what that gentleman wants, but only to put your mind at ease."

The two of them slowly approached the viceroy's table. His wife along with two other royal ladies were chatting and whispering horrendous things about Andrea. Then, the viceroy's wife stopped whispering and spoke in a normal tone. "She is such a vulgar individual who has no respect for the men of the Lord."

Her lady companion added, "She must be a very sinful woman."

Their other friend added, "It is in such bad taste to present yourself as you are like that, without a fancy wig and the elegant makeup at this fine, royal celebration."

The viceroy's male friends all agreed on what one of them said, "I love her hair and skin."

Another gentleman added, "Such beautiful bright eyes as I have never seen before in all my life."

Another gentleman said, "And such an alluring presence."

When Andrea reached the table the women became instantly silent. They looked at her with distaste in their envious eyes. The men greeted her graciously. The viceroy stood up to welcome Andrea. Even though Andrea was not extremely tall, she towered over him. Andrea was about five feet, five inches tall and the viceroy was only around five feet. He signaled a service man to assist her in taking a seat at his table. He understood and followed his instructions. Andrea sat next to the viceroy. He said, "Is there anything I can do to help such a beautiful creature enjoy this party?"

Andrea answered, "It is a perfectly nice party already."

The viceroy insisted, "In three days, I will have a more reserved party with only my closest family and friends, and I would like you to join us."

Andrea glanced at him. He added, "And I will not accept 'no' for an answer."

The viceroy's wife asked, "What party, dear?"

The viceroy answered, "You will not attend it since you will be busy with other important matters."

The viceroy's wife insisted, "I did not know about any other royal party. Why have you not mentioned anything to me yet?"

The viceroy answered, "You do not need to know all my business of high importance, woman, go find me the duke immediately."

The viceroy's wife placed a hand on her chest. Then unhappily answered, "Me? Find someone, but I am your wife?"

The viceroy said, "Yes, you are, unfortunately, but what are wives for? Other than to annoy you all they want and bore you for the rest of your life."

The viceroy's wife, offended, stood up, looked at her friends, and said, "Let's go to the ladies' room." The three of them stood up and followed her.

Andrea stood up as well and said, "Thank you for your invitation, Your Highness, I hope you enjoy the party."

The viceroy stood up to say good-bye to Andrea, and vowed, "I will send someone to find you in the evening and you will be escorted to my party. You will have a grand time, you will see."

Andrea said, "Your wife may not like it if I go since she is not invited."

The viceroy added, "Do not worry, dear, I will invite her if it soothes your mind, she will be there too."

Andrea was saying her good-byes when a gentleman suddenly invited her to dance. She danced with him happily. Many important royal gentlemen in the party asked Andrea for a dance that night. Each of them waited for their turn patiently to be able to dance with the most beautiful woman at the royal party. One by one the royal gentlemen asked her to dance, and Andrea enjoyed herself with each of them through the night.

A few years later, Andrea was having a conversation with her teachers. Charles said, "Andrea, dear, we have been very happy here in the New Spain." Salvador agreed, "Yes, we have. Happier than we would have thought."

Dianne squealed with delight, "It's been just lovely living here, and you finally received your royal title here in the New Spain!"

Valerie added, "If we could have known we would be living such a good life here, we would have come sooner." The five of them laughed.

Andrea said, "Yes, I love it here, and I am officially a countess now." She smiled. "I would have never imagined I was going to get my royal title here in this new land, life has been good to all of us here."

Charles said, "I agree, dear, but there is something that worries me a bit. What is going on between you and the viceroy?"

Andrea's smile disappeared. "Nothing of importance."

Charles insisted, "Something must be going on between you two. You have been seeing him for some time now." He added, "He is always looking for you personally or sending someone to find you, and you have been spending a lot of time with him, more than usual, for many months now."

Salvador intervened by asking, "Is there anything you would like to share with us, dear?"

Andrea answered, "I have absolutely nothing of consequence to share at this time."

Dianne said, "Come on, gentlemen, you already have an idea of what is going on here."

Valerie added, "I don't think there is anything to worry about, we have trained her well."

Dianne advised, "Andrea, always remember not to get sentimentally involved with him or you're lost."

Annoyed, Andrea answered, "I know, you lot have mentioned that many times before. Like Valerie said, there is absolutely nothing to worry about."

Charles stood up, and said, "All right then, since you insist so much that everything is well, I believe you." He narrowed his eyes, then added, "However, he looked very impatient and nervous when he asked me to find you, saying he needs to speak with you urgently, and in private of course."

Andrea asked, "When? Where?"

Charles replied, "The viceroy is waiting for you in his big saloon, and he looked like he had something of great importance to tell you."

Dianne said, "If it wasn't for the clear circumstances, I would assume he is pregnant."

They all burst into laughter, except for Andrea. In her usual way, she slowly and calmly said, "As I stated previously, there is nothing serious between us. Still, I will find out right away what he wants." She added, "I will see you all later." Andrea walked to meet him.

While the viceroy's door was opening, Andrea's face lit up with excitement. The young, handsome priest, Peter, had opened the giant door and invited Andrea into the saloon where the viceroy was anxiously expecting her. Andrea looked at Peter with her big, bright, intense green eyes. She moved closer towards him and whispered in his ear, "What a pleasant surprise to find you here, Peter."

The viceroy was looking at them attentively. Peter nervously stepped back from Andrea, and announced loudly, "Sir, Viceroy, the countess is here." He added, "The viceroy has been waiting for you, dear Countess."

The viceroy stood up from his seat, and said, "Go ahead, Reverend, go fetch me the bishop so I speak with him about these important matters I mentioned."

The young priest said, "I will bring him right away, sir."

The viceroy sighed impatiently, "I told you to call me 'Your Highness.'"

Embarrassed, the priest said, "Please, forgive me, Your Highness."

The priest left and the viceroy closed the big doors behind him. He grabbed Andrea by her waist with both of his hands, and said, "My beautiful Countess, my love, don't play with me like this." He kissed her on her arms and shoulders. "I saw how you were looking at the priest, but he is not for you or any other woman." He added, "Remember, he will dedicate his whole life to serving others, don't you ever forget that he is a man of the Lord. I have given you everything you ever wanted, what else would you like? You don't know how important you are to me. Anything you desire I will get for you with a snap of my fingers! I have been thinking for a long time now, and I finally made a decision. I want to be with you forever." With great excitement, he added, "This is the important matter I was discussing with the priest, and he will bring the bishop here to end our agony once and for all. You deserve a lot more than what I have been giving you, you deserve a respectable place by my side."

Andrea looked at the viceroy attentively. She asked, "What do you mean?"

He hugged her, stood on his tiptoes to kiss her on the neck, then said, "My beautiful Countess of Stonemason, I know what you must want, and I want to please you."

Confused, Andrea held her chin with two fingers, and asked, "What are you saying, Viceroy?"

The viceroy said, "My dear Countess, my Andrea, I am asking you to marry me."

Andrea laughed out loud. Her laughs echoed inside the big saloon.

The viceroy asked, "Andrea, what is so funny? Are my feelings worth nothing to you? I am the most important man in the New Spain, and you are mocking me, are you not? I am offering you everything I have, even my pride. I want you to marry me and be with me forever."

Andrea, still laughing, controlled herself enough to say, "Me? Marry you? But you are already married."

The viceroy said, "Do not worry, my love, I have thought about everything, and this is a little detail I will fix with the bishop. Soon I will be a free man, and we will get married and live happily together for the rest of our lives."

Andrea laughed even louder. She said, "Marriage? Moi? Marry you?" She continued laughing hysterically, and said, "Why would I want to marry anyone? Even if you were a free man, why would I want to marry you?"

"One of the reasons for you accepting a marriage proposal from me could be in consideration of elevating your royal position." He added, "You are the Countess of Stonemason now and you could be more than a countess. Very soon, you will be my wife if you desire."

"Why would I want to be your wife?"

He insisted, "My darling, my beautiful Countess, do not say no. There are plenty of reasons for you to consider my proposal."

Andrea looked down at him, and slowly said, "I can find more reasons on why this is a bad idea. First, and the most important one, you already have a wife. Usually that is for life, and second, even if you manage to get rid of her like you are plotting, I would certainly not like to take her place, regardless of what you offer me. Me? Chained to a man forever in marriage? Never!"

The viceroy stared blankly at her. In a serious tone, he said, "Andrea, you have the opportunity of a lifetime, I want you for my wife, don't you understand what this means?"

Andrea said, "Your wife?" She continued laughing uncontrollably, and said, "I don't want to be anybody's wife, but especially not yours."

Surprised, the viceroy asked, "You mean, you don't want to marry me? I thought you were going to be pleasantly surprised with my proposal and you were going to have feelings of excitement and happiness when you heard about my plans for us. Are you sure that you don't care for it?"

Andrea replied, "Me, excited about the possibility of marrying you? Of course not." She continued laughing and walked away from the viceroy. She left, bubbling with laughter. "Marriage? Being a wife?" She stepped outside without being able to sustain her balance from laughing so hard. She was stumbling with so much laughter, almost like being in a drunken state.

Big tears rolled down the viceroy's cheeks. He locked his jaw and closed his fists with force. A few minutes after the countess left, the bishop arrived. The bishop said, "Let me tell you that what you want is very difficult, almost impossible, marriage is for life!"

The viceroy answered, "That is not the main concern anymore, Bishop." The viceroy added, "My mind is clear now, forget about everything I requested, until further notice."

The bishop left confused but happy. The reaction of the viceroy was better than what he had anticipated. The viceroy gave up the divorce idea easily as soon as the bishop had told him that it was impossible to do. The viceroy sat down on his elegant chair, held his head with both hands and sighed. "What a headache, this has been most unexpected and devastating!"

Andrea was still laughing when she arrived home with her four teachers. They were curious about what had happened at her meeting with the viceroy. Valerie looked attentively at Andrea, and asked, "What happened in your meeting with the viceroy, dear? Something good must have happened, I can see it on your face."

Andrea answered, "No, not really, nothing pleasant or important."

Dianne asked, "What do you mean, Andrea?"

Charles asked, "What did the viceroy want?"

Andrea said, "Well, sit down before you listen to this. The very married man wanted to marry me."

Salvador asked, "What did you say to him? What was your answer?"

"What do you think my answer would be?" She added, "Even if he was a free man, you already know what my position is on marriage. It does not work, and I am not interested." Andrea stood tall and straight. "I am exceptionally beautiful, extremely rich, and very smart. I am a great countess, and I do not belong to anyone." Her tutors became quiet and looked at her attentively with serious expressions. Andrea said, "I do not have the need, and I do not have the desire to be anybody's wife. And most of all, I DO NOT want to marry a hysterical little man who already has a wife and is trying to find who knows what ways to get rid of her."

Charles asked, "How did the viceroy take your rejection?"

Andrea, with her back straight and her mind at ease, slowly and elegantly replied, "I do not really know how he took it. He can take it anyway he likes, my answer is still going to remain the same."

Dianne said, "I hope you gave the viceroy your answer carefully and diplomatically."

Valerie asked, "Andrea, how did you answer the viceroy's proposal?"

Andrea replied, "There is only one way to answer such a ridiculous request, by saying 'no' and that is all. Everybody should know by now how valuable my freedom is, and it is not for sale at any price." Her teachers looked at her with wide eyes. Andrea sighed, and said, "Please, let us change the topic about the viceroy to a more interesting one. I am profoundly bored already."

Charles quickly said, "Yes, dear, let's change the topic."

Salvador added, "I concur with Andrea, let us change our conversation to a nicer subject."

A few months had passed when Dianne looked at Andrea. She asked, "What about the viceroy, dear?"

Andrea asked back, "What about him?"

Dianne said, "He has been showing up everywhere you go, and he keeps sending you presents and asking to see you."

Andrea said, "I have more important matters to attend to. Absolutely nothing about him interests me anymore."

Dianne said, "Dear, the viceroy continues finding opportunities to see you. The royal ladies are already talking about it. However, when the rumors come to your attention, you do not seem to care much for them, no matter how bad and exaggerated the gossip gets." Andrea was still in silence, submerged in her thoughts which was shockingly unusual for her.

The next day, Valerie looked at Dianne. She said, "The royal ladies are commenting about how the viceroy does not want Andrea anymore because he got tired of her." She added, "They also think that he will probably decide between trying to make his wife happy or finding a new diversion."

Dianne answered, "If what they are saying is true and if those are the only two options for the viceroy, you know the answer to that already, don't you?"

Salvador said, "The new diversion."

Dianne rolled her eyes, "I know, those pompous women are dumb or pretend that they do not know the viceroy."

Charles piped up, "The royal gentlemen have a very different opinion on this matter, they have been wondering why Andrea is not interested in the viceroy anymore."

Salvador said, "Some of them think she does not want him anymore because he is very stubborn and self-centered."

Charles added, "And others are saying that she is no longer interested in him because of his short temper, which is no bigger than his physical stature."

Andrea's mind wasn't entertained by thoughts of the viceroy or anything about him anymore. She said, "This beautiful land, the New Spain, I like it very much in a way that I would have never imagined before. The sun here warms me up comfortably the whole year round, but this environment— the royal environment—disgusts me, and I cannot stand it any longer. The environment is worse than I ever imagined. It is corrupt, extremely dull, and it asphyxiates me. This is why I wish to leave the city to go to the many small towns where I have my properties to find something more exciting for my life. I might be able to find the happiness that I have not been able to find here with all these unpleasant nobles. I have decided already that I am going to leave the city for some time to go and live with my family."

Valerie cried out, "I thought we were your family."

Andrea answered, "Yes, you are, but you are not the only family I have. You already know you are the family that I chose, love, and enjoy having around, but I have my other family with whom I do not have the best relationship with, but they are still my family."

Valerie said, "It's all right if you want to go and visit them, but you know how bad we four are when away from civilization, so we will not be able to accompany you on this trip."

Dianne said, "Do not take too long to come back, we will be awaiting your return."

Charles said, "Take good care of yourself, my great and beautiful Countess."

Andrea replied, "You know I will, you do not have to worry about me."

Salvador added sweetly, "If you need us in any way, let us know, and we will be there with you as soon as we can."

Andrea said, "I know, and if I did not know all of you four well enough, I would believe you are starting to get sentimental."

Dianne said, "You already know we are not the emotional type, but you are very special to us."

Andrea said, "I know, and all of you are very dear to me. You four are the best friends anyone could ever find, but I must take my leave now."

Valerie insisted, "You are going to be on your own, are you sure you are ready for that, darling?"

Andrea replied, "My life might get dull being away from you four, but the royal environment has turned suffocating, I simply cannot stand it. Spending twenty years around these unpleasant royals has turned into a long time. Besides, as soon as my mother found me here in the New Spain many years ago, I left her in one of my properties and seldom came back to visit her. Then, when my grandma passed away, my sister came to live with my mother, and they have been living together ever since. It would be nice to see my mother and my sister, and this time not just for a visit, I want to live with them again."

Valerie said, "We have been living in the New Spain for twenty years, but it doesn't feel that long to me."

Charles said, "Time waits for no man!"

Salvador looked at Andrea. He said, "I remember when your mother came looking for you, and she was so happy to find you here with us."

Andrea said, "I also remember, maybe I did not receive my mother with the affection she deserved." She added, "You know, I have never been very affectionate with anyone, and maybe I have not shown enough attention toward my mother." She sighed, and added, "Anyway, I will come back and visit the four of you someday. Do not keep melancholy in your hearts about my departure and remember that you will see me again." They all embraced Andrea one by one, and she rode away in her carriage.

Andrea saw royal people walking around the downtown streets of the New Spain. She was looking at the important, rich merchants passing through. She passed the big churches. As she continued to look through the carriage window, surprised, she asked, "Horseman, who is this young man of the cloth walking hurriedly by himself?"

The horseman answered, "That young man is Friar Peter."

The countess firmly ordered, "Stop the horses!" Trembling with immense emotion and a fixed look in her big, intense green eyes, she said slowly, "Bring him to me!"

The horseman gently pulled the horses' reins, and said, "Whoa, whoa." He stopped the horses, scratched his head, fixed his hat, then said, "Yes, my lady." The horseman stood in front of the priest, and said, "Good afternoon, Friar Peter. My lady the Countess of Stonemason wishes to see you, and she is expecting you inside the carriage."

The kind friar looked at him. He said, "Good afternoon, Brother, I have no time to lose right now, but I can spare a minute to see what she needs." The handsome Friar Peter opened the carriage door. He asked gently, "Good evening, my lady the Countess. How can I serve you today?"

Andrea looked at him with her big, bright, intense green eyes and excitedly extended her hand. She said, "Please come in, darling, I need to speak with you!"

He looked away from her, and said, "Please tell me from here because I have somewhere to be."

The countess said, "Come in here so I can tell you." She offered her hands to him and helped him inside the carriage.

He stepped inside and sat down in front of her, closed his legs, fixed his cassock, and placed his hands together on his lap while looking at her with his kind green eyes. She took his hands and placed them on her waist. Then, she slid her fingers through his hair and offered her naturally red lips for him to kiss. He tried to back away. He moved away from her as far as he could in the confined space, and said nervously, "Please, dear Countess, do not do this to me."

She started to kiss him on the lips, embrace him passionately, and said breathlessly, "Why not, Peter? Oh, I have waited so long for this moment. I know you desire my touch as much as I desire yours."

The horseman could not believe his ears and opened his eyes wide with a smirk on his face while inching closer to the carriage to hear better. He said to himself, "You chose the only man that wouldn't see you in that way, beautiful countess." He shook his head and added, "No woman can make him fall to taste the carnal pleasures of this world."

Meanwhile inside the carriage, Andrea kissed the friar's ear while she whispered sweet nothings in it. Friar Peter trembled, and with a weak, nervous voice, said, "Please don't touch me anymore, I have to go." He gently took her hands off of him and then she pushed her bosom onto his chest. He looked at her neckline and then he looked up fighting to escape the temptation.

Andrea ordered, "Do not look away, handsome. Look directly in front of you. I am here!" She added, "I am right here, and I want you, do not resist me, enjoy the moment just as I do. I know you want this as much as I do!" She kissed him passionately while still caressing his hair with both hands.

He took her hands away from him very gently. He glanced shyly at her and was instantly mesmerized by her beauty. She kissed him again and cornered him inside the carriage. He kissed her back gently on her cheek. His mind was filled with doubts. *Would I be able to resist? Could this temptation be stronger than my own will? Or is it my own life's purpose that has changed? I don't know anymore, the only thing I know is that she is so beautiful, and I'm falling madly in love with her.*

She held his hands in hers and kissed him once more. He let her kiss him this time. He looked at their hands, together, and then he looked at her. He caressed her hands. Then, he caressed her hair, her shoulders, her back. Then he planted a sweet kiss on her rosy lips. His kiss demonstrated the great passion she always showed him every time they saw each other. After all, she was the only woman who had dared to stir his most hidden desires. She was the most beautiful woman he had never had, not even in his deepest and wildest dreams.

The horseman knew it was too late for the man of faith to recover his spiritual vocation. The smirk disappeared from his face. Instead, he shook his head with worry and felt discontentment wash over him. He looked up to the sky and made the Signum Crucis. He wanted to be pardoned for his complicity in this sin. A simple game he thought before, but it ended in a rather unexpected way. *Peter was a heavenly man, not a man like him or anyone else. How could he fall for the traps and the temptations of the flesh? Peter was supposed to be stronger than the other men. The strongest of them all, but he wasn't.* Then, in a whisper, he tried to comprehend what was happening, and said, "A faithful man, young—yes—but well respected, humble, eager to help and do good deeds, but still just a mortal man, like all the others, another man like every one of us."

Later that same day, Andrea asked Peter, "Are you sure you do not wish to accompany me to my estate? It will be fun!"

Peter replied, "I can't. There is something I must do first."

Andrea shrugged, "Suit yourself, if you change your mind, find me at one of my estates in the East."

Peter agreed. "I might do that later. Besides, I have a lot of thinking to do first."

Andrea raised her voice, and said, "Horseman, we are going back to where we found Friar Peter."

The horseman replied, "Yes, ma'am," and hurriedly turned the horses around.

Later on, Peter stood at the same spot the countess had found him. An old friar was walking by. He looked at Peter, and asked, "What has happened to you, Brother? Are you hurt?"

Peter nervously replied, "No, why do you say that, Brother?"

The old friar said, "I have never seen you in this state before. Your clothes are all wrinkled, your hair completely disheveled, you look as if you just got robbed."

Peter's face turned beet red. He looked down and in a low voice, said, "Maybe I have."

The old friar asked, "What valuables did you lose?"

Peter asked, "Who can steal material valuables from one who has none, Brother?"

"Some unseen things are a lot more valuable than what the eye can see, Brother."

Peter agreed, and with a low voice said, "Yes, Brother."

The old friar said, "Our faith, to mention one of them."

Meanwhile Andrea, the Countess of Stonemason, continued on her way to her estates. Feeling content, she said to herself, "I will find my happiness in one of these places."

When she arrived at the estate, her mother was very happy to see her. Christine, Andrea's adopted sister, was happy to see her as well.

A few years later, Andrea looked at her mother, and said, "I have spent some time in many of my houses and could not find my happiness. Not even my lovely adventures bring me any joy these days."

Her mother mused, "Maybe you haven't found the right person for you, but you will someday."

Andrea said, "The right person does not exist for me, Mother." She added, "No man deserves my complete love and attention."

Marie sighed, "I wish you could see around you, Andrea, focusing only on yourself all the time makes it extremely difficult for you to find the happiness you're seeking."

"As always, you do not care how I feel, Mother."

"On the contrary, it is me who would love to see you living a happy and fulfilled life, my daughter, but I know your ways will not bring you happiness."

The butler stepped into the house at that moment. He said, "My lady, the Countess of Stonemason, I am sorry to interrupt your conversation, but there is a gentleman in the gardens who is asking to see you."

Andrea asked, "What gentleman?"

The butler replied, "He said his name is Peter."

Andrea smiled and walked towards the gardens. Marie followed from a distance. There he was, dressed as a regular man, the one known by most as Friar Peter. Andrea looked at him, and said, "Good afternoon, Peter, what took you so long?" She added, "I am glad you decided to join me. I see you finally decided to take a vacation here with me, and you will not regret it. It is good you did not bring your priest cassock, and you will hardly miss it, you will see."

Peter took a step closer to Andrea, embraced her with his eyes closed, kissed her sweetly on her cheek, and said, "Let's get married, I will be a good husband to you."

Andrea laughed out loud, and she could not stop laughing.

Peter was confused. He said, "My darling, it is only natural that we get married after all that has happened between us, and to be truthful, I am profoundly in love with you."

Andrea laughed even harder. She could not believe what she was hearing. When she was able to calm down, she said, "Friar Peter."

Peter interrupted, and said, "Not anymore, I am no longer a priest. I told my superiors what happened between you and I, of course I excluded your name when I was confessing my weakness as a man. Soon, the church will pardon my faults and allow me to marry you."

Andrea said, "Peter, I thought you loved being a priest. How could you renounce it?"

Peter said, "I renounced it for you, for us, for our love. I thought about it for a long time, and I came to the conclusion that I prefer you to being a priest." He added, "I want to love you and start a family with you."

Andrea laughed again, and said, "Listen, Peter, it was pleasant what we had around those rude nobles, and then we had lots of fun inside that carriage, but it was nothing serious." She added, "I have never been interested in marriage or in starting a family of my own. You are welcome to stay here with me for some time if you like."

Confused, Peter asked, "You mean you don't love me and you were just having fun with me?"

Andrea replied, "I hope you do not feel bad about it. It is nothing personal, not even the richest men have convinced me to get married." She added, "If matrimony is what you seek, forget about me. Go back to your church and live the life you were living before our paths crossed."

"My life as a priest is now over, and I cannot return to it."

"There must be so many commoners in the church where you served that would be delighted to marry you."

"I now see how you feel about me, and I don't blame you," said Peter. "After all, it is my fault; I should have been stronger to resist temptation. I guess the only thing left for me to say to you is good-bye."

Andrea asked, "What about my offer of staying here with me for some time?"

"There is no point in that."

"We are going to have lots of fun, you will see!"

"That is not what I left the priesthood for, and I am not interested in anything else."

Andrea said, "Good-bye then, Peter." She went back inside her house.

Peter left in silence.

Marie said, "Andrea, you might have been very happy with him; he seems like a very nice young man."

"No, I do not think so, Mother."

"Then you should have left him to live in peace as a priest."

"Do not accuse me of misconduct as you always do, Mother, because if you do you will be mistaken," said Andrea. "I did not do anything wrong, on the contrary, I did him a favor as he had no priesthood vocation, or he would not have shown up here today."

Marie looked at her daughter, the Countess of Stonemason, and said, "You haven't given him an opportunity to see if this relationship can go further, maybe you settling down with him is the happiness you are looking for."

Andrea looked away from Marie and pushed her hair to the side. She said, "Please, Mother, do not bore me with talk of the ex-priest anymore."

Peter walked away slowly from the countess's estate. His head was down as he wiped his watery kind green eyes with his sleeves.

Andrea looked at her mother and sister, then said, "I have been constantly traveling from one of my estates to another, and I have spent some years in each of my houses, except one. I have to go to that house where I have not been in many years. I must go to that house of mine and stay there for some days to see how everything is functioning. I know everything must be well as is customary at all of my properties. I have excellent administrators at each of my houses, but I have to be certain. Besides, I do not know what to do with my life, everything is tremendously monotonous and tedious at every turn. Also, I want both of you to know I am delighted with your presence and acceptance to accompany me to my new destiny. Where finally, after many years I have decided to return to my house in Púcuaro and spend some quality time there again."

Mary and Christine both looked at her with a smile. Mary said, "Daughter, I am overjoyed to follow a new path and live a new life with you at my side. The three of us will continue together on our new journey, and it fills my heart with joy."

Christine with wide and excited eyes, exclaimed, "I am thrilled that the three of us are going to begin this new chapter together!"

Andrea with a bright smile, replied, "Your excitement and happiness is contagious. Now I am just as excited and glad to go to Púcuaro! I will soon find my happiness, and when I do, it will last forever!"

Christine with a big smile on her face looked at her and said, "I hope all your dreams of happiness will soon come true for you, Andrea."

Marie looked at Andrea with a tender look in her eyes. She smiled with hope and held her daughter's hand in hers. She said, "It is my dearest wish that any day now you may make the decisions that will lead you to your true happiness, my beloved daughter."

Andrea looked at Marie and took her hand away from her mother's. Then, she glanced over at Christine. She looked at them both with a serious expression. "I have everything anyone could ever want." Andrea added, "I am very rich, I am very powerful, I have always been very beautiful. I am the great Countess of Stonemason, and someday I will also have the greatest happiness in my life."

Chapter Six

Meeting Alfonso

The carriage was fast approaching its destination, the hacienda in Púcuaro. The Countess of Stonemason had been enjoying the view of her extensive lands for the past hour. The pastures were as green as could be. The wildflowers were tall, colorful, and they emitted a gentle alluring scent. The sun shone brightly on the dark brown galloping horses. Jaime and Angel were at the front of the carriage, in charge of the horses. Suddenly, they all saw it. A wonderful view. A unique, beautiful horse with a strong handsome man at its side. The horse looked very tall and strong, more so than most of the horses the countess had ever come across.

She exclaimed, "Boys, this is the biggest and strongest horse I have ever seen in my entire life! I have never seen a horse like this anywhere, and I have been plenty of places to know that this is an extraordinary animal."

Angel replied, "Oh yes, it is really big and strong, no doubt about that."

Jaime said, "And also wild, very, very wild. We would do best to steer clear of him." He added, "I don't want to be close to that huge, wild, and unpredictable beast."

The countess said, "Look at the way he jumps, so strong yet exceptionally graceful at the same time."

The handsome man approached the horse and lassoed him with his rope. The horse resisted the man, and his enormous strength helped him to free himself almost immediately. The man continued lassoing the horse with his rope, and the horse continued to free itself with each graceful movement. The lean young man with no shirt threw his rope on the side and mounted the horse with a single jump. He was so agile and vigorous. The horse jumped repeatedly, bucking and evading the man's maneuvers.

The sun glared down relentlessly, casting man and horse into a single shadow. But it shone brightest in their big, deep, brown eyes. The man and the horse were quite similar. The horse stopped jumping and the man caressed the horse gently on its face and neck.

The countess asked, "Who is that gentleman?"

"He is one of your workers, my lady," replied Angel.

"I have already assumed that. What else can you tell me about him?"

Jaime answered, "His parents live in Acámbaro, past the Lerma River."

Angel added, "He is the only child they had."

"His father is a Spaniard," Jaime said, "and his mother is a native."

Angel said, "His father renounced his family's great fortune when he decided to marry his mother. His family was not happy that he was not going to marry one of the fine and wealthy Spaniard ladies they wanted for him."

The countess asked, "What is his name?"

Angel and Jaime replied together, "Alfonso." The horse jumped again, and Alfonso held on to him as if they were one. They both looked like a single creature moving gracefully and wildly at the same time.

The countess observed them, then with a smile fixed her big, intense green eyes on them and said, "Such magnificence, gentle yet at the same time savage. What a divine and beautiful beast!"

Jaime and Angel asked together, "You like the horse?"

The countess replied, "Of course."

"He is such a fine and unique animal with such strong willpower," Jaime said. "I would stay away from him if I were you. He is just too wild for anyone to be around him."

"Yeah, he doesn't follow anyone's lead. No one can control him," agreed Angel.

The Countess of Stonemason looked at them both with a smile, and said, "I see you have made up your mind about him, but I still like him profoundly." She continued, "He is exceptional… He is extraordinary… He is so, very…" She could not finish her thought. It was unusual for the Countess of Stonemason to be at a loss for words to describe something or someone. She was very eloquent, but this time she was thinking on what words to use. The emotion and excitement were playing games with her mind. The Countess of Stonemason said, "What an interesting creature, with such a strong will." She added, "He is very attractive and possesses such physical and mental strength."

Angel and Jaime looked at each other. They asked, "The horse?"

The countess answered, "Of course, what else have we been talking about all this time? As patient as I want to be, low-class people exasperate me."

"This long ride made me very hungry," said Angel.

"I know what you mean. I could eat the whole horse we just saw, roasted of course," added Jaime.

Angel said in disbelief, "Well, you would have to catch him first if you really want to roast him, and I would like to see how you are going to do that. It is a good thing that in all the Countess of Stonemason's houses the food is delicious and plentiful as if she was there all the time. We will eat very well when we get to her estate."

The Countess of Stonemason gently shook Marie's arm. She said, "Mother, we have arrived at our destination." She added, "Christine, Mother, both of you wake up." The countess looked at her two employees, and asked, "What is that crowd all about? That many people walking together, what are they doing and where are they headed?"

Angel asked, "Where?"

Jaime replied, "Over there, Angel." He pointed with his hand to the people still far away. "Those are the people of the surroundings who celebrate Lent by praying and walking together in the procession with the son of the Lord, but today is a much greater day. They are celebrating Holy Thursday, expecting Good Friday, and on Sunday it will be the mass celebration for Easter."

Angel added, "Yes, and the church will be full, so we have to get there early."

The countess shook her head in annoyance, then rolled her eyes, and slowly said, "Year after year I have borne witness to their ignorant beliefs and I still do not understand them." She added, "WASTING THEIR TIME, that is what they are doing, since they do not have anything important to do around here." Looking around, she asked Jaime and Angel, "And where is the son of the Lord you are talking about?"

Excitedly, Angel answered, "He is right there in the middle of the procession."

Jaime nodded his head.

The countess said, "That is not Him, what those men are carrying is a statue and nothing else. As you can see, it is very heavy and they already look exhausted."

Jaime said, "You are right, my lady. It is a statue *representing* Him, the real son of the Lord is in Heaven looking at us from above."

Angel added, "My lady, the Countess of Stonemason, those men don't mind if it is heavy as their sins must feel heavier, they have faith that He can lift their spiritual burdens."

The countess chuckled. Then said, "He cannot take their sins away as He is a man-made idol and a very heavy one as we can all attest."

Jaime said, "Yes, my lady, the one they are carrying is man-made, but the real one is looking at them and their intentions."

Angel added, "Yes, my lady, their good intentions and their love for the son of the Lord and for each other is appreciated and valued by our Creator."

The countess shook her head again, looked at Jaime, and said, "Tell me, Jaime, have you gone to Heaven, looked with your own two eyes at who is really there, and returned to Earth to be able to make such an outrageous claim?"

Jaime blushed. He said, "No, my lady, I haven't, but I have faith in who is there and what is expected from us here."

The countess looked at Angel. She said, "Tell me, Angel, do you believe this nonsense too?"

Color started to seep into his cheeks as Angel lowered his head. He replied, "Yes, my lady, I do, that is what my parents taught me since I was a child."

The countess said, "'Your parents, OF COURSE. You obviously do not have a mind of your own, but tell me, Jaime, what is expected from you in Heaven?"

Jaime, still red in the face, said, "To love each other and be well-intentioned all the time with everyone, but this is expected from everybody, my lady, not just from me."

Angel added, "Yes, my lady, our Creator wants us to be good to each other."

Jaime said, "But even knowing what He wants from us, we do not do His will at all times." He added, "Most of us care about our carnal body more than our spirit."

Angel asked, "What do you believe in, my lady?"

The countess replied, serenely but firmly, "Well, like you, my mother and my grandmother taught me about all of this, but I have always questioned everything no matter where it comes from, and since I have not seen any of this with my own two eyes, I cannot assure you or give you my word that there is any truth to it." She added, "Anyway, even if it is true, all of these time-consuming processions do not make any sense at all." The Countess of Stonemason, as usual, completely sure of herself, said, "You see, the beings in Heaven would be all powerful and with absolutely no need for all of these insignificant tiny ants to do anything for them; these poor ignorant people should be helping themselves first."

Angel smiled, and said, "I see that today is not the day we will convince you to believe in the spiritual life, my lady."

The countess said, "No, that you will not do today, but do not feel bad about it, not even my own mother or grandmother were able to convince me to believe in what I cannot see with my own eyes." She continued, "But we should not be worried about all of these foolish people, we must get on with our plans and look away from those absurd 'beliefs.'"

The carriage stopped as they arrived at the house.

Jaime climbed down from the carriage, offered his hand, and said, "After you, my lady."

Angel said, "At last we are going to eat, I want a big, juicy steak."

Jaime smiled at Angel, and said, "I don't think that will be possible today. I am sure Doña Gabriela has ordered some Lent food to be cooked today, so no meat for you, Angel."

Angel asked, "No meat? But I was sure I was going to eat very well today?"

Jaime said, "And you will, but without the meat."

The hallway was illuminated by the sunlight filtering in through all of the vast windows. The colorful flowers left a trailing scent of perfume scattered throughout the huge house. Many young men and women were working in the house when the countess arrived. The house administrator was ordering the young men and women around the kitchen. A woman over sixty, Doña Gabriela, like everybody called her, ordered them to get the fine silverware, plates, and the gold cups set up at the table for the Countess of Stonemason.

The hacienda had many spacious rooms. The walls were made of *adobe* and the ceiling was vaulted. Higher than any regular house. The house stayed cool on hot summer days. At night the rooms felt even colder, and very thick blankets were used to keep people warm. In the kitchen there were always many different pots and pans on the stoves and on the main kitchen table. On this day, there was steak and potatoes, black beans, tomato rice with peas and carrots, cactus salad, stuffed hot peppers, and seasoned spinach with other greens. Jaime said, "So you will get your steak after all, Angel."

Angel said, "That is good to hear after a long day of work. Thank you, Doña Gabriela."

Doña Gabriela answered, "You are welcome, Angel, but tomorrow is Good Friday and no meat for sure." She added, "Maybe a chicken soup for anyone who would like it and if they are feeling ill, but most of the meals are going to be Lent meals and you already know, 'no meat.'"

Angel said, "It is all right, Doña Gabriela, your food is always good no matter what it is. I know it will be delicious, thank you for cooking!"

Andrea, Marie, and Christine were eating together on a giant cedarwood table. Marie said, "This silverware is fabulous. If there weren't so many plates and cups, big pitchers, and soup bowls, I would swear that they are made from real gold."

Christine nodded her head. She said, "I agree with you, my lady Marie. However, who would spend such a fortune on cups and dishes to eat?"

Marie said, "Mother, Christine, I prefer when you call me mother."

Christine agreed. "Yes, Mother."

Confused, Andrea asked, "And why not, ladies? I deserve all the gold dishes I want, that and much more." She added, "Anyway, it is not as expensive as one would think. This place and its surroundings are full of silver and gold, and it is not out of the ordinary to have such things made of gold and silver."

Christine said, "It is not out of the ordinary for you, Andrea. You have always liked the most beautiful, extravagant, and expensive things." She added, "Which is fine and normal if we are talking about you, but it doesn't seem normal for everybody else, no matter how rich they are."

Amazed, Marie said, "Look at the design. It is beautiful!" She added, "It is a work of art!"

Andrea said, "And wait until you see the others. This is the simplest design of them all."

Marie asked, "There are more dish sets of real gold and silverware like this one?"

The Countess of Stonemason said, "Of course, Mother. Many more, and each of these dish sets has a distinguished, beautiful design."

In the kitchen, some of the employees were eating together with clay silverware. Among them were Angel and Jaime. Alfonso came into the kitchen and everyone seemed happy to see him. Angel excitedly shouted, "ALFONSO, YOU ARE HERE! COME AND EAT WITH US!" He added, "You must be ravenous after fighting that beast!"

Jaime agreed, "Yes, Alfonso, eat with us. You deserve a good meal with even better company after risking your life training that monster."

Alfonso said, "Well, thank you. It will be nice to eat with you all. I agree, this is great company."

Angel said, "Alfonso, tell us about the big horse you are training."

Alfonso replied, "With respect to the horse, we were merely playing together; we are now friends, and everything is working out very well between us."

The countess, sitting at her table and looking into the kitchen, said, "Gabriela!"

Doña Gabriela answered, "Yes, my lady!"

The countess asked, "What is all that commotion in the kitchen?"

Doña Gabriela replied, "Oh, nothing, my lady, it is Alfonso. One of your cowboys who just got here and is going to eat in the kitchen."

The countess asked, "In the kitchen? Please, invite him to come and eat here with us."

Confused, Doña Gabriela said, "Alfonso is one of your cowboys. You are telling me to invite him to eat here with you and your family? He just got back from taming a giant, wild horse. He is very hungry, tired, dirty, and sweaty. And he has very rough hands from the ropes he uses to lasso the horses to domesticate them. Are you sure you want this Alfonso at your table?"

The countess insisted, "Yes, this is the Alfonso I am talking about. Invite him to my table, Gabriela." The countess added, "Do not make me repeat myself again."

Doña Gabriela said, "Yes, my lady!" Gabriela added, "I was just making sure I understood what you wanted. I will bring him straight away."

The countess replied, "Thank you, Gabriela."

Gabriela walked into the kitchen to give Alfonso the message. She looked at him and said, "Alfonso, the Countess of Stonemason wants you at her table." She added, "I think she wants you to join her and her family for dinner right now."

Alfonso removed his white hat, scratched his head, and asked, "Me, eating at the countess's table? What for? Are you certain?"

Doña Gabriela replied, "Yes, son. I am one hundred percent sure. Let's go to the family table. Don't make them wait for you."

Alfonso took a bite of his tortilla, and said, "I don't belong at the countess's table. No, no, thank you, but no. I am all right here. Besides, I am too hungry to show good manners at this moment. I just want to eat in peace, and without fancy people watching me eat."

Doña Gabriela said, "Alfonso, I am not asking you what you want to do. And it's not me who decided this. This is a direct order from the countess, so you cannot say 'no' this time."

Alfonso said, "I just want to eat in peace, is that too much to ask?"

Doña Gabriela looked at him with a reprimanding gaze. Alfonso saw her and said, "All right, if it is that important to you, Doña Gabriela, I will go." He finished chewing the first bite of steak and walked into the dining room. He stopped ten feet from where the countess was eating and greeted her calmly. "Good evening, madam. Welcome to your hacienda."

The countess stood up and offered her hand to him. Alfonso walked up to her and with his rough hand held hers to kiss it gently. Alfonso said, "Please, sit down, madam. Continue enjoying your meal. Don't mind me."

The countess said, "Alfonso, honor us with your company. Be so kind as to sit down and dine with us please."

Alfonso agreed. "Yes, madam, as you wish." He fixed the chair for the countess to sit. A girl who was following Alfonso with a big tray, placed Alfonso's plate on the countess's table next to him. He sat down, looked at the girl, and said, "Thank you." The girl went back into the kitchen.

The countess and Alfonso chatted animatedly about horses. Christine and Marie, ate quietly at the table while they observed the couple.

Meanwhile, in the kitchen Doña Gabriela was listening to the dining room conversation and sent a young girl named Lola to serve a new meal on the gold flatware for Alfonso. The girl said, "I would love to serve anything to Alfonso, but not now that he is next to the countess." She added, "I am sorry, Doña Gabriela, but that woman makes me very nervous, and I don't want to be next to her, it will be better if you send Lucia."

Doña Gabriela asked, "Girl, when are you going to learn to do as you are told?" She added, "You and Maria are making me crazy. Neither of you two ever listen to me or anyone else. I cannot believe Lucia, who is only sixteen years old, can be the most helpful and reliable person here. She is always nearby to help with any chores needed around the house."

Lucia was sent to serve the meals to the main table, and she did it happily. When they were done eating, Alfonso asked to be excused from the table. Alfonso, extremely handsome and manly, looked at the countess with his big brown eyes, then said, "Madam, thank you for your kindness. I am a little tired and would like to be excused to rest, if it is all right with you."

The countess replied, "Of course, this must have been a long and tiring day for you."

Alfonso said, "Not very different from the other days. I am all right, but I would like to rest and be ready for tomorrow. Have a good night, ma'am." He looked at Marie and Christine and said, "Good night, ladies."

The Countess of Stonemason smiled and said, "Have a wonderful night, Alfonso." She offered her hand for him to kiss. Alfonso gently kissed her hand and left for his room to rest.

While he was walking through the kitchen and the hallway to reach his room, the other employees were murmuring. A young boy named Danny, about Lucia's age, said to James, "I want to eat from the gold plates at the family table too."

James answered him, "Don't we all, boy, don't we all." All of the employees were laughing with discretion in the kitchen, except for Lucia and Doña Gabriela who were serious and quiet.

Lucia whispered to them, "Doña Gabriela is mad at you all because she doesn't like your comments much."

Doña Gabriela said, "I see you did not work enough today. You have your minds full of silly thoughts. You already ate, and you should go to sleep now to clear those minds of yours. All of you. Only you can stay here with me, Lucia. Let's finish cleaning here so we can go and take our rest as well."

Meanwhile at the main table, they were still finishing up the conversation about Alfonso. Christine said, "He seems like a very nice young man."

Marie said, "Alfonso is very attractive, polite, sophisticated, and manly." She added, "He must have many beautiful girls crazy about him."

The countess laughed, and said, "Of course, many poor and insignificant girls, that is all you are going to find around here, and Alfonso deserves more than that. Someday, he will find a fine lady worthy of his love." The three of them agreed and said good night to each other. They each went to their rooms to sleep.

The next day, Alfonso got up from bed as usual at 4 a.m. He headed out with a couple of horses, pulling a carriage toward Acámbaro. He needed to buy some things for the newly trained horse. On his way there, he stopped by Refugio's house, his girlfriend. He waited outside for a few minutes and then he saw her coming out of the house. Refugio was almost as tall as Alfonso, still considered slim, but she was thicker than most girls around there. Her tan skin shined with the sun while she watered her mother's many plants. Her black hair was straight and fell to her shoulders. White lace held her hair in place and out of her face. She wore a pink-and-white dress with pink laced sleeves to the middle of her arms. The dress covered her neck and was tight at her waist. It flowed freely below her waist and came down to her knees. The bottom of the skirt was trimmed with pink lace. Alfonso blew a low whistle, and whispered, "Refugio."

Refugio turned her head and caught sight of him. There he was so manly and handsome gazing at her with his loving brown eyes. When she looked at him with her compelling brown eyes, a big smile covered her entire face. She threw her watering can on the grass and walked quickly over to her boyfriend to greet him. Smiling, she asked, "Alfonso, what are you doing here?"

Alfonso held her hand, smiled, and answered, "I came to get provisions for the horses, but you know my main reason for being here."

Refugio said, "I'll fetch water for the horses." She hurried and returned with a bucket of water.

Alfonso stopped her and held her hand in his again. He said, "Thank you for the water for my horses, but that's not the main reason I am here. Stay here with me, let me tell you what it is."

Refugio said, "Let me bring you some water for you to drink first." She left and brought a clay jar with fresh water for him to drink. Refugio said, "You must be thirsty."

Alfonso tenderly said, "I am, my love. I am extremely thirsty, for your love. I miss you so much when I am not with you. I cannot wait for the glorious day when we get married and we don't have to live so far away from each other anymore."

Refugio said, "I miss you too, Alfonso. I am glad you are here with me today. Go ahead and drink your water."

Alfonso drank some of the water and left it on top of the carriage to hold Refugio's hands in his. Alfonso looked into her eyes, and said, "It has been too many days without seeing you. The days are so much longer when I don't see you, my love." He held her by her waist and gently pulled her toward him. He said, "I love you!" Alfonso got closer to kiss Refugio gently on the lips.

Refugio hugged him by the neck and kissed him too. She said, "Mama is making tortillas, let me bring you some for your journey back." She went inside her house and brought back a clay bowl filled with beans, tomato sauce, fresh cheese, and tortillas on top.

Alfonso left the bowl of food on the carriage to hold his girlfriend's hands in his and look into her eyes. He said, "My love, I have missed looking into your beautiful eyes so much."

Refugio said, "I feel the same way, Alfonso, I have missed you a lot."

"My love for you is greater than anything I can think of."

She blushed and giggled.

He said, "I am serious, Refugio, I love you for real."

Refugio smiled, and said, "Go ahead and eat your food before it gets cold."

He kissed her cheek, drank all of his water, and started rolling his tortilla to eat. Alfonso said, "This is the most delicious food I have eaten the whole week since the last time I saw you."

Refugio said, "I know very well that's not true. Everybody talks about the great food prepared at all of the countess's houses. There is delicious food cooked in all of her haciendas every day, waiting for the day when she arrives. Each one has a great cook and an abundance of hot, delicious meals for all of the employees to enjoy daily."

Alfonso said, "Yes, my love, but nothing tastes better than these soft beans, tasty sauce, and delicious cheese with tortillas. The food you give me with your own hands is the most delicious of all."

Refugio smiled. "I did not even cook it. Mama cooked it."

Alfonso said, "It doesn't matter. You give it to me with your love and it tastes wonderful. It must be the love that you give it to me with. I wish I could be here with you every day, eating these heavenly meals you give me filled with your love." He continued, "Believe me, I prefer to eat beans with cheese every day if I can be next to you rather than eating delicacies far away from you. This is the best meal in the world. I can look into your eyes and feel your love in this food with every bite I take."

Refugio looked away from him, giggled. She said, "Now, that is true, I give it to you with my love. I have to go and finish my chores. When are you coming back to see me again?"

Alfonso said, "You know I cannot stay too long without seeing you. I would love to come every day, but I have to wait to see you just once a week. At the hacienda there is much work to do as always, and with the countess there now, we have even more things to do."

Surprised, Refugio asked, "The countess is there? How is she? I heard she is extremely beautiful and always wears the fanciest clothes and jewelry. And that she gets everything she wants all the time, oh, and that she doesn't accept 'no' for an answer."

Alfonso said, "I see you know a lot about the Countess of Stonemason. You have described her well. Who told you all of this?"

Refugio said, "I have heard it from my mother and her friends. They have talked about her for many years. She seems like the most important and powerful woman. The countess is extremely beautiful and elegant like I mentioned. I wonder why she has never been married?"

Alfonso, with a serious expression on his face, said, "She is all right. Now that you mention it, I think I know why she has never married." His expression changed and with a little smirk on his face, he said, "Why would she want only one man to boss around, when she can have them all, making her wishes come true at all times and without compromise?" He laughed loudly at his own joke.

Refugio smiled, and asked, "Can't you be serious?"

Alfonso said, "I just don't know why she has never been married. She seems to be a nice lady, and you have described her as if you already met her. She is a very interesting and distinguished lady, but I don't want to talk about her anymore. Let's talk about us."

Refugio agreed. "Sounds good, when are we getting married?"

Alfonso kissed her on the cheek gently, and in a low voice he said, "In my heart, we are already married, my love. If you want, I can take you to my father's house right now, and you can live there until I have enough money for us to be wed. This way we don't have to wait to be together. I cannot wait anymore. I feel great anguish waiting for the day we finally live together."

Refugio's expression changed to a sad one. "I cannot leave home like that. My parents deserve more respect from me than that. I will not live with you until we are married. Even though it is my greatest wish that someday we can be together forever."

Alfonso said, "Your wishes are very important to me my love. I almost have enough money for your dress, the church decorations, and the food for the party, but I still need to save some more money to buy furniture for our home. The good thing is we already have a house. My father gave it to me long ago thinking of the day I would find love and wishing for us to be happy living in it."

"Alfonso, we don't need to spend that much money on our wedding. We can just ask the priest to marry us and use the money you have saved for the furniture."

"My love, we must have something to offer our friends and families celebrating our union with us the day of our wedding. No one is as impatient as me about this. But if we are going to have a wedding, I want to do it right. Don't worry, we almost have enough. We just need to wait about six more months for the big day. In the meantime, I am going to ask my father and my mother to come to your house and ask your parents for your hand in marriage."

Refugio nervously asked, "What will your parents think about it? I hope they like me."

Alfonso said, "Oh, they will like you, you will see. You are the most lovely and wonderful girl in the whole world."

Refugio laughed softly, then said, "Oh, Alfonso, I am so nervous about meeting your family. I hope they like me."

Alfonso kissed her softly on the lips, and said, "I love you so much. Don't be nervous, everything is going to be all right."

Worried, Refugio asked, "What if your family does not like me?" She continued, "What are we going to do then?"

Alfonso smiled. "Why would they not like you? They will like you very much when they can see all that I see in you, my darling. They will love you when they get to know you better. I have already talked to them about you and how much I love you. They are eager to meet you. Don't worry, my love, everything is going to be all right." Alfonso added, "I have to go now. Take care, and I hope you dream about me. I dream about you every night. I am going to miss you, my love. I will come back to you soon."

Refugio said, "Good-bye, Alfonso, I will be waiting for you."

"And remember to let your parents know I will return soon with mine to ask for your hand in marriage." Alfonso kissed her on the cheek, and said, "Ask my mother and father-in-law when is a good day for us to visit them and set our wedding date. Good-bye, my love." He kissed her on the lips and held her by the waist. Refugio kissed him back with both of her arms around his neck.

Refugio's mother yelled from the inside of her house. "Refugioooo, are you done watering the plants?!"

Refugio quickly pulled away from Alfonso. He was still holding her hand in his. He looked deeply into her eyes, and Refugio gave him a loving smile. They smiled at each other, looking deeply into each other's eyes, delighted. Alfonso said, "Say 'hi' to my mother-in-law. Good-bye, my love."

Refugio waved her hand and blew him a kiss. "Good-bye, Alfonso. Don't take too long to come back." She waved again and smiled sweetly. Alfonso left in his carriage with his two horses.

Upset with her daughter, Refugio's mother said in a loud voice, "This is getting worse every time. You are getting bolder and bolder each time you see this boy. I hope your father doesn't hear about this. Or your grandparents. You know how many people are watching you kissing and messing around with this man. What must they be saying about you? You have no shame."

Refugio said, "What are they going to say, Mother? That I love him? People can say that if they want because it is true. They can say that we love each other." Refugio glanced up at the blue sky and sighed. "Yes, we do, we love each other very much."

Refugio's mother said, "Oh no, they are not going to say that, Refugio. You don't know how people are. They are going to say other things a lot worse than that, many other things that don't have anything to do with your 'love,' you silly girl." Her mother added, "Just finish watering the plants since you cannot reason at this moment. I am just glad your father is not here to hear your nonsense. You already know your father has a bad temper, and I don't know what he would do if he knew anything about this."

Surprised, Refugio said, "I did not do or say anything wrong."

"Like I said, your father is not going to like this. His daughter talking and doing who knows what else with a stranger. Your father is going to be so mad at you when he finds out, and even madder at that Alfonso. I don't know what he will do."

Refugio walked silently as she continued watering her mother's plants. Then, she whispered to herself, "Yeah, yeah, my father's bad temper, but I have never seen it. He is a lot more reasonable than you, Mother." Refugio continued whispering. "I think it is your own bad temper, but you blame it on Father."

Refugio's mother screamed, "What are you saying, Refugio?!"

Frightened, Refugio respectfully said, "Nothing, Mother, nothing."

"Stop blubbering nonsense to yourself and do your chores. You are too distracted thinking about that stranger. Go get the groceries from the list I gave you so we can prepare lunch."

Refugio said, "Yes, Mother."

"Go now and stop thinking about that stranger."

Refugio whispered, "Even my thoughts you want to control. One is not even allowed the liberty to think in peace in this house."

Refugio's mother said, "Stop talking to yourself and finish cleaning the kitchen. Did you hear what I said?"

Refugio replied, "Yes, Mother."

Meanwhile, Alfonso was on his way home to the Countess of Stonemason's hacienda. He looked at all the beautiful wildflowers. He sighed at their magnificent perfume and beauty. It was a combination of different delicate perfumes. The fragrance was so strong it was difficult not to pay attention to the thousands of flowers in the fields. There were many luminous yellow flowers, fire red flowers, rosy pink flowers, bright purple flowers, pure white flowers, and unusual blue flowers. The tall flowers were dancing elegantly and flirting with the wind over the vast green land. The short flowers, firm and strong, were hesitant to dance around with their graceful friends. It was a beautiful, natural, and unforgettable sight.

Alfonso said to himself, "Oh, what beauty. All of them look so very different yet similar at the same time. It is a perfect view to see them all together, to smell them all together, and to enjoy them all together. There are certainly more similarities than differences between them. They all form a beautiful tapestry." Alfonso closed his eyes to enjoy the fragrance from the flowers. Then, he opened his eyes and said, "How I would like for my beloved Refugio to be here enjoying these pleasant fragrances and the beautiful sight of these colorful flowers with me. I would like to cut them all and take them to my love, but no I cannot do that. My love would not be able to enjoy seeing all these beauties for long if I cut them off from their source of life. The only way she would enjoy them is if I bring her with me so she can see their beauty and smell their fragrance from here, close to them, but without disturbing them. This way, my love would be happy, as happy as I am because I love her and she loves me back."

Alfonso spent hours riding his horses with the carriage back to the countess's hacienda. He was daydreaming about Refugio on his way there. He was still smelling the perfume from the flowers and he wanted his love to smell them and see them and enjoy them with him. He also wanted his dear Refugio to enjoy the warm, soft breeze with him. Everything was beautiful and awakened all his senses, but it would certainly be more mesmerizing with his love by his side. He wanted Refugio to be there right next to him to experience everything that he could not completely enjoy without her presence. It was going to be great when they could be together so they could savor their love and the beauty of their surroundings together. That was going to be the happiness he had never before dreamed could exist, until he met his beloved Refugio. It was his dearest wish for him to be with his sweet Refugio forever.

It was almost midday when Alfonso returned to Pucuaro. He stopped to see the Good Friday procession. People at the front of the procession were dressed in white, and they sang praises to the Lord. Then, after the chorus, they walked and prayed in low voices. Others carried statues of Jesus and the Virgin Mary. People stood on the sides of the streets, watching the procession. They prayed together in a low voice. Doña

Gabriela and most of the female employees from the hacienda were there praying with wooden rosaries.

The countess, her mother, and Christine watched the procession too. The countess looked at her mother. Then, she looked at the procession, and asked, "Where could Alfonso be at this time?"

Doña Gabriela gave a wooden rosary to each of the three ladies. Marie and Christine said thank you, but the countess just looked at the rosary, rolled her eyes, and placed it inside her purse, saying, "If I liked to pray, my rosary would be made of gold, silver, and jade, not this cheap wooden thing."

Marie corrected her daughter. She looked at her, and said, "Andrea, prayer is powerful, and it is a way to communicate with the Lord and praise Him. Praying from the heart is what is important on this day."

Christine was praying with her wooden rosary already. Andrea raised her face and slowly said, "I do not believe in these unintelligent beliefs, nor do I want to pray using this worthless, wooden piece of junk necklace." She took it out of her purse and threw it on the ground, and said, "I cannot stand all these sanctimonious, unimportant, insecure women with their dumb heads covered."

Then, she looked up behind the women praying. There he was, handsome and manly. The Countess of Stonemason's big, intense green eyes sparkled with excitement. Alfonso came near them, and said, "Such a nice view to see these good women of the Lord with their beautiful veils covering their heads and praying with a rosary in their hands. It is one of my favorite things to see on Good Friday during the procession."

The Countess of Stonemason picked up her wooden rosary from the ground. She took the veil from her shoulders and put it on her head. She was looking at Alfonso with her big, bright, intense green eyes. She sighed and with a sweet voice said, "Alfonso, you are here, darling, I am so glad to see you." Then she added, "I love praying the rosary, it is one of my favorite things to do every day, and especially on Good Friday. I pray the rosary several times on this day." She looked at the women around her, then started to pray holding the beads from the rosary.

Alfonso looked at her and at all the other women around her. He smiled at them. Marie and Christine looked at each other, stopped praying, and stared at Andrea in surprise. Marie, smiling and looking at her two daughters, said in a low voice, "Miracles still happen, Christine, we have to believe."

Christine looked over with a smile at Andrea and Alfonso. In a low voice, she said, "Yes, Mother, I believe in miracles too."

Andrea looped her arm through Alfonso's and continued to clutch her rosary with both hands. She looked at Alfonso, and said, "Alfonso, pray with me, darling." And she continued praying.

Alfonso said, "Yes, my lady, I would have never imagined you knew how to pray the rosary that well." He started praying with her and the other ladies around them.

Then, when the rosary prayers ended, the countess looked at Alfonso. She asked, "Alfonso, should we follow the procession, dear?"

Alfonso replied, "Yes, my lady, you should."

The countess asked, "What about you? Don't you want to be part of the Good Friday procession too?"

Alfonso said, "No, my lady, unfortunately I have things to do that cannot wait until tomorrow. I have to go back and check on the horses, especially the one I am training." He continued, "Please go with all the ladies, I am sure you will enjoy it together as much as I would if I could go." He looked at Doña Gabriela, Marie, Christine, the girls, the countess, and said, "Enjoy the procession, ladies, and pray for all of us who cannot be there today." They all nodded their heads and started their prayers with their rosaries in their hands once more. Alfonso said good-bye with the tip of his hat and left.

Andrea was furious. She watched Alfonso leave and threw her wooden rosary into the bushes, then said, "This is ridiculous. I am not going to be walking and wasting my time on silly things with all the riffraff."

Marie said, "Let's just finish these prayers and we can go back to the house."

Andrea said, "You finish them if you want, I am going back now." With a very discontent face, she fixed her veil on her back and shoulders the way she liked it. She said, "I have more important things to do."

Marie said sweetly, "I would prefer if you continued praying here with us but do as you please."

The countess closed her eyes and looked away. She said, "I am going home."

Christine nodded her head and continued praying with her wooden rosary in her hands. She looked at Marie, and whispered, "Mother, would you like us to follow the procession?"

"Not really, Christine, they will be walking too far away." Marie watched Andrea as she was leaving, and said, "Let's stay here and pray."

Christine nodded her head and continued praying with Doña Gabriela and all the girls. Andrea walked quickly, trying to catch up to Alfonso. She called out, "Alfonso, wait!" Unfortunately for her, he left on his horse before seeing or hearing her. Andrea continued walking to her house. An old man who saw her calling Alfonso said, "Today is not the day for disturbances or screaming." He added, "Try to stay in peace at least on Good Friday."

She looked at him, and said, "Just what I needed, an old, poor man telling me what to do." She added, "You have no idea who you are speaking to." She left in a hurry.

Alfonso got to the horse's corral and started his routine with his wild horse. Some young men saw him, and asked, "Why are you going to work, we never work on Good Friday, remember?"

Another boy added, "Today is a day of peace and prayer or story time with the boys—whatever you want."

Another one said, "It is a day of reflection, and nobody works on Good Friday."

Alfonso smiled, and answered, "I know, but this is not work. This is an important project I want to complete. Do not worry, boys, I am doing it of my own free will. I already prayed, and I will meditate as soon as I finish with my strong friend here. I hope I can catch up with you guys for story time another day."

One of the boys said, "I see that you love that horse too much to stop from seeing him even for a day."

The other boy said, "Do whatever you have to do, but we are going to the house to pray, meditate, and rest."

Alfonso agreed. He replied, "Very well, we are all doing what we like to do." He added, "I will see you all soon, do not get behind on your prayers because of me, please go on."

The two young men answered, "We will."

One of them said to the other, "Working on Good Friday, whoever heard of such a thing?"

The other boy replied, "We did, today, with Alfonso, there is always a first time for everything."

The horse appeared happy to see Alfonso. He seemed to resist his training, but at the same time he came back to show he could not be tamed. Both seemed to enjoy the game. They seemed to know what they liked and respected about each other.

Some hours later, Alfonso said good-bye to his horse and went to the kitchen to eat his dinner with his coworkers like he did every day. It seemed like any other regular day, but it wasn't. His coworkers were gathered at the kitchen table to eat, but today they were behaving differently. They looked at him in a strange and secretive way. They were not speaking to him. Instead, they whispered things about him to each other. He ate his dinner quicker than usual and went straight to his room.

He opened the door to get into his room and everything was different. There was a new bed covered with new sheets and red wool blankets. The bed was surrounded with new furniture all around it. The windows had new fancy curtains, and thick carpets were laid out on the floor around his bed. Next to his bed there was a night table with a big bouquet of fresh perfumed flowers. He was still looking around and processing what had happened to his room when Doña Gabriela knocked on his door, and said, "Alfonso, it's me, son, open the door."

Alfonso opened the door and saw Doña Gabriela and her sixteen-year-old helper, Lucia. Alfonso smiled at them, and said, "Doña Gabriela, I am glad to see you and Little Lucia. What are you two doing here? I am very pleased to see you both."

Doña Gabriela answered, "We are here to see if you like the new arrangements to your room."

Excited, Lucia added, "I helped Doña Gabriela with the decorations. Do you like the carpets and the curtains? It was me who arranged them for you, 'Poncho.'"

Alfonso said, "So it was you two who did this? I was about to leave the room. I did not know what was happening, or why everything looked different. For a moment, I thought I had entered the wrong room. Why did you do all of this? I liked my room simple, just the way it was before. It did not need anything else."

Lucia asked, "Does this mean that you do not like it?"

Alfonso answered, "Of course I like it. I like everything you do, Little Lucia." He added, "You always do nice things, and Doña Gabriela also. Thank you to both of you, everything looks nice. However, it wasn't necessary. I was comfortable the way it was before but thank you to both of you."

Lucia said, "Don't thank us, 'Poncho.' Thank the countess, we were just following her orders. These changes were her idea. She wanted you to feel more comfortable, right Doña Gabriela?"

"Yes, my girl. It is true, we were just following orders, but still I hope you like it, Alfonso."

"I don't want to bother anyone but thank you again for your hard work."

Lucia giggled. "Good night, 'Poncho.' Doña Gabriela and I will soon go back to work at San Cristobal for some time, and I will see my grandparents every day."

He said, "Maybe I should do the same and go to San Cristobal, closer to my parents' house."

Doña Gabriela said, "All right, my son, remember to thank the countess too as this was her idea, and we were merely following her orders."

Alfonso yawned. "All right, Doña Gabriela, I will do that."

"Good night, son."

"Good night, Doña Gabriela, and good night to you too, Little Lucia."

Lucia giggled. "Good night, 'Poncho.'"

Alfonso went to sleep on his new bed with his new soft, red blankets. There was a knock on his window. He was too tired to get up to check who was there. He continued lying on his bed with his eyes closed, but the knock on the window continued and became more insistent. Then he felt it on his hair. It was Refugio's touch. She was caressing his hair. He was too tired to wake up and continued lying on his bed, besides he was enjoying his love's touch. She caressed his hair on his forehead. She touched his face with both of her hands while kissing him on his eyebrows. She kissed his closed eyes, and finally she kissed him on the lips. It was a warm, gentle kiss full of love. It was a soft but long kiss, the longest kiss they had ever shared before. He wanted to hug her and to tell her how much he loved her. He wanted to kiss her back too. He wanted to return his love for her with his touch and all his love. She continued leaning on his bed to kiss him. Alfonso looked at her and slid his fingers through her long, soft black hair. He held her head gently and kissed her lips softly. They looked into each other's eyes. The moonlight was reflecting on Refugio's hair, face, and especially in her eyes. Her eyes were glowing and looking at him with profound love. Alfonso looked into her eyes again and grabbed her by the waist. He gently placed her next to him on the bed. He hugged her and pulled her on top of him. Again, he kissed her lips softly. He looked at her and brushed her hair away from her face and continued kissing her. She took his hands from her waist and held them on hers while resting atop him. He took one of her hands and kissed it gently. Then, he did the same with her other hand. He placed both her hands on his chest and continued kissing her while holding her face gently.

Alfonso said, "I love you, Refugio, my beloved Refugio."

She answered back, still kissing him. "I love you too, Alfonso."

"I have waited so long for this moment."

"I know, my love, I feel the same way." She added, "I am so happy and very excited tonight that we can be alone together at last." They continued kissing with profound love and even greater passion.

There was a knock on the window again, but this time louder. Alfonso opened his eyes, now completely awake, and looked around his dark room. It wasn't pitch black, as the full moon was still glowing through his window. He looked around him, but he could not see her. Alfonso searched the bed sheets all around his bed, but he could not find her. He even called her name in a low voice full of love. "Refugio, my love, I'm here." But she did not answer him.

He got up from his bed and went to the window. He opened it and felt the soft breeze, warm on his face and little branches full of flowers blew against his window. Every time the branches knocked into his window, the tiny fruit blossoms fell and were carried away by the wind, spreading their faint citrus fragrance all around. The branches continued knocking on his window. That was the knocking he had heard. It was all just a sweet dream, one of the many dreams he was used to having about the love of his life, Refugio. The lemon, lime, guava, pomegranate, and peach trees were dancing a slow dance with the soft, warm wind. Their little blossoms continued being carried away by the wind, leaving an enchanting scent through the night that awakened all his senses. The water from the river seemed to sing a melodious song for the souls in love who were ready to give their hearts away to their beloved ones. The enormous silver full moon was the witness of his love for her. He could not sleep peacefully anymore until she was there with him. He continued to stand there, leaning his arms on the window, looking at the gigantic glowing moon in front of him. He smelled the fragrance from the tree blossoms that the soft wind was blowing all around. And the river still sang its magical sweet song for lovers. Everything was perfect for a romantic night. The landscape was offering a magical experience for the ones in love. The breeze continued caressing Alfonso's face, his hair, and his shoulders. How sad it was that Refugio was not there to share this magical moment with him. That was the only thing missing on this beautiful night.

"Refugio, my beautiful Refugio, I need you more than you can imagine," he whispered, and the wind carried away his words to his beloved Refugio on the fruit blossoms from the trees. The moon was witness of his great love for her.

Alfonso stepped out of his room, sighing and meditating about his beloved. He continued to gaze at the giant full moon. The river continued to sing a song for him and his dearest Refugio. Suddenly, he heard some footsteps behind him and a female voice calling out to him. "Alfonso, my love, I know what you are doing here! You, like I, cannot sleep thinking about our love. My sweet Alfonso, I now know how you feel, I know you love me." It was the Countess of Stonemason. "I love you too, my love, do not suffer for me, anymore. I am here for you, darling. My heart is full of love for you! These feelings I feel for you are the greatest and the most extraordinary love I have ever felt with the strength of an erupting volcano. Everything I have is yours to take, darling, my body too, take anything you want, take everything, including my heart, my mind, and my body." She added excitedly, "Take me! I cannot live without you anymore. I want us to be together forever. Say yes, my love, say you love me too. I know you do. I will make you happy if you stay with me forever. I will never leave you. This is my promise to you. My dear Alfonso, say yes, please darling."

She was crying to convince him of her love. Big tears fell down her cheeks as she held Alfonso in a tight hug, her face on his bare chest and her hands on his shoulders. *What else can I do to conquer Alfonso's love? I have no other option, but to be the one to pursue him. After all, I have tried many of my most effective flirting tricks with him and none of them have worked. I have no time to lose. This time I must be direct and hold him in my trap of love to keep him with me forever.*

Alfonso had his hands behind his body while leaning on the balcony. His thoughts ran wild. *I do not know what to do with such an embarrassing situation. I do not want to be rude to her, but I do not want to plant any false hopes about a love that does not exist. I have my true love waiting for me, the one who makes me dream sweet dreams of love and hope. I know the countess is not in love with me either. She just wants to see if she can find happiness through me, the happiness she has never found in anyone for she has never looked within herself.* He was right, even if she had looked inside of herself, how could she find happiness in the emptiness of her soul?

The countess was insistent and continued begging for his love. She said, "My love, I will make you the happiest man. You will be the owner of everything I have." She added, "I will make you immensely rich and powerful, and I swear that I will never leave you. I will only have eyes for you. I promise you, I will be with you forever. Please, believe me, it is true. I will always be with you to love you and please you all the days of our lives. We are going to be together, living our love and enjoying my riches forever."

Embarrassed, Alfonso did not know what to do or what to say to her. This was the magnificent Countess of Stonemason with the finest, prettiest clothes that no one else had ever worn before his eyes. The extraordinary, beautiful woman with the most elegant presence. The one who did not bow to any man because she did not need any of them to be happy. The best, the perfect, the most powerful woman he had admired and respected since childhood. He was speechless. His admiration and respect turned into a mixture of emotions. The only feelings left in him for the Countess of Stonemason were a mixture of pity and rejection. He looked at the river, wishing to throw himself in it to get rid of such an uncomfortable situation, but it could be fatal. He valued life too much to do that.

The countess continued promising him everything she could think of, then said, "I will make you the greatest man of all the New Spain. Alfonso, my love, do not suffer for me anymore. I am here. Take me, and my love will make you happy forever."

Alfonso looked at the countess, and replied, "My lady, this is a misunderstanding. It is true that I could not sleep, but it is not for the motives you are thinking."

She put her finger on his lips, and said, "Quiet, Alfonso, do not say another word, darling."

"You don't understand, my lady, I could not sleep because I received bad news from my family in Acámbaro, and I am worried about them." He added, "Worried as I am, it was impossible for me to sleep, but it was nothing else. It is only worry that has kept me awake on this night. I am sorry if my behavior tonight misled your thoughts and feelings."

The countess dried her eyes with a fine handkerchief, then said, "Very well, I want you to go to Acámbaro early in the morning to see your family and comfort yourself with this visit. However, know that my wedding proposal is still in place." She continued, "I am in love with you, and I want to marry you. I will live with you forever and I will make you the most happy, rich, and powerful man in this land. I will give you anything you wish for from now on."

Embarrassed, Alfonso replied, "I am sorry, I don't—"

"Sssshhh, my love, do not say anything, I understand. You might be confused, but you will feel it soon, as profound as I feel this love for you. You are the lucky man who will have my love forever. Do not say no to me or you will regret it for the rest of your life. Soon you will understand that this is best for both of us."

Alfonso insisted, "But I do not feel—"

The countess quieted him again, but this time with a kiss on the lips. Then she said, "Do not speak, my love, just go to sleep. In the morning go to Acámbaro, and we will talk when you return from visiting your family. Take the cart with the horses."

"I prefer to take my own horse."

"You can take the big horse you worked so hard to tame. You have worked so hard it is only fair that you keep it." She added, "That powerful horse is yours, and besides, everybody else is afraid to ride it."

He looked at her, and she said, "Since you are going there, I will give you a letter for the priest who owes me many favors, so he can arrange the wedding."

Alfonso answered, "But, my lady—"

"Shhh, silence darling, you will not regret this. Do not think about it, do not think about anything else, only think of giving your love to me, just do as I say." She added, "I will make you the happiest man in the world as soon as you come back to me. Do not worry about anything. Just go and see your family, take this letter to the priest, and come back to me as soon as possible."

The countess entered Alfonso's room, got a piece of paper and a quill, and she used the light of the full moon to finish writing the mentioned letter as fast as she could. Alfonso considered himself brave, courageous, and decisive. However, at this moment he was pale, sweating, and his hands were shaking. She looked at him intently with her big, intense green eyes as she handed the letter to him and gave him a strong hug. She whispered in his ear, "Do as I tell you, my love. You will not regret it."

Alfonso stood outside his room on the balcony, frozen for a minute. The soft, warm, scented breeze caressed his hair and face once again. He did not know if this was really happening. Was his beautiful dream about his true love Refugio suddenly turning into a nightmare? He wished it was a nightmare from which he would soon awaken, but it was not. He was awake, and he was conscious of everything that was happening. The Countess of Stonemason kissed him on the lips again and hugged him desperately.

Alfonso stood there immobilized, with his hands behind him holding the balcony, still not knowing what to do. He gently pushed her away from him, and in a low voice said, "It is time for me to go."

The countess answered, "Yes, my love. You are tired, go to sleep so you can go see your family in the morning. Today, before dawn, while you go to Acámbaro to spend some days with your family, I will go check on my properties not too far away from here so we can reunite soon. This visit to your family will relieve you from your worries so you may focus on our love when you return to me."

Alfonso walked quickly inside his room. The countess walked back to her room. Once indoors he quickly locked the door for the first time since the day he had started working there. He sat down on the bed with his head in his hands, thinking. He was in that position for a few minutes. Then, he laid down on his bed looking at the ceiling of his room. He was tired, but he could not sleep thinking of what had just happened with the countess.

He got up from his bed, hurriedly put on some clothes, and walked to his horse. He got on his horse and rode away from that place as fast as he could. It was still dark, and millions of stars were shining brightly in the sky. On this beautiful night, he could not enjoy it. He felt a heavy burden over his shoulders like he had never felt before, the heaviest of all. At least Alfonso felt free, riding on his horse away from the problems and toward freedom. He rode away from there as fast as he could, running freely like the wind and the water in the river next to him, and the galloping of his horse added to the melodious sounds of such a beautiful but stressful night.

CHAPTER SEVEN

The Wedding

Alfonso rode his horse as fast as he could. Their silhouette looked imposing under the moon. They were meant for each other, both strong-willed, agile, and decisive. Alfonso had the letter the countess gave him in his pants pocket. He touched it to make sure it was still there. Then, he continued his adventure with his horse. Everything was still dark since he left at 3 a.m. The road was empty and pitch black as the clouds covered the moon. The wind stopped blowing. Everything was quiet. The only sound now was the galloping of his horse.

It was 6 a.m. when Alfonso got to Refugio's house. He sat next to a big tree close to her home and waited to see her. He took the letter out of his pocket. He stared at it, and whispered, "Wedding? Whose wedding?" The envelope was sealed. Alfonso gulped. He slowly reached to touch the plants beside him. The leaves reluctantly buckled under the delicate weight of his fingertips, as the dew dripped onto them. Alfonso pulled back, and used the moisture to carefully open the letter, beginning to read. The letter was directed to the reverend of the biggest church in town, and it said:

Dear Reverend Chava,

Please listen to Alfonso, the young man I have sent to deliver this letter to you. Follow his instructions to prepare the great wedding I have entitled him to prepare. I need the wedding vows ready to be taken as soon as possible. Do not hesitate for economic reasons. Use as much money as necessary to make it the most beautiful wedding for everyone to remember. You already know me very well and I will compensate you for everything you spend, and I will also make sure to compensate you significantly for all your time and effort.

Sincerely,

The Countess of Stonemason

Alfonso finished reading the letter, folded it the way it was folded by the countess, and put it back in its envelope. He closed it the same way it was closed and put it back inside his pocket. *I knew it. Everything in this letter is exactly as I thought, but I had to read it to believe it.*

His horse was grazing next to the tree where he was sitting. Alfonso watched Refugio's house until he saw her open the door and quickly walk down the street. He tied his horse to the tree and quickly walked after her. Refugio heard the footsteps behind her and turned her head to see who was following her. She saw Alfonso, gave a big smile, then asked, "Alfonso, what are you doing here?"

Alfonso looked at her, and asked, "That is all you are going to ask me? What am I doing here? Aren't you going to tell me that you are happy to see me, and you have missed me so much?" He got closer to her, closed his big brown eyes, and offered his mouth for her to kiss him.

"Alfonso!" she said, smiling and amused. He continued walking quickly to keep up with her speed.

Alfonso insisted, "Come on, my love, just a little kiss. I have been dreaming of you every day and for a long time."

Refugio stopped and kissed her boyfriend. They hugged and kissed each other. After they kissed, Refugio said, "Of course, I have missed you a lot, and I do love you very much."

Alfonso said, "Maybe you do love me, but you don't love me more than I love you, and you don't miss me more than I miss you."

She quietly smiled at him. Alfonso added, "And I am completely certain you don't dream about me like I dream about you every night."

In a low voice, she answered, "That's what you think, but I do dream about you." Then her tone changed to a louder but calmer one when she said, "I dream the same dream every night. We are happily talking to each other and then suddenly you leave and never come back. I keep waiting and waiting and asking for you and nobody seems to know where you are."

Alfonso asked, "Wait, let's talk, where are we going walking so quickly?"

"I have to get the bread for Father, he came from the fields for his breakfast, and he wants to take some food for his farmers too. You know my father; he is in a hurry all the time."

Alfonso said, "Yes, my love, I know him, but I would like to know him better. I asked you to let me talk to him about my intentions with you, and you never arranged for us to meet."

"I have tried, but my mother does not like this idea. She thinks my father is not going to be very happy about it. You know she says he has a bad temper and would not like his daughter to be in a relationship with a stranger."

"I am still a stranger because he hasn't agreed to meet me yet."

Refugio entered the bakery and Alfonso followed her. She chose pastries and some French bread. She put it all on the tray and was eager to pay for it. The bakery owner, a man in his fifties, said, "I see you are in a hurry today. It did not even take you one minute to choose all those pastries, and you usually take your time to choose the sweetest and crunchiest bread."

Refugio answered, "I know, but today is different. I am in a hurry because Father is waiting for me to eat his breakfast with his workers. They are all very hungry and waiting to eat." Refugio paid in a hurry and left the bakery.

Alfonso was right next to her and helped her with the four bags of bread. They continued walking hurriedly and Alfonso looked at Refugio, and asked, "Can we slow down, I need to talk to you, Refugio."

She continued walking at a fast pace while looking ahead. "Alfonso, I am in a hurry. Father is waiting for this bread to be able to eat his breakfast with his workers."

Alfonso insisted, "Refugio, I have something very important to tell you."

"All right, fine, you will tell me as soon as I deliver this bread."

"What if you have to go back to do your chores and I cannot tell you what I came for?"

Refugio answered, "Don't worry, there is always next week."

Alfonso insisted, "No, my love, you don't understand. There is no more time left for this, I have to tell you today."

"Alfonso, you're scaring me, why can't you tell me later?"

"Later, it won't matter anymore."

Refugio's father came out of the house and saw them walking. He went back into the house. Immediately, Refugio's mother came out of the house, yelling at Refugio, "You just never listen! I told you your father is in a hurry and he doesn't have time to waste!"

Refugio said, "Mother, I went as fast as I could to get the bread for Father."

Refugio's mother answered in disbelief, "Mhh, fast, oh yeah, talking to this man, very fast of course. You won't listen until your father decides to lock you inside the house so you can no longer be fooling around with the first stranger you meet."

Refugio's father approached her with a young man about Refugio's age. Her father said, "Daughter, this is Juan, and he is the son of my best friend. I've been wanting you to meet him for a long time."

Juan extended his hand to say hello to Refugio. "I am very pleased to meet you, Refugio."

Refugio shook his hand. "Nice to meet you, Juan."

Refugio's father, Don Aaron, looked at Juan like he was trying to tell him something, and Juan understood him. Don Aaron said, "Let's get inside and eat something together before we leave." Don Aaron offered his arm to his daughter and looked at Juan while nodding. Juan nodded back and offered his arm to Refugio as well. Puzzled, Refugio scratched her head and looked at Alfonso. Don Aaron took Refugio's arm and Juan did the same with her other arm and they walked inside the house. Refugio was following along, but she was looking back to see her beloved Alfonso.

Alfonso stood quietly and watched them go. Refugio's mother, Doña Rosaura, slammed the door in his face, and said, "Now it's family time." Rosaura had pots with food boiling in the kitchen. Chicken soup, steak in tomato sauce, tomato rice with green peas and carrots, vegetable soup, and black beans. On the table were the hot homemade tortillas, fresh cheese, sweet corn, sweet pumpkin, tomato sauce, a big bowl with freshly washed fruits, and hot cocoa to drink. Rosaura told Refugio, "Set the table. We are going to eat."

Refugio quietly followed her mother's directions. Juan looked at Refugio with a big smile on his face, then Aaron said, "Refugio, how old are you, Daughter?"

Concerned, Refugio answered, "You know, Father, I'm twenty-seven."

"I am twenty-seven too," said Juan. He looked at Refugio with a big grin on his face.

Aaron said, "I thought you were twenty-three, Juan."

"Twenty-three is almost twenty-seven, no big difference."

Rosaura added, "Love has no age!"

Aaron added, "That's true, and speaking of love, my dear Refugio, twenty-seven is a good age to get married."

Juan took a tiny pink flower from the flower bouquet on the table and gave it to Refugio. He smiled and blew her a kiss. Everybody ate happily, except for Refugio. She listened to the conversation and rolled her eyes. Aaron said, "I would like you to know Juan better, I have a feeling you two will get along very well, and Juan's father thinks the same." He added, "If everything turns out as planned, we will be celebrating your wedding in one or two months."

Juan looked attentively at Refugio, winked at her, blew her another kiss, and said, "That wait is going to feel like an eternity."

In surprise, Refugio's eyes opened wide. "Plans? What plans, Father?"

Rosaura intervened. "Show your good manners and let your father speak without interrupting him, Refugio. Your father knows what is best for you."

Aaron said, "It is time for us to go, Juan, soon we will continue with this conversation."

Juan said, "Next week my parents will be here for dinner to make it official."

Aaron, Juan, and Rosaura put the pots with the hot food in a big wooden box for the farmers. Meanwhile Refugio prepared a smaller pot with a little bit of food and covered it with a plate. She placed it in a basket and was ready to leave when her mother stopped her at the door, and said, "Everything has changed now that you have a fiancé who deserves your respect. You are not going out anymore until you get married to Juan and you will go out only with your husband. He has rights over you right now and deserves your respect as your fiancé."

"Fiancé?" asked Refugio, surprised. "I DO have a fiancé, but his name is Alfonso, and he is a real man, not a young boy like the one you would have me marry."

Rosaura directed her daughter to her room. "This is for your own good and your happiness with Juan depends on it." Rosaura closed the door and locked it from the outside. "I don't want you to continue to shame your family and your future husband."

"What are you doing? Please let me out, Mother?" Refugio, hoping to get her mother's attention, screamed, "Mother, please unlock the door!" There was no answer. Rosaura had gone to finish her chores.

Refugio left the pot of food on her night table and hurried to the window. It was covered by long red iron bars. She could see Alfonso outside sitting on the ground still looking at her front door, waiting for her. She tried to get out through the bars, but she could not fit. Her head and upper body were out, but the rest of her body was stuck. Refugio said, "Maybe I need to get rid of this big dress." She took it off and put on a plain white shirt and skirt.

She tried to get out through the window again, and after a few minutes of trying, she made it. She tried to get the pot with food she had prepared for Alfonso, but the pot could not fit through the bars. She took the plate with tortillas and cheese from the pot, but some of the food fell to the floor spoiling her clothes with beans and tomato sauce. She walked to Alfonso. He smiled when he saw her, and said, "I thought you were not going to get out of your house today."

Refugio said, "I know, I thought the same thing, but here I am."

"These two long hours felt like years waiting for you," said Alfonso.

"I know, Alfonso, I am sorry that I kept you waiting. Let's eat."

"There is no time, my love, save it for later. Today is the day we start our new life together."

Refugio looked at him, and asked, "What do you mean?"

"There are people who have other plans for our lives and if we don't start a new life together, we are going to end up living a life we don't want, and it would make us unhappy forever. I have the feeling something really bad might happen if we don't make a decision now."

Distressed, Refugio said, "I am not going to live with you without being married."

"I know, and that is what we are going to do today, we are getting married." He caressed her hair and kissed her on the cheek. Refugio held his face with her hands and smiled at him. He held her by her waist, and she put her arms around his neck. They hugged and kissed each other tenderly.

He mounted his horse, helped Refugio get on behind him, and they left together. The horse galloped as fast as he could. Refugio hugged Alfonso tight. The sun was in its highest position in the sky, and it was warming their bodies more and more with every minute. They began to sweat as the sun beat down on them. They were hungry, extremely thirsty, and lost in their own thoughts.

Alfonso's horse continued to gallop as fast as he could. As the sky started to change, the wind began to blow with more strength. The clouds moved across the sky and covered the sun. In a few minutes, the sky switched from blue to dark gray. Then it started to rain. Soon, it was pouring down. Refugio was cold and shivering. The sky was getting darker and darker and became illuminated by the lightning that struck. The shadow of three silhouettes merged on the road—the horse, Refugio, and Alfonso. One bolt of lightning struck and broke a tree just after they passed by it, if the horse would have been any slower the tree would have fallen on them. Thunder crashed and another bolt of lightning hit the tree ahead of them and it fell across the road. Alfonso pulled the reins, and the horse majestically jumped over the enormous tree. This was nothing new for the horse, he was used to such maneuvers along with his friend Alfonso. Refugio's heart was racing and she held onto her boyfriend's waist as tightly as she could.

Two hours later, they arrived at his parents' house. It was a different scene there with a clear, blue, beautiful sky. The sun was shining and warming everything under it. There was a gentle, enjoyable breeze. The grass was shiny green, the colorful roses were blooming all around, and the ground was completely dry. The storm had not passed there. Alfonso got off his horse and helped Refugio down. She said, "Such beautiful flowers."

"Yes, my love, they are beautiful, but they are missing a little something."

"Are they? They look perfect to me."

"That is the problem, they are too perfect," he said. "They are all the same size, the same kind, the same color, it is just kind of boring." Alfonso knocked on his father's door, and said,

"This is unusual, this door is never closed; maybe no one is here."

A tall strong man in his late fifties opened the door and hugged Alfonso. "My son, you are here; we were not expecting you."

Alfonso hugged him back, and said, "I was starting to think there was no one in the house." He added, "Father, this is Refugio, the girl I have told you and Mother about, the one I am going to marry."

Alfonso's father looked at Refugio, gave her a handshake, and said, "Hello, ma'am, so you are the one who has stolen my son's heart."

Refugio smiled a little as she shook his hand, and said, "Nice to meet you, Mister."

Alfonso's father said, "Your mother went to visit a family in need, and I was taking a nap." He added, "If you were to work with me it would make your mother and I very happy, but you have decided to work far away."

Alfonso said, "I used to think nothing exciting happened around here, but I have changed my mind and I want to come back here and work with you, Father." He added, "I would like to use the house you gave me next door to live with Refugio, after I marry her today, if it's all right with you and Mother."

Alfonso's father looked at Refugio from head to toe, and said, "Son, I need to talk to you in private, let's go to the library. Would you excuse us, ma'am?"

"Of course, sir." Alfonso's father closed the door. Refugio stood there, she was very tired but did not want to sit down and soil the chairs with her muddy clothes. She was all wet.

"Father," said Alfonso, "we are getting married today. We will be living here, and I am going to be working with you as you have asked me many times."

Alfonso's father said, "Now, now, don't you think you are rushing into this? Everything sounds great, except for the marriage part. It's too soon for you to make that decision, give it some time and then if you still feel the same, then you get married."

Alfonso said, "Father, I am twenty-nine years old, and I have been planning this wedding with Refugio for more than two years."

"Yes, but a little more time would be good."

"No, I am not going to wait anymore."

Alfonso's father said, "You know that I have always been supportive of you in the decisions you have made, but not on this one, Alfonso. I don't want you to ruin your own life. You are welcome to stay here with us and nothing will make your mother and I happier, but no marriage."

"Father, I have never thought you would be against my plans of marrying the woman I love and the one I want to be with for the rest of my life." Alfonso added, "I have spoken to you and Mother about it many times before, and neither of you have ever been opposed to it. Why are you against my happiness now, why have you changed your mind about it?"

His father looked at him, and said, "Well, you have been very mature and a good decision-maker, until now." His father cleared his throat. "What have you seen in this girl that another one does not have? You can get any girl you want, why her, and why marriage? Let's do this… You can live with her for six months and if you still feel the same in six months, you will marry her, and everybody will accept her happily."

Alfonso said, "I am sorry you feel this way, but we are getting married today. Refugio is the woman of my dreams. The one I have chosen to spend the rest of my life with, and no one will make me change my mind about it, not even you, Father."

Alfonso's father asked, "For goodness' sake, Alfonso, don't you see? She is so quiet, shy, ignorant, unimportant, unattractive, dirty and I don't want you to ruin your life by making a decision you will soon regret." He added, "You will live with her for six months and if after this time you still feel the same, I will support you in this crazy decision. You have always been smart and wise, but this is not your best decision. Even if I let you continue with this ridiculous notion, you will soon regret it, and that is what I would like to avoid, Son." His father asked, "What is it that you see in her, I just cannot understand. What do you see in this girl? You are so blind, my son. The house is still yours as I promised, but with the condition that you marry her in six months if you still feel the same about her by that time, not sooner."

"No thank you, Father, you can keep your house as it is not going to be of any service to me with your conditions. Say hello to Mother, and I'll come back to see you both another day." Alfonso opened the door and looked at Refugio. She was all wet, her hair all disheveled, her plain clothes all dirty, and her face serious with a sad look in her eyes. She looked tired and nervous. She had only one shoe on and one bare, muddy foot. Alfonso took her hand, and said, "Let's go, my love."

He mounted his horse and helped her do the same. His father stood shaking his head in disbelief and disapproval.

They got to the closest church and asked the reverend there to marry them. The reverend looked at them, and said, "Where are your parents? Your family? Who is going to be present in this ceremony?"

Alfonso said, "Only us, Reverend."

The reverend said, "I cannot marry you today if you have taken your girlfriend without her family's consent. You need to go back to her home and ask for forgiveness, invite them and your family to be present at the sacrament, and if everyone agrees, I can possibly marry you in a month."

Alfonso insisted, "We want to get married today."

Refugio said, "Please, Reverend, you can do it if you want to."

The reverend answered, "Impossible, you're not getting married today."

They left the church and walked for a few minutes, then sat down on the grass to think. Refugio asked, "What are we going to do?"

Alfonso replied, "I should be taking you to eat lunch and to buy you some new clothes and shoes, but I left all my money in my room at the countess's hacienda."

Refugio said, "And I dropped the plate with tortillas and cheese I had for us to eat. Anyway, we would not be able to eat them as they would be all soggy by now. We should have drunk some of the water from the thunderstorm, I am so thirsty."

Alfonso replied, "We will find a solution, don't worry." They sat quietly deep in thought for a few minutes, then Alfonso said, "I know what to do, let's go, my love." He kissed her on the cheek. They went to the river and drank water along with the horse. Then, they rode the horse until hours later when they reached the San Francisco church. Alfonso asked for Reverend Chava and gave him the letter the countess had given him in the morning. The reverend looked at Alfonso from head to toe, did the same with Refugio, shook his head, and asked, "Where are your parents?"

Refugio answered, "It's only us, Reverend."

Alfonso added, "They are unable to attend the ceremony today, Reverend, but soon you will meet them."

The reverend shook his head again in disappointment. Then, he looked at the countess's letter one more time. The reverend shrugged his shoulders, and happily said, "Let's prepare everything for your marriage."

Refugio said, "Reverend, please just marry us like this, we don't need anything else, we just want to be married."

Alfonso added, "Yes, Reverend, please marry us now, we are ready."

The reverend laughed out loud, and said, "The things love can do, but no, you are going to get married in a nice way as the letter asks me to do even when you took your girlfriend without anyone's consent. I am going to follow the letter's directions as best as I can, but don't worry. We will prepare everything swiftly."

They both insisted again. "Please, Reverend," Refugio said, "please marry us like this and marry us now. We don't want anything else. We just want to get married."

Alfonso said, "Please, Reverend, don't spend any money on us, Refugio is right. We just want to get married, that's all."

Reverend Chava said, "I said no, this is going to be well done like everything I do or I won't do anything." He added, "Don't worry, my children, you are very tense and nervous." Smiling, Reverend Chava said, "It must be because you are getting married today."

Elvira, Reverend Chava's assistant, came out of his office. She looked at him, and asked, "How can I help, Reverend?"

Reverend Chava smiled, and said, "Elvira, you're very timely, please ask two female missionaries to help this young woman get ready for her wedding."

Elvira smiled, and said, "Yes, Reverend, is there anything else you need?"

"Ask some of our Franciscan friars to go and order simple food to be cooked as soon as possible for the wedding."

"Right away, Reverend. What about the fireworks? A wedding is more exciting when there are fireworks for the celebration."

"You don't miss a thing. Very good, Elvira, make sure the fireworks people get here for the ceremony today."

Elvira smiled with excitement and went to take care of the requests.

After four hours, the food was almost ready, Refugio was dressed in a beautiful white long dress, hand embroidered with colorful flowers, leaves, birds, and butterflies. Her long hair flowed down to her shoulders and was fixed with a neat bow. She wore a crown made of many tiny white, pink, and red flowers with their green leaves still attached. She had a handwoven, thin, white shawl covering her head, and she wore natural-colored leather sandals. Alfonso looked at her with profound love. There she was, the love of his life at the doors of the church entrance where they were going to promise to love each other for the rest of their lives. This was the moment they had wished for. He was excited to finally unite his life with his beloved Refugio.

Alfonso was dressed in a typical mariachi suit, and it highlighted how manly and attractive he was. As he approached Refugio, he kissed her cheek, and said, "You are so beautiful, my love, and soon you are going to be my wife forever." He held her hand.

The giant bells from the tallest tower of the church started to call people from all around town to come to the mass ceremony. They were going to get married during the seven o'clock mass. The church was filled with colorful wildflowers everywhere. The carpet was red and new. The big church was full of people by the third call from the bells. There was no more space on the wooden benches to sit. People coming into the church had to stand to be able to participate in the mass. Reverend Chava gave a nice and reflective ceremony about marriage. He was the best at weddings, according to the people of Acámbaro and its surroundings. This was the reason many couples chose him to marry them, and even waited for many weeks for the honor to be married by Reverend Chava. His wedding sermons made some women cry and at the same time inspired a few men to get married. The mass was a delight, like every mass ceremony celebrated by Reverend Chava. Some parishioners were happily participating in the sacrament. A few others criticized the couple in love. They wondered why there was no one from their families around. Hymns praising the Lord were sung by the church choir formed by young men and women. Some of them played guitars animatedly.

At the end of the ceremony, Reverend Chava asked, "If there is anyone who objects to this marriage, speak now or forever hold your peace." A deep silence reigned in the church at that moment. Alfonso looked at Refugio and held her hands in his. Refugio looked at him and they smiled at each other happily. Their hearts and faces were emanating love and happiness all around them. Finally, the reverend said the words they had been wanting to hear for a long time. The reverend asked, "Alfonso, do you take Refugio to be your wife? Do you promise to be faithful to her in good times and in bad, in sickness and in health, to love her and to honor her all the days of your life?"

Alfonso said, "I do." He smiled at Refugio. She had an intense warm feeling inside of her that she had never felt before. She felt like floating in the air. It was like a sweet dream, but the best part of it was that she knew it was not just a dream, it was really happening this time.

Reverend Chava looked around him like he was looking for someone, but the assistant priest was not around. Then he focused on the couple again. Reverend Chava asked, "Refugio, do you take Alfonso to be your husband? Do you promise to be faithful to him in good times and in bad, in sickness and in health, to love him and to honor him all the days of your life?"

Refugio said, "I do." She gave him a subtle smile. Alfonso felt immensely happy, a happiness stronger than he had ever experienced before.

Reverend Chava looked at the congregation. Then he looked at the happy couple and with a kind and firm voice, he said, "What God has joined together, let no one put asunder." Then, Reverend Chava glanced at the assistant priest and made a sign with his face and hands. The assistant priest did not seem to notice the urgency in Reverend Chava's eyes. Reverend Chava came closer to him, and whispered, "Where are the rings?"

The assistant priest asked, "What rings?" Then he opened his eyes wide and looked at Reverend Chava. "Oh my, we forgot about the rings!"

Reverend Chava nodded, and said, "It's fine, they are already married with or without rings." He looked at the pair in love, and said, "You are joined now in holy matrimony in the name of the Father, the Son, and the Holy Spirit, amen. Congratulations to the married couple." He added, "The mass has ended, you may go in peace."

Alfonso kissed Refugio's cheek and they looked into each other's eyes and smiled. Alfonso held his wife's hand. They walked together, and everyone's eyes in the church were on them. Some were sincerely happy for them. An old couple looked at them tenderly. The man wiped a tear from his eye and said to his wife, "The bride reminded me of you on our wedding day, and during the whole mass she also reminded me that we haven't seen our granddaughter, Refugio. The bride kind of looks like her."

The new married couple passed by as the old lady looked at her husband and opened her eyes wide. She raised her voice, and said, "She looks like our granddaughter, Refugio, because she is Refugio!"

The grandfather opened his eyes wide, and asked, "Refugio, our granddaughter?"

The old couple looked at each other. The lady said, "Yes."

The gentleman lowered his voice, and said, "It couldn't be, they didn't invite us to the wedding."

"This is very suspicious." The old lady looked around. "Her parents are not here." She added, "They didn't invite anyone, not even their own parents; I'm going to find out what is going on when we're out of the church."

He said, "It cannot be, Refugio wouldn't do this."

Not everyone was happy for the new couple, as they were criticized and others already found something wrong with their wedding. Three ladies watched the new married couple. One of them said, "I don't like her dress."

The next lady said, "And what fine lady gets married wearing sandals?"

The third lady said, "Keep on criticizing them instead of praying and you are not going to be blessed today."

Refugio and Alfonso heard the comments, but they paid no attention to them. Their deepest, most important wish just came true and the little stones on the road did not bother them on this day. They held hands and walked together happily. They felt like they were in a new world. A new and beautiful world where the most important thing was being together. The most important feelings were their feelings for each other, and the most intense feelings in their hearts were love and harmony.

When they got out of the church, a couple of priests invited everyone to eat vegetable tostadas with sour cream, cheese, and salsa. They also had red rice with chicken, mole sauce, and hibiscus cold tea. Refugio said, "I forgot how hungry I am."

Alfonso said, "Me too, I was very hungry, but during our wedding mass I forgot all about it. My love, this is the happiest day of my life."

Refugio said, "Oh, Alfonso, I love you so much, I am very happy that we are finally together."

Alfonso held Refugio's hand, and said, "Let's go get some food, my love."

As they walked together, they overheard a conversation. Two Jesuit priests were discussing an important matter between themselves. One priest said, "This is the third time bandits have stolen our products and money. I don't know who to trust anymore."

The other priest answered, "I know, Brother, and we have no one to do the trading tomorrow or to bring the products to sell early in the morning."

Alfonso intervened in the conversation, and said, "Good evening, Brothers, I could not avoid listening to your conversation. If you need somebody to work for you here, I can do it. I will be happy to work for you. I am honest and reliable. You will see that you can trust me and I am a good worker."

The priests said, "It is a very time-consuming job. You will need to leave here at midnight to be there at around 2 a.m. The trading will take a couple of hours and you will be back at about six to check the merchandise, which will take from one to two hours, and if everything goes well, you will be done by 8 a.m. This needs to be done weekly. Then I would like you to supervise and help with the construction being done at our chapel every day, five days a week. You will be done by 3 p.m. every day. Are you interested? If you take the job, you can live with your wife in the little house by the chapel. It would be convenient for us to have you near."

Alfonso said, "Yes, Reverend, I am glad to work for you. Refugio and I will be happy living in the little house next to you." The sky gave a burst of fireworks while the band played music, and people of all ages danced. It was almost 10 p.m. when the wedding party ended. The last fireworks of the night went off as people watched them happily.

Alfonso tenderly looked at his beloved wife, and said, "Refugio, I have to go to the new job the Jesuits offered me."

Refugio answered, "You mean right now?"

Alfonso said, "Yes, my love, tonight will be my first night working for them." He added, "First, you and I will go to our new home, and when you are there safe and comfortable, I will go to work. Do not worry, my love, I will see you tomorrow after 3 p.m. As soon as I finish my work."

Refugio said, "All right, Alfonso, let's go."

A few minutes later, the two priests showed them their new home. One of the priests said, "As you can see, this is a small house, but it has everything a new couple needs to be comfortable and happy." He added, "I hope you like it here."

Alfonso looked at Refugio, and asked, "What do you think, Refugio?"

She answered, "I agree with the priest, this tiny house is comfortable enough and has everything we need. We are going to be very happy here, Alfonso, you will see."

Alfonso said, "Yes, my love, we will. Now that you are here, safe in our new home, I can go to work happily, and I will see you soon." He got near her, and whispered, "Meanwhile, rest and dream nice dreams about me."

Refugio smiled at her new husband. Alfonso kissed her on the cheek. They both looked at each other and smiled with profound love. Refugio said, "Do not worry, my love, I will be all right here waiting for you to return."

Alfonso nodded and left with the priests who were waiting for him outside.

Refugio stayed inside their new home and watched them from the window. She went to the kitchen, and said to herself, "There is nothing to eat here, and I didn't eat well at our wedding. I will drink a jar of water and go to sleep."

She walked through her new home and sat down on a chair by a small, round table. Then she got up and sat down on another chair by a rectangular table. She wiped the dust from the small table with her hand, and said, "It never crossed my mind that someday there was not going to be any food to eat at home. It was nice to have a lot of food to eat back there at my parents' house, but I think we will manage living here. We will have everything we need. For now, the most important thing is that we are together." She stood up from the chair and went to the well to get some water. She took out the bucket, rinsed it, and tossed out the water. She got some more water, took some in her hand, and drank from it many times.

Friar Augustine saw her, smiled, and whispered to himself, "It is very nice to see someone enjoy drinking water so much, she must be very thirsty." Then, he got closer to Refugio, and said, "There is a nice water jug nobody uses, would you like to have it, Sister Refugio?"

Refugio splashed water all around her mouth. She wiped her mouth with her arm and said, "I am sorry, Brother…"

He said, "There's nothing to be sorry about, Sister. The Lord likes it when you take care of yourself, and drinking water is one of the ways we can take care of our bodies." He added, "If you want the jug, I will bring it to you straight away. What do you say?"

Refugio smiled, and said, "Well, if nobody uses it and if nobody will miss it, the truth is it will be very useful to me, Brother."

The priest said, "I will bring it right away, Sister." And he did.

Chapter Eight

Christine Has a Boyfriend

The sunny, warm evening was scented with a sweet, citrus breeze that welcomed the Countess of Stonemason back to her estate. As usual, she returned to her house in San Cristobal without any previous notice. She did the same with all her houses and arrived without announcing it before she got there. The only difference was that this house, at this time, was very special. This was the home where her family was currently living. San Cristobal was near Acámbaro where Alfonso's family resided. The Countess of Stonemason felt near her dear Alfonso who in her mind was in Acámbaro to visit his family. Alfonso, with his delicate, bronze skin. Alfonso, with his deep, mahogany eyes. Alfonso, who was to be her future husband.

Or so she thought.

Her mother and sister were always waiting for her wherever they were but without really expecting her. Andrea talked to herself and her big, intense green eyes were glowing when she said, "I want to announce it to my mother and Christine and everyone, that the powerful, beautiful countess is soon to be married to a handsome, manly, and young gentleman who desires my love." She added, "There is going to be a wedding in the family, the most important wedding in the New Spain, the most important wedding of all." Andrea laughed out loud and her eyes sparkled. "I am going to get married—my own wedding—the great countess's wedding." Andrea was so eager to share the news that they were going to have the greatest party of all. At last, she had found the man of her dreams, the one who was worthy of spending his life with her. She knew this was going to be the greatest wedding in the New Spain.

Andrea forgot her thoughts for a minute when she saw her sister holding hands with an elegant gentleman. They looked into each other's eyes, talked, and giggled. This was the first time Andrea saw such a thing from her sister Christine. The Countess of Stonemason could not believe her eyes. She whispered to herself, "The little sanctimonious spinster has found herself a boyfriend, I cannot believe it." Andrea looked at the enamored couple, and said, "How have you been, Christine?"

Christine stepped away from her boyfriend, blushed, and answered her sister's salutation. "Andrea, it is good to see you. When did you get here?"

Andrea announced, "I have just arrived, and you are the first person to see me. Where is Mother?"

Christine replied, "She must be busy with the girls, you know how they follow her around, and she likes teaching them."

"I see she still enjoys wasting her time on others." She added, "I am not surprised at all, that sounds exactly like her!"

"Yes, Mother loves helping others, especially women with children!"

Andrea rolled her eyes, and said, "Those dumb women have a bunch of impoverished children and then go crying to Mother because they have no means to feed them or educate them."

"Nobody asked Mother to do it, but she does it from her own desire to help them," said Christine.

Andrea sighed, and said, "I do not desire to continue this conversation anymore." She looked at Christine's companion, and asked, "Who is this gentleman?"

Christine replied, "Oh, I am sorry, I did not introduce you two. He is my fiancé, and we are going to marry soon. Andrea, this is Simon. Simon this is Andrea. She is my sister, the countess, and the owner of everything as far as you can see around here."

Simon looked at Andrea, and said, "It is a pleasure to meet you, Countess of Stonemason."

Andrea looked at her sister, and said, "Excellent introduction, Christine, except you forgot to mention that I am the most powerful, rich, beautiful, intelligent, and important woman in France, Spain, and here in the New Spain."

Amused, Christine said, "Well, there is no need to say that anymore since everybody knows that, and now you have said it yourself."

Andrea raised her face and eyebrows when she looked at Simon from the side, and said, "To explain it briefly, I am the most beautiful and significant woman in the world."

Simon watched Andrea. Christine looked at Andrea, and asked, "Should we go and find Mother? I am sure she will be delighted to see you."

Simon got up and went to the carriage to ready the horses, and said, "Ladies, please give me the honor to take you to see your mother." Andrea got inside the carriage and Christine followed her. They left together.

As they rode, Andrea said, "I really hope Mother is happy when she sees me, for I am here to stay with you two for some time while I make preparations for an extremely important event."

Christine looked at Andrea with her big, brown eyes, smiled at her, and said, "I am glad you finally decided to live with us and get used to the simple but peaceful life we have here."

Andrea answered, "Do not get confused, Christine, my being here does not mean I would be willing to live an absurd, tedious, despairing life like you and Mother."

Christine said, "Andrea, you have always lived life the way you have liked, and I do not intend to change that nor change you either."

Simon stopped the horses, and said, "We have arrived, ladies." The three of them entered the enormous estate.

There were colorful flowers everywhere, fruit trees all around, beautiful horses, peacocks, vegetable gardens, and wild chickens flying from tree to tree. Marie was sitting on a bench teaching a bunch of young women to read. Suddenly, overcome with emotion, she stood up and said, "Andrea, honey, you are here."

Andrea replied, "Even the way you greet me, I do not like. I miss Father and the way he treated me. Do not worry, Mother, still I am here because I have missed you, and I want to be with you and Christine."

Marie smiled, and said, "That is good to know, Daughter, you will be happy here with us, you will see."

Andrea answered, "I think I will, Mother."

Simon interrupted, "Dear ladies, you must have a lot of things to talk about, and I must take my leave now."

Marie said, "Have a good night, Simon."

Andrea said, "Good-bye, Simon."

Christine said, "I will accompany you to the entrance." Simon smiled lovingly at Christine, and said, "Thank you, darling, I was hoping you would say that." They both left holding hands and giggling. Marie looked at them happily. Andrea looked at them curiously.

Andrea looked at her mother intrigued, and asked, "Why do they want to get married?"

Marie looked back at her daughter with love and with patience, and replied, "They love each other, and they want to spend the rest of their lives together."

Confused, Andrea asked, "How so? I thought Christine was never going to marry!" She added, "I do not understand, how she can be so naïve as to waste her youth on marriage."

Marie said, "She is not that young anymore, and someday you will understand, Andrea, when you fall in love and you feel like she is feeling." She added, "I wish you would find a good man who loves you as much as you love him. I wish you both would get married to be able to have someone to spend the rest of your life with and be happy."

Andrea's expression changed from a mix of befuddlement and curiosity to a mix of anger and skepticism when she asked, "What are you talking about, Mother? You never married anyone, why do you want me to get married if you know marriage does not work?"

Marie said, "I never said that, and I do believe in marriage." She added, "I was profoundly in love with your father, and I wanted to be with him for the rest of my life."

Andrea interrupted, "But he did not love you!"

Marie said, "That is not true, he did love me very much too."

Andrea abruptly said, "He did love you, but not enough to marry you."

Frustrated, Marie said, "Andrea, your father and I loved each other very much."

"But not enough to live together for the rest of your lives."

Marie got a little more frustrated and sighed. "No, no, it was not like that. We did love each other greatly, and we both wished in our hearts to be together forever."

Defiantly, Andrea answered, "You and Father can say that all you want, but I do not believe either of you. If you felt such grandiose love as you both have professed so many times, you would be married and living together now, but instead you are living your own separate lives. Neither Father nor you desired to waste your youths on a marriage together. So please stop lying to me about your magical love story that you never really have felt in your hearts as you affirm."

Marie's expression became filled with sadness, and she said, "I know it must be difficult for you to comprehend this, but we are not together because of the obligations we had to our own families."

Andrea said, "Naturally, your own families, and what am I to you then?" She added, "So I was not worthy enough for you two to form your own family with me?" She furrowed her eyebrows. "I was not important enough for you two to leave your parents and offer me a home full of love, the love you two always vow and proclaim to me?" Andrea answered her own question. "Mother, your existence has been only to please your mother, and my father's existence has been to please his father and gain power."

Marie's eyes filled with tears. "Andrea, I only have your happiness in mind when I tell you my deepest feelings. You are the most important person to me and the one I love the most. I want you to follow your heart and be happy, unlike your father and myself. I do not want you to make the same mistakes your father and I have made in the past."

"Mother, you never married, Father is unhappily married, and I am going to live my life the way I desire. Marriage has never been on my mind, as you already know." Andrea added, "Furthermore, when I get married it is going to be because I have decided to, not because you tell me to do it. Also, I want you to stop telling me how to be happy and how to live my life. It is very illogical to listen to unhappy people giving advice on how to live a happy life."

Marie lowered her voice, and said, "I hope you find your own happiness someday."

"I do not have to look for happiness for I have always had a voice. I do anything I want when I want, and this in a way must be happiness, do you not agree, Mother?"

"Christine and Simon are in love and they want to share their lives together, and someday you will find someone to share your life with as well. This is my deepest wish for you."

Andrea said, "I have already found happiness and the man of my life, but not because you want me to live like that, but because I have made up my mind about it." Andrea frowned and furrowed her eyebrows again. "Christine might be dumb enough to be in love, but Simon is not, he is just after my money, and he will get none."

Marie said, "Please, Andrea, do not interfere in their relationship, let them choose their own path and live peacefully."

"Mother, my mother, always troubled over other people's lives more than worrying about her own daughter."

Marie said, "Andrea, you are my daughter, and you are the one I love the most in the world, and I am sure you already know this." She added, "However, I have seen Christine grow up by your side, and she is like a daughter to me too." Marie looked at Andrea. "And even though I love you the most, I love Christine very much and I want her happiness as much as I want yours."

Andrea calmly said, "I do love Christine, too, Mother. We grew up together and I know she is my sister even when we do not have the same blood running through our veins. We are sisters." Andrea added, "But I am not going to let astute men lie to my mindless female family members and get away with it."

Marie said, "Andrea, please, respect your sister's wishes on how to live her own life, let her be happy!"

Andrea said, "And I will, if in a few weeks she still feels the same."

Two teenage girls interrupted the conversation between Andrea and her mother when they asked, "Madam Marie, are we going to continue with the reading classes?"

Marie turned her back on the girls, and she wiped her eyes. Then, she faced them, smiled, and said, "Yes, my darlings, the reading class is still on for today, let us continue."

The girls giggled and held their notebooks, and Marie looked at them with affection. Andrea glanced at them, shook her head, and left. "Some people never change!" She added, "My mother is always worried about helping the riffraff's children more so than caring about my own life—me, the most beautiful, the most powerful, the richest and the most important woman in the whole world." Andrea looked at the girls from afar in disgust and shook her head. "Why do these poor people have so many children anyway? They do not even have enough to provide for them, nor have the knowledge to educate them."

Andrea took a deep breath, walked through her estate, and saw her young employees working. Some were taking care of the fruit trees. Others were taking care of the many different farm animals. They were all sweating, covered in dust and working hard. Some of them were making jokes and laughing, others were singing, whistling, or just working peacefully. The Countess of Stonemason looked at them, and said to herself, "How can all of these poor people be so happy? They have so little, work so hard every day, and still it seems as if they are enjoying their miserable lives. This does not make any sense, how can they look so happy when they do not have anything, not even freedom to do what they would like to do. On the other hand, I have everything I want and still I do not feel even remotely happy. I do not understand. I could have been married to one of the richest, the most powerful of nobles, or a very handsome prince, any man that I desired, but I never really wanted any of them, at least not for my whole life. They were not happiness to me. Now, I have a lot of money and power, yet this has not brought me happiness either. I did everything I wanted during my youth, and still I do not feel happy about it. I never let anyone, not even Mother tell me what to do. Everyone always did as I wished, but it still did not make me happy. There is something painful inside of me, it hurts me deeply, but I don't know what it is. I feel infinitely empty inside. I thought I would never say this, but I am starting to feel lonely. I never needed anyone before. It is different now, I know I need something or someone to make me happy, but I do not know what it is that would bring me the happiness I desire. Who would bring me the happiness and the company I desperately need now? I have never felt this melancholy before. I never cared for anyone else and I never needed anyone, but now I feel horrible when I see couples being happy together."

She continued talking to herself. "Why do I feel like this now? I am soon going to have a young, manly, handsome, intelligent husband, and I will walk by his side so everyone can see how happy I am with him." She added, "But first, I will fix Christine's life." Squinting her intense green eyes, still watching her employees from a distance, she said, "How can all of these miserable, ignorant, sweaty, dirty workers I have feel happier than I am?" She saw the adolescent girls leaving and she hurried to catch up to them. "Do not leave so soon, girls, I would like to chat with you for a few minutes."

One of the girls responded, "Yes, my lady, what would you like to talk about?"

The other two girls listened attentively, looking at Andrea. She said, "I have many dresses I would like to give to one of you, they are very expensive and elegant dresses."

Another girl asked, "Beautiful dresses like the ones you wear all the time?"

Andrea replied with a naughty smile on her face. "Exactly, all of these dresses are the finest, most expensive dresses imported from France, and they all are going to be yours, a whole big trunk full of them."

The girls giggled excitedly, and said, "Thank you, thank you."

Another girl said, "We love your dresses, my lady, all of them, thank you for being so generous."

Andrea said, "But before you get them you need to do me a little favor."

"Anything you want, tell us."

Andrea said, "I simply want you to catch a gentleman's attention and if you can get him to hug and kiss you, the dresses will be yours."

Confused, the girls looked at each other. One girl asked, "Pardon me, dear Countess of Stonemason, who is this man we are speaking of?"

Andrea answered with a naughty smile on her face. "Simon, my sister—Christine's—acquaintance."

The three girls answered quickly one by one.

"No."

"No."

"No."

One of the girls said, "He is Ms. Christine's boyfriend."

Another girl exclaimed, "He is her fiancé!"

The other girl affirmed, "Ms. Christine is not going to like this, and I do not want to do it."

The other girl added, "My mother will give me a lick for sure if I do that."

Andrea said, "You are no fun, trio of cowards." Andrea added, "It is just a game. Christine will not care about it."

With a worried look on her face, one of the girls said, "I don't know, it doesn't feel good to think about doing that."

Andrea slightly pushed two of the girls from behind, and said, "Come on, stop being so dull."

One of the girls asked, "Wait, what?"

Andrea whispered, "Sssshhhh, he is coming, and the one who can hug and kiss him will get the beautiful dresses, and any of my perfumes of her liking too."

Simon passed by, and said, "Good night, ladies."

Andrea stood in front of him, and asked, "Why are you leaving this early? These girls were just telling me so many interesting things about you."

Simon looked at them, and asked, "Really? What can these very young girls know about me?"

Andrea gave the girls a stern look. The girls looked at each other nervously. Andrea asked the girls, "Tell Simon what you were saying about him, about how handsome he is."

The girls giggled, and one by one said, "Yes, he is handsome."

"Very handsome."

"So handsome."

Simon stopped smiling, looked at the girls, and said, "Girls, you are far too young for me, you need to find some boys your own age."

Andrea said, "They are not that young. Girls, how old are you?"

They continued giggling, and one said, "I am eighteen."

Another girl said, "Nineteen."

"I'm twenty," replied the other one.

Andrea exclaimed, "See?!"

Simon said, "You girls are still too young for me. Go find some eighteen or twenty-year-old boys."

Andrea said, "Oh, but they do not like young boys like them. They like handsome, manly, interesting full-grown men like you, Simon."

Simon looked at Andrea, and said, "They did not say so, it was you who said it, Countess of Stonemason. It doesn't really seem like it is them who said those things about me."

Andrea stood in front of him and caressed his face with one hand. "Not just handsome, but intelligent. You have detected my feelings."

Simon blushed, and said, "You know I am seeing Christine, and we are soon to be married."

Andrea said, "That is of no importance to me, if I wanted a husband, I would already have one." She added, "I just want someone interesting to talk to, and Christine will not mind. Besides, she does not have to know about it."

Simon said, "I do not think this is a good idea, it is time for me to leave now."

"Do not be afraid, Christine will not know."

"I will know, and I do not think this conversation is such a good idea."

Andrea asked, "You are a man, or are you not?"

Simon answered, "You are my sister-in-law!"

"Not yet, let us have some fun before you become a married man." Andrea got near him, her lips next to his, her chest closer to him, as her hands held his and wrapped them around her waist. She whispered, "Come on, Simon, just a little kiss and you will never see me again. I will continue my traveling and you will be happy with Christine here in my big comfortable hacienda." Andrea held him by his shoulders, and whispered, "You are so strong, just one little kiss, Simon."

He looked into her big, bright, intense green eyes with long eyelashes, and he felt like he was becoming trapped in their beauty. Andrea kissed Simon passionately. He kissed her back. The girls stopped giggling and left in a hurry, afraid of what had happened in front of them. Andrea held Simon's hand and pulled him behind a giant tree. Simon held Andrea by her arms against the tree and kissed her desperately. Andrea's ribbon fell from her hair to the ground, and her curly, golden hair fell down her back and face like a waterfall. Simon pulled his own hands away from her. She put Simon's hands on her waist again and continued kissing him passionately.

A carriage passed by carrying two elegant ladies—Marie and Christine. They saw Andrea and Simon kissing. Christine instantly became quiet. Marie was frightened of what Christine had witnessed, and said, "I am very sorry, my child. I wish this had never happened. I wanted you to be happy with Simon, I am sorry you had to see this."

Christine was still quiet, but a few teardrops fell down her cheeks. Marie asked her, "What are you thinking, Christine?"

Christine replied, "I am all right, Mother, do not worry about me, I am fine."

Marie hugged Christine, and said, "I love you, Christine, I have considered you my daughter since your birth mother died, and I want you to make the best decisions for your life and for your happiness." She added, "Whatever it is that you decide, I will support you in your decision. You can still marry Simon, leave this place, and be happy with him far away."

Christine was calm but lost in her thoughts, and said, "You have always supported us, Mother, and I thank you for all your time and your dedication. You have been an extraordinary mother to both of us, thank you for everything."

Marie's eyes were watery. She hugged Christine, and said, "Oh, Christine, my sweet child."

Christine hugged Marie back, and said, "I love you too, Mother."

When they got home, Christine went to bed and covered herself with her blankets. Marie laid down next to her on top of the blankets. She said, "Christine, I do not want you to be sad, and I want you to know that whatever you decide, I will support you."

"I know you will, Mother. I do not want to talk about this anymore, I want to sleep."

Marie caressed Christine's hair. "Sleep, my child, sleep."

Christine was silent as big tears soaked her pillow.

Early in the morning, Lucia knocked on Christine's door. "Miss Christine, Mr. Simon is waiting for you by the fruit trees."

Marie looked at Christine, and asked, "Would you like me to go with you to see him?"

Christine answered, "No, Mother, that is not necessary, I will go on my own."

Marie nodded in agreement.

Christine walked calmly to where Simon, her fiancé, was waiting for her. She saw him, walked back toward the girl, and said, "Little Lucia, I have changed my mind. Tell Mr. Simon I cannot see him, and tell him not to come back here anymore."

Lucia nodded. She walked to Simon, and said, "Mr. Simon, Miss Christine does not want to see you, and she asks that you do not come back here again."

Simon looked up from the ground to Lucia, and said, "Little Lucia, tell her I will not move from here until I see her."

"I will tell her, but I do not think she will change her mind about this."

"Thank you, Little Lucia. Wait a minute, why do you think that?"

"My friends already told me about you and the Countess of Stonemason liking each other and falling in love at first sight."

Simon said, "No, no, all of you girls got it all wrong. That was not love, it was not even a little adventure or a careless fling, it was just a stupid kiss." He thought for a moment, and asked, "How could I have transformed myself into such a thoughtless, inconsiderate brute?"

Lucia's big brown eyes opened wide as she listened to his words.

Simon looked at her and corrected himself. "What am I saying? I should not be talking about this with you, Little

Lucia. Just please go get Christine for me. I will not leave until I speak with her."

Lucia left and found Christine. "Mr. Simon is very sad, regretful, worried, desperate for your love, and he will stay here forever and ever until you accept to see him and talk to him."

Christine opened her eyes wide, and said, "He wants to hear it from my mouth, very well, I will tell him."

Lucia said, "He loves you very much, Miss Christine, and my grandpa says there is no perfect man. My grandma says we must have forgiveness in our hearts."

Christine looked at Lucia, sighed, and said in a low voice, "Thank you for your insights, Little Lucia, they will surely help me. I will go see him now."

"You are very beautiful, Miss Christine, on the inside and out, you can do this."

Christine looked at Lucia, smiled at her, and said, "Thank you, Little Lucia, your grandparents have taught you well."

Simon saw Christine and his eyes sparkled with excitement. He approached her and hugged her gently with his strong arms. "Christine, the love of my life. You know that I love you so much, let's get married right away and go far away from here."

Christine said, "That will not be possible."

Simon asked, "What do you mean?"

"I do not want to marry you anymore, here is your ring."

"If this is about Andrea, I do not care about her. I love you and I want to marry you as soon as possible and go far away from here where we can love each other and live peacefully together."

Christine looked at him with her big brown eyes, and said, "I do not want to marry you anymore."

Simon said, "But we love each other."

"Love is not enough in a marriage, Simon, trust and respect are important too."

"Andrea planned this all along and you are falling for it, Christine." He added, "Are you going to let Andrea ruin our plans for marriage and our happiness?"

Christine said, "It was not all Andrea's fault, you have to take some responsibility for your actions too."

Simon said, "All right, I accept all the responsibility, but let's get married right away, let's leave this place and be happy together as we had planned."

"That will never happen now," said Christine.

Simon looked at her with his big brown eyes, and said, "I cannot change what already happened, Andrea was very insistent. You know how she is!"

Christine sighed, and said, "I know, she has always been like that, but she is my sister, and she will always be my sister." She looked away from him. "And I could not be happy living with you after what happened between you and Andrea."

Simon said, "Nothing happened between me and the countess, it was just a stupid kiss. Forgive me, Christine, I love you."

Christine said, "I forgive you, but I do not feel the same love for you anymore."

Simon said, "Christine, do not let pride and a little mistake I made separate us and make us both unhappy for the rest of our lives."

"There is no other way."

"Christine, forgive me, this will never ever happen again. Please marry me, I love you."

Christine said, "It already happened, and we cannot change that You did not love me enough to resist temptation."

"Do not let Andrea get her wish of separating us."

"Did I do that?"

Simon replied, "All right, it was me who let her get away with this, but it will never happen again. Please forgive me, my sweet love." Simon looked at her with sincerity in his heart, and asked, "What about all of our plans, and the children we were going to have?"

Christine was firm and serious. "I am sorry, Simon, good-bye. I wish you well."

Simon cried and hugged Christine in desperation.

"Please, do not touch me. Nothing will ever be the same between us, just leave."

Simon sobbed. "I will give you some time to think about it and I will come back to ask for your forgiveness. My marriage proposal is still on."

Christine said, "My answer will remain the same, do not come back here ever again." She turned and walked away.

A few minutes later, Andrea saw Simon silently crying and looking down, so she went to speak with him. She looked down from her sorrel horse, and said, "You look inconsolable, Simon. What happened to you?"

Simon replied, "If you have come to mock me and make me feel bad for being so stupid as to fall for you, do not waste your time. I already feel terrible."

Andrea said, "And 'terrible' you are, making Christine suffer like that. The good news is, you still have me, the most important one, the Countess of Stonemason to marry and be happy." She added, "You will have the most beautiful wife, and you will be richer than you thought."

Simon stopped crying, looked at Andrea, confused, and asked, "You want to marry me?"

Andrea laughed out loud, and then said, "Of course not, you simpleton. I am the magnificent Countess of Stonemason and too much of a woman for you. I might marry soon, but my groom will be heroic, manly, and the most special man in the world. I will never know what my sister saw in you."

Simon looked down, and said, "I wanted to marry your sister, not you, Countess of Stonemason, but you would never understand. Now I see why everyone around you is so miserable, because you control everybody's life and since you are not happy with your own life, you do not allow anybody else to be happy either." He raised his eyes to see her, and added, "I see you find pleasure in other people's sorrows, and you don't even care that you caused your own sister's suffering and bitter tears."

Andrea asked, "How stupid can a woman be to cry over the love of a man? Do not tell me now that you did not enjoy it. You had your fun in playing with two fine ladies in the same family!" She continued to look down at Simon. Then looked away from him, and said, "I should not waste my valuable time with an unfaithful, unintelligent, boring, unimportant, and tragically lonely man. Excuse me, sir, but I must take my leave now."

Simon continued to cry as he walked away from the estate. Andrea left on her sorrel horse, laughed out loud, and said to herself, "The time has come now to announce my wedding plans to Mother, Christine, and everyone." She remembered the young man she liked and felt a joy she had not felt before in her life. Great emotions overcame her. She was feeling the deep excitement of expecting a new life with the young, handsome man, her new love she had found for herself. She felt happy imagining the new life with the young gentleman she had chosen to be her husband. She caressed her own hair and pulled it back. Her cheeks were rosy. Her big, beautiful, intense green eyes sparkled. "I will finally have my complete happiness with the young, handsome, manly, intelligent, and most special man I have found. The one who will soon be my dear husband, Alfonso."

Chapter Nine

Walking to the Darkness

The countess rode her horse excitedly through her expansive lands. She rode tall and proud, as usual, when she saw two Jesuit priests riding their horses toward her. She asked them, "What are you doing here, priests?"

The old one said, "It is so good to see you, dear Countess of Stonemason." He added, "We are here to bring you an important message from the parish priest at the San Francisco church in Acámbaro." He gave her a letter from his satchel, and she read it silently. Her exuberant expression went from surprise to rage. Her eyes squinted. Her eyebrows furrowed as she read the letter. Then she raised her head to look at the priests, and she asked, "What is this, a joke?"

The young priest answered, "No, ma'am, this is no joke. We were sent to bring you the news you have been waiting for."

The countess said, "I do not understand the message you are attempting to convey here. Nor what this ridiculous letter filled with nonsense is all about." She raised her hands, one holding her horse's reins and the other palm side up. "What wedding ceremony did Reverend Chava celebrate?"

The old Jesuit priest answered, "The one you asked him to do for the nice, young couple deeply in love that you sent to us. That is what was said in the letter you sent to him." He added, "You said you wanted them to be married soon and with a nice wedding and that is what we did."

The young priest added, "The wedding was as beautiful as you asked for with delicious food and fireworks. The church was full of people just as you wanted it. Even though the couple didn't ask for much, a party or even any type of celebration, it was still done in the best possible way with the little time we had to prepare every detail."

The old priest said, "It was very nice to see them get married. Both so young and in love."

The countess was furious and yelled, "WHO GOT MARRIED?!" She repeated the question with tangible rage on her face. "WHO?"

Both priests looked at her in fear, and the old priest answered nervously, "I to-told you, my lady, the nice young couple you sent to us, Alfonso and Refugio."

The young priest intervened. "You should have seen them, my lady, they were so happy and the bride looked so beautiful. We bought her a beautiful dress because before she was all dirty and she didn't even have shoes on. The poor helpless girl." He added, "They looked genuinely in love, and where there is true love, anything is possible."

The old priest said, "It was very nice of you to show this gesture of kindness and solidarity to your young brother Alfonso and sister Refugio. Now if you allow us, we will need to go to Alfonso's room to get his belongings."

The countess calmed down, but she could not hide the serious expression on her face. "Of course, get whatever you need and leave."

The priests left. Then, to herself, she said, "Imbecile, inept, low-class, and good-for-nothing priests." She continued talking to herself. "One little thing they had to do, and they could not do it right. And you, Alfonso, you, the lucky man who was the only one who could have had my heart. The only one I chose to be my faithful husband. Look what you have done to me? You could have had everything you ever dreamed of—riches, a high place in society, a royal title, power, but most importantly the most beautiful, powerful, and important woman in the world. The one nobody could ever keep for themselves, and you could have had me. You could have had it all. Everything no one ever had before." With her eyebrows still furrowed and her fists holding the reins tight, she slowly said, "You dumb, stubborn man. You did not follow my orders. Instead, you chose to go against my dearest wishes, but you will pay for this. Nobody dishonors nor says no to the great Countess of Stonemason." She added, "Nobody humiliates the great Countess of Stonemason without regret." She felt a growing resentment and desire for vengeance. For the first time in her life someone dared to go against her wishes.

The priests entered Alfonso's room. The old priest said to his colleague, "Here it is, the pot with all of Alfonso's savings. He told me to give them to the Countess of Stonemason to cover the wedding expenses, but she doesn't need more money." He added, "She has more than enough money already. Besides, Alfonso was one of her employees, and I am sure she would be very happy to contribute a little toward his wedding. On the other hand, Alfonso's savings will do a lot of good to the poor, and we will make sure they get it." He looked at his friend, and said, "Anyway, we will keep this little detail to ourselves for the greater good." He looked at the young priest, and asked, "Do you understand, Brother?"

Surprised, the young priest just looked at him and nodded. The priest poured all of Alfonso's savings from the pot into his satchel, filling it full of silver and gold coins.

As they left, the countess tried to hide her rage. She looked at them, and asked, "Priest, where is this new couple going to live?"

The old priest answered, "They are already living with us in the small house next to our chapel, you know, the Franciscan and Jesuit chapel."

The young priest said, "It was very good that you helped them, you know, this is very weird, but I think they might be afraid of something because she never leaves their home by herself, and Alfonso brings her everything she needs. Anyway, you don't have to worry about them, my lady. Refugio is safe there with us, and there are many other priests like us to protect her from whatever it is that she needs protection from."

The old priest added, "Yes, my lady, it was a very good idea of you to send them to us. They will be safe with us, my lady. You can be sure about that."

The Countess of Stonemason held her head with one hand. She felt the world around her start to turn and she began to sweat profusely. She could not hear anyone anymore, and loudly said, "Say no more, priests, and leave already. I have important matters to attend to. Good-bye."

The old priest asked her, "Is there anything else you, our dear lady the Countess of Stonemason, would like the parish priest Reverend Chava, his Franciscan priests, or us the Jesuit priests to do for you?"

She replied, "Nothing else, Priest, you have done enough already, and a lot more than what you were asked to do." Then she whispered to herself, "You grotesque, lonely, disgusting, penniless priests have done more than enough already."

The priests did not hear her but saw her negative expression. Confused, the old priest asked, "My lady, is something bothering you, and if there is, how can we help you?"

The countess answered, "Nothing bothers me, Priest. Stop wasting your time talking and go finish whatever you came here to do. I want you two off my property as soon as possible. Stop prowling around my hacienda, do what you need to do, and leave!"

The priests waved their hands good-bye and left in a hurry. The Countess of Stonemason continued to whisper to herself. "This is not the end of it. Alfonso will regret not having followed my orders. My vengeance will be great. He and the insignificant barefoot Refugio will suffer a lot before their horrible and painful end. They have done what no creature has dared to do before. They disobeyed my orders." She added, "They played with my honor and are still laughing about it, but they will not continue to do so for long. They went against my most intimate wishes, against my deepest desires. They will pay a high price for it, mindless fools. Nobody mocks the magnificent Countess of Stonemason without paying a high price for it!"

She went home to see Doña Gabriela. She found her talking with her mother and overheard their conversation. Gabriela said, "And that is how I am going to spend the last days of my life, going on a mission to teach the word of the Lord to the ones who don't know it."

Marie smiled. "That is a promising dream, Gabriela. I would love to do the same when my daughters get married and have a life of their own."

Andrea entered the room, and with a raised voice said, "That is the most ridiculous idea I have ever heard."

Marie and Gabriela looked at Andrea attentively. They waited for her to say everything she wanted to say to them. Andrea looked at Marie, and said, "You wanting to waste all your time teaching others about religion, such an absurd idea."

Marie's smile disappeared, and she said, "That is what I would like to do, but not now, Andrea, someday in the future when you and Christine have a life of your own."

The Countess of Stonemason lost her composure, and angrily said, "As always, you do not know what you are talking about, Mother." She spoke louder and added, "I have never been like you and Christine. I have always had a life of my own, if you have not already noticed. I do not need you, but you do need me. You have everything with me. And if you go on that dumb mission you are going to die because of your foolishness."

Marie lowered her head, and said, "I have to go now, I am going to see how Christine is feeling."

The countess said, "Leave if you want to leave, and remember, I do not need you, I do not need anyone!"

Doña Gabriela was busy arranging the kitchen. The countess approached her, and said, "Gabriela, send two men to look for 'Fast Shadow' and 'Little Shadow.'"

Doña Gabriela answered, "My lady, why would you need those two? They are no good, I am telling you, no good."

Annoyed, the countess answered, "Gabriela, just follow my orders, I am not asking for your advice."

"Yes, my lady, I will send someone to get those two men as you have asked."

The countess said, "And tell them that I want to see them tonight, do you understand? Tonight—no excuses."

Doña Gabriela nodded her head and sent some errand boys to do as the Countess of Stonemason had ordered.

Later that day, Little Shadow came back with the boys. The countess welcomed him to her estate. "It is good to see you, Little Shadow."

"What is it that you need from us, Countess of Stonemason, that could not wait until morning?"

She replied, "I need you to clean up a mess for me."

Little Shadow asked again, "Can you give me more details on what exactly you want me to do for you?"

She stated, "Let me get straight to the point, you and I both know what you do for a living." She added, "I have a need for your services, and you will be well compensated for your work upon completion."

He asked, "How many and who are they?"

The countess said, "You do not need to do anything at this time but bring them to me, and I will do the rest."

Confused, Little Shadow asked, "You mean that you will finish the job and I just have to bring them to you?" He added, "Easy, who are they and how many of them? What have they done to you? And why do you want them alive? How do they look?"

The countess replied impatiently, "You ask too many questions, and that is my business, not yours." She added, "Your only job is to follow my orders and that is all. First, you will bring Refugio to me, she lives in a little house that belongs to the Franciscan priests and is right there next to their chapel. Then, after you bring her to me, you will deliver a letter to Alfonso." The Countess of Stonemason continued impatiently. "I do not know how she looks, young I assume, insignificant, poor, a plain peasant. Just bring her to me."

Little Shadow shook his head in disapproval. "I will not be able to do this favor for you." He added, "My business is with men only. I don't harm any ladies." He shook his head, and said, "Also, I do not get involved with people living in churches and with priests, it goes against my ethics."

The Countess of Stonemason, said desperately, "Ethics? What ethics? You have morals? Unbelievable! I need to talk to your cousin. I understand if you are afraid to do it. Anyway, your cousin is a lot stronger and braver, he will do it."

Little Shadow said, "My cousin will tell you the same thing, as we have the same business policy." He asked, "What could she have done to you to deserve what you are wishing upon her if you have not even met her? What do you plan to do to her once you have her here?"

The countess said, "That is none of your business. It was a waste of time to send for you, as you are too much talk without any action. You do not represent your fame. I would never have imagined that Little Shadow was a coward."

Little Shadow said, "I do not hurt women, I only handle men."

The countess insisted, "You only need to bring her to me, and I will take care of the rest."

"I would not do that, either, and with her living in a church I would not even get near her. No is my last word, no matter the amount you have planned to pay me, I will not do it. Good-bye, Countess of Stonemason."

She asked, "Where are the brave men when you need them?" She opened her big wooden door, looked at the men outside her living room, and ordered, "Take him back to his home and do not come back until you bring his cousin to me."

The men replied, "Yes, my lady, but he wasn't at home the first time we went."

She replied, "Then, wait for him and do not return until you bring him to me."

The young men left in a hurry to follow her orders.

Many hours had passed until the men brought Fast Shadow to her. The tall, strong man looked the countess in the eye, and asked, "The rich and powerful, Countess of Stonemason, what is so important to you that it could not wait until tomorrow morning?"

The countess answered, "I need you to bring me a girl who lives by the Franciscan convent."

Fast Shadow looked at her, and asked, "Why don't you send your employees with the invitation?"

The countess answered, "She will not accept any invitations, and this is why I need you to bring her to me by any means necessary."

Fast Shadow shook his head. "This job is too easy, and you should not have sent for me." He added, "I only handle men, not women."

Frustrated, the Countess of Stonemason said, "You will be paid anything you want, a lot better than if you were handling the most dangerous men, just set the amount and you will get it."

Fast Shadow asked, "What will you do with this woman?"

"That is of my concern, limit yourself to do your work."

Fast Shadow said, "That is the problem with this request. My job only involves men, no exceptions."

"What if I tell you that I only wish to talk to her, and nothing else, no harm will come to her."

"Under those circumstances, everything changes, if you are not going to harm her and you just want to talk to her, I can bring her to you." Then, he asked, "This means I can take her back home when you are done talking to her?"

The countess said, "That I will do, you just bring her to me, and you will leave as your work would be finished."

"Bring her from where? Where does she live?"

"She lives by the convent where the Franciscan priests live."

Fast Shadow shook his head. "I was considering it, but I do not get people from churches. I will not do it."

Frustrated, the countess whispered, "Another scared fool." Then she looked at him and said, "I never would have imagined that you were religious. It is not like you are going to Heaven anyway. Why is it that you cannot do this one favor for me?"

Fast Shadow said, "My job doesn't involve women and it doesn't involve churches either. My final answer is no."

The countess insisted, "Who can do it then?"

Fast Shadow replied, "If I do not want to do it, nobody else will do it. I do the dirtiest work around here, no one will agree to do this."

Fast Shadow got up to leave, and the countess continued planning her vengeance. She said to herself, "I will do this even if it is the last thing I do in my life! I do not care how long I have to wait or how much I have to spend, but I will do it." With anger in her big, intense green eyes, she exclaimed, "I will avenge myself!"

The countess stood there as Fast Shadow opened the living room door to leave. She looked at her employees, and said, "Continue to search for someone to do this special job for me." Her employees brought many men to her. However, one by one they gave her the same answer she did not like to hear. She asked herself, "Are these the fearless men of the region? They commit the most horrific acts around here, but they are afraid of churches, priests, and a defenseless girl. Why? Why are all of these lawless men afraid of one church and one girl? They are the men with the worst reputations in the region, but still they will not accept my challenge. The job is easy. They know I would pay them a fortune, but in spite of that they will not do it because it involves a church and a girl. These detestable men have no logical way of thinking. They prefer to continue to commit their horrific acts for peanuts rather than to bring a girl to me and become rich for the rest of their lives. What am I going to do?"

She heard Pedro quietly walking away from her. She said, "Pedro, I know you are here, you do not need to hide from me. Tell me, what is stopping these dumb scums from being of service to me? I am asking them to do the type of work they are already used to doing. Are they not the bravest men around here? What are they afraid of?"

Pedro said, "If they said no to you, they must be rethinking their ways. They must be afraid of the only force that can get them, the divine justice, my lady, and we all should be cautious of it."

She dismissed Pedro's idea and signaled him to leave. She said to herself, "As soon as they knew they had to go inside a church to get *that Refugio*, no one was interested, no matter the fortune being paid for it."

Pedro approached the countess and looked at her with his big dark eyes. "My lady, is there anything I can do to help you before I leave?"

Andrea replied, "Yes, Pedro, take me to The Goat's Cave."

"All right, my lady, but there is no guarantee we will get there before dusk."

"Pedro, it does not take that long for us to get there, which is why I built these subterranean passages long ago so I could transport myself secretly and save time."

Pedro said, "You are right, my lady." He added, "But even if we could get up there before dark, we would return at night for sure. Even though coming down is much faster than going up, there is not enough time to go and return before the sun sets."

The countess looked at him and said, "Pedro, I am not afraid of the dark, the night has never stopped me from doing as I please."

"I know you have no fear, my lady, but we have to be more careful at night if we want to keep you safe." Pedro continued, "And now we have to be more careful than ever, since one of your underground paths almost collapsed the other day."

Andrea said, "Pedro, Pedro, always so careful, nothing happened and it is not going to collapse, do not worry."

He took a deep breath, and said, "All right, my lady, let's do as you wish."

Andrea looked at him happily, and said, "Very well, Pedro, you know nothing pleases me more than when my orders are followed through to even the smallest of details."

"Yes, I know, my lady." Pedro stood at the window and extended his arm to the countess. She accepted his help to get into the underground cart. When they were both inside the cart, she said, "I have an idea. I can build another underground path to get to the Franciscan chapel, and like my other underground paths, nobody will know about it. That is exactly what I am going to do. I will send for the most important architects in the surroundings."

Two weeks later, a group of the most prestigious architects visited her. The head architect looked at the Countess of Stonemason, and said, "Ma'am, the underground path you want is a very difficult thing to do."

She said, "Nothing is impossible, sir."

He agreed. "No, you are correct, not impossible, but it would be extremely time-consuming and an exceedingly expensive project."

Andrea said, "Money, I have lots, do not hesitate on account of the price. You will have as much money as you need for this project."

Another architect added, "It might not be worth the time and the money spent on it."

An engineer shook his head and interrupted. "There is a big risk in building an underground path under the Lerma River. It is not something I would recommend doing. It would be too dangerous for the workers."

Andrea said, "I do not believe those minor risks can stop you, and that is why you are the ones who are going to do it, because you are the best of the best in the building industry."

The eight men agreed and continued discussing their underground construction plans, while glancing at Andrea from time to time. The men continued talking among themselves. Then the head architect asked, "Countess of Stonemason, are you sure you are willing to take the risk? Also, it might take a much longer time, considering we have to do it under the river. You know, combining tunnels and water is not a good idea. I still think it might not be worth it."

Andrea said, "No matter the risk it represents, the amount of money it might take, or even the time which you may consider to be too long. I assure you, to me, it will all be worth it. Do as I say, and I will pay you as much as you need to complete this project. Patience, I will have plenty. Nevertheless, I will be waiting anxiously from today until the day you are done with this project."

The head architect said, "I understand this is a project of great importance to you."

She nodded, and said, "Nothing in the whole world is more important to me than this."

The men agreed. The engineer said, "My men and I accept this challenge."

Andrea gave him a big sack of gold coins. Pleased, the head architect said, "We will be working diligently and will let you know how it is progressing." The team of building experts left her hacienda before dusk and she was content.

The Countess of Stonemason stood up and watched the horizon for some time. She was lost in her own thoughts. Suddenly, her eyebrows furrowed and her big, intense green eyes glared ahead into the distance.

Gabriela said, "It is always a joy to look at the horizon to see the sun setting, my lady."

Andrea continued to glare at the horizon.

Gabriela stood next to Andrea, then looked at Lucia, and said, "Lucia, take the dishes from the table and—"

Andrea interrupted her. "Gabriela, what is that place deep in the forest I can see from here?"

Gabriela asked, "What place, my lady?"

Andrea slowly said, "The only structure deep in the forest that is made by men and can be seen from here. Other than that, you can only see the trees and the vegetation all around. How come I have never seen it before?"

Gabriela's expression changed from relaxed to anxious. "That is the prohibited temple, and no one is allowed to go in there. The few who have been curious enough to risk their lives have lost them for their curiosity." Gabriela warned Andrea, and said, "My lady, setting foot in that temple is absolutely forbidden."

Confused, the countess asked, "There is a temple there? How come I have never seen it?"

Gabriela said, "It is hidden within the vegetation." She added, "That is where unexplained things happen, and where the pagans meet. The ones who never accepted the new beliefs."

The countess asked, "What new beliefs are you talking about, Gabriela?"

"The beliefs most of the people around here have, including you and I, my lady." Gabriela added, "But those heathens never accepted the new religion, and to keep their own beliefs they went to the extreme of doing unspeakable things that cannot be undone. What is done is done and they have been carrying around this curse for generations."

Andrea looked at Gabriela and her eyes sparkled. "What else, Gabriela?"

"You don't want to know more than what I have already told you, my lady. I have said too much already." She added, "What you should know is that everybody avoids passing by that place, and you should do the same. It is tremendously dangerous, ne-ver e-ver go there, my lady."

The Countess of Stonemason's eyes opened wide and with a distinctive glare in them, she said, "Provide me with more information, Gabriela. What happens in that temple? Why does nobody want to go there to pray?"

Gabriela replied, "You don't understand, my lady, that is not a common temple." Gabriela's face looked mortified, and with a trembling voice she said, "Please, my lady, don't ask me anymore. I cannot tell you the secrets that are not mine, but remember to stay away from there or you will regret it."

Andrea shook her head in disbelief and in her usual arrogant, elegant voice said, "Gabriela, Gabriela, the poor and their superstitions, when are you going to understand the real world?"

That night, as soon as everybody was asleep, Andrea walked to Pedro's room and knocked on his door. When he opened the door, he was naked, covering his body from the waist down with a blanket. "My lady, what do you want here and at this time?"

Mocking him, she said, "Pedro, Pedro, that is why you have never been married, you have no perception. Anyway, I want you to come with me to the temple."

Confused, he yawned, rubbed his eyes, scratched his head, and asked, "My lady, can't you wait till the morning to go to church? Or why don't you go to the small chapel here, in your house?"

Frustrated, she said, "None of those places you mentioned are the special temple where we are going. Hurry up. I would not like anyone else to overhear what we are doing."

Pedro covered himself with his blanket and put his pants on. Then, he got up from his bed and put the rest of his clothes on. He grabbed his boots and his brown serape and sat down on his bed. "Should I bring the horses or the carriage?"

The countess said, "No, we do not want to attract any unwanted attention so we are going to walk there."

Pedro scratched his head and looked around in the dark night. "Walking, my lady, do you know how long that would take?" He looked at her, and asked, "With all due respect, when would you like to get there?"

Pedro's door was open and the countess pointed her finger in the direction of the hidden temple. "Silence, Pedro, and listen, we are going to that prohibited temple, the one many are superstitious about. No matter the time it takes us to get there. Do not begin to express any absurd fears to me because I do not accept irrational beliefs."

With a worried expression, Pedro said, "No, my lady, you don't understand, that place is forbidden, and if we go there we will not come back ever again."

The countess said, "I will vanish you myself if you start behaving like a weakling and do not follow my directions! Anyway, you will just take me there and you can come back to sleep."

Pedro sat on his bed, holding his head with his eyes closed. She shook him, and said, "Pedro, wake up and listen carefully. I want you to take me to the secret, forbidden temple, but I want you to come back as soon as I get there." She added, "I would go there by myself, but I could get lost."

Pedro opened his eyes, scratched his head, and said in desperation, "But, my lady, that is a very dangerous place and—"

"Enough, you are going to take me there, and I ORDER you to return as soon as I get to the temple. I do not want any obstacles there with me."

"But, my lady, you cannot be there alone. It is not safe for any lady."

She shook her head, and said, "You are wrong again, Pedro, as I am not just any lady. You should know that by now, there is no lady like myself."

Pedro said, "All right, but we should at least take a horse with us so you can return faster in case you have the need for it."

She arranged her hair slowly and carefully, then nodded her head. "All right, we can do that."

Pedro got one of her horses nearby and they continued to walk at a fast pace for about forty minutes. They walked through the forsaken woods toward the forbidden temple. Pedro said, "You are a fast walker, my lady. We are here already, as you wished."

The countess said, "Now leave, go back as I ordered you before, Pedro. Leave now or I do not know what will happen to you if you stay."

Pedro looked at her, worried, and asked, "Are you sure?"

The countess said, "Completely."

Pedro nodded and whispered, "As you wish, my lady."

Pedro tied the horse to a tree with an easy knot. He patted the horse lovingly and whispered, "Take care, King." Then, he left, walking at a medium speed, not the fastest he could but not too slow either.

The countess looked around the temple and between the vines. She walked around and touched the walls with her hands, trying to find something. The moon came out from behind the clouds and shined on the forest. It helped Andrea to see a little bit while she looked for an entrance into the forbidden temple. She spent a long time trying to find the entrance to the temple without success. In a low voice, she said to herself, "I have been here for hours and I have not found one entrance. How can a temple not have any entrances? There has to be at least one. I will have to come back another time. The sun will be rising in one or two hours."

She untied the easy knot of the rope to get her horse and go back to her estate, but she heard a noise. It was a menacing, deep growl coming from within the trees. She stopped and looked around. She saw the vegetation begin to sway and a big, hairy creature shook within it. In between the plants, she could see two big, dark shiny eyes. Andrea's eyes widened. *It must be a savage dog, a coyote, or a wolf, but whatever it is, it is an enormous one.* She walked very slowly toward King, her horse. *I better get away from here fast.*

She mounted her beautiful black horse and whispered in his ear, "We must get out of here as fast as we can!" The strange creature emitted another deep, loud growl. King reared and whinnied. Andrea held on tight and controlled her horse with the reins. She whispered, "I see I am not the only one scared here, horse, but you are frightened and out of control. You silly, fearful horse. You almost threw me off your back, and that big hairy thing would have eaten me." King ran fast. She added, "Go faster!"

Later, after minutes of riding her horse at a very high speed, they neared her house. She said to herself, "More than a quarter of an hour has passed and that strange creature is still following me, how can it be as fast as a horse at full speed when it looks half the size?" Once she arrived at her hacienda, she stopped the horse, and while dismounting, she fell to the ground. Her black embroidered blouse with silver flowers was ripped on the front. A piece of cloth hung from her chest to her abdomen. Her delicate, shiny black skirt was all dusty and torn. Her knees and right elbow were bleeding. She had a big red scratch on her left arm, and she had another red scratch covering half of her chin. Some of her hair covered her face and sections of it were dusty. Even though Andrea was in pain, she got up from the ground quickly, and yelled, "Gabriela, boys, someone come, hurry!"

Gabriela and some of her adolescent workers came from their rooms still in sleepwear to see what was happening with the Countess of Stonemason. Gabriela asked, "What is happening, my lady?"

Andrea answered, "A growling, savage animal is following me." She pointed to the thick vegetation in the garden. Five boys went together into the foliage to look for the animal. Some minutes later, they returned without having seen any animal as described by the countess.

One of the boys said, "We didn't see any dangerous animals in there."

Gabriela looked at Andrea, and said, "My lady, you are hurt."

Andrea said, "These are only scratches, Gabriela." The five boys stood there looking at Andrea. She asked, "What are you all doing here? Go back to sleep."

Gabriela said, "Let me clean your wounds, my lady."

"No, I can do that myself. You go back to sleep too."

Everybody went to sleep. Maria was sitting on a chair with her room door ajar, looking at the countess. Andrea said, "Maria, why are you not sleeping?"

Maria came out of her room, and said, "I'm not sleepy anymore."

Andrea said, "Then come and help me get dressed."

Maria helped Andrea get dressed and she also helped her fix her hair. Andrea said, "You may go and change your clothes and get ready to do your chores now." Maria nodded her head and left. Andrea looked in her big mirror, and asked, "What kind of creature was following me? Is that temple full of ferocious things like the one that followed me and that is why there are not any doors? The savage creature was running as fast as the horse. It could have jumped onto the temple if it had wanted to. That is it, the temple is the home of these beasts!"

It was almost dawn, and Andrea walked by herself into the garden and heard the growl again. She saw the growling animal, but there was something strange about it. She whispered to herself, "This creature is changing. It is starting to look less hairy, skinnier, smaller, and smooth brown skin is starting to appear. It looks familiar. More than that, it is starting to resemble a human being." Without blinking, she asked, "Who are you, and what do you want?" Then, she answered her own question. "You are a person who can turn into an animal at will, and you are free to roam any place without being recognized. This is amazing!"

The naked man, still with some hair on his body, shook his head and looked at her. He opened his big snout and growled. The countess, with wide eyes, asked again, "What are you?" Then, answering her own question again, she said, "I know what you are, you are a nahual. All the ignorant people around here were right, nahuals actually do exist. You are a nahual, and you are not free anymore. I saw you and I am going to tell everybody what you are, unless you do as I say!" She added, "I can see your desperation, anger, and thirst for vengeance, and you cannot deny it because I know I am right, and I can clearly see those strong feelings in you."

He had completely turned back into a man, and said, "We can help each other if that is what you want. You see, we offer you freedom, the freedom we got when we started to live the way we wanted."

The Countess of Stonemason said, "I do not need anybody's help. I have always had everything I ever wanted."

The nahual said, "No, you don't. All of us nahuals are like this because there is something we could not get on our own, and we had to get it by force. Some of us want more money. Others want power, freedom to do what they want, and others need just plain justice."

The countess said, "I have all of that and more, everything you cannot even begin to imagine."

The nahual said, "Yes, you have a lot of money and in many states of this country you have extensive lands. Everything as far as you can see is yours with beautiful and comfortable houses full of servants, your fine clothes imported from France, your jewelry and all your extravagances. You have the recognition and favor of the most important people, and all of this gives you a lot of power."

She interrupted him. "Yes, I already told you. I have everything."

"But there is one thing you could not get. The man of your dreams is not yours." He walked around her, and added, "You, the beautiful and powerful Countess of Stonemason, the one who no man could ever resist. The woman who left so many weeping for the rest of their lives, could not get the only man she ever wanted. The only man who ever made the great

Countess of Stonemason even consider standing still with one man! In one place! One love, for the rest of her life. Yet, alas, he did not accept her."

The Countess of Stonemason yelled, "Stop it! I do not wish to hear this any longer." She added, "Actually, I have already decided what I want." She looked at him, and said, "I have always been free so I have absolutely no need for the freedom you offer me." He looked at her attentively while he stood deep within the plants that covered him from the waist down. Making eye contact with him, she said, "I understand you wanting freedom, but I have always had it." She added, "Anyway, there is something else I would like you to do for me."

"What is it?" asked the nahual.

"I want you and another one of your men to work for me. If you can do as I say, I will pay you very well. I know you are not afraid, and you are capable of anything! Or am I wrong?"

The nahual said, "You could say that. Which reminds me about the secret tunnels you use to transport yourself without anyone noticing, and the new passageway you have under construction down below the Lerma River. I am fully aware of its purpose!"

The countess said, "How can you possibly know if I have not told anyone about it?"

The nahual replied, "Oh, but you know our society possesses great knowledge, and I can share this knowledge with you." He cut a long plant with big leaves, covered his chest with it, and said, "You want to get to Refugio, the one you blame for your unhappiness." He added, "You want to get her and make her suffer in front of her beloved Alfonso for not doing what you wanted." His expression changed into anger. "This is your immense thirst for vengeance and the motive of all your thoughts and doings since the day you found out about their love."

The Countess of Stonemason said, "Stop talking, I do not want to hear any more of your knowledge. Let's see if you work as well as you talk." She added, "And do not worry about the money, you and your partner will be very well compensated for your services if I like them." She added, "It is time for us to part ways. I have spent enough time with you today."

The nahual asked, "Tell me, Countess, what do you want us to do for you?"

"All in good time, let's just say that I want your company and protection when necessary." She asked, "Can you dispose of the dangers around me?"

The nahual replied, "Well, working with me is a great danger already."

Andrea said, "I still want to associate myself with you. Anyway, I have always liked living dangerously."

"Then, you got yourself a deal," said the nahual.

"Go get one of your friends and wait for me here with him," Andrea replied. She went back into her house and into her room, put her head on her silk pillow and comfortably fell asleep.

In the late morning when she was having breakfast at her big, elegant table, she watched Gabriela organize the workers. Andrea saw the adolescent boy named Jimmil. She stared at him. *He is very handsome and manly. He looks so much like Alfonso, but younger, and a little shorter, and a little darker, but still very handsome.* The countess looked at him, and asked, "What is your name, dear?"

The boy answered, "I am Jimmil, but everybody calls me Jim."

The countess invited him to her table, and said, "Come sit with me, Jim. Let's have some breakfast together."

Jim opened his eyes wide, and said, "Are you serious?" He immediately answered his own question, and asked, "Why wouldn't you? I mean, I am handsome, funny, a better worker, younger, and with much better taste than that Alfonso." He sat right next to Andrea and started eating some grapes from the table. The countess, amused, looked at him, and said, "Gabriela, order Jim some breakfast."

"Yes, my lady, coming right up." Then, in a lower voice, her faithful server Gabriela added, "This dumb boy." She reconsidered, and said, "What am I saying? Double breakfast never hurt anyone."

Lucia brought him the breakfast and looked at him in surprise. He had a wide smile on his face. The countess said, "I am leaving to check all my properties and will stay a few days in each of my haciendas. Would you like to come with me?"

Jim answered, "Of course, let me get my things ready! When are we leaving?"

The countess answered, "We leave as soon as you are ready to go." She added, "Bring the carriage on your way back so we can leave."

Meanwhile, Andrea went back to where she told her new employee—the nahual—to be. She walked outside her house and into the vegetation where they had conversed. There he was, with one of his friends. He smiled, and said, "You are here, as you said you would be." He added, "I thought you might reconsider and change your mind about our alliance."

Andrea said, "Of course not, I know what I want, and it is very difficult for me to change my mind. You already know who I am, and I would like to know who you are. I don't want to be calling you 'nahual' in front of my employees. They might get scared."

He stood in front of her. His beautiful dark skin was shining from the rays of the sun on his face. "I am Yooko and this is my friend, Masawa."

Andrea said, "I will visit some of my properties and houses not too far from here. A friend of mine will come with me, and your job will simply be to protect us on our way there."

Yooko looked up at his friend. Masawa, who was making eye contact with Yooko, then said, "That is not too hard."

Andrea said, "We will be leaving soon."

Yooko asked, "How soon?"

"As soon as my friend returns with the carriage." She went back into her house.

Jim was returning with the carriage when he heard Maria and Lucia talking. Maria sat on the grass in front of Lucia, and said, "You know what I have always wished for, Lucia? To know what is inside the countess's room that she never uses or lets anyone inside of, not even to clean it."

Lucia said, "Doña Gabriela says there are old fragile things from France and Spain in that room, and I think they might be very dusty." She added, "There must be dust everywhere in there, and I don't want to go in there."

Maria said, "You don't know what you are saying, Lucia, maybe the countess brought a king or a prince from France or

Spain and he is living in there with her." Maria added, "That's why she's never been married, because she has her lover locked up in that room."

Lucia laughed a little, and said, "You are crazy, Maria. He would have died of hunger by now with the long trips the countess takes."

Still sitting on the grass, Maria said, "That's it, you are right, Lucia, she killed her lover and has him in that room mummified."

Jim's eyes opened wide and he hurriedly made the sign of the cross. Lucia shook her head, and said, "I didn't say that, Maria! We better go back to our work. Doña Gabriela will be looking for us soon."

Jim thought, *I have to go in that room and see what the countess has in there.* He went quietly with the carriage. He walked slowly with the horses and looked at them. "Shh, we have to be quiet to see that room." He stopped the horses near the countess's room and went around to look inside the window of the mysterious room. He looked inside. *I can't see anything!*

The countess, who was in the next room and heard the horses, came out of her room to see who it was. She saw Jim trying to look inside the window, and said, "You will not be able to see what is inside with the curtain I have in that window." She held his hand, and said, "Come with me, darling. I will show you what is in there."

Jim smiled and followed along. Once inside, she got a big key from her drawer and with it she opened the back door of her room. They entered and she opened the curtains of the room to let in the sunrays. It was a long room full of stuff. Jim put a tall, colorful headdress on his head. The countess said, "I love that penacho with quetzal feathers." She added, "You have good taste."

Jim continued looking through the room with curiosity. He took a bunch of gold coins with both hands and let them fall in the clay pot slowly. Then, he found a wooden chest. He opened it and it was full of precious jewels. He moved the gold tiaras with shiny stones to the side next to the big heavy bracelets. Then, he took a long gold necklace with a thick, big, gold medallion with some inscriptions on it. He put it on. Then, he found a long gold necklace with a big, green jade stone in the middle of the big medallion. He put it on his neck as well. The countess said, "It is time for us to go on our trip."

Jim said, "Why so soon? Let me see all the stuff you have in here!"

"Maybe another time, let's go now."

He took the headdress off and put it back where it was. Then, he looked at the two necklaces hanging from his neck and held one in each hand. He said, "Wait, let me take these off!"

The countess said, "Keep them, I want you to have them. Let's go!"

He touched both medallions and smiled from ear to ear. She gently pulled him by his arm, and added, "I do not want us to be late for our trip!"

Jim opened the carriage door and offered to help her inside. She said, "I will sit next to you for now to chat a little and keep you company." They were soon sitting up near the horses, in front of the carriage and ready to leave. Andrea looked at Jim, and said, "Two of my workers will be joining us too."

Disillusioned, he said, "I thought it would only be you and me on this trip."

She said, "Do not worry, it will feel as if it were only the two of us." And she kissed him on the lips. He hugged her and kissed her back but with a more passionate kiss, and said, "I feel better now that I know for sure I am the one you are interested in."

Andrea looked at him with her chin up. Then, looking away from him, she narrowed her eyes, and with a look of disdain, said, "Do not get too certain about it."

Jim looked at her. Then, he looked around and with curiosity, he asked, "Which are the two workers who are coming with us on this trip, and why are they coming?" He touched his two medallions, and asked, "Are they honest people?"

Andrea answered, "You do not know them. Their names are Yooko and Masawa and they are coming to protect us."

Jim opened his eyes wide. He put his two big gold medallions inside his shirt. Then he said, "When you are with me, you don't need anyone else for protection." He put his hands up in front of him and the countess, and added, "That's what I will do with these hands, protect you."

Andrea said, "It is better to be prepared and have extra hands. It is getting late, let us continue on our way."

Jim held her hand and helped her into the carriage. At that moment, Yooko and Masawa appeared. Andrea looked at Jim, and said, "Let them drive, and you come in here with me." He did as she said and jumped into the carriage and sat in front of her. They both chuckled while the other two sat in front to drive the carriage. Jim and Andrea talked animatedly during the trip while Yooko and Masawa sat in silence.

Dusk had fallen by the time Andrea and her three companions stopped to rest and enjoy a snack in the meadow. Jim could not keep his hands off of Andrea. Yooko said, "I will walk around to investigate the place a little better. If I don't come back in ten minutes, continue the trip without me."

Jim opened his eyes wide, and asked, "Are you crazy? There are ferocious animals around here that would love to catch you for dinner."

Masawa replied, "Don't worry, I will be with him in case he needs any help." Jim watched the two men disappear into the vegetation. Yooko was tall and strong, with dark skin and big, brown eyes. Masawa was taller and thinner, with tanned skin, gentle facial features, and hazel eyes. Both nahuals were far enough and unable to hear what the countess and her companion were talking about.

Jim looked at the countess, hugged her tightly, and said, "Alone at last, I could not wait any longer for this moment."

The countess looked at him, and said, "And how long was that?"

Jim answered, "A long, long time, since breakfast this morning." He held her by her waist and kissed her impatiently. Then, he invited her inside the carriage with a big smile. The countess laughed and got in. They played and giggled inside the carriage.

Some minutes later, the countess asked Jim, "Look for Yooko and Masawa."

Jim walked outside around the carriage, and said, "They're nowhere to be found, and in this darkness, they could be far or near and we wouldn't know the difference." Jim yelled their names and his words traveled far away with the wind. He screamed, "Yoookoooo, Masaaaawaaaa!" Nobody answered, but they heard a deep and loud growl.

Startled, the countess jumped, and said, "It is time for us to go."

Worried, Jim said, "But they are not here."

"They will catch up with us."

Jim nervously said, "I don't think they will be able to do that without a horse!"

The countess said, "I am sure they will not mind if we leave without them."

"All right, we don't have to wait for these fools if they don't even want us to wait for them." He grabbed the reins, and said, "Let's go, Countess." The carriage took off while a growling animal seemed to run along with the horses, quickly through the vegetation. Then, another noise near them caught Jim's attention. He asked, "What is that flapping noise I am hearing?"

From inside the carriage, the countess replied, "It has to be an owl."

"I haven't seen any owls this big, with wings as powerful and big as I am hearing." He continued, "This is no ordinary bird, I am telling you. It is a hawk or an eagle, but whatever it is I don't like that it is flying so low. That is not normal."

Andrea looked at Jim, and with a smirk on her face asked, "Are you afraid?"

Jim replied, "No, ma'am, I am not afraid, but you should be, these big birds of prey know who is the weakest to attack. Good thing I am here with you to protect you."

"Of course," said Andrea, with a cynical smile. She added, "We are almost there."

Jim asked, "Are you sure? How can you know in this pitch-dark night?"

The countess answered, "It is easy, I know all my estates like the palm of my hand, and even in the darkness I know that when I see this cabin, my estate is not far."

Jim asked, "How can you see the cabin? I don't see anything, only trees."

The countess replied, "That is exactly the sign, my cabin is surrounded by trees."

Jim opened his eyes wide, and asked, "Why do you want a cabin when you have a giant, comfortable house close by?"

Andrea inclined her face, looked outside the carriage window, and held her chin with two fingers. "I have always liked trees and I wanted to have a place to rest next to them." She added, "However, I have not really used this small cabin much."

Jim stopped the horses, jumped down, and got into the carriage with Andrea. He gently pulled her by the waist toward him, and asked, "Let's go see it?"

Andrea answered, "No, it is going to be full of dust. Nobody knows about it, and nobody cleans it either."

Jim insisted, "Come on, let's go see your cabin, or are you afraid of me?"

Andrea laughed out loud, and answered, "Me, afraid of you?" She laughed some more, and asked, "What can you possibly do to me?" She looked at him curiously, and asked, "Tell me, frankly, what do you think of me?"

Jim answered, "What do I think of you? I think you are a very important woman, the Countess of Stonemason, and you have great intelligence."

Andrea said, "Of course I am the very important, intelligent countess and I am the greatest, I already know that." The countess looked at Jim with content, and asked, "What else do you think of me?"

Jim looked at her, and said, "Well, you are extremely elegant, and beautiful, kind of old for me, but I don't care, because I like you a lot, not to marry you, but still I like you a lot!"

Her expression changed drastically. With a piercing look, she raised her voice and slowly asked, "What did you just say?"

Jim got nervous and could not speak. He said, "I, I…"

"Insolent fool, you should feel lucky that I even paid attention to your insignificant self." Her voice got louder. "There is only one of me, and I can find many of you. You will not have a woman like me ever again in your miserable existence."

Jim interrupted her, and said, "I am sorry, I didn't mean to hurt your feelings."

She got out of the carriage, and screamed, "Get down from there and follow me!"

He immediately followed her orders and with one quick jump was next to her. He followed her and tried to calm her down, but he continued to get more nervous. Trying to fix things, he said, "I would probably marry you, yes, I think I would if we continue to get along so well."

She yelled, "You, ignorant, pathetic, low-class individual! I did not even want to marry the most important men from France, Spain, or the New Spain. What makes you think I would want to marry you?"

She suddenly changed her mind and in a decisive tone, said, "We will go see the cabin."

Scared, Jim said, "We don't have to see it if you don't want to, let's continue on our way, as you had originally planned."

The countess yelled, "I said we are going to see the cabin!"

Jim replied, "Yes, ma'am."

When they got to the cabin, Jim stood inside by the door. He held his head with his shaky hands and looked down. The countess said, "Do not just stand there, light the candles and sit down."

Jim said, "Yes, ma'am, I will gather some wood for the fire." He lit the candles with his trembling hands.

The countess said, "There is no time for that, sit down now!"

"Yes, ma'am!" He sat down carefully on the floor.

She screamed, "Not there, on the chair next to you!"

He used his hands to find the chair, and said, "It is not easy to see in this darkness."

She hurriedly took a thick rope from the window as he sat down on a fine and very detailed handcrafted wooden chair. The countess said, "It is not that dark anymore with the light from the candles, and it is time to play now."

Jim answered, "Play? It is a little late and I don't want to play anymore. I want to go home. Let's forget about all of this. I will take you back to your estate and I will return home to my family. They didn't want me to leave, and they must be worried about me."

Jim's eyes started to adapt to the darkness of the cabin, and he could see her. Her eyes changed as well as her expression. She had an evil and haughty look in her eyes as she tied him to the chair with the rope, and said, "Come on, just a little game, why leave so soon?" Jim didn't move a finger to stop her mad game. She added, "The fun is just beginning, sooo, you were calling me 'old.'"

Jim let her tie him down. He tried to convince her to let him go while still sitting on the chair. He said, "Let's play another game, I do not like to be tied."

She repeated, "You were calling me old."

Then, he tugged on the ropes attempting to free himself unsuccessfully. Tiny drops of sweat rolled down his temples, and he started stammering. "N-n-no, no, I, I, I, d-d-d-didn't mean 'old.'" He added, "I am the one who is old." More drops of sweat rolled down his forehead. "I am eighteen already, yesterday was my birthday, and my father told my mother, let him go, he is old enough to leave home and see the world. You see, being old is not bad, it is a good thing. It allowed me to leave my home and be free so I could come here with you."

The countess rolled her eyes. She glared at him, shook her head, and whispered, "So much nonsense." She closed the door, then yelled, "Stop talking!" Her glare was sharper than a spade, and she raised the rope in her hands to placate the hate she felt inside. The Countess of Stonemason wanted to appease her thirst for vengeance, and she used the rope to punish the young man irrationally, ruthlessly, and viciously.

Jim's painful screams could be heard from a distance. A flock of birds in the nearest tree broke away into the sky. Unfortunately, there were no other people around to hear him lament. Given that she had closed the door of the cabin, and she made sure no one else could hear Jim screaming in pain. He was there for hours, hoping she would get tired of hurting him. Unfortunately, that didn't happen that night.

Before dawn, Yooko and Masawa arrived at the cabin. Jim was still tied to the chair. He was unconscious and his shirt was stained with dirt and blood. Confused, Masawa asked the countess, "What is going on here?"

Yooko could see what she had done, and asked, "What have you done?"

The countess answered calmly, "He insulted me. Me— the Countess of Stonemason, the most beautiful, the most powerful, the richest, and the most important woman in the world." She added, "And he deserved it, now dispose of him."

Masawa asked, "Is he alive?"

"If he is still alive, then finish the job," she replied.

Masawa held his head with his hands and looked at Jim's inert body.

Yooko, looked at Jim, and said, "You, Countess, are supposed to be a fine, delicate lady, but look what you have done. You have opened a door you will not be able to close." Yooko added, "We will not be able to help you with this, hurting the innocent was never part of our deal."

Andrea calmly said, "But you are practically monsters, and you eat people. What is the big deal?"

Masawa, white as a cloud, said, "Nahuals are not monsters and we don't eat people."

Andrea calmly said, "Look, I will do whatever you want if you help me."

Yooko looked at Masawa, and said, "The only way to solve this is to help her become a little more like us."

Masawa said, "It has never been done with someone like her."

Yooko said, "The only way we can help you with this is if you swear to follow our beliefs and follow our doctrine step by step." He added, "We will teach you how to do it, but you need to participate in all our rituals."

Masawa said, "Then you will be a little more like us, and we will be allowed by our ancestors' teachings to help you with anything."

The countess said, "I will do it, but help me with this."

Masawa looked at her, and said, "Understand that you will become like us, we don't exactly know the results because it has never been done with a woman or with anyone out of our society, but it is the only way out to solve your problem and for us to help you."

Yooko said, "The results of your change will depend on your own heart and your inner self, and we do not know what the results of that will be on you."

Masawa added, "And there is no turning back from this, the transformation and the results are irreversible."

Yooko added, "This will be permanent, like ours is. You have to understand this."

The countess said, "I said yes already, stop wasting time with so much unnecessary talk and help me solve this little problem."

Yooko made a sign to Masawa to help him take Jim out of the room. Yooko put Jim's arm around his neck and Masawa did the same with Jim's other arm to help his friend carry the young man. They both left the little cabin. Masawa said, "I'll get rid of him."

Yooko agreed. "Make sure nobody sees the body." The flapping of big strong wings was heard. Yooko looked at the sky, and soon Masawa and Jim were nowhere to be found.

Andrea came out of the cabin and looked at Yooko. "The sun is coming up soon, take me back home."

He looked at her attentively without knowing what to think of her.

She said, "Stop staring at me and open the door."

Yooko opened the door for her, and she got into the carriage. She rubbed her hands adorned with fancy, extravagant rings and bracelets. She said, "Oh, my poor hands, I need to be more careful with them." Yooko got up into the front of the cart, held the reins and drove her back to her home where she had met Jim the day before.

Andrea was home by sunrise and all her employees who saw her looked at her in surprise. As she ate breakfast, her employees watched her in disbelief. They whispered among themselves. A gentleman said, "I have never seen the countess like this before."

Another male employee added, "Her clothes are dirty and torn."

Surprised, a third said, "She has disheveled hair!"

Joseph added, without whispering and in his regular voice, "And a ve-ry tired look!"

The countess heard and looked at him outside the window. He was young, but manly. He was an attractive young man. He was tall and strong but still had an innocent look on his face. It could be his nineteen years of age combined with his simple way of living. He still had a lot to learn, even how to whisper. She stood up by the window, looked at him, and asked, "Who are you?"

Joseph answered, "I am one of your gardeners."

The countess continued looking at him attentively. "Do you have a name?"

"I'm Joseph." He tipped his hat to salute her. "Excuse me, ma'am, I need to get some fertilizer for these flowers. If there isn't anything I can do for you, I'll be on my way."

The countess said, "I have some business to attend to, but we will continue our conversation later."

He tipped his hat again and left. She walked through the rooms while two of her young female employees followed her. She looked at some of her rooms one by one. They were all very spacious, comfortable, elegantly decorated, and each of them was different from the others. They had the finest details. The most expensive curtains from the time and the softest, shiniest bedsheets imported from France. Great cushions and the finest and most detailed furniture. Every bedroom had two night tables, one on each side of the bed, a big closet, a chair, a dresser with a big mirror and a stool. Even though all the bedrooms had similar furniture, they all had different designs and colors. Each room had a combination of bedsheets, curtains, and carpets in the same color, and every room had its own stylish color. Andrea stopped at one room, and said, "I will be here for now."

Surprised, the two girls looked at each other, and together said, "This is the white room!"

The countess answered, "I know, I never liked this room before, all white and boring like my life is now, but today I want to sleep here."

One of the girls closed the curtains, the other fixed the sheets and helped her take her shoes off. Both girls tried to help her into the fine silk bedclothes, but she refused. She threw her fancy, dirty dress on the white carpet and got herself into bed. The white bedsheets got soiled. The girls covered her. She uncovered herself, and said, "I don't need you anymore. Both of you out of my sight and let me sleep."

They left and closed the door behind them. A little while later, one of the girls walked by the countess's room to make sure she was still asleep and to see if she needed anything. She saw a brightness under her door. Without blinking, she looked at the illumination escaping from under the door, and asked herself, "What could that be? We covered the windows to ensure she could sleep during the day without the sun or any daylight getting inside." She walked quickly to the kitchen where the other girls were.

Another girl looked at her, and asked, "What happened to you? You are so pale and frightened, like you saw a ghost."

She answered, "It is nothing. I just like being with all of you instead of by myself." Still shaking like a leaf but trying to hide her fear, she asked, "Why would I be afraid during the day?"

By dinnertime the countess woke up, had a bath, got her hair done, and put on a beautiful new dress. She ordered them to take the white, dirty carpet out of her room and replace it with a new one. In a flash, four workers entered the room and replaced the dirty carpet with a new one as white and puffy as a cloud. The countess looked at the four men. Two were around their forties and the other two in their twenties. The two older handsome gentlemen saluted her attentively. She looked away from them and paid attention to the two younger gentlemen. They were both attractive and manly young men. One was tall, strong, athletic, fair-skinned with big green eyes and short golden hair. The other one was of medium height, slim, athletic with bronze skin, small dark eyes, and long thick hair. She got closer to them, and said, "You two, come here and sit by me. I want us to have a conversation."

Confused, the two young men looked at her. One said, "Yes, ma'am." The taller, stronger boy stood in front of her and moved the tip of his hat up to see her while the other boy sat down on a small bench by the wall and took his hat off. Both boys looked at her attentively, waiting for her to express her wishes.

The countess asked, "Which one of you gentleman would like to be my companion for some days?" She added, "Life here is very dull, and I would like to have someone compelling to amuse me, you know, someone with whom I can have an entertaining dialogue."

Confused, the shorter, young man looked at her, and in a low voice said, "Yes, ma'am."

The other one looked at her, confused as well, but asked, "What do you mean, ma'am?"

Andrea said, "I am inquiring about your presence for a few days to keep me company in this lonely place."

The green-eyed boy asked, "Oh, you mean working here for days without going to see my family?" He answered his own question. "No, sorry, I cannot do that, I have to go back today, no matter how much you pay I have other things to do besides work."

The other boy said, "Ah, you want someone to stay here and work for you for some days. I can do it if you pay me well, but I need to go back home to let my family know where I will be."

The countess said, "Do not stress about this matter. I will send someone to your home with the message that you will be back in a few days." She called her maids. "Girls, come and bring him anything he would like to eat and drink, he is my guest."

The girls looked at each other, and said, "Yes, my lady." They approached the boy and asked him what he wanted.

The countess turned to the tall, green-eyed boy. "And you, come with me, I need to show you something before you leave."

The tall boy agreed reluctantly, after which they promptly mounted horses at the countess's insistence.

After galloping for some minutes, the boy asked, "Is it much farther from here?"

She said, "No. Not that far."

About a half hour passed before they finally arrived at the cabin. After tying the horses to a post, they entered. Before the boy had a chance to take in his new surroundings, the countess left, locking the door from the outside. She said, "Wait here for a few minutes, I will be back." He was bewildered, but she seemed unbothered. As she strode through the grass, she said to herself, "Insolent boy, not accepting my friendly invitation and not wanting to please me—ME, the great, the beautiful, the powerful, the richest, the Countess of Stonemason." She continued talking to herself, and said, "Yooko and Masawa will solve this."

The boy screamed, but through the thick walls of the cabin, it was only a whisper. "Let me out, please, I have no time for this. I have to go back home!" He added, "Come back, let me out!"

Sadly, nobody could hear him. The thick walls trapped all sounds inside. Undisturbed, the countess walked back to her house.

She continued with her day, eating, drinking, and chatting with her new, young male companion. He asked, "Where is my partner? He was in a hurry and he hasn't come back?"

Andrea said, "He wanted to go home and he must be there by now, but let's not talk about him." She offered him another fine pastry and a new drink.

In the evening, she walked for some minutes around her house and asked to see her employees together in the party saloon. She played the piano with her long, soft fingers covered in fine jewels, but unlike her glamorous parties in previous years where her songs were happy ones, this time her melody was melancholic. Her employees entered the saloon and sat down. She continued playing the saddest melodies she had ever played before. Then, a middle-aged man named Antonio who was in charge of everything when she was not there, approached her, and said, "My lady, all your employees are ready for the meeting."

Andrea answered, "Very well." She walked around the saloon and looked at all her employees, paying special attention to the young men. Most of them were wearing their cowboy hats they used for sun protection during their daily work routines. Most of them raised their hats to see her better. There she was in front of them with her elegant and astounding presence.

Their important, powerful, royal, female boss and the owner of everything as far as they could see was right there in front of them. They were attentive to their superior's wishes. She who they had always admired and respected. They were all very careful and focused on her words, wanting to understand her.

The countess said, "I want all of you to know that my visit here is different than any others before." She added, "This visit is not related to business. My stay here is simply for having leisure time and as such I ask not to be disturbed in any way." Then she said, "If there is something you would like to communicate to me, go and discuss it with Antonio as you have always done before. If it is important enough he will convey it to me."

Antonio said in a low voice, "I hope everyone will understand your wishes with the unusual and elegant vocabulary you use, my lady."

Andrea didn't notice Antonio's words as she looked at her employees. "I need volunteers to give me a tour around my property. I want you to stand if you are able to do this for me."

Everybody stood, except for a couple of new employees. One of them told the other, "I know you are like me. We would volunteer but we don't because we're new here and need a tour ourselves."

Joseph entered the saloon, and said, "I made it, what is this gathering all about?"

The countess asked him, "Joe, reveal the reason for your delay."

With a confused look, Joseph wondered what she was saying. She asked him again. "The rationale for your tardiness?"

Joseph held his hat with one hand while scratching his head with his other hand. He looked at her, still quiet and puzzled. He did not understand what she was saying. Antonio intervened and rephrased her words. "Why are you late?"

Joseph answered, "Oh, that. I was working far from here and I did not know about the meeting until I got here a few minutes ago, and my name is Joseph, madam."

The countess said, "Joe, Joseph, not a big difference. Anyway, if you show me around my territory, it will be easier for me to remember your name."

Joseph smiled, tipped his hat, and said, "It will be my pleasure to show you around your lands, madam, I will bring the horses as soon as you are ready."

The countess steadied her gaze on him, and said, "I am ready now." She looked at the rest of her employees, who were still standing, and said, "This meeting is over, you may resume your daily routines."

Joseph had the horses ready and helped the countess to mount one of them. At that moment, Yooko and Masawa showed up and stood next to Antonio, who was standing next to the countess. Antonio looked at them with wide eyes, and asked, "What are you two gentlemen doing here?"

In a hurry, the countess answered, "They are my employees too. Show them to their rooms."

Antonio replied, "What is their job position?"

"They are my companions and protectors."

"Very well, madam, I will show them to their rooms. Gentlemen, follow me please." The three men left together in silence.

Yooko and Masawa were both around six feet tall. Yooko with a strong and muscular build, Masawa taller, slimmer but muscular as well. Both men in their thirties. Antonio was in his late forties. He was around five feet, seven inches tall and had a dark complexion. His hair was black and wavy accompanied by a pair of kind dark eyes. Yooko asked, "I know that you have recognized us. Is there anything you want to tell us?"

Antonio replied, "You know that I don't agree with you two, and I never will, but if you stay out of trouble, we can work next to each other." Antonio then said, "What am I saying? You don't like to follow rules. Just mind your own business with the countess and stay away from the rest of us."

Masawa said, "Clear enough, we won't bother any of you."

Yooko added, "If you respect us, we will do the same, I can assure you that."

Antonio replied, "These are your rooms, gentlemen. Good-bye." Antonio left and they watched him walk away.

The countess rode her horse side by side with Joseph while he guided her around her land. Yooko and Masawa appeared, and the countess stopped her horse to talk to them. She asked, "Are you looking for me, gentlemen?"

Together, they replied, "Yes."

The countess looked at them, and asked, "What do you need?"

Yooko replied, "We need to talk to you in private."

"Whatever it is, you can tell me in front of Joseph."

"I don't think that's a good idea."

"'Think.' Think? You are not here to think. You are strictly here to follow my commands."

Following her lead, Masawa said, "The underground construction is ready, and you will be able to transport yourself unnoticed as you wanted and much faster than riding any horse. There are many different tunnels that go to the main parts of the city as well as to the exact place you wanted, the Franciscan chapel and its residencies."

Andrea laughed out loud as she had many times before, but this time her laugh lasted much longer. In some way, this long laugh was a little different from all her other laughs. It had a mean little twist to it. She said, "I have waited so long for this day, and it has finally arrived." She glanced at Joseph, and said, "You may go on, I will catch up with you shortly." Joseph nodded his head and left on his horse.

The countess looked at Yooko and Masawa, and said, "You are my good employees."

Yooko said, "Yes, ma'am, but I thought you were going to reconsider what you were going to do as some time has passed and you have had time to think it over many times."

Masawa whispered to Yooko, "No thinking, remember?"

The countess answered, "No matter the price, I always get what I want, and do not expect me to change my mind." She added, "You will use the tunnels to get Refugio and this way Alfonso will come to me begging for her life." She laughed uncontrollably, and said, "I will torture her in front of him so he can suffer and feel the humiliation and pain I have felt with his abandonment."

Masawa, in disbelief, asked, "Madam, why do you feel so much hate when you don't even know this woman, Refugio?" He added, "I'm sure she is very ugly and poor compared to you, such an elegant and beautiful royal. It is not even worth paying attention to her."

The countess said, "If I am not happy, Alfonso will not be happy either. This is my revenge." She added, "Nobody plays with the destiny and honor of this beautiful, elegant, intelligent, rich, great, and magnificent royal woman without paying dearly for it. Besides, I do not have to explain anything to you, delinquent peasants. I am the one who makes the decisions and asks the questions around here. Your job is to strictly follow my orders. Limit yourself to do this only. We are going to the tunnels."

Together, Yooko and Masawa asked, "When?"

The countess yelled, "Immediately!" She added slowly, "Oh, how the peas-an-try irritates me."

The three of them rode together, caught up to Joseph, and continued riding for hours until dawn. Then, it was just the countess on her own horse and Joseph on his, riding along with two other horses. Joseph stopped, and asked, "Where are the two men?"

The countess answered, "Do not worry about them, they will catch up to us soon."

Joseph insisted, "What do you mean, 'They will catch up to us soon'? You mean walking or running? They can be fast, but these are horses. No man is faster than a horse. Did they get mad or tired and turn back?"

The countess asked, "Tell me, Joseph, how old are you?"

"I am twenty-eight."

The countess laughed out loud. "Twenty-eight?" She added, "You are very charming, but you have to tell me the truth."

"I am nineteen and soon-to-be twenty."

"How soon?"

"In six more months."

The countess said, "Age is not important, you are well-mannered and charismatic."

He kept quiet. She stopped her horse, and he did the same. She caressed his muscular arms with both hands. Motionless, he looked at her happily. She offered her natural red lips to him, and he kissed them. She held his hand and took him into the fields.

A couple of hours passed when they heard noises. Joseph said, "Do you hear that growling?"

The countess answered, "What growling?"

Joseph insisted, "Those growls coming from a big, strong animal." He added, "This is very strange. It could be a mountain lion, but a lot bigger and stronger. Let's go back to the horses and continue our trip to wherever we are going."

The countess said, "What is the rush? Do you not enjoy keeping me company?"

Joseph said, "I don't like it, my lady, I love it. You just don't know how much I have been waiting for a lady like you to cross my path, but I don't want to risk our lives, especially yours."

The countess said, "There is nothing to be afraid of, even the savages know who their chief is, and they obey me." She started to kiss him.

He said, "I never thought I would say this, but—"

The growling got louder. He opened his eyes wide and screamed, "No, I am leaving!"

"You are not going anywhere. You will do as I say," said the countess. She held him by the throat with both her hands.

"My lady, let me go, I don't want to hurt you."

The countess laughed out loud, and yelled, "You! Hurt me?" She added, "Ignorant fool!" She scratched his face with both hands. He pushed her away and she fell to the ground abruptly.

Joseph touched his painful, bleeding face with both hands, and asked her, "Are you all right?"

The countess looked up at him from the ground, in pain, feeling humiliated with her fancy dress all dusty. Her dress was covered with straw and leaves. He offered her his hand, and she bit it. Joseph held his injured hand with the other. He looked at her, and asked, "What are you so mad about?" He added, "Stay down on the ground if that is what you want. I am out of here." He got up, mounted his horse, left the countess there sitting on the ground, and rode away as fast as he could.

The countess screamed, "Yookooo, do not let him go! Punish him for his audacity!"

Something big and hairy snatched Joseph into the fields. The growling got louder and more sinister. Joseph cried out a desperate and painful scream. "Aaahhh, aaahhh!" His screams were so loud that they could be heard at a great distance. "Noooooooooooooooo, stooooop, aaahhh!!"

Unfortunately, there wasn't anyone around to help him. Then, suddenly everything became quiet. The countess felt calmer and continued riding her horse through the night until almost dawn. She reached Acámbaro where her new tunnels and modern method of transportation awaited her.

Yooko, her guardian that night, said, "You are risking yourself way too much."

The countess said, "What are you talking about? There is no risk involved at all." She added, "Nobody will know anything about this, and even if they knew, there is nothing they can do about it. I do whatever I please, and they have no say in it. And, if they do not like it, they can leave at any time. Besides, they all deserved it. Jim called women old, Joseph hurt women… If anything, I am just doing this world a favor by liberating it of bad men." She thought to herself, *They looked so much like him, and were just as disobedient as well.*

Many male workers stood at the entrance of one of her tunnels. Some of them were middle-aged and others were in their twenties. They were all covered in dust and talking with each other. Then, most of them left, leaving only two of the youngest men behind. Andrea shook her head, opened her eyes wide, looked at Yooko and Masawa, and said, "Go and see what is happening here."

They looked at each other, then walked toward the two young men. Masawa said, "Good afternoon, fellows, where is everybody going? Aren't all of you supposed to be working together on the tunnels?"

One of them answered, "We were working, but we had to come back up here into the open."

The other young man interrupted. "We are lucky to be out here, we almost got trapped in the part of the tunnel that collapsed."

Yooko asked, "Do you mean that this big tunnel has collapsed?"

The young man, named Kasper, answered, "Not all of it, but the part closer to the river. What were the engineers expecting when they made all of us dig under water?"

The other young man, named Alvaro, said, "Kasper, we are not supposed to talk about this with anyone who does not work with us, remember?"

Kasper said, "He is right, good-bye. Let's go, Alvaro." They walked by the countess and Kasper said, "Excuse me, ma'am."

Alvaro also said, "Excuse me."

Andrea looked at both of the manly, handsome young men. She asked, "Gentlemen, would you like to escort me?"

They both looked at each other. Kasper scratched his head. Alvaro crossed his arms and put one hand on his chin and cheek. Kasper, asked, "What?" They both looked at Andrea.

Alvaro asked, "Who are you visiting, ma'am?"

"I am not visiting anyone, these lands, as far as you can see, are mine."

Surprised, Kasper said, "You mean, you are the Countess?"

Alvaro asked, "The Countess of Stonemason?"

Andrea said, "Of course I am."

Alvaro said, "I should not be asking, it is obvious as there is no other woman like you around here."

Andrea said, "Or anywhere else I know."

Kasper said, "Nice to meet you, Countess."

Alvaro said, "Nice to meet you, we have to go home. Our work here is done."

Andrea said, "What do you mean, 'is done,' if you just said part of the tunnel collapsed."

Kasper said, "And that is why it is done. None of the men are coming back, and I don't think we should either."

Alvaro said, "It will be safer to find another job."

Andrea looked at them, and said, "That is why I am inviting you to service me personally."

Alvaro looked at Kasper, hugged him, distanced himself from the countess, and asked, "What is the fancy countess saying?"

Kasper looked at her, then he looked at him, and said, "I am not sure about what she wants. I think she is trying to tell us something."

Alvaro said, "It will be better if we get out of here, maybe she is saying something bad."

Kasper agreed. "I think you are right. She must be saying something really bad. Let's go home." Kasper looked at Andrea, and said, "Good-bye, ma'am."

Alvaro said, "Good night, ma'am."

Andrea screamed, "Stop them!" The young men walked away in a hurry.

Confused, Yooko looked at her, and asked, "Stop them for what?"

Masawa added, "They haven't done anything wrong."

Andrea yelled, "I said, stop them!"

Yooko got Kasper and Masawa got Alvaro. They sat the two simple young men by a big rock in front of the countess. With her big, intense green eyes piercing through the young men, she said, "You insolent, undeserving, low-life rodents. How dare you reject my invitation?"

Kasper and Alvaro looked at each other. Alvaro whispered, "What is she so mad about?"

Kasper raised his shoulders. They looked up at the powerful, angry lady. The Countess of Stonemason looked at her partners, and said, "You know what to do with them."

Yooko looked at his friend, and said, "We have to get rid of these two also? I am getting tired of vanishing everyone for this capricious woman."

Masawa said, "I'll do it. You can go ahead and keep her company."

Yooko asked, "Are you sure? You were very upset about this the first time it happened, but I see that you have accustomed yourself to the idea of disposing of them."

Masawa nodded and held the men by their collars. Alvaro asked, "Where are you taking us?"

Masawa calmly replied, "Far, far away from here where you cannot disturb the countess."

Kasper asked, "But why? We didn't do anything."

Masawa replied, "Don't feel bad about this. It is not your fault you are immature."

Yooko and Andrea continued on their way to her house not far from there. Later, when they got to her house, she said, "I will ask Gabriela to take you to your room so you can rest."

Yooko said, "No need for that, Countess, I am used to resting in the fields and I enjoy it."

Andrea said, "Do as you please. I will go to my room and rest." She entered one of her rooms, took her clothes off, and lay down on her comfortable bed.

Yooko took off his serape, put it on the ground next to a tree, and lay down with his feet up against the tree. The Countess of Stonemason enjoyed the night by lying down in the opulence of her room. Yooko, the idealist, preferred lying down amongst the abundance of nature. They rested for hours and through the night.

It was very early in the morning, still pitch-dark when Lucia awoke and wanted a cup of water. She sat on her bed. Doña Gabriela asked, "Lucia, it is still too early. Sleep, girl."

Lucia answered, "I am going to get a cup of water. Would you like some water, Doña Gabriela?"

Doña Gabriela replied, "No."

On her way to the kitchen, Lucia walked by the room where the countess slept. Lucia looked at the countess's closed door and quietly asked herself, "Where is that golden bright light coming from? Everything is dark and the candles don't have a strong light like that." She added, "And what is that sound?" Lucia came closer and put her ear to the door. She heard a noise, and in a low voice said, "It is snoring, or a growl, maybe something came inside and ate the countess." She ran from there and went back to her room. Shaking, she said, "Doña Gabriela, there is something very scary happening in the room where the countess is sleeping."

Gabriela asked, "What do you mean, 'something scary'?"

Lucia said, "There is a scary animal growling or snoring inside and there is a golden light coming out of the room."

Gabriela said, "It must be the light of a candle."

Lucia disagreed. "The light is too bright and golden to come from a candle."

"Then there must be the light of many candles."

Convinced otherwise, Lucia said, "No, not even the whole room filled with candles would have that kind of bright light coming out of the room."

Gabriela said, "You look so pale and are shaking with fear. Did you drink water?"

"No, I forgot about the water and I got too scared to keep on walking to get to the kitchen," replied Lucia.

"Young girls and their wild imagination, go back to sleep then. Soon it will be time for us to get up and start our work."

Lucia nodded her head and covered it with her blankets. She was shaking with fear.

The next morning, Andrea was eating two fried eggs, a tiny pineapple pastry, and some orange juice. Yooko was eating three fried eggs, yogurt, beefsteak with onions, freshly chopped pico de gallo, fresh tortillas, and some orange juice. Masawa was eating the same thing as Yooko. Masawa went to the kitchen, and said, "Doña Gabriela, I would like to have twenty hard-boiled eggs and a lot of tortillas and pastries if it isn't too much to ask, please."

Doña Gabriela said, "Of course not, I will have them ready soon."

The countess asked, "Your hard work makes you eat well, I see." She looked at Yooko, and asked, "What about you, do you want the same thing?"

Yooko said, "Not today. You know, Masawa has always had a greater appetite than me, and he has been working harder these past few days.

Andrea looked at them, and said, "I need you to investigate when they are going to repair the collapsed tunnel. I know the architect who is the head of the construction project will let me know, but I am sure you can find out faster than that."

Yooko said, "Masawa and I will find out for you." After they ate, they left.

Meanwhile, Andrea went to her stable and saw the men working in it. Some were cleaning it. Others fed the cows and horses, and others helped a cow deliver her calf. Most of the men stopped what they were doing to look at Andrea attentively, except the two workers who were with the pregnant cow. The countess looked around and went to speak with the two tall, strong, handsome, dark-skinned young gentlemen who were helping deliver the baby calf. She looked at both of them, and asked, "What are your names, gentlemen?"

The cow was lying down. They shifted their attention from the cow to Andrea. One said, "I am Benito."

The other one said, "And I am Esteban."

She asked, "Which one of you gentleman would like to come with me to ride my horse? I do not want to go alone." Benito, looking at Esteban, asked, "Do you want to go?"

Esteban replied, "I want to finish helping Perla deliver her calf."

With a serious expression Benito said, "Then I'll go."

Esteban said, "Go ahead."

Benito grabbed his hat from a pile of straw, put it on, looked at Andrea, and said, "I am ready, ma'am."

Andrea looked at him, and said, "Find us two horses for the ride." He brought the two horses and helped her get on one. He mounted the other and they left. He let her lead the way.

After a few minutes of riding their horses in the wild, Andrea brought her horse to a halt. Benito asked, "Is there something wrong, ma'am?"

"I wish to speak to you."

"What do you want to talk about?"

"Let's sit down to rest and chat for a little while," she said.

Benito agreed by nodding his head and got off his horse. Then, he walked to her and offered his arms. She accepted his help to get off her horse. He took his outer shirt off and put it over a big rock. He said, "Go ahead, my lady, sit down." He still had on his white undershirt. He took his hat off and sat down on another rock not far from the one he offered the countess. She looked at him, and asked, "What do you think about me? I would like you to be honest."

Benito picked up a blade of dry grass from the ground, put it in his mouth, took it out, looked at it, and said, "I don't know. Nothing I guess."

With a calm expression, she said, "Well, look at me. What do you think when you look at me?"

"My lady, you are my boss, and the owner of everything around here as far as I can see."

Andrea looked at him with the same calm expression, and she asked insistently, "What else do you see?"

"What do you mean, my lady?"

Andrea sighed, but remaining calm, asked again, "Would you like to keep me company for a few days while I am going to be at my estate here?"

Benito asked, "Oh, you mean like right now? Guiding you through your lands and helping you stay safe?"

Andrea chuckled, and said, "Yes, something like that."

"I will be happy to serve you. Anything you need, just let me know and I will help you."

"Now that you mention it," she said, "I have been feeling very lonely lately. Your company will make me happy."

Benito said, "There are many girls in your house who would be very happy to keep you company, and I am sure they will have a lot more things in common with you to talk about so you won't get bored."

Andrea stood up, got closer, and offered him her hand to kiss, and said, "Right now, I prefer the company of a strong man like you."

Confused, he looked at her and shook her hand gently.

"Stand up," she said.

He stood up.

"Kiss me."

He looked at her, confused. She got closer to him and kissed him passionately. He let her kiss him.

"My lady, before you hear it from somebody else, I want you to know that I have a girlfriend and soon-to-be wife."

Andrea looked at him, and asked, "Did you like our kiss?"

Benito responded, "Yes."

"Then do not agonize over it, you should know that I do not wish any serious engagement with you. We can enjoy each other's company, and then you can go back to your normal life as soon as I leave."

"If that is what you wish, my lady."

"That is exactly what I wish." She hugged and kissed him passionately. He accepted and returned her advances.

A couple of hours later, Andrea said, "It is time to go back to the house, there is some business I must attend to."

"As you wish," said Benito.

Andrea had grass and dry straw all over her clothes and hair. He started to brush it off of her. She said, "Let it be, I will fix everything as soon as I get to my house."

Benito insisted, "But people are going to see you like this and they are going to talk, let me help you tidy up a little."

Andrea shook his arm away from her and raised her voice. "Leave it! It is unnecessary."

He stopped, and said, "Very well."

He helped her mount her horse, mounted his, and they continued on their way back to the house. A couple of young gardeners saw them and continued to work. Around ten maidens looked at her, then continued to clean the house. Gabriela said, "You and you, go ask the countess if you can help her."

The two teenaged girls went to her, and one asked, "How can we help you, my lady?"

The other girl said, "How can I help you, my lady?"

Andrea stopped, looked at them with a serious face, and said, "First, help me get clean clothes." She walked into one of her rooms. The two girls followed her quietly. One of the maidens went to Andrea's wardrobe, and asked, "What dress would you prefer to wear, my lady?"

The other girl said, "I am going to prepare the water for your bath." Soon, Andrea was in her flower-scented tub sprinkled with rose petals of a variety of colors: red, yellow, light pink, bright pink, orange, and white. When she was done, the countess was again as well-groomed as usual. She looked at her young female employees, and said, "Go fetch Benito for me."

The girls walked quickly to the stable. There was Benito delivering the little calf at last. The girls waited for some minutes. The cow was licking her newborn, cleaning and welcoming it to this world. Together, the girls called to him. He looked at them quietly. One of the girls looked at him with a serious expression, and said, "The countess is asking to see you."

He stood up and quietly walked with the girls to where the powerful woman was waiting for him. They spent the day together, and the night.

The next day, early in the morning, Benito got up to ride his horse. The countess was still sleeping. Lucia was sent by Doña Gabriela to serve breakfast in bed to the countess. Gabriela said, "My lady the countess hasn't eaten since yesterday's lunch and she must be hungry." She added, "I want you to take some breakfast to her room and leave it there next to the bed for whenever she wakes up, in case she wants to eat."

Lucia agreed, and said, "What food do you want me to bring her, Doña Gabriela?"

"The usual, girl, but hurry up before she wakes up."

Lucia said, "All right, I can quickly squeeze the orange juice, boil two eggs, make a quesadilla with fresh cheese, prepare some diced papaya with pomegranate on the side, and get one of the little delicious French cakes she likes. Though, I still don't know why we serve her so much food when she is only going to eat half of it at the most."

Gabriela said, "Lucia, we should never limit the meals for our lady the countess. We should always offer her enough of what she likes and if she doesn't eat it, it is because she doesn't want it, but never because we didn't offer it. Remember this girl."

Lucia answered, "Yes, Doña Gabriela."

Another girl, Maria, who was listening, said, "I wouldn't make or take any breakfast to the countess's room. She is not going to eat anything you take to her, by the time she wakes up her breakfast will be cold and she will ask for a new one. You are wasting your time and preparing this breakfast for nothing because the countess will not eat it. I'm telling you."

Gabriela said, "Maria, when are you going to learn to follow directions without protesting? Even if the countess does not eat it and we end up making a new breakfast, that is our job." Gabriela added, "Maria, it would be good for you to stop protesting when we have to do something. You even protest when it is not you who is going to do it."

Maria said, "I'm just saying, Doña Gabriela."

Gabriela said, "You always have something to say, Maria, and you, Lucia, are you almost done with that breakfast?"

Lucia said, "The countess's breakfast is ready, Doña Gabriela."

"Then take it to her room, Lucia."

Maria said, "If I were the countess, I would throw it in your face for disturbing my sleep."

Gabriela looked at Maria, and said, "That's why the Lord does not give wings to scorpions, Maria."

Lucia looked at Maria. She did not mind Maria's comments, in part because she was used to it, but mostly because she was nervous about going to the countess's room after having witnessed weird events from her doorway.

Gabriela said, "My lady the countess said she wanted her breakfast in her room early in case she had to leave, but even if she changes her mind we have to do our work well, and that means taking care of her and following her orders." Gabriela continued organizing the gold dishes. She looked at Maria, and asked, "So you would throw the breakfast away, eh girl?" She added, "I see it is very good you are not the countess, Maria, and you, Lucia, don't just stand there, go on girl."

Lucia nervously said, "Yes, Doña Gabriela, I'm going."

It was almost dawn. Lucia got the tray with food and walked to the countess's room. She stopped and stared at the doorway, whispering to herself, "I hope the countess doesn't wake up mad and throws her breakfast in my face for waking her up." She continued looking at the door, and said, "I will be very quiet." But just as she reached for the doorknob, Lucia noticed something. Lucia asked herself, "What is that light under her door?" She looked at the burning candle that she had on the tray of food and whispered to herself, "How many candles are making that big, bright light?"

Lucia opened the countess's door very slowly and carefully. She did not make a sound. Slowly she entered the room. Even though it was dark, she did not need the candle as she could see everything in the illuminated room. There was an intense bright light in the middle of the darkness, and it was coming from the bed. Lucia saw the table where she was going to place the tray. Then she looked at the bed and was immobilized by what she saw. Her eyes grew as wide as the plates on the tray. She could not take her eyes away from the big animal sleeping on the bed and exhaling fire from its nose and mouth. Lucia wanted to scream, but she could not. She wanted to run away from there, but she was paralyzed with fear. Then she looked to the door, and she was able to move again. Carefully and quietly, she exited the countess's room. She was still holding the food tray with both hands. She held the tray with her left hand and tried to close the door carefully with her right hand. The tray almost slipped from her hand. She held it with both hands again. The sleeping mule started breathing harder and more fire came out of its nose and mouth. Lucia fixed the tray again and held it with her arm, hand, and abdomen while she quietly closed the door with her right hand. She walked very carefully away from there. As soon as she turned down the hallway away from the rooms, she started to run while holding the tray with both hands. The candle she had on the tray went out. The kitchen was not far but to Lucia it was not close enough. When she reached the entrance of the kitchen, Lucia tripped and fell, dropping the tray on the floor. Maria looked at Lucia, started laughing, and said, "I told you she wasn't going to eat it."

Gabriela said, "Maria, it is very late, and you have not swept the garden halls."

"In a bit, let me just see what happened to this one. She is as white as a flour tortilla." Maria looked at Lucia, and asked, "What happened to you?"

Lucia, lying on the kitchen floor, stared at nothing, pale and quiet. She did not even blink. Gabriela looked at Maria, and said, "Go sweep, I will see what is going on with this girl."

Maria took a broom and before leaving, she said, "Sweeping again, every day sweeping, why do we have to do it over and over again every day?" Maria continued talking to herself and said, "I have to do everything around here. I better start sweeping away from the kitchen before Doña Gabriela asks me to clean the big mess Lucia made when she threw the countess's breakfast all over the kitchen floor."

Startled, Gabriela said, "What is going on with you, Lucia? What is the big rush? It is not like you to be running around the house. What got into you?"

Lucia got up from the floor. Still pale and trembling with fear, in a low voice she said, "Doña Gabriela, you are not going to believe what I saw on the countess's bed!"

Gabriela said, "Look at you, so frightened and pale these past few days. What is going on with you, Lucia?"

Lucia's knees and voice shook. "There is a mule dressed in the countess's elegant clothes and she's sleeping on her bed, but this is a different mule. It breathes fire from its nose and mouth as it sleeps."

Gabriela's face turned red and her voice came out loud and desperate. "You silly girl, if anyone hears what you are saying, they will punish you harshly and nobody will help you when you receive a well-deserved punishment for your impudence." Lucia, still pale and with scratched knees and elbows, left the kitchen.

Doña Gabriela looked out the window and saw Lucia leaving as fast as she could. Gabriela looked at the other girls, and said, "Ask some of the boys to make sure Lucia gets home safely. She was so frightened that she might be going back home."

One of the boys who was gardening offered to help. He said, "I will follow Lucia to make sure she gets home safely, Doña Gabriela."

Maria heard, and said, "I'll follow her too, Doña Gabriela, and I will go with him to make sure Lucia is all right."

Gabriela said, "Very well, Maria, do not get distracted on the way." Gabriela looked at the boy, and said, "That goes for you as well. Do not get distracted, not even for a second. Whatever happens, do not take your eyes off Lucia."

The boy said, "Yes, Doña Gabriela." Gabriela stood there and watched the teenagers walk away. Lucia was walking the fastest of all three. Diego was walking fast right after Lucia, and Maria was walking right after Diego. After walking for some minutes, they saw two men drinking on the street, talking and laughing. One of the men saw them coming, and said, "Diego, come and join us."

Diego said, "I can't, Baltazar, I'm busy."

Baltazar walked along with him. "You can bring your friends, too, if you want."

Maria looked at Baltazar, and he asked her, "What is your name, beautiful?"

She giggled, and said, "Maria."

Diego looked at Maria, and said, "Keep on walking, Maria. I need to talk to him."

Maria looked at Diego, and said, "You keep on walking."

Baltazar said, "Maria, I would love to invite you to dinner tonight."

Maria said, "All right."

Diego said, "Come on, Maria. Lucia is getting too far ahead."

Maria said, "So you go follow her, I can take care of myself." She ran her fingers over her hair and moved it to one shoulder. Baltazar smiled at her.

Then he looked at Diego, and said, "I will keep her company, don't worry. You go ahead with the other girl."

Diego insisted, "Maria, we came together and we must return together or Doña Gabriela is not going to like it."

"Doña Gabriela is not here, and you are not my boss."

"Come here for a minute before I leave you here. We have to follow Lucia, remember?" Baltazar stood watching them from a distance as Maria got closer to Diego. He looked at Maria, and said, "That Baltazar is a womanizer. He plays with women, gets bored, throws them away, and finds new women. That is his life, and you are going to be his next game if you accept his advances."

Maria said, "I don't believe you. You're just jealous of him because he is handsome and charming."

"Maria, listen to me," said Diego. "I don't want you to fall for him. His father is a rich businessman from far away, but Baltazar just comes around here to have fun with the girls and leaves them devastated."

"I don't believe you! And if it's true it's because they're stupid, but I'm not like them. So, you said he's rich, eh? That's why you are jealous of him."

"Me? Jealous? The only thing he does every day is drink and cheat on women."

"You're lying," said Maria.

"Pedro is not going to like you going out to dinner with another man. I'm sure of that," said Diego.

"He doesn't own me. Besides, I already left him."

"So you don't care about what he thinks? He's your fiancé and in less than a month he will be your husband."

Maria laughed, and said, "Unless I find a better husband."

"I already told you how Baltazar is, but it seems like you want to be one more on his sad ex-girlfriend list."

"You go ahead with Lucia, I will stay and chat with Baltazar."

Diego shook his head, sighed, and said, "I already warned you, but I might have wasted my time, and now I don't see where Lucia is anymore. I am going to look for her. Good-bye, Maria."

Maria grumbled, "Hmph," and started walking back to where Baltazar was.

Diego walked ahead looking for Lucia, but she was nowhere to be found. He quickened his step and some minutes later he reached Lucia's grandparents' house. The door was open and Diego stuck his head inside, and said, "Hello, Lucia? Who's here?" He didn't see anyone, so he walked into the hallway leading to the back of the house. There at the end of the long, wide hallway was Lucia's grandfather. He was chopping wood for the stove, but he stopped when he saw Diego.

The grandfather asked, "What are you doing here?"

Diego nervously replied, "I'm sorry, sir. Me and another girl were supposed to accompany Lucia and make sure she got home safely, but we got distracted on the way here and lost sight of Lucia. Is she here already?"

Her grandfather replied, "She's here and her grandmother is with her in the room."

"Excuse me, sir, can I say hello to your wife and good-bye to Lucia?"

"I don't think that will be possible. She is in bed feeling sick and her grandmother is keeping her company."

"May I help you with the wood cutting then?"

"Don't you have to go back to work?"

"Not until I know how Lucia is doing."

"All right, you can help me finish that uncut pile while I fix the rest of the wood."

After a few hours, Diego asked, "Excuse me, sir, can we see how Lucia is doing?"

Lucia's grandfather left the ax on the tree stump, and said, "Let's go see." Grandpa knocked on Lucia's door gently, and asked, "A boy is here asking how Lucia is?"

Her grandmother said, "Wait a minute." Then, she came out of the room and closed the door behind her.

Diego asked, "Good afternoon, ma'am. How is Lucia?"

"She is very scared, she saw something evil in the countess's house, and she can't get it out of her head."

Her grandfather asked, "Is Lucia feeling better?"

"No, she is the same as when she first got here, pale and weak." Her grandmother looked at Diego, and said, "You should leave that place, too, before you see something wicked like Lucia saw. The devil is in that countess's house, leave before you see it too."

Diego didn't know what to say. Then, he asked, "Can I come back tomorrow to see if Lucia has recovered?"

Her grandmother said, "Yes, you may come back and bring with you more of Lucia's friends."

"Thank you, I will bring some friends with me."

Her grandfather said, "Good night, boy."

Diego tipped his hat, and said, "Good evening, sir. Ma'am."

"Good night, son."

Lucia's grandmother said, "Be careful there at the countess's house. You saw what happened to Lucia. The fear is killing her." She added, "Leave that job and never return there, something very evil is in that place."

Diego agreed with a nod of his head and left Lucia's house. Her grandparents stood by the door of their house and watched him leave. He walked at a normal speed back to his work when he saw Baltazar still standing at the same spot. Diego said to himself, "That might be his favorite spot in this whole area, and who is he talking to? Is it the same guy he was talking to before or is it a different one?" Then he saw them getting closer together and embracing each other. Diego said to himself, "They are smooching? Who is that other person? That can't be what I am thinking. Oh, but it is, my worst fear has come true. Maria is the one still there with him, and she is in his arms." Diego scratched his head. "What am I going to do?" Immediately, he answered, "Nothing, there is nothing else I can do about it, except for…" Then he screamed, "Maria! Aren't you going back to work? Doña Gabriela must be worried about you."

Maria, in a loud voice, replied, "Tell her not to worry, 'cause I'm good!"

Baltazar yelled, "And tell her Maria will not go back to work anymore because she's with me and I will give her anything she wants! Her only work from now on is to keep me company." Maria giggled, and they both continued laughing and kissing.

Later that evening, Diego returned to the hacienda. Doña Gabriela saw Diego, and said, "At last you are back, boy, how did it take you this long to take Lucia home?"

Diego, with a serious expression, replied, "Don't ever send me with that Maria to do anything ever again. I had to take care of Lucia and babysit Maria too."

Doña Gabriela said, "You're mad because you haven't eaten anything all day long, come and eat." She asked, "How is Lucia?"

"She is at home with her grandparents, resting, but I couldn't see her. Her grandmother said she is very scared and that the devil lives here at the hacienda."

Gabriela made the sign of the cross, and said, "Where is Maria?"

"She stayed with her new boyfriend, Baltazar."

"And you let her?"

"She doesn't even listen to you, Doña Gabriela, what makes you think she would listen to me?"

Gabriela served him a plate of food, and said, "That's true, boy, that girl doesn't listen to anyone, eat your food in peace."

Pedro entered the kitchen, and said, "Good evening, Doña Gabriela. How are you doing, Diego? Where is Maria?" Diego and Doña Gabriela looked at each other.

For better or for worse, Pedro did not see his fiancée with her new boyfriend. Maybe it would have been good for him to see her with his own eyes so he could abandon his dreams about living a life with her for once and for all. Even though others already knew about Maria's playful heart, Pedro didn't and maybe it was better this way, at least for now. Anyway, there is not one secret that can last forever.

Some days later, Diego asked, "Doña Gabriela, Lucia has been absent from work for so many days, almost a week. This is not like Lucia. She must be really sick."

Doña Gabriela said, "I know, Diego, and I don't like it either."

"Maria's father went to see Baltazar's father," said Diego. "He wants his daughter married since she is already living with Baltazar."

"I hope that goes well," said Gabriela.

"I don't know, Doña Gabriela, it will not go very well, I know that."

She asked, "Why do you say that, boy? Don't give me more worries than the ones I have already."

"Everybody who knows Baltazar's father says he is very rich and stubborn. He raised Baltazar into a brat and wants a rich and fine lady for his son to marry, not just any plain, poor girl like the ones we have around here."

"What are you saying, boy? All the girls around here are very pretty and good. Besides, where did you get these ideas about Baltazar's father wanting a rich girl for his son?"

"Maybe the girls around here are the way you say, Doña Gabriela, but being pretty and good is not enough for Baltazar's father. And it's not like all the girls around here are as good as you think either, Doña Gabriela, at least not Maria. She's as stubborn as a mule and doesn't listen to anyone."

"Maybe that is going to change now, Diego, and when Maria is a married woman she will change her ways and listen to her husband and his family."

"What makes you think that, Doña Gabriela? If Maria doesn't listen to her own family or you, I don't think she is ever going to listen to anyone."

"The good thing is, Maria is going to marry that Baltazar soon. Marriage might soothe her."

Diego said, "I don't know about that, Maria needs to be very rich before Baltazar and his father agree to that marriage, you will see."

"Stop giving me bad news, boy. Don't you have anything good to say today?"

"Don't worry, but it's the truth, and it is better that you know it." He added, "Oh, and I didn't make that up, I heard it from my uncles who used to work for Baltazar's father a few years ago."

Gabriela asked, "How can Baltazar's father say no to Maria's father after they have already been living together and all the people in the surroundings know about it? He has to say yes, he just has to…"

Meanwhile far away from there at Baltazar's house, Maria's father was talking to Baltazar's father. "Marry them we can," said Baltazar's father, while lighting a cigar, then he added, "if each party meets the requirements. Marriage is an association where the family business and fortune grows with the union. A lot of my family money and assets belong to my son for the day when he finds the young woman he will marry. What does your daughter have to offer to this business union that is called marriage? Can she at least match the goods my son has? If it is like this, we can marry them straight away." He made eye contact with his visitor, and asked, "What riches does your daughter have?"

Maria's dad lowered his head and left quietly.

Meanwhile, Diego saw Maria at the store, and said, "Maria, if you leave that guy, I believe Pedro will still marry you as if nothing has happened."

"You are crazy, Diego," said Maria. "Everybody knows that I have been living with Baltazar for the past week."

"Pedro doesn't care about what everybody says about you, Maria. Think it over, he will still marry you if you want."

Maria said, "Pedro is too good for my taste, and too poor also. Tell him not to send you with these silly messages. Don't come back to ask me this again, I will soon be the wife of a rich man."

"If that is what you want, Maria, I will not come back again. I hope you know what you are doing." He added, "Just one more thing. Pedro doesn't know I came to talk to you. I came of my own free will." He turned and left, and Maria continued doing her shopping at the store.

A bunch of guys who witnessed the conversation between Diego and Maria called to Diego. One said, "How are you doing, Diego?"

Diego looked at him.

Another guy said, "Come with us, Diego. We are going to get some drinks." Diego shook his head. The six of them surrounded him and walked with him.

One said, "Only one drink, Diego, you will feel so much better."

They all entered a nearby restaurant and ordered food and drinks. One of the men gave Diego a bottle, and said, "A little drink will not hurt you, but it will make you feel so much better."

Diego said, "I will take this drink another day. I have to go. Doña Gabriela is waiting for me back at the estate." He left while the men continued chatting and drinking together.

The countess was eating breakfast with Benito when a girl came to them, and said, "My lady, there is a man asking to see you."

Andrea asked, "What does he want?"

The girl said, "He has a letter for you from your most important project, that is what he said."

"Very well, bring him in."

The boy entered the room, and said, "Good morning, Countess, this letter is from your—"

The countess interrupted him. "I know who the letter is from." He handed her the letter. She read it, shook her head, and said, "Ineptitude, that is what they have, and they have plenty of excuses for it. Anyway, I have to wait until they finish their work, no matter how long it takes. I have been waiting for a long time, and a little more makes no big difference at this point."

Benito asked, "What is that letter about?"

Andrea looked at him attentively, and said, "You look so much like him." Then she screamed, "Girls!" The girls immediately came to see what she wanted. Four of them stood in front of her, waiting for her orders.

One of them asked, "My lady the countess, what do you need?"

"Where are Yooko and Masawa?"

A couple of girls raised their shoulders, the two others shook their heads. One of them said, "I haven't seen them in a couple of days, my lady."

Andrea shook her head, and said, "I am surrounded by worthless good-for-nothing peasants." She waved her hand to Benito, and said, "You, wait for them."

Benito scratched his head, and asked, "Me? Wait for whom? And what for?"

The countess said, "Tell Yooko and Masawa to take you with them and finish the job."

"What job?"

"They will know what to do, you just wait for them here and tell them that."

Not worried, he said, "All right."

Concerned, the four girls looked at each other. The countess said, "I have to leave. Tell them to go find me as soon as they get here." She wrote down a few words to indicate the place where she was going to be and gave the note to one of the girls, then turned to the other girls. "Go ask the men to prepare my carriage, I am leaving right now."

After some minutes, the countess left in her carriage. Benito waited in the gardens for Yooko and Masawa as he was told by the countess. One of the girls approached Benito quickly and silently. She was medium height, thick, and with dark skin. Her hair was long, straight, and braided. She had dark, almond-shaped eyes. She looked at him and said in a low voice, "Benito, go home, and don't come back here ever again."

He looked at her, nodded, and asked, "Why do you think I should leave?"

The girl answered, "The countess continues traveling to each of her properties alongside the Lerma River, and she continues choosing the most strong, manly, and youthful workers as her companions." She added, "Then, after a few days she discards them and continues to choose a new one."

Benito laughed nervously. Then he said, "You are imagining things, but I will leave because I am tired of waiting for those two." He turned to leave. The girl who warned Benito continued talking to herself. She sighed, opened her eyes wide, and said, "If what I am saying is true, my cousin could be dead by now, but I am not going to give up until I find out exactly what happened to him and the other boys who have disappeared."

Unfortunately, she was not too far from the truth. On the other hand, she was not the only one with this kind of suspicion. There were many parents looking for their sons in the surrounding area already.

The news spread all around that many of the countess's most handsome, young workers had disappeared after being involved with her. The gratitude and affection shown by her employees was turning into fear and despair.

Andrea continued traveling to her houses along the Lerma River and the Balsas River.

Andrea traveled to her house in Tuxpan. She was welcomed by her many workers and given good food and all the attention, just as she was accustomed to. There was only one difference, the boys here inclined their heads and covered their young faces with their hats in fear, trying to stay alive longer. None of these boys wanted to be the most handsome, the most manly, nor the chosen one for the Countess of Stonemason. She was very observant, but she did not notice they were trying to avoid her as she was not feeling well.

Her butler said, "You look different, my lady, your cheeks are not rosy anymore. Actually, you are extremely pale." He asked her permission to touch her by putting his hands in front of her face. "I would swear you have a fever. Can I check you, my dear Countess of Stonemason?"

She with a sick and tired look, nodded her head and got near him. He touched her face with both hands, and said, "You are burning, my lady. We will fix this immediately." He turned to some female workers. "Girls, help our lady, the Countess of Stonemason, get her into bed to rest." The girls promptly helped her.

The butler went to the kitchen, found the cook, and said, "Prepare a chicken soup with vegetables as only you know will help the sick recover."

The cook said, "Immediately. Who is sick?"

"The Countess of Stonemason."

Andrea slept for some hours. Then, as soon as she woke up, she was offered chicken soup. She looked at her butler, and asked, "Tell me, have you ever felt very sick and afraid of dying?"

Her butler answered, "Yes, my lady."

"And what did you do to get better?"

"I was kicked by a horse, once. I was very ill, and I thought I was going to die."

The countess asked, "How did you get well?"

"It took me a long time to recover. I thought I wasn't going to make it."

She again asked, "What did you do to get better?"

The butler said, "The first thing I did was to ask our Creator to help me, and I promised Him I was going to be a new and better person. I repented of my sins and became a better person as I promised. I still have my faults, but not as big as I used to have." He added, "I plan to keep my promise for as long as I live, and I am very grateful for our Creator's mercy. That is what has kept me alive and well since then."

The countess said, "Will I get better if I promise to be a better person and to do only good and promise not to harm anyone?"

Her butler looked at her, smiled, and said, "I am sure you will if you do it from your heart, my lady." He added, "Now eat your chicken soup to recover your strength." He offered her a tray with the chicken soup with vegetables. She was so pale, sweating, and feeling weak but accepted the tray of soup, and said, "I promise to be a better person if I recover from this fever." Then, she ate her meal peacefully.

After finishing her nutritious meal, she slowly walked outside. She held a tree with both of her hands. Then, still feeling weak, she stumbled. Before she fell down, a handsome, manly, middle-aged man caught her in his strong arms. He was tall, with tan skin, dark hair, a mustache, and wearing a uniform. He held her in his arms and looked at her closely face to face. She opened her eyes slowly. He kept looking into her eyes, and said, "The immensity of the forests, nor the depth of the seas could be a more impressive sight than a look from your beautiful eyes!"

Still in his arms, she weakly said, "How dare you touch me without my permission?"

He said, "I had no choice, or you would be on the ground with a split head by now." He helped her sit on a bench nearby and looked at her. "How do you feel, my beautiful flower?"

"You bold, insignificant peasant. How dare you speak to me in that manner, you must be the one with a split head."

He put both his hands over the left side of his chest, and said, "A split head I do not have, but you just broke my heart!" He added, "It wouldn't be the first time, as I always have liked my women beautiful and evil. But I promise, you will be my last woman if you care to get to know me. Nothing would make me happier than spending the rest of my life with you by my side."

She said, "You dare to want to marry me? Do you know who I am? I am the most important person you have ever met, and I am the owner of everything and the boss of everyone around here!"

He chuckled, and said, "We have something in common then. I am the boss of a whole army. I am the captain, but in front of you I feel like a defenseless bunny."

Color came back to her face, and she firmly asked, "What are you doing here anyway?"

"I almost forgot, I have a message for you." He handed her a letter, and said, "I know deep inside you like me, but I have to go now." He added, "There is some important business I must attend to, but if you decide to give yourself the opportunity of having a real man who will love and care for you, let me know. You know where to find me."

She looked him up and down with narrow eyes. "I never needed a man to take care of me and I never will."

"You can still catch the last boat to happiness!" He cleared his throat, and said, "I mean you and me both can still find happiness together before it is too late for us!" Then he left on his horse.

She ignored him and looked at the letter, then said to herself, "Could this be about my most inner wish, my most important desire, what I have been wanting for such a long time?" Her appearance started to change. Her still pale cheeks began turning rosy again. She was not sweating anymore. Her hands felt steady. She read the letter and was happy with the news. She looked up, and said, "At last, my most important project is ready."

The butler reminded her about her health, and said, "My lady, you should rest and continue recovering until you feel well."

The countess said, "Thank you, but I feel so much better now and with the energy to continue with my most important plans."

The butler said, "As you prefer, dear Countess."

She laughed out loud, and said, "After such a long wait, I will be able to finish what I started, and nothing will stop me this time, nothing can stop me now! I always do what I want, and I have been wanting this for such an extended period of time." She continued laughing, then asked herself, "How dare they go against my dearest wishes? Nobody goes against me without paying for it—me, the most beautiful, powerful, rich, and important woman in the world." She smiled maliciously, and said, "At last they will be at my feet for their insolence, and no one can stop it now." She ordered, "Bring me my carriage!"

Her employees looked at her, confused and frightened. She was helped into her carriage and taken to see her new and final underground road. An hour had passed when she started feeling sick again. She called her riders, and asked, "Gentlemen, how is the weather?"

Confused, the riders looked at each other. One of them answered, "It is a sunny and warm day, my lady."

The other rider added, "That's why we are sweating, like most days riding at this time."

The countess said, "I am sweating, too, but these are very cold sweats. I feel very cold! One of you, come and keep me company."

They whispered among themselves. One rider looked at his partner, and in a low voice said, "You should go, and I'll keep driving."

The other rider whispered back, "Me? No, you go!"

The countess said, "I think I am going to faint."

One of the riders said, "I'll go," and handed the reins of the horses to his partner. He went inside the carriage, looked at her, and said, "What happened to you, my lady? You are very pale!"

She said, "I feel sick and very weak. I feel worse than ever, and every second I keep feeling worse!"

The young man asked, "Do you give me permission to touch your face? You might be running a fever."

She said, "Yes, go ahead." He touched her forehead and her two cheeks and took his hands away from her immediately, and said, "You are burning!"

The countess ordered, "Quick, take me to the closest doctor! I need to recover my health and my strength."

The young man said, "The closest doctor lives four hours from here."

"No, then take me back to my closest house as fast as you can."

The other young man, driving the carriage, said, "My lady, we will go quickly and be there in less than an hour."

"I do not know if I will be able to last that long. I have never felt this sick before."

Then she fainted.

The young man next to her shouted, "She stopped talking! It will be better if I keep her company while you take us back to her house."

The rider said, "We are on our way, keep on checking her, make sure she is all right!"

The gentleman in the carriage checked her wrist. Then, he checked her neck. He said, "Her pulse is weak, and she is hardly breathing."

The rider said, "I hope she can make it home alive." They were quiet for the rest of the way. They were going as fast as the horses could carry them. The rider said, "Finally, we are here again at your house, my lady." He shouted, "Help! Help! The Countess of Stonemason is sick!"

Many workers came out of the house, some came from the stables and a few others came from the orchards to see what was happening. The butler ordered, "Bring her some water." The girls looked at her, frightened by her condition. One of the youngest girls came with a cup of water. She offered the golden cup to her. The countess held it, but she wouldn't drink from it. The countess's weak arm fell and dropped the gold cup with water, letting it roll out of the carriage. In her physical weakness she was unable to speak, and she thought, *I am so thirsty and so cold, but I do not have the strength to open my eyes and tell them so they can help me.*

The butler said, "There is nothing we can do for her here. We must take her to the doctor."

The rider said, "But it is four hours from here."

The butler insisted, "We have to try and help her, that is all we can do." The butler and the young girl who gave her the water got into the carriage with Andrea. He asked a preteen boy, "You, boy, come with your sister, we might need you."

He got into the carriage with them, and said, "We have no time to lose."

The butler held the countess gently, and the rider went back with the other rider to help with the horses. The riders rode the horses as fast as they could.

"The countess is panting, and she has a weak pulse. She is very cold," said the butler.

"Continue checking her, sir, in case her breathing changes. We can tell the doctor when we get there," said the girl in front of him.

The butler nodded his head and agreed. "You are a wise, young girl."

She said, "I am eleven years old, and my brother is twelve."

"Then, why have I been thinking you two are the same age?"

The girl said, "I don't know, maybe because we are the same height."

"And because the two of you look alike." He checked the countess again. Startled, he said, "The countess is not breathing, and she does not have a pulse. She is very cold!"

The countess thought, *I do not feel cold and thirsty anymore, and I am able to see my own body lying on the carriage next to my employees who are trying to help me. I try to touch my own body, but I cannot. My physical body cannot move, and I cannot get back in there as I am trying. Yet, I can see without my physical eyes, and hear without my physical ears, and mostly I can feel what others are feeling for me.* She felt desperate. *They have only sad feelings for me. I can feel their fear, compassion, sadness, and pity. I want to go back to my physical body to yell at all of them as loud as I can that I do not need them, and that I am the most rich, beautiful, powerful, and important person they will ever know, but I am unable to.* Her tone lightened and a beautiful and unique cast of light flashed across her face. *I have never seen such a delightful light like this before. It feels wonderful. I can feel that only the greatest good is in that light.*

CHAPTER TEN

Love is Recovered

Christine walked away from her sister's house. She was surrounded by the vegetation all around her and lost in her own thoughts of sorrow. Every day she walked alone for hours since that sad day when she lost her fiancé. Then, she saw several of Andrea's young employees looking attentively at something and surrounding it. She also saw Lucia with her grandparents. Christine got closer, and asked, "What is happening here, boys?"

"We found him in the meadow and brought him here."

Christine looked at the little one wrapped in a man's shirt. Lucia said, "Poor little baby, he is lucky the coyotes did not find him first." The baby was crying.

Christine held him in her arms, and said, "Do not be afraid, little one. I will protect you until we find your parents. We will find your mother, do not be afraid."

One of the boys said, "Miss Christine, I do not think his mother is going to be able to take care of him."

Concerned, Christine asked, "Why not?"

Another boy answered, "His mother has mental problems and is not well enough to take care of herself, much less take care of a little baby."

Lucia said, "That is true, Miss Christine. Poor defenseless baby does not have a mommy or grandparents to take care of him. When my parents died, my grandmother and grandfather took care of me, but this little one has no one else, only us."

Lucia's grandparents looked at each other and smiled. The grandmother, with tears on her cheeks, hugged Lucia, and said, "You are all right, Lucia. I was afraid we were going to lose you."

Lucia's grandfather hugged them both and cried. Her grandmother looked at Christine, and said, "This is the first time she has spoken and shows some sense after a month of being sick and absent-minded. Earlier today I was mad at my husband for insisting on taking Lucia on a walk, being sick like that, but I was wrong. This walk has resulted in a miracle."

Christine looked at them, and said, "I am happy for you three that Lucia is all right." Then she looked at Lucia, and said, "Do not worry, Little Lucia. We will take good care of this baby." Christine held the baby in her arms, looked at Lucia, and said, "I am very happy to see you here, Little Lucia." Wanting to humor and make small-talk to Lucia, she smiled and asked, "Have you been following me all this time?"

Lucia said, "Miss Christine, when I saw you, I remembered Doña Gabriela said somebody had to take care of you today."

Her grandmother whispered to her grandfather. "Today? Today she has been with us the whole time and no one else."

Her grandfather whispered back, "Shhh, at least she can talk now."

Christine smiled, and said, "Poor Little Lucia, you are only sixteen. I should be the one taking care of you."

"Oh, but you do, Miss Christine. We all take care of each other around here."

Christine nodded in agreement. The young men turned to head back to work. One of them said, "Take good care of our baby for us, please, Miss Christine!"

"I will do that, boys." She smiled down at the baby boy. The baby was crying desperately.

"He must be hungry," said Lucia. They both went back to the house. Christine held the baby in her arms, and Lucia stood next to her looking at the crying baby. Marie was happy to see them and smiled as she walked toward them.

Christine looked at Marie, and said, "Mother, we have to find someone to feed this little one."

Marie looked at Lucia, and said, "Little Lucia, go ask Doña Gabriela which women in the area have young babies. One of them must want to help us feed this little one. We will pay her well." Christine cuddled the newborn, and Marie watched with tenderness. Marie put her arm around Christine's back, and asked, "Darling, where did you get this little fussy baby?"

"You are not going to believe this, Mother. I feel like the Lord put him in my arms so I could do something for him."

"Tell me, Christine, what happened?"

Christine calmly explained, "I was very sad and confused, like I have been for so long, just walking without knowing where to go, thinking nothing mattered anymore. I did not know what I was going to do. I wanted to leave and go far away from here and never come back again. I felt miserable, ruined, without hopes or dreams, but today I decided to change my life for the better and I was praying to God to clear my troubled head." She held the baby against her chest, looked up at the sky, and said, "Then, I saw all the young men had stopped working and were surrounding him. I knew they were looking at something very important because they had stopped working. There he was on the grass, so tiny and fragile, crying from the top of his lungs like he was asking someone to save him." Christine's tone changed to a more tender one and with her eyes full of tears, she said, "Mother, when I saw this little one, I remembered life is so valuable, so precious, and it is worth living even with all of its difficulties." Big tears ran down her cheeks. She looked at Marie, and said, "Life is like a great treasure that we must protect."

Marie said, "I agree with you, Christine, life is worth living, and it is such a precious gift."

Later on, there were two babies lying on the fancy bed. Both were dark-skinned with a big mane of thick, black hair on their little heads. Their eyes were big and brown. The one with a mother was a lot bigger and stronger. The one that Christine found was such a tiny, delicate, defenseless baby. Lucia's grandparents were still watching Lucia from a distance. They were still astonished to see their granddaughter being talkative again. However, they wanted to make sure she was all right and not leave her out of their sight.

Lucia approached Christine, and said, "Miss Christine, Pedro is very sad."

"That is very strange. Pedro is usually in a good mood, Little Lucia."

"Today is different. He found out Maria, his fiancée, left him. She doesn't want to marry him anymore because he is a poor man. First Pedro didn't want Maria, he said she was too young, but she insisted, even asked him to marry her. Finally, he agreed and bought her a beautiful wedding dress, only for her to leave him for another man with more money. They would not have been happy anyways. Even though she was the one pursuing him, she was always complaining about how poor he was. Now Maria is pursuing her dream of finding a rich man, but I feel sorry for Pedro. He is such a nice guy. He did not deserve being left like this, after spending so much money on his bride's wedding dress. She begged for that dress and now that he bought it for her, she does not want him anymore. What will he do with the dress?"

Christine said, "Do not worry, Little Lucia, Pedro is a strong man. He can handle it. It is better that it happened now rather than after getting married."

"But he looks very sad, and I have never seen him like this. I wish you two would have fallen in love, Miss Christine. You know, Pedro always liked you, but because you didn't like him back, he accepted Maria."

Christine sighed, and said, "Lucia, it is not that I did not like him, I have always liked Pedro, a lot!"

"Then why didn't you accept him? Don't get mad at me, please, Miss Christine, I know this is none of my business."

Christine looked at Lucia tenderly, and said, "It's all right, Lucia, I will tell you why I never accepted Pedro. I thought he was too young for me, and that someday he was going to prefer a younger woman his own age. I did not want that to happen."

"Pedro is a good man, Miss Christine, and he has always loved you. I don't think he could wrong you, he likes you too much. Besides, he is way too formal and serious to be mean or disloyal to anyone." Lucia added, "You and Pedro would look good together, Miss Christine. I don't think anyone would notice any difference in age."

"Maybe you are too young to understand age differences at this moment."

"My grandfather says that a difference in age between a couple is not important when both of them are adults," said Lucia. "Did you know that my grandmother is seven years older than my grandfather? And they have been very happy together all their marriage. My grandfather still likes and loves my grandmother."

"That is a beautiful thing, what your grandparents have, Little Lucia. I wish I was only seven years older than Pedro."

Lucia said, "Pedro and you are adults, and if you love and respect each other, age is not that important."

"I wish it was that simple."

"It is simple, Miss Christine. Think about it, it is your decision." Lucia placed her hands on her own chest, one over the other, and sighed. Then she said, "You have the right to be happy with the man of your dreams!"

"You are very young, and such a romantic girl, Lucia, but I am starting to think that everything you have been talking about makes a lot of sense, you know." Christine added, "Maybe it was me who was creating all these limitations in my head." The baby started crying. Christine said, "It is all right, little one, you just need dry clothes."

"You are a very good mother, Miss Christine."

"Thank you, Little Lucia, I wish he really was mine." Lucia caressed the baby's head, and said, "You have a nice mother, little baby, you only need a nice father. I am going to pray that you get one."

"I'll help you find some clothes for him, Miss Christine."

A loud voice was heard. "Luciaaa! Doña Gabriela wants to see you in the kitchen."

Christine said, "Go ahead and help Doña Gabriela. Do not worry, Little Lucia. I can handle this cute little one."

Lucia nodded, and said, "I'll see what they want, and I'll be back to help you with your baby, Miss Christine."

A female's loud voice was heard again. "Luciaaa!"

Lucia left in a hurry but looked back to see Christine and the baby. She said to herself, "I wish I could spend the whole day helping Miss Christine take care of the little baby."

When she got to the kitchen, she asked, "What do you need help with, Doña Gabriela?"

Doña Gabriela hugged Lucia with a big smile and tears rolled down her cheeks. "I thought I saw you from far away, but I had to make sure it was you, girl, my girl, my Little Lucia." Gabriela added, "I am so glad to see that you are all right, Lucia. Come and sit down while we cook the Lent meals."

"You always want me to help you with that, Doña Gabriela. What do you want me to do?"

Gabriela wiped her tears with the inner part of her apron, and said, "You are right, my girl, I need your help with the Lent meals. Help me get everything done, if you want. You can start by frying the seasonings for the lentils. They are almost cooked."

"Yes, Doña Gabriela," said Lucia.

She poured a little grease into a pan. When the grease was hot, she added the diced onions and stirred them for a minute. Then she added the ground garlic and stirred it for a few seconds. Then Lucia added the cilantro and the diced tomatoes. After a few seconds, Lucia added the fried condiments to the pot. She let them boil for a minute and then took them off the fire carefully with a thick kitchen rag. Lucia looked at Doña Gabriela, and asked, "Did you put salt in the lentils, Doña Gabriela?"

Gabriela looked at Lucia, and said, "Yes, my girl, I added the salt ten minutes ago. They are ready." She added, "Now sit down next to the stove and help me toast the big poblano peppers, but watch them, I don't want them burned."

Lucia put the big, fresh, dark green poblano peppers on the flat griddle. She watched and turned them. Doña Gabriela said, "Don't burn them, my girl. Remember we want them well toasted but not burnt. As soon as they are toasted on one side, turn them to the other side."

"Yes, Doña Gabriela, I am doing that. I am being very careful and I won't burn them, don't worry." Then, Lucia started cutting fresh cheese into long, thick slices.

Doña Gabriela asked, "Where are the peppers?"

"The toasted peppers are wrapped with a napkin so they can be easy to peel when they get cool, as you taught me to do, Doña Gabriela."

"Well done, girl, make sure those pieces of fresh cheese are the right size to fit and fill those peppers. What about the tomato sauce for the peppers?"

"It's coming. I will put the tomatoes, garlic, and onions on to cook right away." A boy came into the kitchen, and said, "It smells really good in here, is the food ready?"

Doña Gabriela said, "We will call you in a few minutes when everything is ready."

Lucia smiled, and said, "Pablo, have you seen Pedro?"

"Yes, he was drinking." Pablo added, "Don't look at me like that, you have to see it to believe it. I wouldn't believe it, either, if I hadn't seen it with my own eyes."

Lucia said, "Doña Gabriela, everything is almost done. Pablo can help you finish the meals, but please let me go get someone who can help Pedro."

Doña Gabriela said, "You worry too much for your age, Lucia."

Pablo asked, "What do you want me to do?"

Lucia said, "Just grind the tomato sauce for the stuffed peppers and put the cheese inside them. That's it."

"All right, I'll do it."

Doña Gabriela said, "Wash your hands so you can help us, Pablo."

"When have I touched food without washing my hands first, Doña Gabriela?" he said. "I'll wash my hands right here where you can see them."

"Very well, boy."

Lucia left to find Christine. Lucia's grandparents were still watching her from a distance. Christine was lying down on a bed next to the baby. She watched him attentively while he slept. Lucia ran into the room, and said, "Miss Christine, Miss Christine! Pedro is still drinking, and he never drinks. He needs someone to save him. He will listen to you. Oh, why did he have to do such a silly thing? This is no good, Miss Christine. Please, help him."

Christine carefully took the newborn boy in her arms, and said, "All right, Little Lucia, take me to where he is, I will try to help him. I do not promise you anything, but I will try to stop him from drinking."

Lucia walked ahead in a hurry. Christine said, "Not too fast, Little Lucia. I have a baby in my arms." Lucia slowed her pace and walked closer to them. Some minutes later they got to where Pedro was. Christine stood a few feet in front of him, and asked, "Pedro, you have never liked drinking before."

Pedro sat on a chair, holding a cup next to a bottle on the table. He looked away from the bottle for an instant, took another sip of his drink, and said, "I thought I would try it today." The baby sneezed. Pedro opened his eyes wide and looked at the baby and at Christine holding him. He asked, "Whose baby is that? Is it your baby, Miss Christine? No, it couldn't be, is it?"

Lucia stood next to them, and said, "The poor little one has no father to protect him, Pedro."

Pedro put his wine cup to the side, and said, "So, it is yours, Miss Christine." He stood up and said, "My offer is still the same, or even better. I will protect you and your baby if you permit it. I can be a good father for that little baby if you let me. We can get married and live a happy life far away from here."

Christine looked at him and smiled while holding the baby in her arms. "You are a good man, Pedro, you always have been." She added, "And even though I am the one who wishes the most to go to a new place far away from here, I cannot do it at this time. I need to stay here until my newborn baby stops breastfeeding and can live on regular food."

His expression changed in an instant from surprised and hopeful to a sad one. He said, "I'm sorry for asking you the same thing again. I already know your answer, you think I'm too young for you, but I had to try one last time since I'm clearing my mind on how I'm going to live my life from now on." He served himself another drink and drank a little bit from it.

Christine said, "No, Pedro, my answer is not the same. I have changed my mind, and I don't think you are too young for me anymore. And to be honest, I have been thinking a lot about you lately and how I have always liked you. I am willing to live my life with you and to raise this little baby together if that is what you really want."

Pedro picked up the wine bottle, looked at it, and said, "Then, I shouldn't be drinking since I have more important things to do." He gently pushed the bottle away, looked at Christine and the baby, then said, "Christine, we are going to be very happy together, and I promise you I will be a good husband and a good father to this little baby. I will always take care of you both." He stood up, walked slowly toward them, hugged Christine and kissed her gently on the cheek, and smiled. Then, he looked at the baby and caressed his head gently.

Christine looked at him and smiled back. "I know you will, Pedro, and if it is all right with you, I would like to live in our new house, your house until we leave this place."

Pedro's eyes opened wide and were full of emotion. He said, "You have said it right, Christine. It is our house from now on, and there will be no one who can disturb our happiness in there. I can assure you of that."

Lucia watched them and her eyes shone with happiness. She clapped her hands quietly and closed her eyes in excitement. She whispered to herself, "That is a real man." Then, with a bigger smile, she opened her eyes and looked up at the sky, and whispered, "Thank you, thank you, thank you. Everything is going to be all right after all, thank you."

Meanwhile, a couple of priests arrived and walked through the countess's estate. They asked Pablo, "Where is Doña Gabriela?" The boy pointed to the kitchen with his hand, and they walked toward the kitchen.

Marie was not far from there, looking at the beautiful garden and sunbathing, while waiting for her two daughters. She wanted to make sure everything was all right with each one of them.

As they entered the kitchen, one of the priests said, "Good afternoon, Sister Gabriela, we are going to travel to the south to work on the church evangelization mission, as you know already."

The other priest said, "One of the priests is sick and will not be able to accompany us on this mission as he had planned." He added, "Our trip cannot be canceled, and we remembered you had shown interest in accompanying us to one of these missions, so that is why we are here looking for you."

Gabriela said, "I am sorry about the sick priest, is he all right?"

The younger priest said, "He will be better in two or three weeks, after the chicken pox is all gone."

The older priest said, "The poor brother never got them as a child."

Gabriela said, "Poor Brother, I hope he feels better soon." She added, "My greatest dream is to go on an evangelization mission, as I have told you brothers many times before, but it is too soon for me. I still have to do my work here at the estate of my lady the countess. I will make that trip someday, but not yet. I am not ready as I have some pending business here."

The younger priest said, "That is a shame, Sister Gabriela, because there is one space and we thought you would be the perfect person to help us with the mission of the church."

The older priest said, "Dear Gabriela, look deep in your heart and ask the Lord what you must do to help his mission."

Doña Gabriela looked at him tenderly, and said, "I already did, and I know I have to wait some time." She added, "I am sorry, Brothers."

The older priest said, "I feel bad that one space is going to be wasted, so many more things that can be done with one more person to help."

Gabriela said, "I understand, Brother, and I am sorry for not being able to help you this time."

The younger priest said, "I wish we could find the right person to go with us on this important mission."

Marie, who was near them and had been listening to their conversation, approached them, and asked, "Good afternoon,

Brothers, what does this person you are looking for have to be able to do and how is she expected to help on this mission?"

The older priest said, "The missionary we are looking for is a person knowledgeable of the word of the Lord and with the faith and patience to teach it to others."

Marie's expression lightened, and she said, "Look no further, I am the missionary you are looking for." The priests looked at each other in disbelief.

Gabriela said, "My lady, your daughters will be looking for you soon, and they might not like you risking your valuable life on a dangerous mission like this." Both priests nodded their heads, agreeing with Doña Gabriela.

Marie smiled a soft smile and looked at Doña Gabriela and the two priests. Doña Gabriela said, "It is very good to see you smile again, my lady, I haven't seen you smile in a long time."

"Thank you, Gabriela, I know you care for us and you mean well all the time." She continued, "It is true that I was expecting to see my daughters today and make sure they are all right. However, I no longer have young children, and my daughters have a life of their own. It is only natural that I choose my own path as well, in this last season of my life."

Gabriela opened her eyes wide and held Marie's hand. "Are you sure? Going on this mission is what you really want, my lady?"

"I am sure, I want to put to good use the little time I have left."

"What are you saying, my lady? You are such an important, elegant, and fine lady. How could you be traveling with a bunch of priests who limit themselves to eat whatever they have? Whose only goal in mind is to preach the word of the Lord to the ones who don't know Him yet?"

Marie said, "We are all the same in the eyes of the Lord and teaching the word of the Lord to the needy will be good for them, and it will be good for me as well, to have a new life with a new dream to fulfill." She added, "I have always liked helping others and it will be good for my mind to keep it busy with this mission. It will give me new hopes and a new meaning."

Gabriela said, "But, my lady, have you thought of the great dangers you will encounter on this trip and all the bandoleros you will see? That is not a life for a fine lady like you."

"I will be fine, Gabriela, you will see." She looked at the priests, and asked, "What do you think, Brothers?"

The young priest said, "I think you will be very happy on this mission, and you don't even have to spend a cent on it as all the costs have already been covered by the church."

The older priest said, "You are the perfect candidate for this mission, Sister."

Marie asked, "Are there any requirements I need to cover to be able to accompany you on this mission?"

The old priest, smiled and said, "Sister Gabriela's job interview with you is good enough for this position."

The young priest said, "You are the new missionary we were missing. Welcome aboard, Sister."

The old priest said, "We will wait for you while you get a few changes of clothes for the trip."

Marie went into the house and in a hurry came back with a little suitcase filled with a few of her personal belongings. She and the priests said good-bye to Gabriela and left together, excited about their new mission. Gabriela could not believe her eyes and followed after them. "My lady, wait, what am I going to say to Miss Christine and to my lady the countess when they come back and ask for their mother?"

Marie smiled and held Gabriela's arm. "Do not worry, Gabriela, just tell them the truth, that I love them and I wish them to be happy, that I have left to fulfill my wish of helping others, and to help the missionaries spread the word of the Lord through the world."

Marie's words helped Gabriela feel calmer, and she said, "Good luck, my lady, I am sure your daughters will understand. I will catch up to you in the future!"

Marie hugged Gabriela, and said, "Thank you, Gabriela. I know you will, see you then."

As Marie was leaving with the priests, she saw Christine with the baby in her arms and Pedro at her side. They were entering the countess's estate. Marie went to explain to Christine her new plans. "Christine, Daughter, I have told you about my dreams of going to see the world on a mission to teach the word of the Lord." Christine looked at her mother. Marie added, "Today is the day I am beginning my mission with these priests and other people who are waiting for us." They hugged.

Christine looked at the woman who took good care of her after her biological mother died when she was a child. She had many good memories of Marie from her childhood. Christine tenderly looked at Marie, and said, "Mother, you have been very good to me all the time. You took very good care of me after my birth mother died, and I do not want you to leave like this, please come to live with us in Pedro's house." She looked at Marie while holding the baby in her arms. "When the baby is a little older, we will move to a new town where we all will be happy together, but for now, please Mother, come and live with us at Pedro's house."

Pedro said, "It is your house too, Christine."

Marie looked at Pedro, and then at Christine, and smiled. "I am afraid I cannot, Christine, but I am very happy for you."

Pedro asked, "Ms. Marie, can you stay with us at least for our wedding?"

Marie said, "I already gave my word and accepted to go on this mission to teach the word of the Lord, and I cannot wait any longer, but know that you have my blessing and that I wish you two the best." She held Christine's hand, and added, "Leave this place as soon as you can, find a new place as you have in mind, and be happy. Do not look back, nor look further for me as I will also be happy helping others and making this world a little bit better for everyone."

Christine said, "How will Andrea know about you leaving on this mission?"

"Do not worry, my child. Gabriela will tell her, and I left her a letter in my room explaining it to her." Marie added, "I would have loved telling her in person like I am telling you, but she has been very busy with her projects lately. The good thing is none of you need me anymore, you are already grown and capable of living your own lives without me."

Christine hugged Marie, and said, "Thank you for everything you have done for us, Mother, you have always been a good mother."

Marie hugged Christine, and said, "Thank you, Christine, and you have always been the daughter anyone could ever wish for, thank you for that, but now live your own life and be happy with the husband and the child the Lord has sent you."

Christine looked at Marie with a smile and tearful eyes, and said, "Thank you, Mother." She offered an arm to hug Pedro also.

He hugged them, and said, "Thank you for your blessing, my lady Marie. I will take care of Christine and our baby."

Marie said, "I know you will, Pedro."

They said their last good-byes to each other. Marie left in the direction of the two priests. Christine left in the opposite direction with the baby in her arms and Pedro at her side, his arm wrapped around her. All of them left feeling a great peace of mind and with a beautiful new dream in their hearts.

The Other Side

The butler tried to help the Countess of Stonemason recover consciousness, but her physical body was still unresponsive.

What is that light? It is so bright. It is very beautiful. I want to be there. I know there is something amazingly good there, and I want to be there. I feel a very good feeling. A feeling I have not felt for a long time, but it is a wonderful feeling. I remember this wonderful feeling from my childhood. I felt something closer to this a few times in my life. It is the happiness I could never find as an adult. It is over there on that marvelous, beautiful, stunning light. I can feel that light is the source of all good things. I also feel something else. I can feel something great, something glorious, but I cannot explain what it is. It is a feeling so benevolent and so strong as I have never felt before. It might be love, a love like I have never felt before in my life. Yes, I know someone on that side loves me profoundly. I can feel it. The greatest love and happiness that I never knew existed for me are on that side, and I want to be there. I see my mother is there and she looks profoundly peaceful and happy. She is not worried anymore like I used to see her all the time when she was with me. When did Mother go there? I was so busy with my own things all the time that I even missed my own mother's departure. Some of my employees are there too. I would like to be there in the midst of that happiness with all of them, but I do not feel happy anymore. I feel very uncomfortable. Why does it not feel good to go in there?

Something is pulling me away from the light, and I do not like it either. No, do not take me away from happiness, now that I have found it. I want happiness. Mother help me! I yell to my mother for help again. Heeeelp me, please, I want to be there with you! Do not let them take me away. My mother cannot see me or hear me, but I see she is thinking of me. She smiles when she sees me as a young girl in her memories, but then when she sees me as I have been all my life, as I am now, her face becomes sad and I can feel her great anguish for not being able to do anything to help me. She always had the will to help me, but my will to not listen to her was stronger. Now, it is too late to fix things. I should have listened to my mother who wanted to set me back on the right path when there was still time. I feel extreme sadness like I have never felt before. I feel the greatest shame like I never thought I could ever feel for causing so much suffering to my mother. She was not as dumb as I always thought she was. She only taught me good things. She taught me to love and follow our Creator, and instead I followed something else. My mother was right. She was bright, but I never saw it. I confused her pure heart with low intelligence, but I was wrong, and I can see it now. She wanted to save my soul when I thought only money, power, and physical beauty existed.

She wanted to teach me about this side, but I mocked her many times assuring that only what I could see and touch was real.

Now I do not know what to do, being here I realize now that all of my money, power, and physical beauty were only temporary things to enjoy and use for good while on this earth, but I was never able to comprehend this myself. No matter how many different people explained it to me numerous times before, I never accepted any of this. I was not a believer of the other side, and still I am here today crying and feeling sorry for myself and for the sinful life I chose to live. I want to cry but I cannot. Nevertheless, my sadness is much greater than when I was able to cry with my physical eyes.

Something is still pulling me downward and away from the light and from my mother. I do not understand what is happening. Mother, help me! Do not let them take me away from the light! Please, Mother, come and help me!

Nothing happens.

I am still falling down at great speed. If I could at least ask my mother for forgiveness and tell her that I love her, and that I know that she was right and not dumb as I implied to her many times. This abyss in which I am falling must be more profound than any ocean as I have been falling for so long and I am still falling. I am very scared of what is coming to me! Mother, please, do something to help me, you always know what to do to save me. Motheeeer, what is stopping you from helping me? Pleeeeeaaase, Mother! Heeeeelp me, Mother! Save meee, please come to rescue me!

Everything is silent and now I am far away from Mother. She cannot hear me, regardless of how desperate or loud I scream. I am afraid. Actually, I feel terrified, and this other terrible feeling I have is a great discomfort. Oh, I feel great shame for my sins. All the poor boys I hurt. They were very young. I was terribly wrong.

How could I do such horrible things? What was I thinking? That was very nasty and absolutely unacceptable! Why did I do such dreadful things? Who am I fooling?

I know why. I was blind with hate, and I always fed my awful urge to control everything and everyone in my life. I was always controlling everything, everyone, and for what? To satisfy my most vile desires that never ceased. The more I fed these offensive desires, the more I wanted to do harm. I was evil, and evil cannot be in the light, but I could not understand back then. I understand now, all the damage I have caused to the many people who have crossed my path.

This is why my grandmother wanted me to follow the right path. She knew this was going to happen to me, and she even tried to prevent it. And my dear Myles loved me with all his heart. Even though I loved him for some time, I did not care for him and I threw his love and dreams away without compassion. And my caring sister who grew up by my side, who played with me, cared for me, and always loved and respected me. She loved me more than money or any position of power. She loved me and accepted me with all of my defects. And I did not understand or appreciate her love. I knew Christine was in love and wanted to marry. She wanted to share her life with her fiancé, and what did I do? I ruined it for her. I broke her heart, and I drove her true love away from her. All to satisfy my own ego, vanity, jealousy, and most of all, my hate for everything good. I could not stand seeing her so happy with a life that I never thought could make me happy. I had to be so selfish and wicked with my sweet sister, Christine, who loved me very much and never wronged me. And my mother always saw me and my improper ways. My mother always loved me unconditionally, but she could not convince me to change my life for the better. Money, power, and physical beauty was everything I could see and the only things I appreciated throughout my whole life. I was wrong. I was very wrong! I want forgiveness! I want to beg everyone for forgiveness.

And my father who loved me, he was like me and thought happiness was in the physical, temporary things. I do not want the things my father on Earth taught me. I do not want those things anymore. I want to learn from my Father in Heaven, the one who created me and created everyone. Please forgive me, Heavenly Father! I now understand you are the only eternally powerful, knowledgeable, and merciful owner of the universe. Please, Father, forgive me. I do not want bad things in my life anymore. I want to do only good things with the money and power you gave me, I want to use it all for the good of the world you created for us. I will not sin anymore if you give me another chance to better myself. I will be truthful with myself and others from now on.

What is happening? I am not falling anymore, and I am at the bottom of some place. Where am I? It is so cold in here I can barely move. How can I feel so heavy and the worst cold I have ever felt without my physical body? Oooh, and what is that horrible, putrefied smell? I cannot take it anymore. I am leaving.

What is happening? As I continue advancing the temperature changes drastically from freezing cold to scorching heat. I am burning, everything is in flames. I cannot handle this much pain. What are all those creatures? They are exceedingly strong, mad, and scary. They are dangerous monsters. I can see the hate in their eyes. The same hate I felt so many times when I was alive. I can relate to them, and their demonic feelings. They do not need to talk for me to understand how they feel. All of them have immense hate, but that is not all they feel. Some of them feel envious. Some feel controlling. Some feel addicted to the pain and suffering of others. I cannot yell with my physical throat, but all my thoughts can be heard by everybody around me. But I do not feel like them at this moment, and I do not want those feelings anymore. I do not want to hurt anyone. I want love.

Lord, please forgive me! I know why I am here. I am like them, but they are much worse than me. Their hate and their pain are much greater than mine. I reject all the hate and negative feelings. I do not want them anymore. I understand how they feel, but I do not feel like them anymore. I could identify with them in the past, but not presently. I am not like them, please take me away from them. I can change. I want to change. I can be better than this, please Lord, forgive me and give me the opportunity to change. I ask for your forgiveness, I was so wrong. Please forgive me and help me, Lord, please. Oh, their loneliness is terrible, I can feel it too. I do not want to feel their loneliness. I do not want to feel their feelings. I do not want to be part of this. Noooooo, I do not want to be here! I do not want to be alone with them. I do not want to be like them. I want forgiveness, please forgive me.

I can be better than this, please I want an opportunity. I want to go back to my life and do good. I want to be alive and live a good life, please let me go back and do good. I can be good, please help me. I can do it all over again and I will be able to go through problems and tribulations in a good way. I want to do good, and from now on I will resist the bad urges.

I want to go back to when I was young. I want to fulfill my dream of love and marry Myles when he did not like drinking. I want to have a son or a daughter with him and teach them how to live a good life with the Lord. I do not want Myles to cry for me and die an alcoholic. I want to tell him that I liked him too, and that I also loved him, a little. But now, I can love him more for he is good. I mean he was good, and he loved me very much. I want to live again and do everything right. I know what I must do now.

Or I could marry the innocent Friar Peter and be happy with him, instead of leaving him alone and without his vocation and dream life at the church. We could have adopted a child, or even taken care of all the abandoned children. We could have provided a home for all of them, teaching them to be good, and we could have lived a happy life together.

Or I could have married the macho captain and after I trained him to be gentle and nice, we could have lived a good life together. Even if I could just have married the chubby duke who wanted to give me everything I wanted all the time, and I did not care for him because he was older than I was. We could have been both plump and happy together doing good deeds. That could have been a good life too.

Even if I stayed all alone like my mother, I could still help the most vulnerable people like she always used to do, and that could have been a good life too. If only I could go back and live my life again. I could do so many things vastly different than the way I did. I want another chance. I want to live my life the way I should have lived it. I want to do good with all my money and power, but now that is not mine either. The only things I cared for during my life are not important here and I still lost them. I have nothing. I never cared for the things I should have cared for on Earth. I have no one good or close to me to tell them how I feel. All I want now is forgiveness. I want forgiveness. I need forgiveness more than all the material things I loved so much during my life on Earth. It does not matter anymore what possessions I had in life.

I understand now that everything belongs to the Lord. He blessed me with so much and I did not do any good with it. I did not see the opportunity I had to do good in the world and I did not do it when I had the time to do it. I want to be alive and do good. I want to be good to others. I am not going to follow the bad feelings anymore. I do not want them. I do not accept them anymore. I want everything that comes from the Lord, and only that. I renounce all the bad feelings I felt and the wrong things I cherished in my worldly life. I want to follow my Creator and His will. I will not do harm to anyone anymore if you give me another opportunity in life. I will be good. I want to be good. I will resist the bad feelings, and I will do good things only from now on. I do not want to feel all powerful and use it to harm others around me, no, not anymore. I now know the only and most powerful being is my Creator, the Creator of the universe.

Please, Heavenly Father, give me an opportunity to ask for forgiveness to all the people who I have hurt on Earth. Please, give me an opportunity to do something good with all the many material things you gave me there. I promise you that I will be a good administrator of your riches if you give me another opportunity to go back and fix my mistakes. I am being honest this time, believe me, please Lord, try me and you will see I am speaking the truth. I am ready to fix all my mistakes, allow me to fix them, please, let me go back to my life on Earth to ask for forgiveness.

Brilliant golden rays of light warmed her face.

CHAPTER TWELVE

REPENTANCE

"Oh, that nice, warm, bright yellow light. Where am I?" The countess whispered weakly with her eyes still closed while her employees looked at her, puzzled.

Surprised, the girl yelled, "She is alive, the countess is alive!"

The countess whispered so low that they could not understand what she was saying. "I need to reconcile with the Lord, whom I have forgotten for so long." She continued whispering faintly and desperately. "He can wipe my soul clean. I want to have a relationship with Him before I leave this world forever."

Her employees continued to look at her, but they could not understand what she was saying for her voice was so low and weak. She took a deep breath and raised her whispers as much as she could for her employees to hear her, and asked, "Where, am, I?" Feeling weak, she opened her eyes.

"We are taking you to the doctor," said the girl.

"We thought you were dead!" said the boy.

The countess said, "No, I do not have much time. I feel very weak and sick. I do not know for how long my soul will be here in my body. Get me the priest to confess and redeem me."

The boy looked at the countess, and asked, "Which confessor would you like? There is a very important bishop visiting from Spain, would you like him to come and see you?"

The countess recovered some of her strength, and answered, "No, not that bishop, I think I know who he is. We are mad at each other, and he might not want to see me. Anyway, he is arrogant and sinful. That will do me no good."

The girl asked, "What about the humble priest from the town nearby?"

The countess asked weakly, "Is he well-known? Because I have never heard of him. I do not think he is well-known. It is not that I think he is such a low-class individual or that he is such an insignificant being compared to me, no, but he is not knowledgeable enough to become my confessor. I want someone wise who can understand how I feel."

Everybody was quiet and serious. The boy said, "There is a priest who is visiting from Acámbaro. He is wise and humble."

The girl added, "That's Reverend Chava, but he might not be well-known because he has only been in charge of monasteries and all the big churches in the small town of Acámbaro."

The boy agreed. "My parents and many people say he is a nice and wise reverend, but I don't think he has ever been to the fancy churches where the aristocrats visit in the downtown of the New Spain."

The Countess of Stonemason opened her eyes wide, and asked, "Reverend Chava from Acámbaro is here?" That name, Reverend Chava, brought the Countess of Stonemason many memories. The countess thought for a few seconds, and said, "Bring me Reverend Chava. He sure is a good, knowledgeable, and humble man. I want Reverend Chava to be my confessor but hurry up so I can see him on time before I leave forever."

The girl looked at her brother, then looked at the countess, and said, "He can go get the priest and I will get you the medicine woman who cures with herbs and plants."

The countess was in agony. She was extremely weak and felt a profound pain in her soul. "No, no, there is not sufficient time to get both, and I do not want to be alone. You two young and innocent ones stay with me, and let the riders go fetch my confessor."

The butler, who was unusually quiet, looked at the children and the countess with wide eyes, and said, "Good idea, my lady, and I will get the medicine woman."

Each one of the two riders got a horse from the carriage and rushed off. They galloped away to find the priest. The butler started running, but it was too much for him, so he walked as fast as he could. The young girl fixed the countess's hair gently, and said, "Don't be afraid, I will take care of you."

The weak and sad countess said, "You do not understand, young girl. I have seen it. The other world, the one I never believed in, oh, but it is a reality. I wasted all my life in mundane things without paying attention to my soul. I manipulated everything and everyone for my own earthly desires and now that it is time for me to go, I am not ready. I have done nothing for my soul. I have a long list of sins—horrible, terrible sins—

that make me feel disgusted and ashamed of myself. Nobody told me there was life after death, or if somebody told me, I never paid any attention to them. But it is not my fault, how could I believe in something I have never seen before?" She was soaked in sweat. "But now, now is different. I have seen it. I have seen and felt the other world and it is extremely beautiful for some, but it is horrific and terrifying for the ones who lived like me, always in sin without caring, and harming others." She felt so agitated. "I repent of all my sins. I repent of every wicked thing I did here on Earth and all the wrong I have caused to others."

The countess became quiet and closed her eyes. The girl looked at her, frightened. The countess held the girl's hand weakly, and said, "Please, stay with me, do not leave me alone."

The girl answered, "I'm here with you, please don't die." The girl started nervously whispering to herself, "What am I going to do? I have never seen a person die and I have never been alone with a dead person, oh this is bad, this is sooo bad, this is sooo horrible."

The young boy looked at them from outside the carriage and covered his eyes with both hands. Then, the countess moaned and closed her eyes. The horrified girl held her hand and touched the countess's wrist, looking for a sign of life. She whispered, "Her hands are so cold. Did she faint or has she died?" The girl's eyes were wide and her mouth was agape. She closed her mouth, swallowed her saliva, and shook her head, trying to get rid of her fear. Then, trying to convince herself, she said, "She is not going to die, she is kind of young, well maybe not young but not very, very, very old either, and she is rich, very, very, very rich."

The boy looked at them, and asked, "You think rich people don't die?"

"No, no, that's not what I mean. I know everybody dies someday, but rich people don't die like this, or do they?"

The boy looked at them quietly.

The girl said, "I don't know, I guess not."

The boy, wide-eyed and in a serious tone of voice, said, "Rich or poor, when it is their time to die, they die."

The girl whispered, "Do you think this is the countess's time to die?"

The boy shrugged his shoulders and looked at them quietly with watery eyes.

The girl continued talking but then looked away from her brother. She looked up at the sky, and said, "Please don't let her die here, alone, with me, let her see the priest and allow her to confess what her soul needs, to find peace." She started praying the Lord's prayer in a low voice.

Andrea woke up, and said, "Listen, girl, and you, boy, both of you. I want to be taken to my house down the river for the final arrangements." She added, "Remember to let the priest know that I want to go to my house down the river, where my sister and my faithful housekeeper, Gabriela, are."

After some minutes, the priest came without the riders. The girl happily looked at the priest, and said, "Reverend Chava, I am so glad to see you! It is so good that the riders were able to get you!"

Reverend Chava said, "No, it was the butler who asked me to come see her, but he could not make it back. He did a supernatural effort to get the medicine woman, but she wasn't home. As soon as he found me, he had to stop and stay there to catch his breath. Also, he asked some gentlemen to find the medicine woman. I hope they can bring her soon."

The girl looked at Reverend Chava, and said, "The countess did not have a pulse, and was getting very cold and pale. We thought she was dead." The girl, scared, continued looking at the reverend, and said, "Then, after a little while she opened her eyes. Reverend Chava, she has been in the other world where the spirits go after death."

The boy added, "She is desperate and very frightened."

The girl asked, "How is that possible, Reverend Chava?"

The reverend looked at the girl with gentle eyes. Then, he looked at the sky, and calmly said, "Don't worry, my children, He knows it all and the reason why everything happens."

The girl became insistent, and said, "Tell me, Reverend Chava, you know what happened to her, tell me please."

The reverend calmly answered, "You have faith, little sister, you don't need me to explain what you can feel."

With wide eyes, the young boy said, "And the Countess wants to be taken to her house down the river, where Doña Gabriela is in charge, when she dies."

The girl stood quietly looking at the reverend and the countess. Then, they heard a deep growl. Reverend Chava looked at the boy, and said, "There is a big cat out there, come here with us, son."

The boy jumped into the carriage where his sister and the countess were, and said, "A mountain lion!"

Reverend Chava got inside the carriage, too, and left the carriage's door open. "That's what I meant, if you see it getting closer to us, let me know." The children looked out the window and at each other quietly. Reverend Chava pointed to the open carriage door, and added, "The countess needs some air, it's going to stay open."

The countess opened her eyes slowly, then said, "Reverend, you are here."

Reverend Chava looked at the countess, and asked, "How do you feel, Countess of Stonemason?"

In a weak, desperate voice, the countess replied, "Reverend Chava, I have seen the spirit world where no one can come back from. I have been there. I have seen it and I came back to tell you how it is. I am sorry for everything I have done. I repent of my sins and all the pain I have caused the young men I hurt and their families. I do not know how I could have done such atrocities? What was I thinking?"

The reverend replied, "God can forgive it all, but for your repentance to be valid, it needs to be sincere. You have to apologize to the young men you have wronged first and never do it again." He added, "Also, you have to fix the damage you have caused them to the best of your abilities."

The countess shook her head slowly feeling melancholic, and said, "That is not possible. They are not in this world anymore. They lost their precious, young, innocent lives. I took them without hesitation. I was very sad, and very angry, and very lonely, with so much resentment and hate in my heart during those days that I could not think clearly. I was feeling such deep pain, and I wanted them to feel it too. I was wrong. I let the pain blind me, and I stopped seeing the good things I had in my life. I took everything for granted, but I did not think that the end of my life was coming this soon. I repent of all these disgusting sins."

The reverend said, "Then, it is still necessary to fix the damage to the best of your means and abilities."

"I know the harm I have caused, and I want to repair it."

"Let's see, were the boys your employees? Indigenous people?"

"Many of them, most were."

"You need to indemnify their families and make new schools for indigenous children so they can be educated and have better opportunities in their lives."

The countess said, "Yes, Reverend, I will do that." She took a document out of her bosom and gave it to him, saying, "These are the exact places where you can find many of my valuable treasures, including lots and lots of gold plates, silver glasses, jade statues, and many other valuables. Use all of them to repair all the damage I have caused and to bring new good things to the young ones who have been serving me and are still alive. On the back of this map, I wrote where you can find the boys I cruelly took away from their loved ones, make sure they receive the holy sacraments and be placed in holy soil where their bodies can rest in peace."

In a calm voice, the reverend said, "My lady, you understand that in those places, churches must be built for the eternal rest of all these unfortunate souls who lost their lives there, and where their loved ones can go and pray for their souls."

The countess promptly answered, "Yes, build all the churches you need to build to bring peace to their souls, and instead of sorrow and death, their mothers and all the people who visit the churches can find a place to pray and find hope." She added, "Make sure these churches are well-built with paintings of the other world so people can understand what is upon them, and maybe they will be less blind than I have been my whole existence. I hope they will find faith, the faith I never had until today. Make sure the angels in those paintings look like all the people who live here—the French, the Spanish, the African, the Oriental, the mestizos, and do not forget the indigenous people of this beautiful land that I love. Listen to me, Reverend, remember the indigenous people of this kind and warm land, the New Spain. I have seen the paintings with the angels who are blond and with blue eyes, but not all angels look like that. The angels in the paintings must come with all the real faces living in the New Spain. It is not their appearance that made them angels but the kindness of their hearts."

She added, "I want everyone to have the opportunity to redeem themselves before it is too late. I want the children to learn about this, too, since they are young so they can have a better opportunity to live a good life. I want you to make orphanages to take care of the lonely children who do not have any parents to take care of them, to teach them that they have a Heavenly Father who loves them."

"Also, remember to build a school to educate all the women who want to change their lives for the better instead of always depending on a man."

She panted. "Hospitals, build hospitals for the sick!"

The countess looked up to the sky and with a heavy burden over her heart, she said, "Heavenly Father, forgive me for I have sinned. Reverend, please ask him to forgive me. I repent of all my sins. I repent for believing I was the most important being in the world. How could I have believed the riches were mine to do as I pleased, to do terrible things with them, when in reality He is the only owner and the creator of everything in the universe. I was chosen to be the administrator of some of His riches in this world, and I failed at it. I did not use them for the greater good of His creation. I have many other terrible sins, but none of them as horrible as these I have confessed to you already. I do not have the strength to confess all of them as they are too numerous to mention, and I am afraid I do not have enough time, either, for such a long confession."

Her face was sad, her body was weak, and she spoke with great regret when she said, "I now know I was wrong, He is the most important one, please ask Him to forgive me. But, how can He forgive me, after all the evil things that I have done? I would not forgive me if I were Him. Nobody could stop me from doing wrong, and I never knew how to do good things in my life, nor how to listen and follow the tiny whispers of the good feelings in my heart. No, I always had to resist any affectionate feelings, but it was too easy for me to follow the wrong sentiments of my heart. Now I feel desperate to confess everything I can. How can I die in peace carrying all these heavy sins in my soul?"

She took a deep breath trying to maintain the little strength she had, but there was not much left. She said, "I ask for forgiveness, and I will fix at least some of my numerous horrible mistakes before traveling to the next world." Her speech slowed, but still in desperation, with the little strength left in her body she said, "I ask for forgiveness."

The reverend put the saint oils on her head and forehead. He prayed, and said, "May God forgive all your sins in the name of the Father, the Son, and the Holy Spirit, amen."

She had left her physical body already. A warm breeze blew gently, and the birds sang different melodious songs, all of them in different and enchanting notes. The various floral aromas from the colorful, beautiful, and blooming flowers filled the air. The sun warmed everything and everyone around, except for the countess. Not even the shining sun from the New Spain that she loved so much could warm her being anymore.

The countess's hand, with which she was touching the reverend, fell to her side. He closed her terrified eyes gently and fixed her hands on her chest, then said, "Already very cold."

The boy, with panic on his face and eyes wide, looked at the reverend, and asked, "Is she dead?"

The reverend nodded, and said, "Only to this world."

The girl asked, "Is she in Heaven?"

In a low voice, the reverend answered, "Only the Lord can answer that question, my child."

This is how the earthly life of the Countess of Stonemason came to an end on a beautiful, flower-scented, warm day of spring in the New Spain. Bunnies hopped around and the butterflies danced gracefully with the wind. The golden bees visited the flowers all around, and the ants marched on their great parade. A tiny white butterfly posed on the boy's hand and the girl looked at him quietly. More tiny white butterflies flew around the two innocent children. They both looked at the tiny butterfly on the boy's hand, as it slowly flapped its wings. The boy stood still and watched the butterfly with curiosity and content. Then, the girl raised her eyes to see all the tiny white butterflies gracefully dance around them. The boy raised his eyes to see their gracious and tiny little friends. The two children looked at each other in amazement. Their heavy, frightened, and sad moods lightened. They wiped the tears from their faces and faithfully smiled at each other.

CHAPTER THIRTEEN

The Agreement

Reverend Chava looked at the two kids, and gently said, "Let's go, my children, we have many important things to do, and the sooner we do them, the better." In his hand he held the countess's final will and the map where all her most valuable possessions were located. Reverend Chava held those papers tight and close to his chest. He knew that in those documents was the power to help many, and the potential to fulfill her last wishes.

The children and the reverend were quiet. The boy looked at his sister, and asked, "What are we going to do?"

The girl looked at the reverend, and asked, "What are we going to do?"

Reverend Chava put the will in his satchel. Then, he looked at the kids, and said, "First, we have to take the countess to her family." He looked at the two kids, and asked, "Do you know where she lives?"

"Yes, we can take you there," said the boy.

"But we do not know where her family is," said the girl. She added, "My mother said her family lives far away from here."

Reverend Chava said, "Then, we are going to take her to her house, and somebody there will know where we can find her family."

The boy asked, "Reverend Chava, we don't want to be with the dead countess by ourselves, can we sit in the front up there with you?" Both the boy and the girl looked at Reverend Chava hoping to sit next to him.

He nodded, and said, "Of course, my children, sit wherever you feel comfortable, you have been very brave today."

Both kids sighed in relief, and said, "Thank you, Reverend Chava." The three of them rode on the front of the carriage. They watched the horses and the landscape while her cold and pale body lay inside the carriage. They rode slowly to her house down the river. The three of them were quiet for a long time.

After a few hours that seemed like an eternity, they got to their destination. Gabriela was at the gardens by the entrance of the house. She was picking mint and some cilantro from the gardens. Reverend Chava said, "Good morning, I am bringing the countess home, is this it?"

Doña Gabriela replied, "Good morning, Reverend, this is one of her estates, and yes this is one of her homes." She asked, "Where is she?"

Reverend Chava replied, "She is inside the carriage, but there is something I have to tell you." He stepped down off the carriage and approached Doña Gabriela.

She walked toward him, and asked, "Is my lady the countess all right, Reverend?"

Reverend Chava stood in front of Doña Gabriela and held his hands together in front of his chest, and said, "Wait, do not go in there yet, let me finish telling you what I need you to know."

Surprised, Doña Gabriela opened her eyes wide, and asked, "What has happened to my lady the countess, Reverend, is she all right?"

He looked up at the sky with an expression of doubt, nodded his head, held his hands one over the other, and said, "Well."

The boy said, "She might be in Heaven."

The girl looked up at the sky, and added, "If the Lord forgave her." The girl made the sign of the cross with her hand and kissed it twice, still looking at the sky with a peaceful expression. The boy looked at her and did the same, but he did it three times.

Doña Gabriela walked to the carriage at a moderate speed, opened it, and saw the countess. She looked at the children and the reverend. Then, she looked at the countess again and with a calm but worried expression, said, "She is so pale, she has never been pale before, her face has always been rosy, even in her worst moments." Doña Gabriela continued looking at the countess lying there inside the carriage, and asked, "What happened to you, dear? You have always been very energetic and powerful, and now you look so fragile and defenseless." Doña Gabriela got closer to the countess and touched her forehead. Then she held her hand in hers and looked at Reverend Chava, and said, "She is so cold."

Doña Gabriela was calm and able to manage her feelings, but she could not avoid the tears that rolled down her cheeks.

She wiped her face with her shawl, and asked, "What happened to my lady the countess, Reverend? Do not be afraid to tell me the truth. I am prepared to hear it, just tell me the truth, Reverend, please."

The boy said, "She got sick."

The girl added, "And then she got worse and died for some minutes and she went to visit the other world and she was telling us all about it."

The boy's face showed worry and fright as they told her about the countess's death. Reverend Chava interrupted the girl to say, "You don't need to give all the details now, little Sister."

Gabriela's face turned pale and with a serious, worried expression, she asked, "Did she make it? Is she…alive?"

Reverend Chava opened his hands. He opened his arms wide and moved his shoulders back. He looked up at the sky with an assurance that there was hope for the next life. The girl and boy shook their heads. The boy wagged his finger.

Doña Gabriela looked tenderly at the lifeless body, and said, "How are you, my lady?" She caressed Andrea's face, and said, "Still so pretty." Then, she caressed her arm and hand, then her face again, and asked, "Why did this happen to you so abruptly?" She continued, "You were tireless and full of life, why did you leave us like this?"

Reverend Chava looked at Doña Gabriela attentively and tried to console her. "Sister, the time of departure can take a long time for some, giving us the opportunity to say good-bye to our loved ones, but other times we might leave roughly and without notice." He continued, "That is out of our control, and this is why we have to prepare ourselves every day for when this moment comes, leaving everything ready and finishing our work here on Earth before we leave."

Gabriela wiped her tears with her shawl again, then said, "Yes, Reverend, I already knew all of this, but I do not know why I forget it sometimes. Maybe I thought that it would not happen to her, at least not this soon."

Reverend Chava said, "It would be better to live each day as if it was our last one on Earth, hoping that when the day comes, we don't have too many regrets at the end of our journey." He added, "I know, it is easier said than done, but we have to try."

Doña Gabriela said, "Yes, Reverend, from now on I will live every day as if it was my last day, without excuses. I want to be ready when the day comes."

The boy added, "And be good so you won't die so desperate and afraid of the other world like the Countess of Stonemason."

The girl said, "And don't sin too much, and if you do sin, make sure your sins are not too horrible and not too many so you can have enough time to confess them all at once and make amends before you die."

The boy added, "And the people around you don't have to worry about where you went after you are gone."

Reverend Chava signaled for the youngsters to stop talking, but it was in vain for they had to let it all out. He looked tenderly at Doña Gabriela, and said, "Forgive them, Sister, they are very young and naturally impressed by this shocking event."

"I know you are right, Reverend, they don't mean any harm, these poor little ones witnessed my lady the countess's last moments. It is very sad." She continued, "Reverend, please, all of you come with me so I can give you some bread."

Reverend Chava nodded his head, and said, "Thank you, Sister, a piece of bread would be nice to swallow the bitterness these little ones must have in their mouths."

The boy carefully closed the door of the carriage where the countess began her eternal dream, and he shook his head rapidly and wiped his face with both of his hands, trying to forget it all.

Reverend Chava looked at Doña Gabriela, and asked, "Who are we going to tell first about the countess's departure?"

Gabriela said, "We can begin by telling all of her employees, then send a messenger to find her mother who is on a mission with the Jesuits, and then send another messenger to let her sister, Christine, know, and finally send a messenger to let the important people of downtown in the New Spain know about this sad news." She added, "My lady had very dear friends in the New Spain and in the surroundings. Many of them were royalty, like her, and others were her teachers from many years ago. All of them were very good friends of hers. She always referred to them as her family. They were so very important to her, and she used to enjoy their company very much. She even respected them a lot more than her own mother, and I am sure my lady the countess would be delighted to have them attend her farewell ceremony. I will go with you to find the messengers." She stood next to the girl, looked at Reverend Chava, and said, "Reverend, please wait here while I talk to these young men."

Reverend Chava agreed with a nod of his head. Doña Gabriela looked at the young employees, and said, "Boys, something really sad has happened. Go and tell everyone that there is a meeting in the ballroom, and everyone must attend."

One of the boys asked, "What happened, Doña Gabriela?"

"We will tell you all together at the meeting, remember, in the ballroom."

The boys turned and ran off.

As they drove the carriage away, Reverend Chava said, "Doña Gabriela, before the countess passed away, she was very anxious about some mistakes she made during her life here in this world, and she wanted me to help make amends after her departure." He continued, "And that is what I am going to do to the best of my abilities, hoping her soul will find some peace."

"Reverend, let me know how I can be of service to you."

"I will, Sister, I will accept all the help I can get so we can finish these arrangements as soon as possible to fulfill the countess's last wishes." He added, "I would like to tell all of the employees about her last desires and how they can help if they would like to do it. Also, I would like to reorganize the labor duties to match the countess's expectations and be done with all the things she entrusted with me."

Gabriela said, "I can't wait to hear about all of my lady's last wishes."

The girl asked, "Reverend, you cannot say what the dying people's sins are, or can you?"

The boy replied, "He is not going to share the countess's sins, but he is going to do everything he can to try to fix them, remember?" The boy added, "But not even a priest can fix the countess's very bad sins."

Surprised, Doña Gabriela reprimanded the boy. "Son, you shouldn't talk like that about Reverend Chava, nor should you say those things about my lady the countess either."

Concerned, the boy asked, "What did I do? I am just telling the truth, right Reverend?"

Reverend Chava said, "Yes, you are, but it is better if none of you talk about the countess's confession, remember that it is supposed to be between the parishioner and the priest and no one else. This time was an exception as the countess was passing to the next world and it was not safe to leave you two children alone around there where we were." He added, "I didn't want to risk your lives with the mountain lions and other dangers in the region, not even for a confession." Reverend Chava's face turned more serious. "Anyway, please do not talk about this with anyone else, you can tell your parents, but no one else, as it was a confession."

Doña Gabriela said, "How are we going to stop two kids from saying everything they heard in a confession, Reverend?"

"There is no way to stop them, Sister. They are kids and are going to act their age, and we are going to be all right with that." He added, "We can just remind them to talk about it only with their parents and hope for the best."

Doña Gabriela said, "It is that house right there."

Reverend Chava stopped the horses as Doña Gabriela directed him. They entered the countess's house and sat around a small table to eat their bread. Gabriela said, "Eat up, little ones, this bread was made this morning, but it is still good to eat. You too, Reverend, eat while I prepare some hot cocoa for you to swallow your bread."

They sat around the small table, peacefully eating their bread and waiting for their drink when they heard a knock on the half closed door. Gabriela said, "Come in."

A tall, strong bishop entered the kitchen, and everybody stared at him. He asked, "Brother Chava, what has happened to the countess, where is she?"

Reverend Chava, still with bread in his mouth, tried to chew it quickly so he could speak to the bishop.

The boy said, "The countess passed on to the next world." And he made the sign of the cross.

The girl added, "And we are worried and very scared. That's why we are eating bread, so we won't get sick because of the big scare."

Gabriela said, "Eat your bread, children. Let Reverend Chava talk to the bishop." Gabriela kissed the bishop's hand, and asked, "What would you like to eat, Your Excellency?"

Surprised, the bishop replied, "The countess is dead!" He continued, "Where is she? What happened to her?"

Reverend Chava swallowed his bread, and said, "Your Excellency, unfortunately our dear countess's spirit has gone on to the next life." He continued, "Let me show you." He directed him to the carriage, and said, "Would you please help me carry her into the house?"

The bishop's eyes widened and in a higher voice, he asked, "Me? Carry her? Me?"

Reverend Chava said, "Well, I might be able to do it by myself, let me see if I can do it." He carefully hugged the countess and carried her gently. It was challenging for him, and he walked with great effort. The reverend was in his late forties with a slim figure. He carried the countess in his arms, and asked, "How can such a beautiful creature be this heavy?"

The robust bishop asked, "Why didn't you tell me she died?"

Reverend Chava continued carrying the countess with great effort.

The bishop asked, "When were you going to tell me?"

Reverend Chava kept quiet and placed the countess's body on an elegant couch. He covered her body with a fine blanket and carefully covered her face with a black veil she was wearing as a shawl. He gave his entire attention to the countess.

The bishop, trying to get the reverend's attention, said in a louder voice, "Reverend Chava, I am talking to you."

Reverend Chava calmly said, "Your Excellency, I was going to tell you as soon as I could send the message to the New Spain for her friends and family to come and say goodbye to her for the last time. Then, as soon as I returned, I was going to tell you."

Furious, the bishop said, "You have to tell me first, before anyone else, I am the one who must know first!"

Reverend Chava said, "Yes, Your Excellency, and that is what I was going to do, tell you as soon as possible. Now that you know already, I have to send a messenger to the New Spain with the bad news."

Calmer, the bishop said, "You don't need a messenger, I will be the one giving the message about the countess's departure in the New Spain. I was on my way there anyway." The bishop added, "You have to go back to the church immediately and continue with your responsibilities."

Reverend Chava looked at the bishop, and asked, "Your Excellency, who is going to stay here with the countess to take care of her until her holy burial?"

The bishop said, "All right, Reverend Chava, you are in charge of all of it until I come back." The bishop left.

Meanwhile in the kitchen, Doña Gabriela looked at the kids, and said, "I know you are young, but it is time you learned not to interfere in adult conversations unless one of the adults are talking to you." She continued, "When the adults are asking another person for anything, you should not answer a question that is not meant for you to answer."

The boy said, "Doña Gabriela, thank you for the bread, but we are growing and we need more food than this to be healthy."

The girl looked at Doña Gabriela, and added, "What do you have in those pots over there, it must be something really good, can we have some?"

Doña Gabriela sighed and smiled. "Yes, my children, today you can have anything you like. I have sweet pumpkin, black beans, tomato rice with vegetables, zucchini with fresh cheese, tomato sauce, fried hot peppers with onions, and the hot cocoa I am making you."

Excitedly, the two children said, "Sweet pumpkin, please."

Doña Gabriela served a small amount of sweet pumpkin to the kids. The boy gobbled the whole thing in the blink of an eye. The girl moved her pumpkin around her plate with a spoon. She tried it by tasting it with the tip of her tongue but did not take even one bite. She continued moving her food from one place on her plate to another. Gabriela said, "Very good, young man, you have finished the whole thing, would you like a little bit more?"

The boy replied, "Yes, please, this is delicious, better than my grandmother's."

Doña Gabriela said, "Don't you say that in front of your grandmother, please. I want no enemies over a sweet pumpkin dish." She looked at the girl, and asked, "What about you, young lady, you didn't like the sweet pumpkin?"

The young girl's expression was sad. "The pumpkin is good, Doña Gabriela, but I just can't swallow it, I don't know why I'm not hungry anymore."

Doña Gabriela sat next to her, made eye contact with her, and said, "Don't you worry, little one, tomorrow you will feel much better. Today has been a long day for everyone, especially for you two. I am going to find someone to take you both home."

The boy said, "We know how to get home."

"I would like for someone to accompany us home today," said the girl.

"I know you might be used to walking around by yourselves most of the time, and you know all the ways around here." Gabriela added, "But today is a special day, and you have experienced new things, and for that I want someone to take you home today." The children accepted by nodding their heads.

Reverend Chava entered the kitchen, and said, "Sister, the bishop is leaving for the New Spain, we will need no messenger after all. He will deliver the message there."

Gabriela took an embroidered napkin and filled it with bread. Then she put them in a small basket, poured hot cocoa in a big clay pot, and covered it with a clay cup. She quickly walked out to the bishop's carriage, and said, "Your Excellency, here is some bread for your trip and some hot cocoa."

The bishop took them, and said, "Thank you, Doña Gabriela, I will be back in a week if everything goes as planned."

Reverend Chava watched them from the kitchen doorway. Doña Gabriela waved good-bye and returned to the kitchen. "The bishop will be back in a week. It means he will travel day and night." She asked, "Reverend, would you like something to eat?"

He replied, "I don't want to bother you, Sister, you have been very kind to us, and even if I am hungry, it would not be very considerate of me to have something to eat at a moment like this."

Doña Gabriela said, "Say no more, Reverend Chava, I will be happy to feed you, the food has already been prepared, and it is important to nourish your body as well, not just your soul."

The boy said, "And it is delicious, try the sweet pumpkin."

Reverend Chava smiled at the boy, and said, "I will certainly try it after my meal."

The young girl sat still, quietly moving her pumpkin around her plate with a spoon. Reverend Chava touched her head, and asked, "What is wrong, child, you don't like your pumpkin?"

A young man entered the kitchen, and said, "The employees will go to the ballroom for the meeting, what time is it going to be?"

Gabriela looked at Reverend Chava, and said, "The meeting can start when everybody is at the ballroom, is everybody there?"

The young gentleman replied, "No, not yet. They're still coming from work."

Reverend Chava said, "Very well, I will be there soon, as soon as I finish eating Doña Gabriela's good food."

The young gentleman said, "I can see that most of the employees are now walking to the ballroom, they are still far away, but they should all be there in around ten minutes."

Reverend Chava said, "Thank you, young man, that is enough time for me to hurry up and finish eating. I will be there in no time to begin the meeting. Is there anything you want to tell me before I go there and talk to everybody?"

The boy said, "Most of the countess's employees are in the ballroom." He added, "The majority of them are sitting down, and a few of them are standing up or walking around anxiously waiting to hear the news."

Reverend Chava said, "I will be there soon." He continued eating in a hurry.

After a few minutes, he got up, walked to the ballroom, and said, "I am glad to see all of you here, and I want to thank you for coming. The purpose for this meeting is to let all of you know about the countess's last wishes. She made many mistakes when she was alive, but in the last moments of her life she had selfless thoughts about this community. She wanted to redeem herself, and she wanted to help all of you in different ways."

A young woman asked, "Reverend, you mean that the countess is not alive anymore?"

"That is exactly what I am telling you, Sister. She left this world today but not without thinking about all of you and the betterment of this community." He continued, "I want you to know that starting today, new buildings will be built. There will be new churches, new orphanages, a new hospital, new schools for the children, and schools for the adults as well. New employees will be needed for these projects, and if any of you are interested in participating, you will be welcomed to do so."

One young man asked, "You mean that you want us to come after work to do voluntary work for the church, Reverend?"

Reverend Chava looked at him, and replied, "Yes, every one of you is welcome to participate in this project, but it will not be as volunteers. You will be compensated for your work. You don't have to be the ones to do it as you already have a job, but I would like you to tell your friends and relatives about it so they can help us full time with this big important project, as it is in everyone's best interest to finish it as soon as possible." He paused and looked at all the people. They started to talk amongst each other.

A young woman looked at her two friends, and said, "This is very good, constructing new and good places for the betterment of our community."

A young man looked at the people around him, and said, "I am interested in helping after work since they are going to pay us."

A young woman asked, "Reverend, where is the countess?"

Reverend Chava replied, "Her body is inside the house, and it will be prepared for the funeral." He continued, "In a couple of hours, she will be ready for all of you who would like to visit and say your last good-byes to her."

Meanwhile Doña Gabriela and seven teenage girls washed and prepared the countess's body for her funeral. They looked through her beautiful clothes to find something for the countess to wear for her unplanned and special occasion. Finally, she was all clean and dressed up. She wore a long, shiny, black skirt. It was embroidered with string made of real gold. The patterns on the skirt were as golden and as curly as her hair was. Her blouse was black and embroidered with real gold strings as well. The sleeves and neck ended in a silver embroidered pattern, and from the shoulders fell a triangular black-and-silver shawl ending at the back of her waist. These were the most fine and modern clothes anyone had ever seen around this place at the time. Her elegant clothes were all imported from France. A transparent, silver veil embroidered in a floral pattern with real gold string covered her head, and her golden curls fell out of the veil.

She lay there, still. It was unbelievable to think that she was not alive anymore. She seemed to be asleep. For the first time since she passed away, she was ready for viewing, but her most trusted friends were not around, and neither were her ostentatious royal comrades with whom she had shared many adventures. Not even her family was there to cry for her like they had many times before. Her employees sat around her and prayed for her soul. Most of them were adolescents who had learned to be responsible early in life. Their families were also there and other people from the community who came to support the famous, beautiful, elegant, and lifeless countess. They all prayed for her, and one by one went to the front of the ballroom to see her. Some of them had flowers in their hands. One by one they looked at her up close and said good-bye. They put the flowers on the table next to her body. They lined up to pray for her soul.

Many people visited her to say good-bye. Some of them with so much love and compassion in their hearts to offer her, even though they did not know her very well. They felt sorry for her early departure. One by one her visitors said good-bye to her and left at least one flower next to her. A lonely mother came to her with a giant white flower in her hands. She whispered, "I know you are not a mother, but I still plead to the maternal feelings inside of you, please give me back my son wherever you have him. Free him and send him back to me, now that he is of no use to you anymore." She added, "The last time he was seen, he was with you. Please, send my son back home. Release him from wherever you have him, let him come back to me, to his family. I will not judge you or ask you why you kept him away from me for so long, if you return my son to me." She continued to cry and gasp as she placed the big, fresh flower on the countess's chest, then slowly walked away. She was covering most of her sad face with her black veil embroidered with black flowers. Only her irritated watery eyes could be seen while her thin transparent veil caught her tears. The veil was thin, and her tears dripped from it as if it were drizzling.

The sun was still shining, and the air was dry. She left feeling the loneliness she had felt in her heart since the day of her young son's disappearance. The anguished mother felt she was alone in her pain, and that nobody could understand it. How can anyone understand her melancholy? But she did not know there were many other women not far from there who shared the same pain as her. Other mothers like her were crying and pleading for the lives of their beloved sons and waiting anxiously for their return.

CHAPTER FOURTEEN

The New Home

Alfonso and Refugio were having lunch together at their new home at the Franciscan residence. They both had plates of fried eggs, sweet potatoes, beans, green tomatillo sauce, and tortillas. He looked at her, and said, "My love, I have been living the happiest days of my life here with you." He put his tortilla down, held her hand in his, and asked, "Do you like living like this here with me? Are you happy?"

Refugio looked at him tenderly, and replied, "Alfonso, this is the life I have wished for us for so long. How could I not be happy living here with you?" She added, "I always wanted us to be together like this."

"Thank you for living this simple life here with me."

"It might be simple, but it is a beautiful life living it with you. You are a great husband—caring, considerate, responsible, honest, and you love me." She asked, "What else could I ask for when I have everything I need to be happy with the love of my life?"

Alfonso kissed her hand, then said, "I know you deserve to live better than this and you deserve to have beautiful dresses and a house of your own."

Refugio smiled, and said, "We both deserve good things, my love, and we will have them someday, but for now let's enjoy our simple life full of love and affection for each other."

"My love, you don't know how grateful I am that we could overcome the difficulties and the barriers to achieve our greatest desire, our union."

"My love, I am very grateful as well that we could defeat all the impositions we faced, and I know that was possible because of your determination and your dedication to fulfill our dreams of being together."

"I know we have the right to live our lives together and that I must not let anyone intervene against our love."

Refugio hugged him, and said, "The way you are makes me love you more every day."

Alfonso kissed Refugio's cheek, and in a low voice said, "I can't wait to come back from work to be with you, my love."

"I will be here waiting for you. Would you like anything else to drink or eat before you go?"

"I am all right, my love, thank you. Everything was delicious." He added, "Relax and get some rest now. Take care of yourself and I will see you in the afternoon."

"I hope you like your new job, Alfonso."

He smiled, and said, "I do like it, my love, but I don't know if I will be able to concentrate on it today. You know I will be thinking of you the whole time, but I will do my best."

Refugio lovingly said, "Oh, Alfonso, we are so happy together, I love you very much!"

Alfonso hugged her passionately, kissed her, tenderly caressed her soft, shiny black hair, and said, "I know, my love, but I love you a lot more than you love me." He chuckled, then he got serious again when he said, "I am so grateful for the life we have started together, it might not have been easy at first, but we will overcome any obstacle as long as we are together."

Refugio kissed him back, caressed his face with one hand, and said, "Yes, my love, we are together, and we will be for a long time, as long as we live with the help of our Lord."

"My beautiful Refugio, one hundred more years is not enough time to be with you, my love. I would like to stop time when we are together."

Refugio kissed him again, and quietly said, "My dear Alfonso." Then, with firmness, she said, "All right, all right, you have to go now. I know you will do a great job in whatever you have to do today."

Alfonso smiled, and asked, "You really think so? You know me well."

"Of course, you will be great, now go, no more talking, go!"

Alfonso gave her a quick kiss on the lips, and said, "See you soon, my love."

Refugio kissed him back quickly, and said, "Good luck, my beloved."

Alfonso closed the door slowly and quietly. She watched him leave for work through the bedroom window. She sighed and smiled a big smile as she thought about him. She looked at the sky, and whispered, "Thank you, Lord, for all the blessings you give us every day." She added, "And thank you for blessing our marriage and our home." Then, she looked at the wooden table and saw the only thing on it, a folded piece of fabric she sewed and decorated to cover the window. She grabbed the fabric, danced with it in her hands, turned around, and said, "Our home is going to look so much better with these curtains, and I will make tablecloths and pillowcases. Everything in here is going to look so beautiful."

She measured the window with the curtains she was making when she looked out the window suddenly and saw a familiar carriage. A fancy lady got out of it and knocked desperately on Refugio's door. Refugio scratched her head, opened her eyes wide, and nervously whispered, "Mother!" Refugio held her hands together, and asked herself, "What is she doing here?" Refugio's mood changed rapidly from feeling loved and peaceful to a deep anxiety and desperation. She breathed heavily, and asked herself, "Maybe she came to congratulate me? Perhaps she is happy for me?" She shook her head, and said, "No, that couldn't be."

Refugio hurried to the door and opened it for her mother. She nervously and gently said, "Come on in, Mother. I am glad you came to visit."

Rosaura firmly said, "What a horrible, poor place. Let's go, Refugio, the carriage is waiting for us outside."

Feeling doubtful but remaining calm, Refugio asked, "Go where, Mother? Where do you want to go with me?"

Rosaura cynically said, "We are going home, of course, you cannot live under these conditions." She added, "We are going to write a letter to the pope and when he learns how this savage forced you to marry him, this marriage will be annulled. Let's go!"

Refugio took a deep breath, and firmly said, "No, Mother, I will not leave Alfonso." She added, "I have waited so long for him, and now that I have him, I will take good care of him."

Rosaura rolled her eyes, and said, "Two years of seeing him once a week might be very long for you, but it is not that long."

Refugio looked at her mother, and gently said, "You don't understand, Mother, I have met many others, and I had many boyfriends before him, but none of them were like my Alfonso." She looked tenderly at the horizon, and said, "I feel like I have waited for him my entire life. Alfonso is the one I like and the one I love, and I am sure of it."

Rosaura interrupted her, and said, "You love him?" She mocked her daughter. "What a dumb thing to say. Love is for the dumb ones, who else could say such absurdity?" Rosaura's eyebrows furrowed and a fiery anger burned in her eyes when she looked at her daughter, and said, "Alfonso doesn't love you! He just likes you because you are young and beautiful." She added, "Soon you will become ugly and old due to the poor life you live with Alfonso, and he will get tired of you and leave you for another woman." Rosaura, enjoying her own words and ill wishes, continued, "That will be your punishment for being a bad daughter. He will leave you for a younger and prettier girl, you will see." She seemed to gain strength with every ill word she said. As she spoke louder and seemed to enjoy what she was imagining, her face broke into a malicious grin. She said, "And you will come back home, begging me to forgive you, and you are going to look so ugly and old as consequence for the life you are living here with this inferior and poor man. You are so foolish that you don't even realize what you are doing." With fire still in her eyes, Rosaura asked, "Aren't you embarrassed of living here in such poverty in this tiny house that is not even yours because this poor man has nothing to offer you?"

Refugio said, "I have what I want, and I am very happy here with my husband, Mother, no matter what you say."

Rosaura's malicious grin disappeared and in exchange a distressed look covered her face. Feeling agony now, she said, "You are going to make me get sick with all these problems you give me. You will cause my death with all your disrespectful ways. Not to mention all the shame you cause me and our family."

Refugio, worried for her mother, said, "Mother, there is no reason for you to get sick, I do no harm to you in any way." She added, "I am just asking you to respect my wishes and my husband. I will not return home with you, nor will I follow your orders anymore."

Rosaura said, "You mindless woman, preferring such an unimportant man over your own mother. Your mother, the one who gave life to you, the one who gave you everything."

In a calm voice, Refugio said, "You are my mother, and I love you, I respect you, and nothing is going to change that. You will always be my mother, but I will not allow you to ruin my marriage with your antiquated, erroneous ways."

Rosaura spoke even louder and with more rage, she said, "Insolent, ungrateful daughter! I took very good care of you all these years and this is how you repay me? You will pay for this, the heavens will punish you for causing me all this suffering!" Rosaura added, "I am leaving, but you will be the one to blame if I die for your nonsense." She looked around, and yelled, "This is an ungrateful daughter who doesn't love her mother!

She prefers the love of a poor man. Everybody, listen up! She is a bad person, don't trust her, don't talk to her. She is so dumb and a terrible daughter!"

People walking nearby looked at them with surprise and curiosity. Rosaura approached her carriage, her young employee helped her up, and they left. She continued yelling bad things about Refugio as she left. Refugio quietly watched her mother leave. She left feeling powerless for not being able to manipulate her daughter anymore. Rosaura was full of fury and screaming horrible things about Refugio.

A Jesuit priest came to see Refugio, and asked her, "What happened, Sister? Who was that loud woman?"

Refugio could not contain her sadness anymore. She sobbed and big tears rolled down her cheeks. "She is my mother."

The priest said, "That's what I thought, but I could not believe it, until now that I hear it from your own lips."

Refugio nervously said, "She is very upset because she feels lonely and she misses me."

"I heard everything. You don't have to explain it to me."

Refugio wiped her eyes but could not avoid it and continued to cry. The priest said, "Don't cry, sister, don't feel bad anymore. You didn't do anything wrong for marrying your husband." The priest held her hands in his, and said, "Look at you, you are shaking like a leaf. Sit down, I will bring you a piece of bread to calm your nerves."

Refugio wiped her eyes with her hands, and said, "I am all right, Reverend, don't worry about me, I am fine."

"I know you are all right, but I want you to be more than all right, Refugio. You are a very nice young lady, and I don't want you to worry about the unjust accusations your mother has made against you."

"She is usually not like the way she behaved today. Most of the time, she is respectful and a good person."

"I know, I know, don't be afraid of what I might think of your mother." He added, "Sometimes parents make mistakes, too, big mistakes, and they make life more difficult for their own children. Sadly, sometimes they are not able to look further than what their own desires permit them." The priest gave her a small piece of French bread, and said, "Here, Sister, eat the bread so you can feel better."

"I don't want to eat anything, Reverend," said Refugio. "I prefer to drink some water, I am so thirsty."

"No, Sister, no water for you right now, or it will make you ill after the unpleasant encounter you just had." He continued, "Come on, eat your small piece of plain bread and wait a while before you drink water."

Refugio said, "My mouth is so dry."

"I imagine it is."

"Thank you, Reverend." She slowly ate the tiny piece of bread the priest offered her.

"Will you be able to wait to drink water?" the priest asked.

Feeling calmer, Refugio sat down, and said, "Don't worry, Reverend, I will not drink any water. I will wait if you think that's what is safer for me."

"Wait at least one hour before you drink water."

"I will, thank you for caring about me." She added, "I appreciate your kindness. Thank you, Reverend."

"You're welcome, sister." He looked at Refugio, and said, "You look very tired."

Refugio nodded her head. "I feel that I have no energy today."

The priest said, "Try to rest, child. Take a nap to recover your energy."

"Wouldn't it be wrong if I lie down to sleep at this time of the day?"

"Of course not, my child, close your door and rest, and if you need me I will be in the small chapel praying."

"Thank you, Reverend."

The priest left to do his chores. Refugio closed her door and went to bed. More than one hour passed until Alfonso returned home. He looked around and walked carefully toward the bed where Refugio was resting and avoided making noise, trying not to disturb his beloved's sleep. He sat down quietly next to her, looking at her. He was completely mesmerized by her beauty. He felt so much love and was content to have his beloved wife next to him. They were at last living the life they had wished for so long. He watched her attentively and was happy to have her there with him. He let her sleep and dream peacefully.

Refugio felt his gaze and turned over on the bed. She opened her eyes and looked at Alfonso. Confused, she asked, "Alfonso, what are you doing here? Aren't you supposed to be working?"

Alfonso smiled, and said, "Yes, my love, but I had to bring some merchandise nearby. I saw a street food stall with fresh fruit water, and I thought it would be nice if we went together to try some of their drinks." He asked, "Would you like to continue sleeping or would you prefer to go and have a bite with me?"

Refugio smiled, got up in a hurry, and said, "Let's go, Alfonso." She looked at her small mirror on the wall, fixed her hair quickly, and said, "I'm ready."

He held her hand and they both left smiling and holding hands. They walked a couple of blocks and got to the food stall. They approached a lady, and Alfonso said, "Good afternoon, Miss, please give us two cups of fruit water."

The lady looked at them, and asked, "What kind of fruit?"

Alfonso looked at Refugio, and asked, "Would you like watermelon?"

Refugio nodded her head.

Alfonso said, "Two cups of watermelon water, please." Alfonso looked at Refugio, and asked, "What would you like to eat?"

Refugio said, "I'm not really hungry, but you must be starving."

Alfonso said, "You're not going to let me eat alone, are you, my love?"

"Well, I might eat a little."

The lady said, "Have you tried our mushroom quesadillas?"

Refugio shook her head, and asked, "No, are they good?"

The lady said, "They are really good, and the zucchini flower quesadillas are very good too."

Refugio said, "All right, I will try one of the quesadillas."

The lady asked, "Which one would you prefer?"

"Either of them."

"The zucchini one first, what do you think?"

Refugio nodded her head, and said, "Sounds good."

The lady looked at Alfonso, and asked, "What would you like, young man?"

Alfonso asked, "What do you recommend?"

"How do you feel about lentils with pico de gallo, and zucchini with fresh cheese?"

"A plate with both sounds good, please."

Meanwhile, two pairs of piercing eyes watched them attentively from far away. It was Refugio's mother and Alfonso's father who were at another food stall near them. Even though they had not met before, they were there at the same place and not far from each other. Rosaura looked attentively at her daughter and her son-in-law. The boy selling the fresh fruit water on that side offered her a cup of jamaica water and asked her, "Would you like anything else, ma'am?"

She got her water, and said, "That is all, thank you." Rosaura noticed the man next to her, Alfonso's dad, who was also looking at the couple with as much attention as she was. Rosaura noticed, and said, "Mister, there is no doubt they both are young, but there is a huge difference between them." She continued, saying, "I still do not comprehend how such an elegant, great, beautiful being could have fallen in love with such an ordinary creature."

Alfonso's father agreed, and added, "Absolutely, I ask myself the same question every day. How can such a refined person mix with such a low-class individual?"

Both their faces showed disgust, and at the same time they said, "And sooo ugly." They wickedly laughed out loud, and said, "You're right," but their statements were a little different at the end, and both spoke together with great frustration. Alfonso's father said, "That GIRL is very ugly."

Rosaura said, "That BOY is very ugly."

They both opened their eyes and mouths wide in disbelief. They were surprised and outraged with each other. Both looked at each other, and asked, "What are you talking about?"

Rosaura said, "My daughter is flawless."

At the same time, Alfonso's father said, "You are so wrong, my son is perfect."

Rosaura looked at Alfonso's dad, and said, "You are not the fine gentleman I thought you were!"

"And you are not such a fine lady, after all."

Surprised, Rosaura asked, "Your son? But of course, who else could be the father of such a vulgar being."

Alfonso's father stood up, and said, "I better leave, I don't like talking to gossipers."

Meanwhile, not too far from them, Refugio and Alfonso were enjoying each other's company and the happiness of having their own new home. It was a small and humble house. It was a borrowed house. Still, it was their dream home where they were living together, and it was full of their love, kindness, and dedication to each other. Refugio and Alfonso looked into each other's eyes. Her eyes were filled with the great love and devotion she was feeling for him. He noticed her tender look, held her hand in his, and said, "Refugio, my love, I am so grateful that we are together like this after waiting for so long."

Refugio smiled, and said, "Me too, Alfonso, I am so happy that we are together, and I have great hopes that everything is going to be all right for us both."

Alfonso said, "Yes, my love, I have faith that everything is going to turn out right in our lives from now on." They continued looking at each other tenderly, with smiles full of love. Alfonso caressed his beloved's hands. They shared the same feelings of love and happiness for having each other. Both had the desire of living a peaceful life together. And most importantly, they shared the same beliefs and the faith that everything was going to get better from now on just by being together as they had wanted for such a long time.

CHAPTER FIFTEEN

The Countess's Spirit

Doña Gabriela was talking to Reverend Chava. She said, "You have done a very good job of dedicating yourself for so long, helping the young and neediest of people in our community." She continued, "We are so grateful for you, Reverend Chava, for all your good and loving work."

Reverend Chava said, "It was the countess's treasures that helped us make this possible."

"That might be true, but you have dedicated most of your time, with enthusiasm, to build these houses of help for women, children, and the neediest people of this region, and the three new churches too. I have never seen churches built that fast."

"Money helps a lot when you want to finish your projects fast, Sister," Reverend Chava said.

Gabriela agreed. "All the good things you can do when you have the money to do them, and you can do them very fast." Wishfully thinking, Doña Gabriela said, "If only all the people who have lots of money had the desire to do good things with it for their own communities and others, not just keeping it for themselves."

Reverend Chava agreed. "Then we would have a better world, and the younger generations would learn to do the same!"

"Thank you, Reverend, for spending all your time and all her money to help everybody."

Reverend Chava smiled, and said, "That is the least I could do after promising the countess that I would do it." He continued, "I wanted to do everything as fast as possible to be able to keep my word to the dying countess. I also wanted to make sure that all her valuables were used for the betterment of the community, especially for all the people she hurt and their families."

Gabriela said, "I am very happy to see the churches finished, the women's houses and the orphanage open and helping so many in need." Her smile vanished. "I wish my lady the countess could have done all of these good deeds when she was still alive and well." She continued, "I wish she did not have to die so soon, and that she wouldn't have harmed all those poor boys."

Reverend Chava said, "It would have been very nice if the countess could have changed her mind, forgotten her deep resentment in her heart, and resisted the temptation to hurt those poor young men, Doña Gabriela. I would have wanted it the same peaceful way as you do. Unfortunately, she couldn't resist the temptation of power and vengeance."

An adolescent worker screamed. "Reverend Chava, they need you at the construction site! You will not believe what they found there!"

He stood up, and said, "Calm down first, and then tell me—is it good what they found at the construction site?"

The boy said, "One is good, but the other thing is very bad!"

Reverend Chava asked, "Tell me, young man, what is the good news?"

The boy said, "They found many gold dishes and a big pot full of gold coins encrusted in the wall they were smashing, but not far from there on another wall they found a dead man."

Reverend Chava said, "Don't tell me anymore, let's go see it." They left together in a hurry.

Doña Gabriela's eyes squinted. Her eyebrows furrowed and she started panting. "Who could that poor man be?" Teardrops rolled down her cheeks. She started praying in a low voice.

Reverend Chava got to the construction site where they were demolishing the walls, still looking for some of the countess's treasures. The boy who gave the news to the reverend said, "Look, Reverend Chava, those are the countess's treasures and that is the dead man!"

With wide eyes, Reverend Chava quietly looked at the skeleton. He wore simple clothes like all the workers around there. He also had two big gold medallions. One with a big jade stone in the middle of it, and the other one only made of gold, thick and big. Reverend Chava nodded his head. He sighed. Then, he blessed the skeleton with the sign of the cross.

The boy looked at the reverend, and asked, "Do you want me to bring you a big blanket to carry him?"

Reverend Chava said, "Yes, Brother, we have to take him to a church for a Christian burial."

Later that day, Reverend Chava returned to Doña Gabriela. He sat down on a chair just as another boy yelled, "The Cristeros are fighting the soldiers and together they are destroying the new church!"

Gabriela went outside, and asked him, "What church are you talking about, boy?"

"One of the churches made by the countess's orders."

Upset, Gabriela said, "All those uncivilized men." She asked, "Couldn't they go fight someplace else away from the church? I wasn't expecting anything like this." She looked at Reverend Chava, and asked, "What are we going to do, Reverend?"

Reverend Chava said, "First, we have to check the damage caused to the church." He continued, "I hope it is not that much, as we have used most of the countess's money already." Then the reverend lowered his voice, looked at Doña Gabriela, and said, "Except for some of the countess's treasures we have not found yet. I hid the valuables we found today in that new church, thinking they would be safe there!"

The boy shouted. "The Cristeros and the soldiers are still there at the new church killing each other, and nobody can go near them without getting killed by them!"

Reverend Chava said, "You heard, Sister, we have to wait until all of the commotion passes."

Doña Gabriela said, "By then, the treasure will be lost, and everything will be in ruins."

He shook his head, and in a low voice said, "After all the good work everyone has done, that would be a shame."

"Yes, a shame it would be, why do those men have to kill each other to get their message across? And destroying the new, beautiful church, after all the hard work we put into it." Doña Gabriela continued, "And the worst part, my lady the countess will not rest in peace if all her treasures were spent in vain."

Reverend Chava added, "A shame, Doña Gabriela, it would be if the countess's last wishes for the betterment of this community cannot be fulfilled."

"They were fulfilled, Reverend, you made sure of that, but this, who could have guessed this could happen to the last good deeds of my lady the countess." Desperate, she put her hand on her head, and said, "How can this end like this, Reverend, having her good deeds destroyed? Why? What are we going to do to fix it? My lady the countess will have no peace if her last wishes are not carried out as you promised."

Reverend Chava nodded and frowned. "I did promise it to her, and like you said, I completed the work as promised, but I never thought anyone would fight, revolt, and destroy a church." He looked up with a worried expression, and said, "I hope the countess can understand, wherever she is, and that her soul can still find peace."

Doña Gabriela said, "I hope so too, Reverend. I wish with all my heart that my lady's soul can find the peace she deserves."

Reverend Chava said, "Let's pray for that every day."

Doña Gabriela looked up, and with a knot in her throat, nodded her head and wiped her tears away with her shawl.

The next day, early in the morning, Doña Gabriela kneeled and prepared to pray for the countess's soul when she heard horses neighing, cows mooing, and dogs barking. She stood up and went outside the little chapel to check on the animals. There was nothing unusual besides the animals being upset. She said, "I'm not going to pay attention to any of you silly horses anymore because you all are fine." She continued, "Stop making such a big fuss for nothing." She looked to where all the animals were staring, and saw a slim woman dressed in black elegant clothes. She couldn't recognize her because her face was turned and facing in another direction. Intrigued, Doña Gabriela walked slowly toward the fancy woman in black, and asked, "Excuse me, Miss. Is there anything I can help you with?"

The woman turned her back to Doña Gabriela and hurriedly left without saying a word. Doña Gabriela returned to the chapel. Then said, "She must be in a hurry, I wonder who she was?" Shadows covered the countess's place as the sky darkened. Gabriela heard a loud roll of thunder as she knelt to pray.

Then, she heard a horse galloping and someone screaming. "The cows got out of the stable and are stampeding toward the town! Bring the cowboys, where are the cowboys?"

Gabriela got up and went outside to see what was happening. She asked the boy, "How did that happen?"

The boy said, "I don't know, Doña Gabriela, but unless your cowboys bring them back in, the herd will get to town soon and do who knows what."

Gabriela screamed, "Boys, where are you? Where is everyone?" Everything was silent and this was unusual at the countess's house. Gabriela walked quickly toward the stable and looked around, trying to find the cowboys. No one was there.

One of the boys said, "The herd is coming back." The cowboys were directing the herd back to get them into the stable. Doña Gabriela saw them, and said, "I am so relieved you were able to get the herd back on time, for a minute I thought the herd was going to get to town before I could find all of you boys. Where were you?"

One of the boys said, "We were following Fernando and then we saw the herd running, so we brought them back." He added, "Get out of the way, Doña Gabriela, before the stampede crushes you." The boy left with his horse and continued to guide the herd into the corrals and into the stable.

Doña Gabriela started talking to herself. "They were following Fernando, but where, and why?" She continued, "I need to talk to these boys, maybe one of them can explain what happened."

Chapter Sixteen

The Countess's Cave

A group of young men walked up the mountain toward the countess's cave. They were curious and looking for the countess's treasure in The Goat's Mountain, where many people believed it was hidden by the countess before her death. Most of the travelers there were young boys from the area who wanted to make a fortune of their own.

In the kitchen, Pedro was eating, and Doña Gabriela said, "Pedro, there are a bunch of young men looking for you."

"What do they want, Doña Gabriela?"

"They were saying something about you taking them to the countess's cave."

Pedro, surprised, asked, "They want to go to the countess's cave? What for?" He continued, "Whatever they will find there is not going to be good."

Gabriela looked down, nodded her head, and said, "I know, Pedro, but they don't know that, and you have to tell them directly, so they stop with their silly ideas."

Pedro looked at Doña Gabriela, and said, "Then, I will tell them, Doña Gabriela." He walked outside the kitchen and out the corridor. He passed the flower garden, passed the vegetable garden, and he entered the orchard where the boys were waiting for him. They were all happy to see him. Pedro saluted them. "Hello, boys, what brings you here?"

One boy said, "We want you to help us get to the countess's cave."

"If that is all you want, you don't need me." Pedro continued, "All of you know where the countess's cave is and how to get there."

Another boy replied, "We do know where it is and how to get there, but we want to explore it further, and only you and the countess have done that before."

Pedro sighed. "I assure all of you there is only danger inside that cave, and there is nothing good in there for you that is worth risking your lives over." He continued, "Forget about this so you can avoid big trouble and go find yourselves a new job."

A boy said, "There are many jobs, but we are not looking for a job, we want to explore the countess's cave, and you know why."

Another boy, looking at his friends, said, "Maybe he doesn't want to take us because he wants the treasure for himself."

Another boy interrupted, and said, "And don't deny it because even though you and the countess were very secretive about it, all of us saw you many times going in and out of that cave with the countess, and we know that only you and her know the interior of the cave well."

Pedro shook his head, and said, "All you boys are mistaken, there is no treasure in there, but there is great danger. I am telling you, I am not going in there and you shouldn't either."

One boy said, "We want you to come with us, and we will share with you whatever we find there, but if you don't come with us, that will not stop us and we will not share the treasure with you."

Pedro said, "I am warning you, do not go in there because if you do, you may not come out of there alive."

Another boy said, "Look at that, you were going in and out with the fine lady, the countess, many times, and now that we are here to help you with anything in there, you are afraid."

Pedro said, "I already told you there is nothing of value for anyone to get in there, and it is too dangerous. There is no treasure in there as all of you might be thinking, and the only thing you boys will find in the cave are a bunch of dangerous animals. That is all."

The boys started talking at the same time. One said, "Let's go, he is not coming with us."

A second boy said, "We are wasting our time here."

A third boy said, "We don't need him, let's go already."

Another boy said, "We shouldn't have come here."

They all turned to leave, and Pedro said, "Don't go in there, you better listen for your own good." They all turned their backs on Pedro and walked away. Pedro added, "Don't risk your young lives in there, listen to me, boys."

One boy said, "Good-bye, Pedro." The rest of the boys paid him no attention and walked faster.

Pedro entered the house again. Doña Gabriela was waiting for him. Pedro said, "Guess what that bunch wanted?"

Doña Gabriela said, "I heard everything, the windows were open, Pedro."

"They don't listen, and they are going to go inside the countess's cave by themselves, even when I told them how dangerous it was." He continued, "Where did they get this dumb idea about a treasure inside that cave? And if there was one, I sure would have seen it by now, but there isn't any."

Doña Gabriela looked quietly but attentively at Pedro.

He asked, "You do believe me, Doña Gabriela, don't you?"

"Of course, I believe you, Pedro. I know you are a man of your word." She continued, "I'm sure those naïve, impulsive, thoughtless boys will be back from the cave in no time."

Pedro, with a serious and worried expression, said, "That's what I hope, Doña Gabriela, and I hope they all come back in one piece."

She said, "I miss my lady the countess very much. If she was still here none of this would be happening. She knew how to keep everything under control and put everything in order when necessary."

Pedro said, "She did have everything and everyone under control and more than you would have ever imagined."

Meanwhile the four young boys climbed to the top of the mountain to get into the cave, with big illusions in their minds. When they were almost there, one of them said, "Wait a minute, what is that big rock doing there covering the entrance of the countess's cave?"

Another boy added, "That rock wasn't there before, how did it get there?"

Another boy said, "Maybe the wind or a storm moved it and put it there."

The fourth boy said, "It doesn't matter, we will move it away from the cave."

They tried pushing the gigantic rock to the side to remove it from the entrance of the cave. They were pushing and pulling, sweating, even growling, but they could not move the big rock, not even one bit. Then, Ignacio went under a tree to lie down and rest.

One of the boys asked, "What a change, what happened to the sunny day?" The sky was covered with gray clouds, and the wind blew strongly bringing the darkest clouds to the top of the cave. As soon as the sunny day disappeared, it became darker and darker.

"If you all weren't so skinny, we would have no problem moving that rock."

The other boy said, "As if you were the stronger of the bunch, you are the skinniest of us all." He added, "Let's go home, a thunderstorm is coming."

Ignacio had fallen asleep. A boy shook his arm, and said, "Ignacio, wake up, we are leaving, it's going to rain."

With his eyes closed, Ignacio said, "Let me rest for a few minutes."

His friend insisted. "Get up, we are leaving."

Ignacio, still with his eyes closed, said, "Go ahead, I will catch up with you in a few minutes."

The three boys looked at Ignacio. One shook his head, another raised his shoulders, and the three of them continued walking down the mountain. Then one boy screamed, "You better hurry, Ignacio, if you don't want to get hit by lightning!"

Ignacio turned to his other side, and said, "Go ahead, I will catch up to you in a minute."

Big drops of rain started falling as the three boys went down the mountain, but Ignacio was dry. One of the boys said, "Run!" And they did. It continued raining harder on the three boys, and they continued running home. The three of them were all wet when they got to the bottom of the mountain.

Meanwhile, at the top of the mountain, the clouds blew away, the sun started shining, and everything was sunny and warm again. Ignacio continued sleeping. He seemed very comfortable, warmed by the sun's heat, but protected by the tree's shadow. He finished taking his nap, until dusk when he woke up. He looked around him, and asked, "Hey, guys, where are you?" He said to himself, "Maybe they left, I'll take a look at the countess's cave before I leave."

He went to the cave and the big rock was not blocking it anymore, it was off to the side. He was free to walk inside the cave to explore it as his friends and himself had planned before. He looked inside the long, deep, dark cave. He looked at the heavy, big rock, and said, "Oh, they moved it without me. They are stronger than I thought." He went inside the dark cave and took a few steps. He looked back to see the giant rock was slowly and quietly moving and closing the cave entrance with him inside.

He heard a clink inside the cave and turned around to see what it was. Ignacio could see something blinking and he bent to touch it and picked up some gold coins. He said, "We were right, here's the treasure." He put some coins in his pants pockets. He got some more and filled his pockets quickly with as many coins as he could. Then he took his shirt off and put all the coins he could in his shirt. He said, "This will do for now, why is it getting darker in here?"

He got to the entrance and touched the rock with his hands. It was almost blocking the whole entrance, except for a small opening. Ignacio asked, "How did this big rock get moved to close the entrance again? I just changed my mind about not liking being skinny."

He put one foot out to exit the cave, when he heard a female voice. "Everything, or nothing, you take everything or nothing." Ignacio's hands shook, and many of the coins from his shirt fell to the ground. They clinked against each other on their way to the ground.

Ignacio, scared, looked inside the cave, and asked, "Who's there?"

He saw two glowing eyes. Terrified, he dropped the rest of the coins from his shirt and tried to leave. The rock closed a little bit more as he heard the loud, clear, echoing female voice again. "Everything or nothing!"

He took all the gold coins out of his pockets as fast as he could, threw them on the ground, and pushed himself out the cave through the small exit between the big boulder and the cave. He had barely made it when he looked back to the rock, it was closing the cave completely again. He trembled and realized the darkness of the night was there with him already. The good thing was, there was a full moon.

Ignacio walked back home as fast as he could. He looked back to the cave, still in horror, and he started to run down the mountain. He was sweating and panting when he got home safely.

His mother asked, "Where were you, Son?" She added, "You are as white as a cloud, where were you this late?"

Ignacio stuttered. "I-I wa-wa-was at the countess's cave, and someone is there."

"Those crazy friends you have."

"I'm not talking about my friends, it was someone from, from, from—"

His mother interrupted him, and asked, "It was someone from where?"

"The other world."

"Young men and their imaginations, that will not feed you," his mother said. "You need to spend your time working, not having fun at the countess's cave."

"Who was having fun? It was, was, was—"

"Was what?"

Ignacio replied, "Frightening!"

At that moment somebody knocked at the door. Startled, Ignacio jumped. His mother asked, "Why are you startled just from a knock on the door?" She opened the door and saw there was nobody there. She closed the door, and said, "There's something weird about you today. Sleep, some rest will be good for you so you can be ready for the day tomorrow."

The next day, early in the morning, there was some knocking at Ignacio's front door. His mother went to see who it was. Ignacio followed her to the entrance. Five teenagers stood at the door. They all said, "Good morning, ma'am."

One said, "Ignacio, we were worried about you. I'm sure glad you are all right."

Another boy interjected, "They said they left you up there by the cave sleeping, and a thunderstorm caught up to them when they were coming back home."

Another boy said, "Let's go, Ignacio. We are going back to the cave again."

Another boy said, "But first we are going to get more men, as many as we can, so we can move the heavy rock this time."

Ignacio shook his head, but before he could say anything his mother looked at him, and said, "The only place you are going today is to look for a job, and nowhere else until you find one."

Relieved, Ignacio said, "The chief has spoken, you heard her, boys."

His mother looked at him, surprised by his reaction and compliance. He looked at his mother, and said, "Bye, Mother, I will find myself a job today, I will see you in the afternoon." He closed the door of his house, leaving his mother inside, and he looked at his friends, and said, "There is something really bad in that cave. Yesterday, after you left, the rock was on one side of the cave. The opening of the cave was wide open, and I went inside. I saw the treasure you were all talking about, and I even filled my pockets with gold coins. As soon as I did that, the boulder started covering the entrance of the cave again. How could that big thing move by itself so fast without making any noise? For a moment I thought I was going to be locked inside forever. But I am very lucky, there was still a small opening, but it was not going to be there for long as the boulder continued moving and closing the exit of the countess's cave." He continued, "I ran away from there as fast as I could and that is why I am alive to tell you about it."

A boy asked, "Where is the treasure?"

Another boy added, "Where are the golden coins you took?"

Ignacio sighed, and said, "I took them out of my pockets and threw them back into the cave."

Another boy scratched his head, and in a loud voice asked, "You did what?"

"That was the only way to escape alive," Ignacio said. "When the boulder was closing the entrance, trapping me inside, a lady told me to take all the treasure or nothing."

Two boys asked, "Why didn't you take it all?"

Ignacio answered, "Impossible. The treasure is too big for one person to be able to take it all. Besides, as soon as you touch it, the boulder closes, and you will be in there for all eternity. And you will not be in there alone. This isn't just a lady… I heard a haunting voice. The evil ghost of a woman is in there."

The boys together said, "The countess's ghost!"

Ignacio said, "She will not let you take her treasure. You will not leave that cave alive with the treasure, that's for sure."

A boy looked at everyone, and said, "I didn't know you were such a coward."

His bold friend said, "I do not fear ghosts."

Another boy said, "Come on, Ignacio, you will not be alone this time, none of that will happen today."

Ignacio said, "I told you everything that happened to me in that cave, and I am not going back there, no matter how big the countess's treasure is. I am going to look for my treasure elsewhere, but today I am going to find a job and make my mother happy." He continued, "That ghost made me realize how valuable my life really is. Why don't you all forget about that cave and come with me to find a job too?"

"Forget about the countess's treasure?" a boy asked.

Another boy added, "No, we are going without you."

Ignacio said, "If all of you die in that cave I'm not going back up there, not even to bring your bodies back home." He left and walked downtown. His five friends walked toward the mountain to find more friends to get into the countess's cave.

Ignacio spent all his morning walking around the small town and looking for a job without success. He was still walking around when he saw Mr. Frank looking out the window of his carriage. Ignacio loudly said, "Good morning, Mr. Frank! I am looking for a job. I am a very good worker."

Mr. Frank said, "Go to my house and tell them I sent you to help them take care of the cattle."

Ignacio happily said, "Yes, sir!"

By the time he got to Mr. Frank's house it was after two in the afternoon. After talking to Mr. Frank's employees, a young cowboy looked at Ignacio with a big smile, and said, "Time to go home. Remember, we start working early, Ignacio."

He said, "I will be here by five." Ignacio left to go home. Grinning, he said to himself, "I got myself a job. I wish the boys were here to see this. Maybe they're still trying to get into the countess's cave. I'll take a look to see how they're doing."

Meanwhile his friends were still trying to move the big rock away from the entrance, but they had not moved it, not even one little bit. Even though there were ten of them this time. One of them said, "It's so hot."

Another one said, "Let's take a rest."

"We have been trying for hours, and nothing," said another.

One boy said, "There must be a way to move this big rock."

Another said, "Oh man, I need a nap."

"That is what I need, a good rest," said another.

Each of them chose a spot near the cave to rest. The sun was shining beautifully. Its rays were hot and dry, and everyone could feel the suffocating heat on their whole bodies. Four of the boys took their shirts off and went to lie down on the dry grass under a tree. Four others went to lie down under a leafless tree. They threw their shirts and pants on it to make shade. Two boys looked at each other and signaled to the tiny lagoon filled with rainwater. The water was shallow, it came up to their waists. They left all their clothes on a rock to keep them dry. One of the boys in the lagoon said, "This water is so warm."

The other one said, "It is so refreshing, much better than being all dry under the sun."

Dusk had fallen while the boys were resting and cooling off in the water. As they left the water, one said, "I left my clothes on this rock."

The other one said, "I saw you and I did the same."

The first boy said, "Now the clothes are not here."

The second boy said, "You are joking."

The two boys, with their wet underwear stood there looking at the rock where they left their clothes. They crossed their arms over their chests.

The second boy said, "It's not that hot anymore."

The other one said, "Actually, it's a little chilly now."

The first boy said, "Yeah, it feels like a thunderstorm is coming."

Both of them approached their friends under the big tree. The first boy said, "Who took our clothes?" The four boys resting looked at them. One looked at where their shirts were, and asked, "Who took them?"

The second boy said, "We don't know."

The third boy said, "All right, good joke, give them back now."

The first boy said, "No joke, we don't know who took them."

The fourth boy said, "At least we have pants on."

The fifth boy said, "Dry pants."

They started walking around, looking for their missing clothes with no success. The boys under the leafless tree looked at them. The sixth boy looked at them, and asked, "Where are your clothes?"

The four boys looked at the leafless tree, and one said, "They were here on top of this tree."

The seventh boy asked, "You lost your clothes too, huh?" They were all looking for their missing clothes.

Ignacio watched them from a distance, covered by a big rock. He asked himself, "Who took their clothes? I have been here all along, observing their whereabouts and I didn't see anything. I should have paid more attention, but I did pay attention. This is very weird!"

The eighth boy said, "Forget about the clothes. Let's go and move that rock once and for all."

The first boy said, "It's easy for you to say because you have your pants on."

The ninth boy said, "Stop acting like little girls and come help us move that rock."

The tenth boy said, "This is getting too weird, maybe we should go home and call it a day."

The ninth boy said, "Oh no, we are going to finish this job today."

The first boy said, "I'm going home."

The second boy said, "Me too."

The ninth boy said, "We can come back tomorrow."

The boys in underwear walked home. The boys with their pants on went home after them. Ignacio, still hidden behind a big rock, waited for them to walk ahead. Then, he walked home too. He was confused. "Who took their clothes? I am not going into that cave ever again. Something creepy is happening around there."

The next day, twelve boys went back to the countess's cave. It was early in the morning, before sunrise, when they started pushing the big boulder together to remove it from the entrance of the cave. The rock did not move at all. Two boys walked away from the boulder. The boys still pushing the big rock, said, "Don't leave, help us!"

The two boys found big sticks and the two of them started digging under the rock. The other boys continued pushing. After some minutes of digging and pushing the huge rock, it started moving. Little by little, they were able to move it. One of the boys happily screamed, "Finally! We can enter and find the countess's treasure." All the boys went inside the cave.

One boy looked at the boys with sticks, and said, "You two, stay here and watch that rock." Confused, the two boys looked at each other. The boy corrected himself, and said, "I mean, watch the rock and the entrance and make sure nobody gets in. If someone comes near the entrance or if the rock starts covering the entrance, let us know."

"All right, I will let you guys know if someone comes near, but this big heavy thing is not going to move on its own, I can tell you that for sure."

"Fine, we'll be watching." They stayed by the entrance holding their sticks. The others went in.

One said, "It's so dark in here."

Another one said, "I have some matches." He lit one and it went out right away as bats flew over them and out the cave. The boys at the entrance covered their faces with their arms as the bats flew near their heads and out of the cave.

One boy inside the cave said, "Let's go home. I don't like bats."

Another one said, "I'm staying in here until we find the treasure."

Another boy said, "I saw the treasure, shining and moving when you lit the match."

"Light another one," said another boy.

The boy with the matches said, "I will, but it goes out right away, so look for the treasure." He lit another match.

One boy said, "Look, the brightness!"

Another asked, "Did you hear that?"

"What?" asked a boy.

Some boys started screaming in pain. A boy said, "Snakes!"

Another boy said, "That was no treasure, that was the shiny snakes sliding against each other!"

Another boy yelled, "Snake nests!"

Another boy said, "Now, you rattle, you sneaky, bad snakes, you were supposed to rattle before, not after, you bite."

All of the boys ran outside the cave. Some sat right outside the cave entrance. Five of them had snakebites on their arms and hands. One of them said, "Those rattlesnake fangs are sharper than I thought, it surely hurts a lot."

Another boy said, "It is not the bite that worries me, but the venom."

"And not all of them were rattlesnakes," said another boy. "Rattlesnakes don't have those brilliant colors. They were more like coral snakes."

Another boy said, "I didn't see any of them, but surely heard the rattlesnakes."

"If they were coral snakes, we are doomed," a boy said.

One boy pulled up his pants and there was a tiny coral snake chewing on his leg right above his ankle. The boy made kicking movements to get rid of the snake, but the tiny colorful snake was still biting him. The boy said, "Go, go you little poisonous one, stop injecting me with your venom!" He stomped his foot, shaking it and kicking it away from his body, but he could not get rid of it.

One of the boys used his stick to remove the tiny colorful snake from his friend's leg. It fell to the ground and the boy used the stick to throw the snake back into the cave. The boy who was bitten, asked, "Why did you do that, why didn't you kill it?"

The boy answered, "Kill it? It is just a baby!"

The bitten boy said, "It didn't want to stop biting and chewing and injecting its venom into me! That looks like a baby to you?"

The boy with the stick said, "I'm sorry, man, we better hurry to see the medicine man before it is too late."

"What do you mean, too late?" asked one of the bitten boys.

"Soon the poison will take effect and you will not be able to walk on your own."

The other boy by the boulder agreed. "Let's go."

Another boy asked, "What do you think is worse, being bitten by a poisonous snake, or being stung by a bunch of venomous scorpions? Even though I didn't see them, I'm almost sure that's what stung my hands."

Another boy said, "Scorpions got my hands too. I could feel their little sharp claws." He looked at his swollen, red hands.

"What stung me didn't feel like scorpions, they were more like spiders, big hairy spiders," said a boy. One of his hands was also swollen.

The boy who asked the two boys to watch the entrance of the cave was the only one who seemed to get out of the cave unharmed. He said, "I was lucky that nothing got me, not even that bat I touched by accident when I tried to hold the ceiling. Let's get out of here."

Ignacio was carrying oats for the cows at his job when he heard his coworkers talking. One said, "And a bunch of them are very sick at the medicine man's house. Venomous creatures stung and bit them when they were in the countess's cave looking for her treasure."

Ignacio heard that, and said to himself, "I hope it is not the same bunch I'm thinking about."

As soon as he got out of work, he went to the medicine man's house. The door was open, and he went inside. He looked around him. There were sick people lying down on small wooden beds in the big hallway next to the gardens. All the patients had pictures of their health issues. Two boys had drawings of five and four scorpions on their beds. Another one had the drawing of a spider on his bed. Six boys had drawings of a snake nest on their beds. The six patients with the pictures of snake nests were very pale, shivering, sweating, and delirious.

The two with the scorpion pictures were breathing with difficulty, sweating, salivating excessively, and with muscle spasms in their necks, heads, bodies, and eyes. The bed with one scorpion picture at its feet was empty, and next to it was the boy who was lying there a few minutes before. The young artist who drew the pictures, a ten-year-old boy, looked at him, and said, "My mother and father are preparing more medicine for them, you can help us with it."

He nodded his head and followed the kid to the kitchen. The bed with the picture of a spider was empty, too, and the patient was nowhere to be found. The kid looked at his healthy friend, and asked, "Where is he?"

He answered, "He must have gone home."

The kid said, "He must come back to take all his medicine, so he won't be like them."

The friend said, "He must be all right if he left."

The kid said, "Not for long, if he doesn't take his medicine."

In the kitchen, the medicine man and his wife prepared teas and herb ointments. They were in their forties, medium height, and dark-skinned. Their kid said, "The one with the spider sting left without taking his medicine."

"He will come back," said his father.

The lady looked at the boy with one scorpion sting, and asked, "How do you feel?"

He replied, "Very worried about my friends."

She looked at her husband and both smiled. The kid looked at them, then looked at the young man, and said, "My mother means, how do you feel about the scorpion sting?"

The boy looked at his swollen hand, and answered, "Oh, that, it still hurts a lot, but other than that, I feel fine."

The lady looked at him, and asked, "How does your throat feel?"

He touched his throat with one hand, and answered, "Feels fine."

The medicine man asked, "How does your head feel?"

He looked up, trying to see his own head. Then, he replied, "Feels fine too."

Happily, the child said, "You're going to be all right. You can help us heal your friends."

Ignacio stood in the doorway, immobilized, looking at his friends. The kid asked his parents, "What happened to him? He's been like that since he got here a while ago."

His dad said, "He's in shock." The medicine man and his wife held Ignacio and helped him lie down on a bed. The man loosened his shirt and belt. The woman took off his shoes.

Then, she placed Ignacio's feet above his head over a couple of pillows.

The kid covered Ignacio with a warm blanket, and said, "Don't worry, we are taking care of your friends, and they will be all right. Right, Papa?"

The medicine man nodded his head and continued preparing medicines with the herbs.

Meanwhile, the medicine woman looked attentively at Ignacio. He silently got up from the bed, and with a blank expression he walked to the door and left.

"Mama, he is leaving, and he is not well, do something," said the boy.

The medicine woman looked at her husband. He looked back at her and then looked at their son, and said, "We want to help him get better, but we will not retain him here against his will."

The medicine woman looked at her son, and said, "One of these boys will recover soon, so he can go get his friends' families and they can take all of them home. There is no more room in here if someone else needs emergency care."

CHAPTER SEVENTEEN

The Charitable One

"Take everything or nothing," said the menacing female voice inside the countess's cave.

A young gentleman named Ernie asked, "Who said that?" He added, "And I am not here to take anything that does not belong to me. Anyway, how could I take it all when I cannot even see the end of it. This cave must be very long, and even if I had a carriage with me, which I do not have, I could not take it all for there is a lot of gold and other treasures in here. Besides, I was just passing by, and I have no intention of taking what is not mine."

There, in the darkness, he looked toward the female voice. Then, not very far from him, he saw her. A beautiful young lady dressed in black elegant clothes, looked at him, and she said, "I need your help, and I will give everything valuable to you that is in here, to do with it as you please." She continued, "There is only one condition, you need to carry me down the mountain and into the town's closest church so I can be blessed with the holy water inside the church. You need to carry me over your shoulder, but no matter what you hear, or feel, you should not turn back to look at me. You need to keep on going until we are inside the church."

Ernie asked, "Is that all you need from me? To carry you and take you inside the closest church? For a blessing?" He continued, "That is an easy task for a strong man like me, and I will do it to help you even if you don't give me anything. I will still do it as it will make me happy to help such a beautiful, young girl like you, and I want you to feel good and be happy." He asked, "Are you sick? Is that it, and that is why you cannot go to the church on your own?"

The countess answered, "Something like that, you would not understand if I explained it to you." She continued, "I will give you everything you see in here, but we have to hurry, and remember no matter what you hear or feel, don't turn back, and do not stop until you get me inside the church."

Ernie asked, "Why shouldn't I look back, what if I want to see how you are feeling?"

The young countess replied, "I will be all right as long as you do as I tell you to the best of your abilities. Do not ask me why, I need your help, and I need you to follow my instructions implicitly. Can you do this to help me?"

Ernie scratched his head, and said, "It does not seem very clear to me, but I will do as you say to help you." He continued, "It is a shame to see such a beautiful creature like you suffering for not being able to go to a church. Do not worry, pretty girl, I will take you there immediately if you want, and you will get your blessing."

The countess said, "One more thing, do not stop for anything, no matter how tired you get, you must continue walking until you get there." She insisted, "You just have to carry me and look ahead and keep walking until we get into the church."

Ernie said, "Yes, pretty lady. I understood already, you don't have to repeat yourself that many times. I will take you to the church, I will not stop, and I will not look back until we are inside the church. I am a young and strong man, you know." Then, bragging, he said, "I can even take you there and come back here and back to the church again as many times as you would like, you will see. This is just too easy for me."

With a sad expression, the countess said in a serious voice, "You do not need to do this several times, you just need to be strong enough to do it well once. Remember, you have to take me inside the church once and that will be enough."

Self-assured, Ernie smiled, and said, "I am such a strong man and you are such a fragile, young woman that this is too easy for me. You must be one hundred thirty or one hundred forty, maybe one hundred fifty pounds at most. I can easily handle that." He asked, "Are you ready?" He looked at her tenderly and opened his arms wide. "Come to me, beautiful woman."

She said, "Wait, not like that." And she pointed to his arms. "You have to carry me over your shoulder."

He happily said, "Oh right, we can do it any way you want it. Come to me so I can carry you over my shoulder."

The beautiful, young countess ordered, "You come to me and close your eyes before you hold my weight on your shoulder." He walked toward her and closed his eyes. The countess said, "This is the last time I will speak to you. I am too tired, and I will not be able to talk to you on the way to the church, but you have to remember the directions I have given you."

Ernie said, "I understood the first time, you don't have to talk or do anything, you will see how fast we get there."

"I wish I had met you a long time ago," she said.

He asked curiously, "A long time ago? You have been suffering this illness for a long time? Months? Years? A long time ago you must have been a child." He picked her up with both arms and placed her over his shoulder. "You are so cold that even your dress feels ice cold. Don't worry, we will get to the church, the priest will take care of you, and soon you will feel good as new again."

He started to walk with the countess over his shoulder. He held her with his arms and hands, and said, "You are so light, we will be there in no time. It is around eight in the morning, and it took me a couple of hours to get here to the cave. This is such a good way to start my morning, helping a beautiful woman. But now, instead of going back to where I began my walk, I just need to take you to the church and that will take me only half the time, one hour approximately." He smiled and held her tightly. "All right, I have you now. We are going to go very carefully down the mountain to the church as you asked. Sorry, I know you told me you would not be able to tell me anything until we get there to the church, but it is hard to have you with me and not talk to you, you know. All right, I will stop talking now." He added, "Anyway, if I'm quiet I will have more strength and I will focus all my efforts on carrying you."

He started to make more of an effort to carry what he thought was a regular woman. He began to sweat with every step he took as he made a greater effort to carry the weight he had on his shoulder. His face was bright red. Sweat rolled down his forehead, his temples, and down his sideburns. He whispered to himself, "How can you be this heavy? No offense or anything, but you are getting heavier by the minute. And where are all the people that I saw yesterday morning? It is very strange to see these streets empty at this time in the morning. Where did all the people go? Yesterday, when I was walking up the mountain, there were men and women sweeping in front of their houses. Men going to work. People going to the food market. Children playing with their marbles on the streets. People going and coming from buying groceries at the plaza. How can there be absolutely no one right now? Not one single person on the streets, this is very strange."

He continued talking to himself in a whisper. "How can this pretty woman be this heavy? She keeps on getting heavier with every step I take. I don't know if I am going to be able to keep my promise and get her to the closest church. I thought this was going to be much easier." He was sweating profoundly. His face was as red as a cardinal's feathers, and he was walking very slowly and hunched over. He whispered, "I am almost there, just one more street, but she is becoming too heavy for me."

He continued walking down the last street to the church. After that, he just needed to cross the plaza and enter the church with her. *If only I could walk faster with this heavy weight I am carrying.* He raised his head a little bit and looked ahead of him. He whispered to himself, "I can see the plaza.

I'm almost there. The plaza is empty with no people either. How can this be possible?" He added, "There are people at the plaza going to and from the churches every single day. Where is everyone?" He continued walking as fast as he could, which was very slowly. Feeling some relief, he whispered to himself, "I am almost there, just a few more steps and I will be at the plaza where the churches are."

Finally, half an hour later he was going to take the first step into the plaza. He thought, *Just one more step and I will be at the plaza. Everything is going to be easier and faster from now on.* He entered the plaza and started to hear people talking, whispering, and murmuring. He heard some frightened ladies saying, "Let's stay away from him."

He continued to hear people whispering as they moved away from him. Ernie could hear them, but he could not see them. He was focused on carrying the countess as he agreed, until Aaron from a distance asked, "Why are you carrying that?"

Refugio's mother was coming from church, and screamed, "A demonic specter!"

He turned his face and tried to look at the screaming lady and lost his step, falling down with his heavy load. He saw what was surprising the few people around him. With wide eyes and his mouth agape, he asked, "She was turning into a mule? No wonder she was getting heavier with every step I took."

The mule was breathing fire from her snout, and her eyes burned with intense flames of desperation. The charitable man who carried the countess over his shoulder looked at her on the ground with wide eyes, but within a few seconds she disappeared, leaving a few sparks of fire behind her.

At that moment he heard more stirring around him. He looked up, and said, "Where did all these people come from? There were just a few at the plaza and none on my way here. Now there are people everywhere. Where were all these people before?"

He asked all the strangers around him. They just looked at him and walked away. Aaron who witnessed the spiritual encounter came closer to Ernie, and said, "The plaza is always with people, and even more people on a Sunday like today."

Ernie said, "I know, I was confused, too, but there weren't any people before, where did they come from all of a sudden?"

Aaron said, "What do you mean, 'all of a sudden'? There have been people around here all morning. They were here when you got to the plaza today." He continued, "You didn't see them as you were too busy carrying your mule of fire."

Relieved, Ernie sighed, and asked, "You saw that too? Then, I am not imagining it. It is true."

Aaron said, "Of course it is true. Who else saw it? I don't know exactly because everybody is busy with their own things, but, if I were you, I would stay away from trouble and from mules of fire."

Ernie extended his hand to Aaron and said, "My name is Ernie. It is nice to meet you."

Aaron kept his hands to himself, and said, "It is nothing personal, but I don't want anything to do with you." He added, "Go ask a priest how he can help you, I don't know how to help you. He might be able to do something for you."

Ernie said, "I don't need any help, that lady I was carrying is the one who needs the help."

Aaron asked, "What lady? Don't you know that lady—as you call her—was someone out of this world? What did you do to bring her to this world? Were you doing witchcraft?"

Ernie said, "Witchcraft? Me? No, I am not interested in that kind of stuff." He added, "I was passing by the cave at the Goat's Mountain and I waited there to take a rest. Then this young lady with extraordinary beauty, you should have seen her, she asked me for help and I brought her here as she asked me. I wish I could have brought her all the way into the church as she wanted me to do."

Aaron said, "You were at the countess's cave and that mule of fire must have been the countess's spirit." He asked, "You brought her here all the way from the countess's cave?"

Ernie said, "It seemed easy. She was tremendously good-looking and so fragile, and she looked so light until I started walking down the mountain with her weight over my shoulder. She became heavier with every step I took."

Aaron said, "Well, prepare yourself to deal with her from now on. I don't think she is going to give up on you bringing her to the church since you made the first attempt."

Ernie said, "I hope she can rest in peace because I am not going back to that cave ever again." He added, "I am not going back to that cave, not even to get the reward she was offering me."

Aaron asked, "Reward?"

Ernie said, "She wanted to give me a lot of gold and jewelry, a treasure so big that I couldn't take it out of the cave by myself."

Aaron asked, "Didn't you realize, there at the cave, that she wasn't a typical lady? Not from this world?"

Ernie said, "Now that you mention it, her special green eyes had a certain glare to them. I thought she had distinctively beautiful eyes—you know, out of the ordinary—but I didn't think much of it."

Aaron said, "It is not going to be easy for her soul to rest in peace. How can she ever find peace after all the innocent lives she took?" Aaron looked at Ernie, who was quiet. Aaron asked, "What is wrong with you? You are shaking and sweating at the same time, and the sun is too high and hot for you to be cold or shaking."

In a low voice, Ernie said, "I am all right."

Aaron said, "No, you're not. You just saw an evil ghost, and that was not any regular ghost, that was the Countess of Stonemason's ghost. You are lucky to be alive. Let's go inside the church, I will help you explain it to the priest."

Ernie said, "What for?"

Aaron said, "To see what he suggests you do to get rid of those shakes and sweats."

"What can a priest do? Priests pray, that's all."

"And prayer would help you a lot right now. Let's go."

Ernie walked toward a bench, and said, "I'm not going anywhere. I'm just going to sit down and rest for a little while, before I start looking for a place to stay."

Aaron said, "Now I see why the countess confided in you, she saw you were like her, stubborn!" Aaron started yelling, "Priest, priest, come here, over here!" He waved his hands in the air. Ernie sat on a bench, glanced at Aaron and then at the church.

A priest came out of it and walked toward them. He had heard Aaron calling to him. The priest looked at both of them as he approached. The priest was tall, slim, had dark hair, was middle-aged, well-groomed, and freshly shaven. He stood next to them, and said, "Good morning, Brothers. Were you calling me?"

Ernie said, "No."

Aaron said, "Yes. Look at him, don't you think he needs help?"

"He looks pale. Is he getting sick?" asked the priest.

"I'm not sick," said Ernie.

The priest said, "Even though you don't want any help, let me invite you to have something to eat. A bite might help Aaron said, "Sounds good to me, but what he really needs is your spiritual counseling. He just brought a ghost, an evil one, not knowing it was someone out of this world. Then in front of him it just disappeared. How do you think he feels after that, Reverend Chava?"

The reverend laughed covertly. Then, he jokingly said, "Don't fear the ghosts, fear the living." The reverend looked at them both, and in a serious tone he asked, "Have you two been drinking today?"

Aaron said, "I am telling you because I saw the ghost too. I am not making this up. I saw him carrying a mule with eyes of fire, breathing fire from her nose and mouth, wearing very fancy black clothes." Aaron added, "Then he tripped, they both fell, and when he saw what he was carrying, the mule just disappeared in front of our eyes. She vanished, still leaving some sparks of fire behind."

The reverend looked around him, lowered his voice, and said, "There is no such thing as ghosts."

Aaron said, "I saw it, too, and for what he told me it was the Countess of Stonemason's evil spirit."

The reverend got nervous. He put one finger on his own lips, and said, "Shhh, stop talking about ghosts, people are listening and you're going to scare them away from church."

Aaron said, "Let them hear, Reverend, so they know they have to stay away from the countess's cave."

The reverend said, "Let's go into the church. We will be able to speak more comfortably there."

The reverend walked to the church, and the two men followed him. Ernie sat on the back bench of the church. He said, "I'll sit here for a few minutes and will follow you later."

The reverend said, "A good piece of plain bread will make you feel better, come on." The reverend bent down and held one of Ernie's arms to help him get up. Aaron looked at them. The reverend said, "Brother, help him on the other side, please."

Aaron held Ernie's arm and together the three of them walked to the front of the church. Then, guided by the reverend they entered a big room to the left side of the church. The reverend and Aaron helped Ernie sit down on a chair. The reverend opened a door into the patio and returned quickly with a small plate of bread and a cup. He said, "Eat this cheese bread and drink this hot cocoa. It will make you feel better."

Through the same door that the reverend used to get the snack, came a middle-aged woman. "Reverend Chava, Sebastian, the teacher, is here waiting for you."

The reverend asked, "Why is he here, Elvira? It is merely coincidence that I came back, but you know that I was going to be back until late afternoon today."

Elvira answered, "I know, Reverend Chava. I told Sebastian, but he didn't care. He insisted on waiting for you until you came back. It seems like an emergency. I think the school where he works is haunted."

The reverend made a sign to Elvira, covering his lips with one finger, indicating her to be quiet. Then, Reverend Chava looked at his male guests, looked at her, shook his head, and in a low voice asked, "Where do you get these nonsensical ideas from, Elvira?" The reverend added, "Nothing is haunted around here, much less a school full of little angels."

Elvira said, "The little angels are in one part of the school, Reverend, but the evil spirits are in another part. When the children leave, the evil spirits play tricks on the schoolteacher. You will see when you go with Sebastian to the school."

Reverend Chava was embarrassed. "All right, Elvira, let's talk about that later. Sebastian the teacher is lucky that I am back so soon today. Tell him I will see him in a few minutes, after I talk to these gentlemen."

Elvira said, "I will let him know, he will be so happy to know he doesn't have to wait that long to see you." She left the room and closed the door behind her.

Aaron looked at the reverend, and said, "I see we are not the only ones encountering evil spirits today, Reverend."

The reverend said, "The only evil spirit I see today is the one of hunger and dehydration."

Aaron said, "Because you were late to see the real ones. It's starting to bother me that I am trying to convince you to believe. Shouldn't it be the other way around?"

The reverend said, "Don't take it that way. I believe, but I believe in the good word, in the savior, and in the salvation of the souls."

Aaron said, "All the opposite of that exists, too, and this man encountered it this morning just before we saw you, and that's why he is in this shocking state." Aaron continued, "The countess's evil spirit spent a good chunk of time with him today, and it wouldn't surprise me if she came back to see him again. What can you do to help him?"

The reverend opened a drawer and took out a little book. "This is a book of prayers to pray when you feel troubled in some way. Praying will make you feel much better. It will improve your life if you focus on the good things you have."

Aaron said, "That's all? Don't you have a blessed big cross and a big bottle of holy water or something like that to give him?"

The reverend said, "I can find all those things for him if it will make you two gentlemen relax."

Exasperated, Aaron said, "Relax? Who can relax with such an evil spirit following you?"

Ernie ate half of the cheese bread and some hot cocoa, and said, "No spirit is following me, the lady asked me to bring her here to this church when I was visiting the cave and I accepted her petition. That's all."

The reverend looked at both of them, and said, "I wish you would believe in good deeds as strongly as you feel about evil spirits." He added, "I have to talk to the teacher and see what he wants." The reverend subtly smiled, looked at Ernie, and said, "I see you have recovered your color, please come back to see me whenever you have time. I am usually here after 3 p.m."

Aaron asked, "What about the other holy items you were going to give him?

The reverend said, "That will have to wait, but I will have them ready for you the next time you come to see me." Both Aaron and Ernie stood up. The reverend looked at Ernie, and asked, "How do you feel?"

"I am fine, thank you."

Aaron said, "He will be back for his holy items." He placed the little book of prayers in Ernie's hands. They left together. Aaron said, "I will take you home."

Ernie said, "First, I need to find a place to stay."

Aaron said, "I knew you were not from around here. I will help you find a place. Mr. Lopez must have a nice, comfortable room for a reasonable price, and I heard the food is good too."

Meanwhile the reverend invited the teacher into his office. He said, "Teacher Sebastian, please come in. It is very nice to see you. What brings you here today?"

Sebastian said, "Thank you for your hospitality, Reverend. Unfortunately, what I am here to discuss is a little embarrassing and I don't know where to begin."

The reverend asked, "What is it?"

Sebastian shook his head, ran his fingers through his hair, and said, "It is getting intolerable working in that school."

The reverend said, "It must not be easy working with children all day, but are those children in your school really that bad?"

Sebastian shook his head, and said, "It is not the children who are bad. Most of them are very good kids, and I don't have problems with any of them. On the other hand, the school ambience is a nightmare. I always get to school earlier than the students to make preparations for the class, and everything is quiet, but then the noises start."

The reverend asked, "What noises?"

"The sound of a railcar rolling quickly and making sharp scratching noises inside the walls, and the worst part is the lady screaming horrendously!"

"What is causing all that noise, and who is that woman?" the reverend asked.

"It is very uncomfortable for me to say this, but there is no other explanation. It must be a ghost, La Llorona, or some evil spirit in that school."

"There must be a logical explanation about everything that is happening there."

"That is why I came to ask you to go to the school early in the morning before the students so you can bless the school, and especially the classroom where I teach." The teacher added, "There, in the classroom, is where you can hear the loudest of all the howls from beyond the grave. Just thinking about it gives me the chills. It might sound very silly to you, I know, and I am hoping all this nonsense stops with your blessing, Reverend."

"Very well, I will be there early Monday morning." They shook hands and the teacher left. The reverend said to himself, "This is very strange."

Elvira entered the reverend's office, and said, "Not that strange, Reverend, if you ask the monks living in the temple next to us. They have heard the weeping woman too." She added, "She was howling fiercely and scratching inside the walls of their temple. They could also hear the fast cart on the rails."

Reverend Chava said, "Elvira, how many times have I told you it is a bad habit to listen behind closed doors."

"I was just passing by the door, Reverend, and that's when I heard everything."

In disbelief, Reverend Chava said, "Of course."

Elvira looked at Reverend Chava with wide eyes, and said, "Since the death of the Countess of Stonemason, many mysterious things have been happening around her properties and other places."

Reverend Chava said, "There is no such thing as ghosts. When I find out what it is, I will tell you." He added, "I don't want you to believe everything you hear, Elvira. I have heard many rumors, and when I investigated them, none of them were true. If you didn't see it, don't believe it until you see it with your own eyes."

Elvira said, "I don't want to see it, and that is why I believe it. And you will see some of these strange happenings one of these days, Reverend, and that is when you will believe it."

"Elvira, more respect, please."

"I do respect you, Reverend."

"Then don't wish for me to see and believe all those ghost stories."

"I want you to see it so you can understand how all these people are feeling, Reverend." She added, "Then you will be able to help them for real."

"I see I am not going to convince you that ghosts are not real."

"And I see I won't convince you that they are real either," she said.

They both chuckled.

Reverend Chava said, "All right, Elvira, go home now, your family must be waiting for you. I will see you tomorrow morning."

"Yes, Reverend Chava. Thank you and I will see you tomorrow."

Reverend Chava was at the school that Monday early in the morning to see the teacher as he had promised. He knocked on the big wooden door with the palm of his hand. *Knock, knock, knock, knock.* A street dog came near him. Reverend Chava looked at the dog, and said, "Hey, look at you, it is nice to have some company today." He knocked on the door again. The street dog did the same with his paw, only not as loud. Even though he was a big dog, his paw was still small and padded compared to a human's hand. Reverend Chava smiled, and said, "You are trying to help me, thank you, hairy fellow!" The dog looked at him and cocked his head. Reverend Chava whispered, "Where is Teacher Sebastian? Isn't he here yet? I thought he was anxious for the school's blessing. I'll wait for him for a few minutes." He smiled and looked at the street dog. "We have time to get to know each other better, hairy fellow."

He extended his arm and showed his hand. The dog put his paw on Reverend Chava's hand. He grinned. Then, he chuckled, caressed the dog's body gently, and said, "You are a smart, hairy fellow." He asked, "Where is Teacher Sebastian?"

Sebastian was inside, sitting down on a chair in his classroom. His face was pale and his body was covered in a chilling sweat. His mouth was open and moving a little bit, as if he was trying to say something. His brown eyes were wide open. A screeching sound echoed in his classroom. It was an unearthly scream that made all the hairs on his arms stand, and goosebumps covered his entire body. He felt a freezing rush of air run through his whole body; from his back to his chest, then from his neck to his face, and finally his head. He felt an implacable iciness overtake him. His skin was bumpy in all places, and the hair on his head started to raise little by little as if something was pulling it from the ceiling. Then, he heard it loud and clear, a cart rolling quickly on a railroad and an enraged being scratching the wall of his classroom from the inside, then scratching the blackboard, and another horrible scream was heard, this time louder. It sounded like a woman who was lamenting something terrible, something nobody could change anymore.

Outside, a boy passed by carrying a wooden ladder. He looked at the reverend knocking on the school door, and asked, "Reverend Chava, would you like to borrow my ladder? It is small, but it would be big enough for you to reach the roof and call the teacher you are looking for. Apparently, nobody is near this big, thick, wooden door and it is going to be hard for them to hear you from the inside, unless you get up there with my ladder." He stood the ladder next to himself, and added, "You would save yourself some time."

Reverend Chava scratched his head, and said, "It doesn't sound like a very good idea, but at the same time it seems like the most reasonable thing to do right now." He added, "Thank you, your ladder will be very useful."

The boy gave him the ladder. Reverend Chava climbed it, and at the top he yelled, "Teeeeacher Sebaaaastian, I am here to seeee you! I am Reverend Chavaaaa. Open the dooooor please."

Inside Sebastian's classroom, the macabre underworld screaming stopped. Immediately the scratching sounds came to a halt, and the running of the cart quieted down too. The voice of Reverend Chava could be heard faintly inside his classroom. As soon as he could, Sebastian got up from his chair and walked quickly out of his classroom to open the main door of the school where Reverend Chava was. He was still calling his name from the top of the ladder. "Teacher Sebastian!"

As soon as Sebastian opened the school's door, the dog looked inside the school and ran away from there so quickly that it caused Reverend Chava to tumble down the ladder. He clung with both hands to the roof and made a big effort to avoid falling. Sebastian put the ladder back up. Reverend Chava asked, "What happened to that hairy fellow? This is too much for so early in the morning."

Sebastian said, "Come on in, Reverend Chava, I was waiting for you."

Reverend Chava said, "Thank you, young man, for letting me borrow your ladder. It was very useful as you said it would be."

"Anytime, Reverend!"

The boy left, carrying his ladder.

Reverend Chava and Sebastian could hear the dog howling from far away when they entered the school. Both men were inside the school when Sebastian closed the door. Reverend

Chava held his rosary, praying with his deep, regular voice, not too loud but not too low, either, and he sprinkled holy water everywhere.

Sebastian walked slowly and watched the reverend bless everything as he entered the school. He blessed the entrance, the hallways, and the courtyard in the middle of the school surrounded by classrooms. Sebastian stood at the entrance of his classroom. Reverend Chava asked, "Is this your classroom?"

Sebastian nodded, and said, "Come on in, Reverend Chava." They entered the classroom together. Reverend Chava continued to bless the school, praying with his rosary on his left hand and splashing water with his right hand. The drops of holy water dampened the furniture, the walls, the ceiling, and the floor. Sebastian looked around his quiet classroom and put his ear to the blackboard on the wall. He said, "Nothing, where are all the noises? The cart on the railroad, the scratching on the walls, and especially the horrible howling of the woman?" He looked around and added, "Why so quiet now? Please, woman, scream now that Reverend Chava is here."

Reverend Chava looked at Sebastian.

Sebastian said, "Come on, ghost, make all the afterworld noises you always make." He looked around and toward his blackboard. "And where did you hide that underworldly, unwelcoming, icy feeling?"

Reverend Chava looked at the desperate teacher, and asked, "Brother, pray with me."

The sun was shining, and everyone could feel the nice, warm environment of the courtyard and corridors in the school. Anyone who walked outdoors at this time of day, would feel the heat from the sun. Reverend Chava said, "Now that the whole school is blessed, make sure to pray in here every day, and don't overwork yourself, Teacher Sebastian." The reverend added, "Take a rest from time to time, it would be good for you to relax once in a while."

The teacher said, "Please, Reverend, sit down for a little bit here in my classroom, don't leave so soon."

The reverend agreed. He sat down, looked the teacher in the eye, and asked, "Is there anything you want to tell me?"

The teacher said, "Reverend Chava, I want you to hear all the noises I told you about, and you haven't heard anything."

"Don't worry, Brother Sebastian, a blessing not only changes the ambience, but it also eases your mind."

"Thank you for coming here for this blessing," Sebastian said. "I hope appeasing my mind will be enough to stop the restless spirit that surrounds this place."

"You won't hear a thing from now on."

"I wish I was as sure as you are about this, Reverend!"

Reverend Chava patted the teacher's arm, and said, "Teacher Sebastian, don't worry too much. Anyway, I am not far away from here, and I will come back as many times as is necessary." He added, "You just let me know."

"I will, Reverend, thank you."

The reverend stretched his arm out and they shook hands. Then, Reverend Chava left.

Sebastian waited a few seconds inside the school door. A cat jumped onto the roof, looked inside the school, arched his back, his hairs stood up, and he hissed fiercely. Then, he jumped to the next roof and meowed, running away from there. Sebastian opened the big wooden door and left the school.

He closed the door on his way out, did the sign of the cross, closed his eyes, and said, "Enough ghosts for one day, I am going home. A new home, a real home where there is peace and quiet." He walked quickly across the little plaza, and the street dog followed him. Sebastian saw Reverend Chava entering the monks' convent. He stopped outside one of the big windows of the monastery. He thought, *Reverend Chava forgot to tell me where the guesthouse is, and with all the commotion from the horrendous lady ghost, I forgot to ask him. Maybe he is not going to stay for long. As soon as he gets out I will ask him, and I'll be on my own way. It's starting to get too hot out here. I'll sit for a little bit until he gets out of there.*

The teacher sat down on the windowsill, held the bars covering it, and looked inside trying to see through the dark screen. He thought, *It is so refreshing to sit here. Where is that chilling wind coming from?* He answered his own question. *Inside the monks' convent there should not be any wind. Even though it is partially underground, it explains not being as hot as out here, but it doesn't explain the wind or it being that cold. This doesn't make any sense. I should ask Reverend Chava about this. He will know the answer. Anyway, he seems to have an explanation for everything.*

Sebastian continued to look into the window. He thought, *I can barely see anything. This window screen is so dark, and it doesn't let me see well inside, but I can still feel the cold breeze. What is that strange odor? I wish I could see inside.* He had his head in the window as much as the iron bars allowed. His face was against the window screen. He stuck his face in between the bars as much as he could. He used both hands to push the dark window screen in to see what was going on inside.

Someone opened the door nearby, and said, "Don't stay there, Teacher Sebastian. Come on in, you are welcome to come inside."

Sebastian looked up to see Reverend Chava. He blushed, and said, "I forgot to ask you about the guesthouse."

Reverend Chava said, "First, I would like you to meet someone, and it would be an opportunity to show you the monks' convent. You haven't been inside, have you Teacher Sebastian?"

"No, Reverend, I haven't."

"Let's go in, then. You must be very curious about how a monastery looks inside!" Reverend Chava took out a large iron key and opened the ample wooden door. He gently signaled the teacher to go in. Sebastian entered and waited for the reverend. Reverend Chava left the door ajar. He said, "I am sorry, Teacher Sebastian. I should have invited you to come with me to the guesthouse right away after the blessing. I knew I was forgetting something important."

Sebastian said, "I would appreciate it if you would take me to the guesthouse. I want a place where I can rest peacefully at night."

A monk passed by and acknowledged the reverend. "How are you doing, Reverend Chava? We are going to pray the rosary at the chapel. You and your guest are welcome to come and pray with us."

The reverend looked at the teacher, and asked, "What do you say, Teacher Sebastian, should we go and pray with them?"

"That would be nice, but I would rather go to the guesthouse and make sure I have a peaceful place to rest tonight, if you don't mind."

The reverend said, "Not at all, we will do that then."

The monk looked at the reverend, and said, "Reverend Chava, we have a couple of empty rooms here, if you want. You don't have to look elsewhere for a place to stay."

The reverend looked at the monk, and said, "I did not know there were empty rooms here, Jeronimo. This is very convenient." Then he looked at Sebastian, and asked, "What do you say, Teacher Sebastian, would you be willing to stay in here for some time?"

The teacher looked at him with hope, and said, "I don't know what to say. Would it be all right if I stay here? I don't want to be a burden to anyone, but it would be nice to have a peaceful place like this to spend the night after work."

Jeronimo said, "Then you can stay if you like it." The monk added, "You wouldn't be a burden, all the contrary, you could be of big help if you water the plants every other day, and it would be nice to have you pray with us whenever you have the time."

Sebastian had a subtle smile on his face.

Reverend Chava asked, "What do you say, Teacher Sebastian? It would be nicer to live in here than any guesthouse. Will you stay here with the monks? They would be great neighbors."

"Are you sure, Brother Jeronimo and Reverend Chava, that it is all right for me to stay here? Who do I need to talk to?"

Reverend Chava said, "You just talked to the right person, Brother Jeronimo, and you can stay here until there are new monks who need the room or until you decide to become a monk yourself and stay here permanently."

The teacher chuckled a little, and said, "Me? A monk? I don't think so. But I can stay here temporarily if it is all right with you two, and the rest of the monks."

Jeronimo said, "The rest of the monks will be happy to have you here with us." He said, "There are some rules that are important for everyone to follow, including you. If you agree to follow them, you can stay right away."

Sebastian asked, "What are the rules?"

Reverend Chava looked at Sebastian, and said, "I am sure the rules will be no problem for you to follow."

Sebastian said, "I would like to know what the rules are to make sure I will be able to follow them."

Jeronimo said, "For now, the most important rule for you to remember is that we close and lock the front door at seven in the evening when it is time for prayer before bed, and we would expect you to be here before that time and go to sleep by nine so everyone can rest to be ready for the next day."

Sebastian smiled, and said, "I have no problem with that. I will be here before seven in the evening. I will go to bed before nine, and I will be as quiet as a turtle."

Reverend Chava smiled, and said, "Then, it is settled. You will stay here starting today, Teacher Sebastian."

The teacher said, "I will go get my things from school. Would you tell me which one is my room?"

Jeronimo said, "Your room is that one at the end of the hallway, to the right."

Sebastian extended his hand to Jeronimo, and said, "Thank you, Brother Jeronimo, I will be back later with my belongings, and I will stay here starting today if it is all right with you."

"Sounds good to me. I will be waiting for you so I can introduce you to the rest of the monks."

Reverend Chava looked at both men, and said, "Let's go pray with them, if they haven't already finished." They all walked together. Then, Reverend Chava and Sebastian followed Jeronimo into the little chapel.

In the chapel there were two rows of benches with four benches on each side of the chapel. There were three monks on each bench except the last bench on each side. Those two benches at the back were empty and the three went to those benches, kneeled, and started praying with the rest of the monks. The monk leading the prayers, said, "We pray to the Lord for good world leaders."

In unison, the monks said, "Lord, hear our prayer."

The leading monk said, "We pray to the Lord for good community leaders."

The monks said, "Lord, hear our prayer."

The leading monk said, "We pray to the Lord for the church."

The monks said, "Lord, hear our prayer."

The leading monk said, "We pray to the Lord for the community."

The monks said, "Lord, hear our prayer."

The leading monk said, "We pray to the Lord for the sick. We pray to the Lord for the lonely."

The monks said, "Lord, hear our prayer."

The leading monk said, "We pray to the Lord for the dead so they can find eternal rest."

The monks said, "Lord, hear our prayer."

The leading monk said, "We pray to the Lord for the forgiveness of our sins."

The monks said, "Lord, hear our prayer."

The leading monk said, "We pray to the Lord for guidance so we can make good decisions."

The monks said, "Lord, hear our prayer."

The leading monk said, "We pray to the Lord for the neediest members of the community."

The monks said, "Lord, hear our prayer."

The leading monk said, "We pray to the Lord for the peace of our town and the peace of the world."

The monks said, "Lord, hear our prayer."

All of them prayed in chorus, in unity, with selflessness, expecting their prayers to be heard by the Creator of the universe, asking Him for the salvation of humanity. However, they were all secretly wishing the same thing in one way or another, that their prayers would also bring peace, healing, and harmony to their whole town.

CHAPTER EIGHTEEN

ESCAPING THE GHOST

It was nine o'clock at night when Sebastian heard knocking at the front door of the monastery. He was already set up to sleep after reading under the light of the candles. He thought, *Who could it be at this hour? I hope it is not the evil ghost who came after me, and if it is, the wicked ghost has to stay at the door for I am not going to open it tonight.*

The knocking continued, and Sebastian sat up on his blanket on the floor where he was trying to sleep. He scratched his head and thought, *Don't these people know that these monks will not open the door to anyone after nine o'clock?* He stood up and put his coat on. *And maybe they do know, and that is why they are still knocking, waiting for me to open the door. Well, I am not going to open it.*

He heard the knock again. It was not louder, but it was a much longer knock. *I am going to see who is at the door. How can these monks sleep through this much knocking?* He stepped out of his new room and looked down the dark empty hallway. *I just noticed how very long this hallway is.* He stood up and walked carefully through the obscure corridor. Then, in the middle of the hallway he felt a subtle but freezing wind, and thought, *How horribly cold it is in here.*

He walked quickly, got to the door, and opened it. There stood a man in his twenties. The young man looked at Sebastian, and said, "Good evening, Brother. My name is Ernie and I am here to ask for a holy place to stay. I can cook, clean, build walls, fix up things, whatever you need to be done I will do, if you allow me to stay here for some time."

Sebastian said, "You will have to ask the monks tomorrow because they are sleeping at this time."

Ernie said, "Please, let me sleep here tonight. I will be very quiet, and you will not even notice I am here. I have no place to go."

Sebastian asked, "Where are you coming from? Are you escaping from the law or something like that?"

Ernie said, "No, no, the law I have always followed, it is not the living but the departed ones who I am fearing. Please, let me stay here and I will be no bother to anyone."

Sebastian sighed, and said, "I shouldn't be doing this as I don't have the right or the authority to do it, but since you look very scared and in need of help, I will let you stay in my room tonight. You will have to talk to the monks tomorrow to see if they will allow you to continue staying here for a longer time."

Ernie said, "Thank you, Brother."

Sebastian showed him the way with a wave of his hand. Ernie entered the monastery and Sebastian closed and locked the wooden door.

Ernie said, "Thank you, you don't know how much you are helping me by letting me stay here tonight."

Sebastian said, "Let's keep our voices low. We don't want to wake anyone up and get kicked out of here."

Ernie nodded his head and they walked quietly down the long and dark corridor. On the way to the dormitory they looked at each other and hurried to the room at the end of the hallway. Sebastian led the way and they entered the room. He closed the door, went to his bed made of blankets on the floor, picked up a couple of blankets, and said, "Use these to make your own bed. It isn't much, but at least we will have a peaceful place to sleep tonight."

Ernie said, "And we will keep each other company." He added, "Maybe you don't need anybody's company, but I don't want to be alone after delivering the countess's ghost to the church. I can't stop thinking about her. Even when I sleep, she is still there in my mind. I don't have dreams anymore, only nightmares."

Sebastian opened his eyes wide, and asked, "What do you mean, you took the countess's ghost to the church?"

Ernie said, "I took her to the church to help her, you know, to liberate her from the issues holding her back, keeping her here in agony." Ernie added, "I wanted to free her from her curse and help her, but I couldn't make it to the church. We were just a few steps away from the church when we fell down on the ground and she disappeared in front of my eyes."

Sebastian said, "I wanted to ask you if you are serious, but I believe you. The question in my mind is why did you accept to help the countess's ghost, and after you did, why didn't you finish taking her to the church?" He looked at Ernie with curiosity, and exclaimed, "You are very brave!"

"First, I helped her because I didn't know she was a ghost, you know, I never saw anything like that before," said Ernie. "Then, she was getting heavier with every step I took down the mountain. It was very hard for me to get down here, and when I fell, she just disappeared in front of my eyes, but I wasn't the only one who saw her."

Sebastian was lying down, looking at the ceiling, and listening attentively.

"There was another man who tried to help me," Ernie said. "He took me into the church to see Reverend Chava, but the reverend didn't seem to believe us. It is true that before this experience, I didn't believe in ghosts, either, you know, but he is a reverend. Aren't reverends supposed to believe in spirits and what the eye can't see? Well, not this one."

Sebastian said, "I know what you mean. I know Reverend Chava and he doesn't seem to believe in the things he cannot see, like ghosts. Reverend Chava is a good person and tries to help. He prays and seems to have faith, but he doesn't seem to believe in ghosts."

Ernie said, "I wish I was like him, like I was before, the way I have been all my life before this, not believing in ghosts, but I haven't been able to rid my mind of the countess's apparition. I feel her around me everywhere I go, and I fear her. I don't know what to do anymore."

Sebastian gently said, "It is good that you are here tonight and neither of us has to face the horror in our minds alone." He added, "We will keep each other company like you said before, and it will be easier for both of us to forget about our worries. Let's say our prayers and go to sleep."

Ernie said, "Thank you for letting me stay here in your room tonight."

"No problem, I was exactly in your place earlier today, asking for a place to sleep, and the monks are kindly letting me stay here for some time. This is my first night in this room, as it is for you too."

Ernie asked, "What is your name?"

"My name is Sebastian."

"Mine is Ernie. Thanks again for letting me stay here tonight."

"You're welcome. Good night, Ernie."

"Good night, Sebastian."

The room was dark but not completely as the crescent moon could be seen through the window. Ernie felt hopeful in his bed on the floor. He knew that it was going to be better now that he was not alone. Sebastian was a little worried about letting his new friend stay in there with him, but the relief he felt of having company that night was greater. Even though they had just met, there was a connection between them. They somehow knew they could count on each other. They would at least keep each other company and away from the ghost that had been frightening them so much.

The next day, early in the morning, as soon as the sun was rising, Sebastian opened his eyes, looked at the ceiling, and said, "Ernie, Ernie, wake up. It is time for you to go outside and knock on the door so you can talk to the monks and ask them to let you stay here." Sebastian heard a knock at the main door of the monastery. He stood up and walked to Ernie's bed, and said, "Ernie."

There was no one on Ernie's bed. The blankets were folded. A bell sounded in the small chapel. *Ding, ding, ding, ding.* At the same time, he heard a knock on his own door. He opened the door and saw a monk. The monk said, "Brother, we have a meeting at the chapel."

"Now?"

"Yes," said the monk.

Sebastian followed the monk. They walked through the long semi dark hallway. Even though the sun was up, the hallway was dark and cold because the monastery was half underground. They entered the chapel full of monks. Jeronimo stood at the altar with Ernie next to him, and said, "Brothers, this brother came to us this morning asking for help and a place to stay." He continued, "Therefore, I have asked all of you to meet here with us this morning to ask your permission for him to stay with us here in the monastery."

One of the monks asked, "Brother, why are you asking for our opinion when you didn't with Teacher Sebastian?"

Jeronimo replied, "Teacher Sebastian is the teacher of one of our community schools." He added, "Also, Reverend Chava recommended him to be allowed to stay here for some time with us."

Another monk from the benches asked, "Brother, are you asking our permission for this brother to stay with us, because he knows no one in the community?"

Jeronimo answered, "Yes, Brother, that is the reason I am asking all of you for the authorization for him to stay here at the monastery. I would like for all of you to cast your vote here.

He will be living with us momentarily until he finds another safe place to stay."

Ernie said, "My name is Ernie. I am honest and I like to help others." He added, "My stay here will be temporary, as Brother Jeronimo has already stated. I will be of no trouble for any of you if you let me stay."

Jeronimo said, "Please raise your hand to vote for this brother to be allowed to live here for some time with us until he finds another place to stay. Take into consideration that if he stays, he will be sharing a room with one of you as we have no more empty rooms at this moment."

Sebastian raised his hand. All eyes were on him. He said, "Brothers, it is all right for him to stay in my room, you don't have to worry about finding a room for him as my room is big enough for the both of us."

Jeronimo said, "Thank you, Brother Sebastian, it is very kind of you." Then Jeronimo looked at the rest of the monks, and said, "There is one less thing to worry about since Brother Sebastian kindly offered to share his room with Brother Ernie. The only thing left here is for you to cast your vote about agreeing on Brother Ernie staying here with us." He added, "Please, Brothers, I ask all of you to look into your hearts and raise your hand to cast your vote in favor of this brother staying here with us temporarily."

Most of the men raised their hands, including Sebastian, with the exception of two monks. Jeronimo asked, "Please, Brother, each of you say your reasons for not agreeing with this new brother's stay."

The two disagreeing monks stood up. One looked at his colleague, and said, "Go ahead, Brother."

The other monk looked at him kindly, and answered, "Thank you, Brother." Then he looked at Ernie and Jeronimo, and said, "I understand this brother, Ernie, has no place to stay, and that we have to be kind to others. However, it worries me that he may not be what he says he is and would put all of us in danger."

Ernie said, "Brother, I know you do not know me, but I give you my word that I will be of no trouble for any of you." He added, "Believe me, this is as difficult for you as it is for me. I would prefer to stay in the woods by myself instead of annoying all of you with my presence. The problem is, there is a spirit who is following me around, and I found out I am not as brave as I thought I was when beings from the other world are involved. The truth is that I am afraid to be alone. I never thought I would say this in my entire life, but it is the reality. I don't want to be alone anymore and the best place for me to be at this moment is here in this house of prayer, your home."

The monk who expressed his concern calmly said, "I hope you are speaking the truth, Brother Ernie, if that is really your name and that your intentions are only good."

Jeronimo looked at the second monk who did not vote for Ernie's stay, and asked, "What about you, Brother, what is your concern with Brother Ernie's stay?"

The second disagreeing monk replied, "This is a monastery. Is Brother Ernie considering becoming a monk?"

Jeronimo answered, "Not at this moment, but his stay would offer him the opportunity to consider it if he likes the lifestyle here at the monastery." Then Jeronimo looked at Ernie, and asked, "What do you think about becoming a monk, Brother Ernie, is it a possibility in your mind?"

"I feel the need to say yes to have your minds at peace, but the reality is that I have never felt the vocation in all my life to become a religious man," said Ernie. "It will certainly be a new experience for me living here in the monastery, but I don't know if this would really inspire me to become a monk."

Jeronimo said, "Brothers, why don't you give this man the opportunity we all would like to have if we were in his place?"

One of the two monks with the negative vote said, "All right, Brother, let's welcome him here with us." He looked at the other disagreeing monk, and asked, "What do you think, Brother?"

He replied, "It is all right with me too, Brother, let's give him an opportunity." He added, "Teacher Sebastian does not have any objections on his stay, and he has even offered to share his room. Besides, Brother Ernie seems sincere and honest."

The other monk who voted against Ernie added, "We will find out sooner or later what good comes out of having two worldly men living in a holy place."

Jeronimo said, "Thank you, Brothers, for your understanding and acceptance of these two new brothers in this house of prayer." He looked at Ernie, and said, "The morning prayers are going to be said in a few minutes, and I would like you to pray with us, Brother Ernie."

The monks looked at Ernie. He looked at Jeronimo, and said, "That I will do, Brother. Prayer will do me some good, I hope."

As the little chapel was almost full of monks, Ernie sat at one of the last two benches in the chapel. Sebastian sat on the other bench across from Ernie. Both men prayed with the monks. The prayers lasted for about an hour. Then, some monks went to tend the gardens. Others went to clean the monastery, sweeping and dusting. Some cooked, while others fixed the chapel and the monastery. Sebastian said, "Brothers, it is time for me to go to school. Thank you for everything and I will see you after class, in the evening."

Jeronimo said, "The milk is not boiled yet, but you should take a piece of bread with cheese and some water for breakfast."

Sebastian said, "It is very kind of you, Brother, but I don't want to bother any of you more than necessary."

Another monk looked at Jeronimo and Sebastian, then asked, "Would you like me to get the bread with cheese? It will be no bother at all."

Sebastian stood there quietly, feeling grateful, looking at both monks. Jeronimo looked at the monk offering the meal, and said, "That would be very nice, Brother. Yes please, so Teacher Sebastian will have some food in his stomach before teaching his students."

The monk offering the food hurried through the corridors, entered the kitchen, and came back with bread and cheese wrapped in a piece of cloth and a jar of water covered with a cup. The monk looked at the teacher, outstretched his arms with the food, and said, "Here you go, Teacher Sebastian. Teaching children takes a lot of energy, and you need to eat to have strength to do your work."

Sebastian smiled at him, and said, "Thank you, Brother, it is very kind of you." He looked at Jeronimo, and said, "You too, Brother Jeronimo, thank you very much. I will see you both in the evening."

As Sebastian was leaving, Ernie stood next to the two monks, and asked, "What should I do to help here in the monastery? Please tell me what needs to be done and I will be very happy to help you."

Jeronimo opened his eyes wide, and asked, "Brother, would you like to go with Teacher Sebastian and ask if he wants any help in school today? I am sure he will be pleased to have your help for a few days. Why don't you ask him and see if he likes this idea."

Ernie nodded in agreement, and said, "All right, Brother, I'll catch up with him, and be back if he doesn't need any help." He walked quickly after Sebastian. He caught up with him as they neared the school. Ernie said, "Sebastian, I have been trying to catch up to you, but you are such a fast walker."

Sebastian said, "I am sorry to hear that I made you walk all the way here, Ernie. How can I help you?"

"Jeronimo wants me to keep you company at your work and help you in anything you need help with for some days." He smiled at Sebastian, and asked, "What do you say, do you want me here with you today?"

Sebastian looked at him kindly, and said, "That would be very nice, Ernie, but I am just not used to having any helpers at work."

"Should I go back then?"

"No, no, please stay. It would be nice to have someone to talk to while the children get to school."

Ernie said, "All right, but I don't know anything about teaching children, so I hope you will find something extra for me to help you with that doesn't require me to teach or do anything with kids."

Sebastian chuckled, and said, "Don't worry, I will let you know what to do in order to help me in the classroom without having to deal with the boys." He took a big key out of his satchel and inserted it inside the big, thick wooden door. He opened the door and both men entered the school. Sebastian put his key back in his satchel once inside and closed the door. Then they walked through the corridors, around the courtyard, and into the classroom. Ernie left the classroom door ajar.

Sebastian sat on a chair and pulled out a bowl full of stones from his wooden desk. The drawer fell to the floor. It was broken. Sebastian put it back in the desk and it hung to one side. Many stones fell through the crack of the drawer.

Ernie excitedly said, "I can start fixing this drawer while you teach the children!"

Sebastian smiled, and said, "That is an excellent idea, Ernie! You sure are going to be of great help around here. I have been wanting to fix this desk, but never got to it. As soon as the principal gets here, we will go meet her so she knows you are going to be here with me helping me fix the classroom."

Ernie smiled, and said, "Sounds good!"

The wind was whistling, and it opened the classroom door abruptly. Ernie crossed his arms to protect himself from the cold wind, and said, "This is the coldest wind I have ever felt at this time in the morning."

Sebastian wanted to say something, but he could not speak. His teeth started to chatter. Then they heard footsteps— female footsteps wearing high heels. They both looked up at the ceiling, from where they both heard the footsteps. Then, they heard a cart on the rails inside the walls behind the blackboard. They heard a woman's loud, screechy, desperate scream, "Aaaaaaaaaah!" Then, they heard sharp nails scratching the wall behind the blackboard. The coldness intensified in the room. They could see each other's cold breath. They turned pale looking at each other and then both turned their heads to look at the wall with the blackboard. They looked at the door as it closed suddenly with a violent force. Then, everything was quiet for a few seconds. The bowl full of stones slid from the middle of the desk and fell to the floor. The stones flew everywhere. The lock of the door slid slowly into place by itself and locked the door with both men still inside. They heard more footsteps on the ceiling. Then, they heard a jump and heard the footsteps in the room next to them, and a shadow flew quickly between them.

Ernie ran to the door, unlocked it, and quickly opened it. He whispered, "Sebastian."

Sebastian ignored the shadow in front of him, looked at Ernie, and ran to the door. They both got out of the door and Ernie closed it behind them. A middle-aged woman was in the hallway three classrooms away from them, and she asked, "Teacher Sebastian, what is all this commotion about?"

Sebastian looked at her, and said, "Good morning, Principal Sarah. This is Ernie and he will help me fix the furniture and the classroom." He added, "That is, if you authorize him to help me with it."

The principal asked, "Do you know him well, Teacher Sebastian?"

"Yes, I do."

"Are you recommending him to be around our students?" the principal asked.

"He will be around the students under my supervision, and he will be exclusively in charge of fixing the classroom while I teach the students."

The woman looked at Ernie, then at Sebastian, and said, "He can stay for a few days under your responsibility."

Ernie looked at the principal, and said, "Good morning, ma'am."

Sebastian said, "Thank you, Principal Sarah."

The woman said, "You need to drink some coffee or eat something before you start working because you are both so pale and skinny."

Sebastian said, "Yes, we brought something, and we are going to eat it soon."

She turned to go to her office, and said, "You know where to find me if you need me."

"Yes, Principal Sarah, thank you."

Ernie said, "Have a good day, ma'am."

She was far enough away from them not to hear what Ernie was saying. "I can't believe that ghost followed me here too." He shook his head, held his forehead with one hand, and said, "I regret coming here with you and bringing you this, this, this evil ghost."

With wide eyes, Sebastian asked, "What are you talking about? This ghost has been bothering me for some time now before I even got to know you, and it has nothing to do with you." Sebastian scratched his head, and asked, "The only thing I am wondering is why is it getting worse? I thought the ghost would not bother me if I had company, but I was wrong."

Ernie looked at him, and said, "If this ghost has been bothering you before you even knew me, there must be many ghosts in this town." He asked, "I wonder why?"

Sebastian said, "I don't really want to know why." He added, "I just want to know how we can get rid of them for good."

"Does the principal know about the ghost?"

Sebastian replied, "Probably not."

"You haven't told her about it?" asked Ernie.

"No, she would think 'this man is crazy' and she would kick me out of here for good!"

Ernie lowered his head, and said, "Yeah, I would probably think you're crazy, too, and I would replace you with a saner and better teacher."

"Well, thank you very much. It's good you are not the principal!"

Ernie said, "You know, it is not easy to believe in what you cannot touch. Before, when I had not seen anything like this, I didn't believe in ghosts either."

Sebastian opened his arms and raised his hands above his head slowly, and said, "We have to get back into the classroom and clean it before the kids get here for their morning session."

Ernie asked, "Have the children seen anything like this?"

"No, everything goes back to normal when the children are here."

"You mean nothing like this happens when the children are inside that same classroom?"

Sebastian said, "Nothing at all, no ghosts, no mysterious noises, nothing, only children."

"I don't feel like going back inside your classroom, but the pebbles are everywhere."

"I have to arrange the classroom for the kids before they get here, but we can do that later for the afternoon session."

Relieved, Ernie asked, "Really?" He scratched his head, and asked, "Where are you going to teach the children this morning?"

"Right here, in the middle of the playground."

"I am so happy to hear that, I don't ever want to go back inside your classroom."

"I know, me neither, but we have to go back in there and arrange everything, but not now," said Sebastian. "We can fix the classroom when the children go home for lunch, and it will be ready when they come back for their afternoon classes."

Ernie said, "I'm glad we don't have to go in there right now. We will figure out a way to do it later."

The principal opened the school's front door. The children started running into the school. It looked like all of them wanted to get inside at the same time. Their giggles and laughs could be heard throughout the whole school. The principal loudly said, "Boys, enter orderly, slow down, everyone, listen, walk carefully!"

A boy loudly said, "Teacher Sebastian, our classroom is closed."

Sebastian stood in the middle of the playground under a tree, smiled at him, and reassured him. "Yes, Steve, we are having our classes here in the playground this morning."

Many children screamed in delight. And they soon surrounded Sebastian. The twelve of them were attentive and sat down on the ground. Sebastian said, "Good morning, students."

In chorus, they answered, "Good morning, Teacher Sebastian."

He said, "This is Mr. Ernie and he is going to be here with us for some time."

Ernie said, "Good morning, children."

Together, the children said, "Good morning, Mr. Ernie."

Ernie said, "I must say that all of you have such good behavior."

Steve stood up straight, and loudly said, "I am an exemplary citizen, respectful of myself and others, and ready to better my community."

Ernie said, "That was beautiful, can you say it again for me, please?"

Sebastian looked at the children, and asked, "Everyone?"

All twelve students stood up straight, and in chorus proudly said, "I am an exemplary citizen, respectful of myself and others, and ready to better my community."

Ernie said, "Thank you. You are the best students I have ever seen."

The children sat down on the ground around their teacher. Ernie stood next to a tree and watched them.

Sebastian said, "Good job, everyone."

Steve looked at Sebastian, and asked, "Do you want us to gather pebbles?"

Sebastian said, "Yes, Steve, during our last class we gathered ten rows of ten pebbles each. Today I want you to do the same thing, but twice."

The children got up from the ground. Sebastian looked at the children, and said, "Everyone, wait, you know the rules. You can walk around to find your pebbles as far as you want to walk, as long as I can see you at all times, all right?"

All the children replied, "Yes, Teacher Sebastian." They started walking and collecting pebbles. Sebastian watched his students walk around the playground.

Ernie looked at Sebastian, and said, "Aren't you afraid the ghost will scare one of them?"

"No, they are not going to go inside the classroom," Sebastian said. "There are twelve today. Don't lose sight of any of them, could you help me with this, please?"

Ernie said, "Of course, and what are you going to do?"

"The same as you, watch them. When they walk everywhere it might be a little confusing to count them, but the two of us doing the job will make it easier."

"Sounds good to me. I will make sure you have twelve kids and that no one sets foot inside the haunted classroom."

"Please don't say that in front of the children or it will ignite their imagination that is already full of ghost stories."

"Got it, but I don't know if it is only their imagination," Ernie said. "After everything I witnessed today, I would believe anything they say!"

Sebastian said, "Don't believe everything you hear, unless you see it with your own eyes."

"I would prefer not to see or hear anything about ghosts ever again."

Sebastian looked at him quietly. Then, he looked around. The children were all lying down on the grass. Their notebooks were open and the boys were counting their little pebbles. One of the kids sat on the grass. He had his pebbles in his hands and didn't know where to put them. Sebastian asked, "Where is your notebook, Adam?"

He nervously answered, "I forgot it."

Jesus took out a red handkerchief, extended it on the grass in front of Adam, and said, "You can count your pebbles here on Steve's handkerchief, I would give you some sheets from my notebook, but I don't want to move my pebbles and start counting again."

Adam looked at Jesus, smiled subtly, and said, "Thank you, this is all right." Adam's expression changed. He was feeling better. He started to count his pebbles on the handkerchief, but they were piling one pebble over the other. He took his pebbles, put them on the side on the grass and patted the handkerchief with his hands to fix the grass under it. Then, he was able to place the pebbles in lines of ten to count them. He laid down comfortably and continued to fix his counting tools.

Later, Sebastian said, "It is twenty minutes before lunchtime. The students who are finished with their assignments for this morning may put everything away and play a game under this tree near me. If you are tired of lying or sitting down, come and get a rope and start jumping."

Adam put his pebbles on a big leaf, folded the red handkerchief, and gave it to Steve. Adam said, "Thank you for letting me borrow it."

Steve said, "You're welcome."

Adam looked at Steve, smiled, and asked, "Would you like to jump rope?"

Steve nodded yes.

Adam walked toward Sebastian, and asked, "Teacher Sebastian, can I use a jump rope, please?"

Sebastian smiled at him and took a rope out of his satchel and gave it to him.

Adam asked, "Can I have another one for Steve, please?"

"Of course." He took another rope from his satchel and gave it to him.

Adam stood in front of Jesus, and asked, "Would you like to jump rope with me and Steve?"

Jesus smiled, and said, "Not yet, I need to finish my work first."

Adam skip jumped toward Steve with a rope in each hand and offered him one. "Here's yours, Steve."

Sebastian asked, "Before we begin the games, can anyone please summarize what you did today?"

Adam stood up and raised his hand.

Sebastian said, "Go ahead, Adam."

Adam said, "We counted to two hundred by ones, tens, fives, and twos."

Sebastian said, "Very good, Adam, thank you!" There were other children raising their hands. Sebastian asked, "Go ahead, Manny."

Manny said, "We divided two hundred by two, by five, and by ten."

Sebastian looked at him, and said, "Very good, Manny, thank you!"

Everybody else had their hands down. Sebastian looked at Steve, and asked, "Would you like to add anything else, Steve?"

"Yes."

"Go ahead, Steve."

He said, "We observed the symmetry in various leaves, and we talked about being honest and good citizens everywhere we go."

Sebastian said, "Wonderful job, Steve. Very well done, everyone, go ahead and play for a few minutes until lunchtime!"

Adam and Steve started jumping and counting with their jump ropes. They were playing happily. Steve whispered, "My sister told me that the ghost of the Countess of Stonemason haunts her school. She and her friends are afraid of the bats that come out of their chalk board. Her teacher Miss Alma is terrorized by it, but she won't admit it." Adam whispered back, "Boo, the Countess of Stonemason's ghost is here now, and she is going to get you!" Both boys looked at each other and started giggling quietly.

The rest of the students were still dividing their pebbles. Some of them were observing a variety of leaves, dividing them in halves and commenting on their comparisons with each other. Nico said, "This is symmetrical because it has three pointy sides from each half and even though these leaves are different sizes when folding each leaf, one side matches the other side perfectly."

Louis said, "Very good, Nico. Write it down so we can go jump rope."

Nico smiled, and said, "All right, but what are you going to write?"

Louis looked at various leaves, and said, "I already wrote it, let's go jump."

Nico said, "All right!"

Soon all the boys were jumping rope. A couple of them climbed a small tree. Sebastian said, "All right, boys, come down from that tree please. It is time to go home and have some lunch."

All the boys happily screamed, "Hooray!" Except for Adam. He was still jumping rope when the rest of the students were on their way home for lunch.

"Adam, go home and eat. Aren't you hungry?" asked Sebastian.

Adam said, "A little bit, but not much, I prefer to play a little longer."

"Go home, you can continue playing during the afternoon classes. We will have some time to play again."

Adam stopped jumping. He gave the rope back to Sebastian, lowered his head, and walked home. When he left, Ernie said, "Poor little one, he didn't seem too excited to go back home for lunch."

Sebastian said, "He has not been the same since his mother died some months ago. School is the only place some of these kids get some of the positive attention they need, and this is why I always try to give my attention to all of my students in class."

Ernie said, "You are a good teacher, Sebastian, and your kids know they have to make a positive contribution to society. To me that is a big thing you are teaching them."

"All the knowledge in the world would be worthless to them without some moral values," said Sebastian. "Let's eat our lunch so we can finish cleaning the classroom."

"I was afraid you would say that. Do we have to go back into your classroom?"

"Yes, I have no choice. Besides, our lunch is in there."

"I would prefer not to eat today if I could avoid going inside that spooky place again."

"Come on, Ernie, we will be all right. A little ghost and some scary noises are not going to harm us."

"You may have gotten used to the haunted classroom, but not me. I cannot get used to frightening ghosts."

"Let's have some lunch," said Sebastian.

As they both walked slowly toward the classroom, the sun became covered by some thick, gray clouds. The wind started blowing harder. It blew all the children's green leaves around the playground. It blew Sebastian's classroom door open when they got near the door. Sebastian looked at Ernie, waved his hands, and said, "Go ahead, Ernie."

Ernie gestured with his hands, and gently said, "After you, Sebastian."

Sebastian entered the classroom first. Ernie followed him and looked all around the classroom. He picked up a bowl and used it to gather the pebbles from the floor. Then, it all started again. Female footsteps were heard in the hallway outside the classroom. They both stopped what they were doing and looked toward the door, but no one seemed to be there. They both walked out of the classroom and looked for the lady walking around, but they could not see anyone. The wind blew on them, and this time it was colder. They both got chills and went back inside the classroom. Then, they heard it again, a cart on a railroad inside the classroom's walls moving quickly while someone howled in pain.

Ernie looked at Sebastian, and asked, "Do you deal with this every day?"

Sebastian answered, "The lady howling in desperation? Yes, she is here every day."

The cart stopped, and the loud, slow scratches inside the wall were heard by both. They glanced at each other. The scratches were heard moving around the entire classroom and then they stopped where they began, behind the blackboard. The room got darker; it must have been the gray clouds covering the sun. Ernie put his hands together and started praying in a low voice. Sebastian saw him and began doing the same thing. Everything was quiet besides their whispered prayers.

Ernie asked, "What is that scent?"

Sebastian asked, "Is it like a fine perfume?"

Ernie asked, "You can smell it too?"

They looked at each other quietly. Sebastian grabbed their lunch, looked at Ernie, and said, "Let's eat in the playground."

Ernie opened the door and they both walked quickly out of the classroom. They arrived at the playground and sat on the grass in front of each other. Sebastian cut the bread with cheese in half and offered the two pieces to Ernie. He took one and bit into it.

As they finished eating their lunch and drinking water, they heard the children coming back for their afternoon classes. Ernie asked, "Are you taking the kids into the classroom?"

Sebastian said, "Not today. Let's wait for a less intense day to have the children inside the classroom."

"That's a good decision so they don't see the ghost."

"We will go to the plaza this afternoon," said Sebastian.

Later on, at the end of the school day, Sebastian asked, "Who can tell me what time it is?" The children looked at the stone clock in the middle of the plaza. They talked to each other and tried to figure out the time. The kids could not come to an agreement.

One asked, "How are we going to know the time on the stone clock?"

"We look at the clock and use the sun to know the time."

Another kid said, "It has to be after four because we got to school by two and we have done many things already."

Another kid asked, "Where on the stone clock does it say the time is four something?"

Another child said, "We should know the time just by looking at the clock, and it should not take us this long to figure out the time."

Ernie, who was sitting on a bench next to Sebastian, asked, "Can I help your kids figure this out?"

Sebastian replied, "Feel free to do so."

Ernie stood up, looked around the gardens in the plaza, and picked up a small, dried flower stem. He put it in a tiny hole in the upper part around the middle of the stone clock. He said, "Look, children, when you want to know the time on this clock, first you have to find a stick and place it in this hole in the middle of the stone clock."

The children looked at him attentively as he explained, "Then, you find the stick's shadow on the clock, and you read the time by counting the lines around it."

Steve said, "It is almost five, time to go home."

Sebastian looked at his students and intervened. "Yes, Steve, it is almost time to go home." He continued, "Very good job, everyone." Sebastian looked at Ernie, and said, "Thank you, Ernie, very good explanation, but now we have to head back to school so everyone can go home from there."

Steve asked, "Can I go home from here instead of going back to school?"

Sebastian said, "No, Steve, we have to go back to school, and everyone can leave from there."

Steve asked, "Why not?"

Sebastian said, "For many reasons, your parents might want to pick you up from school today."

Adam said, "My parents never pick me up from school, so it would be all right for me to go home from here."

Sebastian said, "We have to say good-bye to the principal before going home so she does not worry about us."

Adam said, "All right, I would not want Principal Sarah to worry about us."

The children walked in pairs with Ernie leading and Sebastian at the back of the line. When they got to the school, the principal was waiting by the door. She asked, "How was your walk, everyone?"

Some of the students said, "Nice!"

Others said, "Fun!"

Adam and a few others smiled at her quietly.

The principal said, "It is almost time to go, boys. Put your school supplies in your classroom and then you may go home.

The children ran to the playground, took their pebbles and leaves, and went to the classroom. Ernie, with a terrified face, looked at Sebastian. Sebastian calmly said, "Let's go with the kids into the classroom." They entered the classroom right behind the kids. They put their things inside their wooden desks and sat down quietly looking at their teacher. The classroom was completely silent until Steve accidentally dropped his notebook and Adam caught it with his hands. They both laughed.

The sun shone through the door and windows. Feeling amazed, Ernie looked at Sebastian, and said, "This classroom is nicer than I thought."

Sebastian said, "It is usually very nice when the children are here." He looked at his students, counted them quietly, then looked at the class list and saw that everyone on the list was there in the classroom. He said, "Good job students, now you may stand up and walk slowly to leave the school and go home to your families."

In chorus, the kids said, "Good night, Teacher Sebastian."

"Good night, children." They all walked in an orderly fashion and left the school to go home.

Ernie said, "What a different classroom."

Sebastian agreed. "It is always like this when the children are here."

Ernie asked, "You mean that you have been scared by this ghost only when the children are not here and as soon as they get here nothing of the sort happens?"

Sebastian nodded his head, and said, "That is the way it happens every day. It's strange, isn't it?"

"It is, but not too much if you think about it. These kids are innocent, with no sins—who would want to scare them?"

Sebastian chuckled, and said, "Now you make it sound like the two of us are sinners."

"Maybe, but the children are the purest form of humanity," said Ernie.

"No one could disagree with you about that." Sebastian added, "I am grateful the kids don't have to witness any of the unholy presences we have to deal with."

Ernie said, "Let's go home to the monks."

"Let's go, Ernie."

They walked out of the classroom. Sebastian closed the door behind him and saw the principal in the hallway. She was leaving. She turned around, and said, "Good night, gentlemen. I will see you both tomorrow, I presume?"

Sebastian looked at Ernie and wondered what his answer to the principal would be. Ernie said, "Good night, Principal Sarah. I will see you tomorrow."

Sebastian smiled at Ernie, then looked at the principal, and said, "We will see you tomorrow, Principal Sarah. Thank you and have a good night!"

Principal Sarah looked at Sebastian, and said, "Please lock the door on your way out."

"I will." And he did.

As they walked to the monastery, Ernie said, "I never thought I would say this, but I miss being home with my family. I had a full belly every day, there were no scary ghosts, and everybody treated me kindly most of the time."

"You might be starving," said Sebastian. "Don't you worry, I will invite you to eat at the plaza as soon as I get my payment in about a week."

"Thank you, Sebastian. I wish I could do the same for you so you could try my sister Clara's cooking." He added, "Someday, when you have a few free days, you should come home with me for some time."

Sebastian said, "Thank you for the invitation!"

Ernie asked, "Are you accepting the invitation?"

"That's a promise. I would love to go with you and meet your family when the horrifying ghost leaves and all of this is behind us."

When they reached the monastery, there was a monk at the door. He received them with a smile, and said, "It is good to see you two. I have been waiting for you. Please follow me to the kitchen." He took a pan out of a bag hanging from the ceiling and served each of them a plate of food. Then he served them each a glass of milk. They smiled at the monk. The monk asked, "Why aren't you eating, you don't like it?"

Sebastian said, "It looks very good!"

Ernie said, "I love molletes. Thank you for saving them for us!" He happily took a bite.

Sebastian took a bite, and said, "Delicious, did you make them?"

The monk said, "No, but as usual, you get the bread, add fried beans, cheese, pico de gallo, and if you are hungry, it is going to be a glorious meal." The monk added, "Brothers, enjoy your meal. I have to get back to my prayers."

After their meal, Ernie took their dishes and washed them next to the well. He used some sand from the ground to scrub the dishes clean. Then, he rinsed them and put them back in the kitchen. Sebastian wiped the table, swept the floor, and asked, "Should we go to the little chapel for the evening prayers?"

Ernie said, "I feel a little tired, I want to lie down."

Sebastian said, "Let's go rest then."

Inside their room, Ernie fixed his bed on the floor.

Sebastian sat on a chair to plan his lesson for the next day when they heard the wind. It whistled outside the window. Ernie shook and covered himself with the blanket for a minute. Sebastian's whole body shook and then he continued writing. In a low voice, Sebastian said, "Someone was whispering in my ear."

Ernie asked, "What did you hear?"

"I couldn't understand."

"Can you smell what I smell?"

"The fine perfume? Yes, I smell it."

"Where is it coming from if neither of us uses any, or do you?"

Sebastian quickly replied, "Of course not, I am almost certain the same spirit from school has followed us here."

Ernie asked, "How can this be possible? So that is why it feels weird in here, and so cold."

Sebastian left his papers and his coal pen on the night table. He looked at Ernie. Then, he looked around the room. They both heard a noise coming from the table. They looked at it and saw the papers and the pen move by themselves toward the edge of the table, gravitate for a few seconds, and then fall to the floor. Sebastian opened his eyes wide, and said, "It must have been the air in here."

Ernie said, "Yeah, the cold air." He added, "I'm tired, good night!"

Sebastian agreed, and said, "It's been a long day, good night!"

It was hard for them to admit how terrified they felt. Both of them prayed silently. They knew someone from the next world was there with them, but neither of them wanted to see it. They continued praying in silence, and then fell asleep with their blankets over their heads.

Later that night, the sound of a howl full of anguish woke them up. It was almost the hour after midnight when they heard it. They both jumped, startled, opened their eyes and looked at the ceiling, mortified of what was coming. The howl intensified, and a cold wind blew their blankets off their bodies. They were shivering. Sebastian sat up and looked at his friend. Ernie, still lying down, took his blanket next to him and covered himself up to his chest. Again, a wind blew the blanket, uncovering his body and then covering his face with it. Ernie threw his blanket to the side and got up on his feet in an instant. Sebastian stood next to the door and opened it. They ran out of the room barefoot. Then they walked quickly and silently, like two timid mice, through the long, dark hallway. There was a tall, dark figure at the end of the long corridor standing and blocking the door, the only exit was close by.

Sebastian held Ernie's arm, and whispered, "Let's go back to the room." And they did.

Once inside their room, Sebastian barricaded the door with a bureau. He put his hands together, and said, "Please, Lord, help us and allow us to sleep well on this night." He added, "Please forgive my sins and I will try to be better every day."

Ernie said, "Yes, Lord, forgive mine too, and I will strive to be better also." He added, "Please Lord, protect us tonight and help us sleep in peace."

Everything was quiet. Sebastian lit the candle and put it on the bureau. They lied down on their beds and covered themselves with their blankets. Sebastian said, "Let's try to sleep some more, Ernie."

"All right, good night."

Then, they heard slow footsteps with high heels walking in the hallway outside their room. Sebastian said, "That must be one of the monks going to the restroom. Good night, Ernie."

Ernie covered his face with his blanket and turned his body to face Sebastian. Sebastian held a big candle in his hands. He took a deep breath in and was going to blow it out to extinguish the flame, but then he changed his mind. He left the candle burning on the bureau. He put it on a plate with water. Sebastian turned around and faced Ernie and covered his body to the neck with his blanket. They were too scared to move, felt cold to the bone, and it took them a while to fall asleep again. A cold wind gusted on their faces and extinguished the candle in the same blow. They kept praying while covering their faces with their blankets.

It was dawn when Ernie squatted in front of his friend and moved Sebastian's arm with his hand. He said, "Sebastian, wake up, we have to go to work. Your children will get to school soon, and we have to be there before them. Come on, let's eat something before we leave."

Sebastian opened his eyes, looked at Ernie, and said, "Let's go, Ernie."

Sebastian got dressed while Ernie waited for him with the door open. They heard soft footsteps and looked at each other, frightened. A monk stood by their door, and said, "Good morning, Brothers. Would you join us for the morning prayers in the chapel?"

Ernie said, "Brother Jeronimo, it is so nice to see you."

Sebastian said, "Good morning, Brother." Then he asked, "How can a ghost be haunting such a holy place like this when there is praying every day?"

Jeronimo looked at them, and said, "That's one of the many reasons we do daily praying, fasting, and acts of kindness, Brothers, to appease any suffering soul surrounding us."

They looked at him with surprise but felt relieved. Sebastian asked, "Did you hear her laments too, Brother Jeronimo?"

Ernie asked, "You heard the ghost too, didn't you?"

Jeronimo answered, "Not a thing."

Ernie smiled. "Of course you heard it. She wasn't hiding from anyone."

Sebastian nodded his head, and said, "She was loud, all right."

Jeronimo said, "Oh, that, you should not pay attention to those things." He added, "The best you can do about it is pray, sleep, and don't mind her too much."

Ernie said, "Please forgive us, we didn't want to bring her here."

Jeronimo chuckled, and gently asked, "You think you brought her here? No, Brothers, she has been here a little longer than you two."

Ernie and Sebastian looked at each other with big eyes. Then, they smiled subtly to each other with a sparkle in their eyes. It was good that neither of them brought the ghost to the monastery. Ernie asked, "How can she be haunting all these places?"

Sebastian asked, "Doesn't she get tired of haunting everywhere we go?"

Jeronimo said, "Forget about that and go eat something before you head to work."

"How can we forget about it?" asked Ernie. "We would love to forget, but how?"

Sebastian said, "I wish it was that easy."

"It is easy," said Jeronimo. "You two are putting your attention on the wrong things around here. Brothers, I have an appointment with Reverend Chava and he will be here any minute now."

Sebastian said, "Thank you for acknowledging it and letting us know we are not crazy."

Ernie said, "Maybe if we leave quickly for work, we will not see it today."

Jeronimo said, "Brothers, please eat. Fasting is for when you plan to stay here the whole day, but since you are going to be working with children you will need all the strength and patience only the Lord and food can bring you. Now go on to the kitchen and eat before you leave, and I will see you brothers in the afternoon."

Sebastian and Ernie waved at the monk and left their room. Sebastian closed their door and they walked to the kitchen. Ernie looked at Sebastian, and asked, "Would you like some flavorful eggs with onions and tomatoes?"

Sebastian looked him in the eye, smiled subtly, and said, "That would be nice. Right now, I could eat anything."

Ernie said, "Very well." He diced a small onion and added butter to a pan. Sebastian fired the stove with some dry grass and sticks. Then, Ernie took some tortillas from the basket that was hanging from the ceiling and warmed them up on the fire. He put three tortillas, a pair of fried eggs on each plate, and a cup of coffee on the side for each of them. They ate their meal quietly. Sebastian washed the dishes with some sand and water and dried them with an embroidered, colorful napkin. Then, he hung the napkin to dry next to the clean dishes. Ernie swept the floor with a straw broom.

Sebastian said, "Done. Let's go to school."

Ernie nodded his head and opened the kitchen door wide. They walked through the corridor and out of the monastery. They heard some footsteps behind them and turned their heads back to see who was coming. It was Reverend Chava. He smiled at them, and said, "Good morning, Brothers."

Both replied, "Good morning."

Ernie's face lit up. He smiled, and asked, "Reverend Chava, could you please come with us to school and bless it, especially Sebastian's classroom?"

Reverend Chava said, "I don't have my blessing tools with me right now, but I could go in the evening when the children go home, if you like."

"That would be nice, and you could come back with us to the monastery to bless our bedroom after blessing the school. Please, Reverend?" asked Ernie.

Reverend Chava said, "The monastery is a holy place where daily prayer is practiced. Continue to do your daily prayers with faith and the disturbances should soon cease."

Ernie insisted, "Can you still bless Sebastian's classroom after his students go home?"

"Let's do that then, I will see you both in the evening."

Sebastian said, "See you later, Reverend."

Ernie said, "Thank you, Reverend."

The reverend started walking quickly toward the San Francisco church. Sebastian and Ernie walked their own way toward the school. Sebastian said, "I like your idea, Ernie. A blessing would be good for our work and living spaces."

Ernie said, "Yes!"

A while later they were in Sebastian's classroom arranging it for the students. Ernie said, "We got here earlier than the children, and we have just enough time to prepare everything for class before the students get in."

Sebastian said, "I'm glad we made it on time and we have everything ready for the students who will be here any minute, and with no setbacks today!"

Ernie agreed. "We made it on time after the little rest we had last night." He added, "I'm so happy the ghost didn't visit us today here in your classroom. Just thinking about her makes me shiver."

Sebastian said, "Let's not think about that or anything scary today, Ernie. Let's focus on teaching the students and you on fixing the classroom."

Ernie smiled. "You got it!"

Hours later, there was a knock on the main door of the school. Ernie said, "What a nice sound that is, announcing Reverend Chava is here." He added, "This is going to be a marvelous evening."

Sebastian smiled. "I see Reverend Chava has the ability to put you in a good mood every time."

Ernie jumped from the chair he was sitting on, and said, "You got me, Sebas, thinking of a life without terrifying ghosts is beautiful, and all thanks in great part to Reverend Chava." Ernie asked, "Aren't you excited about it too?"

Sebastian replied, "It is impossible not to be excited with you by my side, Ernie." Sebastian chuckled. Ernie looked at Sebastian and he grinned.

Ernie opened the main door and there he was. Tall, slim, with big brown eyes and a gentle expression. He said, "Good evening, Brothers. Should we begin the blessing, or would you like to talk first?"

Ernie looked to Sebastian for an answer. Sebastian said, "Go ahead, Reverend, please, and we can talk afterwards."

Reverend Chava smiled subtly and excitedly replied, "Very well!" He started praying and sprinkling water all around them—on the walls, on the floor, on the furniture, even on both of them. He said, "In the name of the Father, the Son, and the Holy Spirit." Ernie had a grin on his face. His eyes sparkled, and he followed Reverend Chava all around the school. Sebastian's face was calm, serious, but still hopeful.

Dusk came upon them during the blessing. The moon's rays shone on Reverend Chava's brown eyes and naturally pale skin. Then they heard it again, that cart on the rails inside the walls of Sebastian's classroom. A roll of thunder followed immediately and almost overlapped the sounds inside the wall. Reverend Chava stopped praying for a moment to look at the two men following him. They looked at him with wide eyes and frightened expressions. He continued praying.

After a few minutes, Reverend Chava said, "Now let's pray together." He knelt on the floor in the middle of Sebastian's classroom and raised his hands. Sebastian and Ernie did the same behind him, and in low voices they repeated everything Reverend Chava said in the prayer. Then, he sat on a chair. Sebastian sat on the other chair in front of him. Ernie leaned on a desk and looked at them attentively. Reverend Chava asked, "Is there anything I can do for you before I leave?"

Sebastian said, "You already did it, Reverend. Thank you for taking the time to come and pray and bless the school every time we ask you."

Ernie said, "Yes, thank you, but there is one thing I would like to ask you."

Reverend Chava asked, "Tell me, Brother, what do you need?"

Ernie said, "I would like you to come back every week or every time you can to bless this school again, please." Ernie shook his head, scratched it, looked at Sebastian, and asked, "Wait a minute, what did you say, Sebas?" He added, "You mean this is not the first time the reverend came to bless this place?"

Without saying a word, Sebastian slowly shook his head.

Reverend Chava said, "Don't be alarmed, Brother Ernie. Constant prayer is much needed everywhere."

Sebastian said, "Thank you again for coming, Reverend. I wish this ghostly presence would go away and never come back."

Ernie had a serious look on his face. He held his head with his right hand, looked at the reverend, and said, "It might be hard for you to believe, but it is true."

Reverend Chava said, "I am sorry, I know I did not believe any of you when you were telling me about the ghost, but I know you are honest." He continued, "I know it is true even though I have not seen it with my own eyes. It might be difficult for you, but I want you to know that there is hope and someday these appearances will cease to be, and you will be happier."

Ernie opened his eyes wide, smiled subtly, and asked, "You heard the cart on the rails inside the wall during the blessing, didn't you?" He added, "And that was just the beginning, if it wasn't for the holy water and the prayers you would have witnessed the whole thing as we have before."

Reverend Chava stood up, looked at them with a serious expression, and said, "It is getting late, and you both must be tired. Let's go and have some rest to be ready for the day to come."

Ernie and Sebastian nodded their heads and walked to the door with Reverend Chava. They saw the school principal at the door, leaving. Sebastian asked, "Principal Sarah, you stayed this late with us, I thought you would be at home by now."

The principal answered, "Not really, I left right away after the children, but I forgot some documents I wanted to check." She added, "Now that I have the documents I need, I can go back home to rest."

Sebastian said, "It is dark, we will walk you home to make sure you get there safe."

Ernie nodded his head.

The principal said, "Thank you, but that is not necessary, you must be tired." She added, "Don't worry about me, I will be safe with Reverend Chava by my side, that is if he will walk home with me?"

Reverend Chava looked at the three of them, and said, "Of course, I will make sure Principal Sarah gets home safely. You go ahead and have some rest, Sebastian and Ernie."

Sebastian looked at the reverend. Then, he looked at the principal, and said, "All right, have a good night, Reverend Chava and Principal Sarah."

Ernie looked at them, and said, "Good night!" They all walked home.

Ernie and Sebastian walked together to the monastery.

Meanwhile, Reverend Chava walked the principal home before going to his own home at the San Francisco church. The principal said, "Thank you, Reverend. It is very nice of you to go out of your way for me."

Reverend Chava said, "Walking is good exercise, and it will be good for me to talk to you on the way to your home. It will take my mind off things."

The principal said, "Can I ask you a question?"

"Go ahead, Principal Sarah, ask."

"Why would a handsome man like you decide to become a reverend? I cannot understand how a man like you made the decision to live alone for the rest of his life?"

He replied, "This is what I like to do, being a reverend, praying and serving the Lord with my life."

She said, "I understand that, but you could still do it with someone at your side."

Reverend Chava said, "I have no doubts and I have accepted my life the way it is a long time ago." He added, "However, I don't understand how a successful, smart, and still young woman like you is not married yet."

She smiled, and said, "I ask myself the same question every night, Reverend, and I don't know the answer to that. It could be that I dedicated all my youth to my career and didn't stop to think about my personal life."

Reverend Chava said, "You can still change your personal life if that is what you want. There is still time to make a new life, if that is what you really desire."

She said, "I would love to do that, but maybe it is too late for me, and I might not be able to have any children."

Reverend Chava said, "Children, you have many at school every day, and you are a very good guide and teacher for them." He added, "Besides, there are many children who need a home and someone who loves and takes good care of them. You can adopt one of those little ones if you want to have a family of your own."

Principal Sarah smiled, and said, "I could do that, Reverend. All of that sounds easy to do, but the hard part is to find a good husband."

Reverend Chava said, "You are at home now, safe and sound. Have a good night, and remember, everything is possible if you pray for it."

She said, "I will, but I have prayed for it already for a long time."

"Then, you are on the right path. Continue praying and just wait for your miracle, it is coming."

"Thank you for walking me home, Reverend Chava. I enjoyed talking to you." She added, "Have a good night."

"It was nice talking to you, Principal Sarah. I will see you in church."

As he walked back home, he saw someone on the street. He thought, *Who is that lady walking by herself at this time?* He whispered to himself, "It's Maria's mother. I better hurry to catch up to her." He walked quickly after her, but he couldn't get near her. He asked, "How can a woman walk so fast that I cannot catch up to her when it is urgent that I talk to her? How can she let Maria live with that Baltazar and not worry about it? She is going to hear me as soon as I get near her." He was breathing heavily. He stopped when he saw Maria's mother knocking at a door. He said, "She is looking for Maria at the guesthouse. That is what I wanted her to do, to find her daughter and take care of her or at least give her some good advice." He took deep breaths, and said, "I thought I was in better shape than this." He walked calmly and looked up at the sky, and said, "Now that Constanza is there to see her daughter, I don't have to tell her anything anymore, thank you Lord."

Baltazar was with Maria in the room. Her mother knocked on the door again. Maria opened the door, and asked, "Mother, what are you doing here?" Maria turned to look into the room at her boyfriend, Baltazar, and said, "My mother is here. I'll be back."

Baltazar looked at Maria and continued to drink quietly. Maria exited the room and closed the door behind her. As she walked with her mother, her mother said, "Maria, it had to happen someday with you always doing what you want, not caring about the consequences. Now, you are a woman and you are going to face the shame of your actions."

Maria said, "Mother, if you only came to see me to tell me how bad I am, you shouldn't have even bothered." She added, "I was feeling better without talking to you."

Her mother said, "Maria, what I am about to tell you will make you feel even worse. Your father has come back from seeing Baltazar's dad."

Maria asked, "Why did he go there without asking me first?"

Maria's mother replied, "He wanted you two to get married since you two are already living together."

"He shouldn't have done that!"

"Were you planning on living like this until he gets bored of you and leaves you?" her mother asked.

Maria's eyebrows furrowed, and she answered, "A married man can leave too, Mother, and nobody is going to stop him when he makes up his mind to leave!"

"Maria, you are so stubborn, at least being married, your shame would be less when he leaves you." Her mother continued, "Baltazar's dad told your father the only way for you two to get married is if you could match the fortune his father has."

Maria's eyes got watery. Her mother saw this, and whispered, "Maria the strong one, and the one who seldomly cries, now crying for a man and for your bad choices."

Maria raised her voice, and said, "I don't care if that man doesn't want me for his son. If Baltazar likes me, he is still going to marry me no matter what anybody says."

"You are so foolish. If his dad doesn't want him to marry you, he will not marry you."

Maria's teardrops slid down her cheeks. "If Baltazar doesn't want to marry me, then I don't want to marry him either. There, we are even."

Maria's mother said, "Shame on you, Maria."

Maria spoke louder and cried. "Shame on me, shame on me only, Mother? Why? Because I am a woman? And what about him? Not shame on him? No, he can do whatever he wants and get away with it because he is a man? That is what it is, isn't it? I have to be worried, full of shame, and thinking about what I am going to do all the time, and the men can do whatever they please and it is all right for them to do so? Everybody wants to judge me and blame me for the decisions I make with my life only because I am the woman in the relationship. Everything I do is wrong because I am a woman and the only free people in the world to decide their lives are men, and the men are saints because all of their mistakes are the woman's fault?"

Maria's mother quietly looked at her daughter for a few seconds. Then she said, "I know it doesn't sound good, but that is the way it is, and it doesn't matter if you like it or not. As soon as Baltazar knows his father doesn't approve of you, he is going to leave you."

Maria wiped her tears with her hands, and said, "Maybe that won't be necessary, Mother. Maybe I am going to be the one who leaves him."

Maria's mother said, "You are as rebellious as always, Maria, and since you don't listen to your parents, life is going to teach you many lessons." She added, "Then, maybe you will stop being so impulsive and stop talking back to your elders." She lowered her voice and added, "I will be waiting for you at home, in case things don't go as you planned."

Maria said, "I haven't planned anything, Mother. Besides, I will never go back home to you and Father, I won't shame you anymore. I know you two feel ashamed of me."

"We do, but you are still my daughter and there will always be a place for you at home." Her mother left quickly with her head down.

Maria stood there and cried as she watched her mother walk home. Then, Maria wiped her eyes again, and went back into the room to Baltazar. She looked at him and screamed, "When are we going to get married?!"

Baltazar put his cup of wine down on the table, looked up, and said, "We are having such a good time, why do you ruin it with silly questions?"

Maria said, "Because your father doesn't want you to marry me because I don't have a fortune like his."

Baltazar said, "I never thought about marrying you, and if my father is opposed to it, that's it, I cannot do it."

Maria said, "Yes, you could if you wanted to."

"You said it, I don't want to. I don't even love you."

"I am with child."

Baltazar took another drink. Maria said, "Say something, didn't you hear me?"

He took another drink, and said, "What can I say, one more, one less, it doesn't matter." He added, "I didn't force you to get pregnant. How quickly our fun has ended because of you."

Maria looked at him, and yelled, "I don't want you anymore, you spoiled brat, good-for-nothing! No, no, wait. I take that back, you are good for something. You are good for drinking and for waiting on your father to solve your problems. You are useless, and I shouldn't have gotten involved with you. I don't want you anymore; I'm leaving you." She slammed the door and left crying.

It was getting darker outside when she left to go to her parents' house. Baltazar looked outside, saw her walking away, came back in, closed the door, and said, "She's gone." He continued drinking.

Some minutes later, on her way home, Maria saw Doña Gabriela on the street and she waved at her. Maria said, "Doña Gabriela it is so good to see you. Can I go back to my job and can I stay there like I used to before?"

Gabriela's expression turned from a smile to a serious one. "Maria, I would love that but what you are asking me is not possible now. Unfortunately, with the death of my lady the countess, everything has changed. Soon, we will have to find a new place to work, all of us. I am sorry, Maria. I wish I could help you. There is still construction work to be done, but it is more suitable work for men."

Maria's sad expression deepened even more when she said, "It's all right, Doña Gabriela, I know this is my punishment for taking everything for granted."

"Cheer up, Maria, you are young and smart. I am sure you will find something better than what you used to do at the countess's house. Why do you need to work? I heard that Baltazar was saying he was going to take care of you."

Maria said, "As you might already know, that did not turn out well." She added, "I have to go, Doña Gabriela. It's getting late."

"Bye, Maria. Take care of yourself and listen to your mother."

"Bye, Doña Gabriela."

Maria hurried toward home. When she arrived, she knocked on the door three times. *Knock, knock, knock.* Her father answered, "Who is it?"

"It's me, Maria."

In a loud voice, her father asked, "What do you want here?"

Maria could hear her mother, her little brother and sister excitedly saying, "Open the door, it is Maria! She came back! Let her in! Hurry, hurry open it!"

Maria's father said, "She is not going to stay here. She is a shame to her brother and a bad example for her sister."

Her mother said, "She is our daughter."

The boy said, "I'm not ashamed, I want Maria to come in."

Mortified, the girl said, "Let my sister come in, Father, please."

The mother yelled, "Open the door for her, you stubborn man!"

Maria's father didn't move, but Maria's mother got up and opened the door. She took Maria by the hand, and said, "Come on in, Maria. This is always going to be your home."

Her father said, "I see why Maria is like that, because she is like you, rebellious, with a big mouth and can never listen." He added, "I'm going to do what I should have done a long time ago—leave you two shameless women on the street where you belong." He held them both by their arms and led them out the door, closed it in their faces, and yelled, "Leave, both of you! Leave and never come back, shameful women."

The children started to cry. The girl said, "I want my mother."

The boy said, "I want Maria to stay with us like before. Let her stay, Papa."

Maria's father said, "Be quiet, you two, and if you don't want me to get the belt, go to sleep."

The children were quiet, still crying, but they did not say anything else.

Maria's mother knocked on the door, and said, "Open the door, you stubborn old man, it's late and dark."

The father said, "I don't care."

Her mother held Maria's hand, and whispered, "Let's sit down here for a little bit, he will open the door eventually."

Maria listened to her mother, and they both sat down quietly outside the door. Crying, Maria said, "I am sorry, Mother, it is my fault that you are on the street with me with no place to go."

Maria's mother smiled at her, and said, "It doesn't matter, Maria. I am so happy to have you back with me that I don't care about being on the street."

Ten minutes passed before Maria's mother said, "Let's go, Maria. We have to find a place to spend the night."

Maria stood up, and asked, "What if Father opens the door for us?"

Maria's mother said, "Then, it is going to be too bad for him because we are not going to be here when he does."

"Where are we going?"

Maria's mother said, "We're going to your grandparents' house."

"How I wish they were still alive," said Maria.

Maria and Constanza walked quickly for half an hour until they got there. It was a tiny cabin in the middle of the flower fields. Maria's mother tried to open the door. She said, "The door is stuck, Maria. Try to get inside through the window."

Maria stood next to the window. It was a circular hole in the wall covered by a big pillow in the middle of it. Maria struggled a little, but she was slim enough to barely make it through the window. Maria said, "The door is stuck, wait, I can open it." She struggled a little but was able to open the door for her mother.

When her mother entered, she grabbed a chair to secure the door from the inside. Maria started making the bed. She found a bunch of scorpions in it, cleared it, and put them all in a bucket. Then, she dumped them outside the window, and said, "The bed is ready." Maria looked under the bed, and said, "Clear!"

Maria's mother scratched her head, and asked, "Did you just throw a bunch of scorpions out the window? Why did you do that? They are going to crawl back into the house and sting us both."

Maria said, "I don't want us to sleep next to crushed scorpions." She started crying.

"It's all right, Maria. Why are you crying now, for the scorpions? It is so rare for me to see you cry this much. Usually, you never cry."

"I'm not crying for the scorpions, Mother. I am crying for my little brother and my little sister. They must be so scared and we are not there to take care of them."

Maria's mother said, "Don't cry, we are going to bring them here with us very soon."

Maria, still crying, asked, "Mother, what happened to you? You are always worried and mad for every little thing, and now that we have many big problems you don't even seem to care."

"I care, Maria, but I just know everything is going to be all right. That's why we don't have to worry anymore. We just have to do the right thing from now on and everything is going to be just fine. Let's pray before we sleep, Maria. We have many important things to do tomorrow."

Maria wiped her eyes with her hands, and said, "Yes, Mother, I'll do the prayer." They both lay on the bed. Maria said, "Thank you, God, for everything you give us. Thank you for the place to sleep tonight. Thank you that my little sister and my little brother are alright on this night. Please, help them to be safe and to sleep well tonight. Also, please help my father to calm down so he can be nice to my little sister and my little brother. Please help us be together again. I know you will give us everything we need because you always do, thank you. Thank you for clearing my mind. Thank you for everything, and I will be a better person as I know you want me to be. Also, thank you for my mother who still loves me and has forgiven me for the mistakes I have made. Please, make me smart so I can become a good person like you want me to be and help me make good choices, amen."

Constanza said, "Amen! Good night, Maria."

"Good night!"

The next day, Constanza woke up before her daughter and left the house. A few minutes later Maria woke up, looked around her, and asked, "Mother? Mother?" She got up, tidied herself, and went outside to the fields. She looked around, and said, "We need some space out here for washing, playing, and resting. These flowers are so beautiful, but we need to get rid of some of them so we can have some space outside." She started cutting the beautiful wildflowers and arranged them in small bouquets, tying them with grass. Maria whispered, "I have to take everything out of the cabin and wash it so it can dry with the sun." She washed the blankets vigorously. Then she scrubbed the big table outside that was behind the cabin. She cleared some space by cutting some of the beautiful wild flowers in the field. Then she moved the rectangular table under a tree about one hundred feet from the cabin. She arranged all her flower bouquets on the table. She had red, pink, white, blue, purple, yellow, green, and mixed-colored bouquets on the table. A couple of ladies walked by and stared at her. They were gossiping about her.

Maria looked at them, and said, "You two are not very good women either, gossipers!"

They looked away from her and left in a hurry. The sound of a horse galloping made Maria look up to see who was coming. It was Baltazar. He stopped his horse, and said,

"Maria, I am not going to marry you, but I want you to know that I have decided to help you with our child."

Maria looked at him, and said, "I don't like you anymore, and that won't be necessary."

Baltazar said, "It is my child, too, and I will help you raise him."

Maria's eyebrows furrowed, and she said, "Stay away from me and don't come back here to see me ever again."

He said, "I have to, you are pregnant with my child."

Maria spoke even louder, and said, "I lied, I am not pregnant, and I don't want anything to do with you ever again in my life." She added, "If our paths were to ever cross again, do not speak to me and go the opposite way."

Baltazar looked at Maria quietly before leaving on his horse. Maria watched him for a few seconds while he left. Then, she continued arranging the beautiful wildflowers in nicely arranged bouquets.

Two other women came walking and selling their goods on the street. One was selling tortillas, and the other one was selling fresh cheese. They stopped by the tree next to Maria's grandparents' house. The lady with the tortillas said, "Let's rest here a little bit under the shade of this tree."

The other woman held her basket with fresh cheese, and said, "You read my mind. Look at these beautiful flower arrangements." She looked at Maria, and asked, "Maria, how much are these flowers?"

Maria looked at them and chuckled. "No, you don't understand…" Maria stopped herself, and said, "Give me whatever you want for them."

The one with the tortillas said, "I'll give you a dozen tortillas for the pink arrangement, no, not for the pink one. I'll take the purple one instead."

Maria stopped arranging flowers on the ground where she was sitting. She stood up and approached the table. She took one pink and one purple flower bouquet, offered them to the lady with the tortillas, and said, "Take them both, and I'll take my dozen tortillas, please."

The lady smiled a big smile, took the flowers, gave Maria the tortillas, and said, "Here, I'll give you a few more. Thank you, Maria, I might come back tomorrow for some more?"

Maria smiled. "That would be nice, please do!"

The other lady asked, "What can I get for a piece of fresh cheese?"

Maria smiled, and asked, "What would you like?"

The cheese lady said, "I cannot make up my mind between the red and the white flowers?"

Maria said, "Then, I will give you both." The lady took the two flower arrangements from the table, smiled widely, put a small, rounded, fresh cheese on the table, and said, "Thank you, Maria, I also might come back tomorrow."

"Thank you, see you tomorrow."

The ladies left conversing amongst themselves happily. Maria heard children laughing. She turned around toward the street, and there she saw them, her two little siblings. Maria said excitedly, "Adela, Leonardo! Mother, you brought them!" The three siblings hugged. Maria said, "Sit down, we are going to eat." She gave each child a cheese taco and a cup of water. The children started to eat happily. Maria said, "Mother, come and eat with us."

Constanza sat down, looking concerned. "Where did you get the money to buy this food?"

Maria said, "From the flowers, Mother. These beautiful flowers." She added, "You know the ladies who are selling tortillas and cheese, not the gossipers, the nicer ones. They liked our flowers and we traded." The four of them sat on the grass and ate together. Maria said, "Someday, I will have a big store right here to sell my flowers!"

Constanza looked at the flower arrangements, and said, "You arranged them beautifully, you are very good at creating lovely things when you put your mind to it, Daughter."

Maria smiled. "And someday I will sell flower arrangements to the whole town, and beautiful dresses made of flowers, and hats, and purses, and shoes, and umbrellas, and many pretty things made with these beautiful flowers." Her siblings giggled.

Constanza smiled. "You are crazy, Maria!" The four of them laughed at Maria's silly ideas.

Thirty years later, at this exact same place, Maria had a big establishment where she was selling bridal dresses and wedding arrangements. She spoke to some of her young employees. "You will get a small percentage for each and every single thing you sell here in my store." She added, "It might seem like a small amount now, but you will see that it adds up. Everyone who works for me will have everything they need to live their life with dignity. I know how it is to be poor, and no employee of mine will ever be poor while working for me."

The adolescent girls and boys looked at her and listened attentively to what she was telling them. Maria said, "I know how it is to be poor, but that was a long time ago." She added, "I have been blessed, and a lot more than I would have dreamed of. I have been married five times, but my late husband was a very nice and exemplary husband—loving, gentle, and especially patient with me. My nieces and nephews visit me sometimes, and I am very happy with my life even when I don't have any children of my own. I have the freedom to think, the freedom to speak, the freedom to work, the freedom to choose my friends, the freedom to enjoy my life, the freedom to be generous with my workers, the freedom to run my business any way I want, and I am very happy with the life I chose to live."

CHAPTER NINETEEN

MODERN TIMES

Over 300 years have passed since the Countess of Stonemason's death. Her beautiful hacienda, a shadow of its former self has been ravaged by the passage of time, and is now derelict and defunct. A bunch of youngsters were exploring the Countess of Stonemason's properties. Armani ran after his older friends around the countess's estate where Pantaleon, his grandfather, did not want him to work. Armani looked all around the estate, and with a shaky voice said, "We better get out of here before the spirit of the countess shows up."

One of the older boys said, "Don't worry, your grandpa must be too tired today and he is not going to notice us here."

The other boy said, "Since Mr. Pantaleon is not near us, we can enjoy the day and have some fun here at the countess's estate!"

The oldest of them all, a seventeen-year-old girl named Jessica, stood tall and elegantly. She walked next to the boys, and said, "I am the most important, powerful, beautiful, and the richest woman in the universe."

One of her friends stood next to her, a sixteen-year-old boy, waved his hand and looked at her, and asked, "Beautiful Countess, may I have this dance?"

The other sixteen-year-old boy next to them said, "The countess will dance with me and no one else." The three laughed out loud.

Armani, the youngest of them all, looked at his friends with wide eyes. He started to shake, and said, "Listen!" Everyone froze. Then, they all heard it—a piano key note. They all looked at each other with concern, and wanted to know who was playing the old piano. Anyway, it was too late for the warning. Armani looked inside the hacienda and there she was. An elegant woman in black could be seen from behind while she sat ready to play the piano. There was a soft movement from the elegant cape that fell from her shoulders, embroidered with shiny threads.

Armani walked around and saw the fancy woman from one side. Her long, skinny fingers were adorned with fine jewels. She started to play the piano. Her bony hands played a mournful tragic melody. Everybody stopped laughing and looked at each other quietly with their eyes and mouths wide open, listening to the unhappy melody.

The older three ran as fast as they could. Armani started to run after them. Jessica was ahead. Then the two boys followed her. The last one still running was Armani. An old piece of wall crumbled and fell over the two boys. Then the sorrowful piano music stopped playing completely. The girl and Armani, with their eyes wide open and pale faces, looked at them, but before they could do something to help, a strong, invisible force dragged the two boys around the ground.

Armani came from behind the girl, and said, "We should not be here." He added, "This would not be happening to us if we weren't here."

The girl was immobilized, looking at the scene. Then, she held Armani's arm, and whispered, "Let's get out of here."

Armani looked at her, and still shaking said, "We cannot leave them here. We have to wait for them."

The girl asked, "Do you want the weeping woman to get us too?"

Armani said, "It is not the weeping woman, she is the Countess of Stonemason!"

A big red truck stopped near them. A couple got out of it, and the woman said, "Excuse me, can you please help us find an address?"

The man approached the teenagers, looked at the two on the ground, and asked, "What happened to them? Don't just stand there, help me get them out of there."

Armani helped him and together they removed the old piece of wall which was pinning them to the ground. The woman showed Jessica a small notebook with an address. Jessica said, "It is not that far away from here, we will take you there."

The lady said, "All right." Jessica climbed into the back of the truck, looked at her friends, and said, "Get in the truck, you three, we are going to take them near Armani's house."

The two boys on the ground stood up. One rubbed his chest and stomach. The other rubbed his arms and shoulders. Armani looked at them, and asked, "Are you guys okay?"

One answered, "I'm okay."

The other one said, "I'm okay too."

However, they walked in pain and stumbled into the truck. They left together.

Armani looked at his friends, and said, "I am never coming back here!" His three friends looked quietly at the road. At least they were all safe now.

It was past midnight when a gang of robbers snuck into what was once just a small part of the countess's incredible property, her favorite in Acámbaro, Guanajuato. They got inside the ruins of the hacienda to hide.

Meanwhile, the watchman, a simple man named Pantaleon, was nodding off, trying to resist his crippling fatigue from watching the old hacienda all day and night. Even though the place was in ruins, Pantaleon had been hired by the new owners to work day and night to make sure the property was left alone with no one to disturb it. Pantaleon, in his sixties, liked his job. It was easy for him to do it, or so he thought. Although it was a little monotonous sometimes, it provided an opportunity for him to meditate about life as he liked. Also, the job allowed him to help his family financially. Pantaleon was an honest man and well respected by everyone in the community. Even though he liked his job, he was conscious it involved some risk. The uninhabited property tempted the lawless when hiding from the law or simply to take an adventure. This unruly group was only one of the many who would pass through these ruins which once were the fanciest place around. This now demolished place, which once belonged to the Countess of Stonemason and entertained the wealthiest and most powerful people in the region, was now the attraction for insurgents and the curious.

The group of thieves was made up of a leader, his two lovers, his sister, four of his friends, and the girlfriend of one of them. The girlfriend was fighting with her boyfriend. "I am tired of running away and always hiding."

Her boyfriend said, "That is part of my job, Caterina."

She said, "I don't like being sweaty and dusty like all of you, and I don't like hiding everywhere we go."

Chucho, the leader said, "Keep it down, you two. The old man is still there, and he might hear you."

One of his friends said, "He can't keep one woman quiet, and you have two over there always following your lead. How do you do it?"

Another friend said, "I don't know how you do it either."

The other friend said, "Handling one woman is a lot of work, I don't know how you can deal with two of them."

Chucho said, "All of you know nothing, you're a bunch of scared mice." He looked at his sister, and said, "Not you, Sister." His sister was tall, voluptuous, with suntanned skin and disheveled hair that fell to her shoulders. Unhappily, she said, "Why can't I be a tiny mouse too, like everybody else?"

Everyone got quiet. Chucho thought, *I have been robbing for a long time, and I have nothing to show for it. I have had many women and none of them ever loved me for real. I have nothing of value. There has to be something more to life than this. I always wanted to go to school and become a lawyer or a priest, but it was not a real option for me nor at my reach, it was just a foolish dream from my childhood.*

The silence grew even louder.

They settled down. Some of them fell asleep. Chucho's sister, Susana, quietly looked through the belongings of her brother's friends and took a few for herself. The men were deeply asleep and snoring, with the exception of Tony, who surprised Susana when she was stealing a necklace from his belongings. He sat up and looked at her, realizing what she was doing. She, in a low voice, said, "I thought everybody was asleep."

Tony said, "Not me."

She said, "I was just looking."

"I know, that is a nice necklace, and it would look very good on you." He took a pair of long gold earrings, placed them in her hand on top of the necklace, and said, "These would look very good on you too. I want you to have them."

Susana scratched her head and looked at him with big eyes. Tony looked at her attentively, and in a low voice said, "Put them on, let me help you." He took the necklace and placed it around her neck. She touched it softly over her neck and looked at him quietly.

Then, she put on the earrings, and asked, "How do I look?"

He held her gently by the shoulders, stared deeply into her eyes, and said, "You are sooo beautiful!"

Susana wrapped her arms around Tony. He laid down and she kissed him on the lips. She said, "Good night!"

He sighed, and said, "Good night, my love."

Her brother's lovers were covertly watching them. Everybody was asleep when they heard a woman's anguished scream. It was a loud, sorrowful howling and with it they could hear the dragging of something or someone on the floor. Everybody but Chucho was at their sleeping spot. His lovers sat up to see what was happening. His sister got up to see what all the commotion was about. His four naked friends stood up, covering their private parts with their hands, to see what was happening. Chucho got up from the ground disoriented and walked slowly, completely naked, holding his head in pain with both hands.

He, not fully awake yet, asked, "Who dares to drag me on the ground when I am sleeping?" Hurriedly, the men answered, "Not me."

"Not me."

"Not me."

Chucho looked at his lovers, and asked, "Who did it?" Both of them shook their heads. He looked at his male friends, and continued to ask, "And why did none of you intervene, what do I pay all of you for?"

The friends said, "My clothes, somebody took them all."

"Mine too," said his other friend.

The other one said, "When we heard all the commotion, we couldn't find you or our clothes."

Susana said, "Who would dare to undress dirty and undesirable thieves?"

Tony looked at Susana with big eyes and smiled. "Somebody must be playing games with us tonight."

Chucho scratched his head, and said, "No, I remember now what happened." His cheeks were covered in dust and scratched from the ground. From the front, his entire body was scratched from the dust and the stones on the ground. His back had ten long nail scratches, red and almost bleeding. Chucho said, "I was sleeping, and the most beautiful and fancy lady I have ever seen sat next to me."

Tony said, "You mean one of the two ladies you had on your side."

Chucho said, "No, not them, a real lady dressed in a shiny black dress."

The two women looked at him in awe.

Chucho said, "I was half asleep and it didn't bother me at all that she was taking my clothes off, until I noticed that she wasn't any common lady." He continued explaining, "She started hiding her face from me, but I could feel she was mad at me. That's why she dragged me with fury across the ground and scratched me with her sharp nails." He took one of his lover's hands and looked at her short nails. Then, he did the same with the other one, who also had short nails. His face was pale.

His sister asked, "You got a scare from a real ghost, Brother?"

Chucho looked at his sister, covered his private part, and said, "Yes, Sister, and she even laughed at me and took my clothes with her."

Susana said, "Let's find your clothes. They have to be around here somewhere." She looked at the men, signaled with her hands, and said, "Us girls will look for your clothes around here, and you men can look over there."

They all looked for the men's clothes in vain. None of the men's clothes were found that night. They couldn't go back to sleep either. They went to the road and mugged three drunk men. While three of them were getting the men's clothes, Tony covered himself with a leafy branch and looked at Susana. She noticed, and asked, "What do you want to tell me?"

Tony said, "It's true, I want to tell you something, but I'm afraid."

Susana asked, "You are afraid of me?"

"No, not of you, but afraid of your answer."

"Tell me what you want, Tony."

Tony said, "I'm afraid you will say no to me."

Susana said, "If you don't ask, you will never know."

"Okay, here you go, will you accept me as your man?"

Susana looked at him, and said, "I like you, but I always wanted to be with an honest man."

Tony said, "I can be honest if you accept me."

One of his friends interrupted and gave him some underwear, and said, "Put them on."

Tony asked, "Why do I get the underwear? I want pants!"

Chucho said, "There aren't enough pants, at least you have something now."

Tony and one of his friends wore the underwear. Chucho and the other two men wore the drunken men's pants. The intoxicated men had to walk home naked.

Following Chucho's orders, the whole group of thieves walked together and by sunrise they arrived at the nearest church. They saw an old priest praying with his rosary at the front of the church near the altar. They walked to the front and sat on the first benches, as Chucho asked them to do. Then, the old priest heard them, turned, and asked, "Good morning, Brothers and Sisters, what brings you to church this early?"

Chucho said, "Reverend, we want to repent of all our sins and become priests and nuns."

His two female companions looked at him with confusion and surprise. One hurriedly said, "Not me."

The other one added, "I don't want to be a nun either."

Both women left in a hurry while one of them circled her index finger around her own ear. His friend and his girlfriend looked at each other and left the church in a hurry too.

Chucho looked at the reverend, and said, "We have a lot of money and valuable things, Reverend. You may have them for your good causes." He looked at the ones still left in the church, and ordered, "Give everything to the reverend!"

One of his friends touched the gold coins and jewels in his handkerchief, and said, "No, I risked my life for this, and I am keeping it."

Another thief looked at Chucho and the reverend, touched his handkerchief, and said, "Sorry, I can't give it to you either."

They both left the church together in a hurry like the others. Only Chucho, his sister, and Tony were left in the church. The reverend looked at Chucho, and said, "Brother, it is very nice for you to come to church with such good intentions, but you don't need to become priests and nuns." He added, "There are other ways to serve the Lord, but you have to look inside your hearts and find out what it is that you have to do to please the Lord with your way of living."

Susana asked, "Reverend, can I serve the Lord if I get married?"

He looked at Susana, and tenderly said, "Yes, Sister, if that is what you really want, you may serve the Lord by following the Lord's will in your marriage and in everything you do."

Tony said, "Reverend, if Susana wants to get married, I want to marry her too."

Chucho looked at the couple with wide eyes. He pointed his finger at Tony and Susana, and asked, "What? You two?"

The reverend looked at the couple, and asked, "Are you two telling me that you love each other, and you want to get married today?"

They both nodded yes.

The reverend said, "Wouldn't you want to clean yourselves, get properly dressed, and come back later for your wedding?"

Tony looked at him, then he looked at Susana.

Susana said, "No, Reverend, we want you to marry us now, please before something happens and stops us from doing the right thing."

The reverend looked at Tony, and asked, "Son, do you feel the same way as her?"

Tony said, "Yes, Reverend, if she wants to marry me, it will make me the happiest man in the world to marry her right now."

The reverend said, "We need to talk before your marriage. I need to make sure you understand what you are getting yourselves into."

Tony said, "I know what marriage is, Reverend. It is loving, respecting, and caring for my wife for the rest of my life."

Susana tenderly looked at Tony, and said, "I agree to do the same as Tony said, Reverend. I will love, respect, and care for my husband for the rest of my life and I will do it happily."

Tony said, "This is the happiest day of my life."

The reverend said, "Very well, there are also a few more things you need to know before I marry you two. You need to set a good example for your children and raise them with love and careful guidance to help them become good citizens as they grow up."

Tony said, "I already promised Susana I will be an honest man from now on, and I also promise to be a good husband for her."

Susana smiled, and said, "I also promise to be a good wife to you, Tony. What else do we need to do for you to marry us, Reverend?"

The reverend nodded his head, and said, "I see you are ready for the commitment of a holy marriage, and I ask you two today in this house of the Lord to always remember your promises of today and follow them with patience and love for the rest of your lives." The reverend looked at Tony, and asked, "What do you say?"

Tony answered, "I will keep my promises."

The reverend said, "Very well, Brother."

Then, the reverend looked at Susana, and asked, "And what do you say, Sister?"

Susana replied, "I will keep my promises too, Reverend."

"Very well, you are old enough and both of you understand the meaning of a holy marriage. There is only one problem, you need to at least be wearing pants and a shirt so I can marry you properly."

The three of them looked at Chucho. He opened his eyes wide, and said, "You already got my sister, and now you want my pants too?" Chucho took off his pants and let Tony borrow them. The reverend looked inside a closet and gave Chucho a pair of pants and a shirt to each man.

The reverend married the couple as they were, and Chucho quietly watched the celebration. When the wedding was over, the reverend congratulated the new couple, looked at Chucho, and asked, "Do you still want to become a priest?"

"Yes, Reverend, I want to be a priest, this has been my dream since I was a young boy. Will you help me?"

Susana and Tony smiled at each other.

The reverend looked at Chucho, and said, "I will, Brother, but first you have to stay here with me for some time so we can prepare everything for you to begin the process of serving the Lord and someday you will become a very good priest, if you don't change your mind that is."

Chucho said, "Thank you, Reverend, I won't change my mind. I have been wanting to do something useful with my life for a very long time, but I didn't know what it was that I had to do. Now that I found my calling, I will persevere until I reach it."

Susana looked at her brother, and said, "I am happy for you, Brother. Sometimes I thought that nothing could make you happy, but now I see that you just needed to find your own purpose in life."

Chucho looked at Tony, held him by his shoulder, and said, "Congratulations, Tony. Take care of my sister and make her happy."

Tony smiled, and said, "I will, Chucho. I am sure our new lives might not be easier than before, but they will be meaningful." They said good-bye and the new couple departed.

The reverend gave a Bible to Chucho, pointed his finger to it, and said, "Read this part." Chucho held the Bible and looked at him quietly. The reverend insisted, "Go ahead, Brother, read it."

Chucho asked, "Are there any priests who cannot read?"

The reverend looked down. Then, he looked at Chucho, and said, "I'm afraid not, but you can learn to read."

Back at the countess's estate, or what was left of it, it was almost noon. Pantaleon was falling asleep sitting down on a big rock. He thought, *Soon I'm going to wash up, eat, and sleep before I come back here again. It is a good thing I don't have to come back for the night until tomorrow. Why do so many people like coming in here only to do bad things?* The very tired Pantaleon took his hat off, scratched his head, forced his sleepy eyes to open, and thought, *It is much easier to work honestly and live in peace than to mess around, risk their lives, and live scared all the time. I wish they would understand that it's not worth it.*

He fanned his face with his white hat. The heat was at its highest and very uncomfortable at this time of day. He stopped fanning himself with his hat and looked attentively at the elegant lady in front of him. She was an impressive sight. She was dressed in fancy black, shiny clothing embroidered in silver, and she was heavily tapping her feet. Pantaleon didn't understand what was happening. *Why is this beautiful, fine woman dancing in the ruins of this place? She doesn't belong here, her fancy clothes are going to get dusty.*

Pantaleon got closer to her, and asked, "Ma'am, do you need any help?"

The fine lady vocalized a few vowels and then disappeared a few steps from him, leaving behind the sound of her footsteps and the stirred up dust. Pantaleon stopped feeling the heat from the sun all over his body, and suddenly a coldness shook his whole being. He was shivering but sweating. He didn't feel hot anymore. He could feel the cold sweat dripping down his face. Finally, when he could move, he walked away from there, and said, "I have no doubt that this place is inhabited by evil spirits. I better go before I encounter the same terrifying spirit again or some of the other many evil spirits that must be lingering around here. I know who the fancy lady was, she was the Countess of Stonemason!"

He left in a hurry as the hot sun started to warm his entire body again. Pantaleon saw the Good Friday procession passing by. First, he saw Jesus carrying the cross. Then, he saw two more men following him and carrying a cross of their own. The Roman soldiers followed them holding whips in their hands. Then, following them was the downhearted crowd. He walked faster, catching up to the procession, and walked with them. He felt a hand over his shoulder. Then he heard a familiar voice. It was a young man. He said, "Grandpa, I found you!"

Pantaleon asked, "I might take you to work with me for some time as you asked me before."

With wide eyes, Armani said, "No, Grandpa, I changed my mind."

Pantaleon said, "I will help you find another job."

"I don't want to go to the countess's hacienda ever again in my life."

Pantaleon said, "I am happy that you changed your mind."

Armani said, "I still want to have a job before I turn fourteen."

Pantaleon said, "No, not at my job, it is not safe, and I don't want you having to deal with all the evil spirits lingering there in the countess's hacienda."

His grandson looked at him, and asked, "Can you tell me the story again, Grandpa?" He added, "When we get home? Can you tell me the legend of the Countess of Stonemason? It has been around for three hundred years since the countess was alive. How many more years will she still be here haunting her haciendas and grieving for her sins, Grandpa?"

Pantaleon patted his grandson on the arm, and said softly, "I don't know, Son." They walked silently, following the Good Friday procession.

Meanwhile, the sound of melancholic piano music was heard within the ruins of the hacienda, where a long time ago only happy music was played and everything there was stylish and glamorous. This place was once one of the most elegant residences in the New Spain. A place of enchantment for the richest royals in the region, and one of the many elegant estates of the once magnificent, beautiful, rich, and powerful Countess of Stonemason.

Giving Thanks

Thank you to my mother for telling me the legends of our ancestors many times throughout my childhood. Thank you to my grandparents for sharing old stories with me when I was little, those were precious times. Thank you to all the people who, through their own point of view, told me these historical events when I was a child. Thanks to all the people who told me the legends of the past, and a special thanks to the elderly people who were the ones who enjoyed taking the most time to tell me these stories numerous times. A special thanks to my heavenly Father, the creator of the universe, who put the immense desire in me to write this book. Thank you to Heidi and Kenneth for all their dedication and effort in bringing this project to fruition. Last but not least, thank you to everyone who took the time to read this book. I hope every one of you will have a wonderful time reading it and can find the power within yourselves to live your lives happily. May you learn something new every day, add your grain of sand to make this world a better place, enjoy life with all its difficulties, and live it to the best of your abilities.